"I love you, Charles," she heard herself saying...

He took a deep breath and his arms tightened around her. Then his mouth came swiftly over hers.

It was clumsy at first, the kissing. Then he moved her head, taking firmer possession of her. And the kisses changed and became like nothing she had ever imagined . . . a demand, a claim, a passionate invasion that left her with no will of her own.

"Be careful," he said . . .

Summer Rain

YVONNE KALMAN

A JOVE BOOK

First Jove edition published September 1980

10 9 8 7 6 5 4 3 2 1

Printed in the United States of America

Jove books are published by Jove Publications, Inc.,
200 Madison Avenue, New York, NY 10016

Part One

Spring into Summer

One

A mud-soaked corpse of a soldier lay on a slight rise, face upward, open eyes staring at the sky. Andrew Fielding noticed that the man had been surprised by death. The face wore an expression of crumpled astonishment and the mouth sagged open in disbelief. He had probably been killed the day before yesterday, when a surprise volley of rifle fire had caused quite a scattering of casualties in this part of the camp.

Andrew wondered why the corpse had not been dragged to the harbor cliffs and rolled down to join the heaping avalanche of slowly rotting comrades on the foreshore. But this poor fellow had not gone unnoticed. Like most campaign victims, he had been methodically stripped of his boots, greatcoat, shirt, trousers, and cap. Whoever had scored the coat had ripped the cavalry insignia from the shoulders and folded it between the dead man's hands like a funeral lily.

Yesterday the campground had been a flutter of low tents,

busy, noisy, and surprisingly cheerful. But this morning all was silent. The men were huddled miserably in their trenches. It was as though the storm which had slashed the tents away had also sucked the vitality from the men it had left alive. Now there was such a lot to be done—clothing to be dried, new shelters to be made from whatever could be salvaged, fuel to be scavenged.

There was no sign of anybody at HQ. That bastard would not be needing him just yet. Andrew squinted into the low sun. Soon he found the outcrop of squat, misshapen rocks. His cousins had been camped just beyond there.

He moved on, stepping with care to avoid the soggiest patches of ground where he might sink past his ankles. His serge greatcoat flapped heavily against his thighs, and the wind whipped nastily at his unprotected face and wrists. He ignored the stinging cold, just as he ignored the tickling at the back of his neck which told him that some of his lice were disturbed by the draft and were moving to a more sheltered part of his clothing. As he walked, he scanned the trenches and shallow caves. Only a few of the soldiers bothered to look up.

The twins were sitting in their trench on a platform of boulders, their backs against the bank. Both Steven and Thomas had their eyes closed, and their faces were slack and weary. Thomas had thrown one arm around his brother's shoulder. It was obvious at once to Andrew that Steven was dead. He stood some feet away, not certain now of how to proceed. Thomas must have sensed his presence, for he shrugged and grunted by way of greeting.

Andrew scrambled into the trench. As he landed, he trod on one of Steven's outflung feet.

"Sorry."

"No point in apologizing to him," said Thomas cheerlessly. "He's been gone some while now."

"Oh, hell," said Andrew. His voice was sincere, and there was sympathy in the squeeze he gave his cousin's damp shoulder.

Thomas shrugged to loosen his grip. "It's going to get us all in the end. I'm done. It's got me. I'll follow him soon, and do you know something? It serves us right, all of us. We've got no business to be here. No damned business at all."

"We had no choice."

"Did any of the medicine get saved from the ships?" Thomas asked as if the answer had no possible consequence for him.

"It all went down. That storm was a bastard."

"Those ships were there a week while grand Lord Longworth played Napoleon and we were ill and starving. I suppose his fresh food and wine was safely landed?"

Andrew nodded. "Furniture and blankets too."

"Oh, God. Oh, dear God. I hope we end up in hell together, me and Lord Precious Longworth both. It's all I can hope for now. If I had the strength, do you know what I'd do? I'd crawl up there and shoot his balls off. Do you know why? To distract him from that Turkish whore. He's not spared one thought for us in this entire campaign."

"You mustn't talk like that."

"Why? Are you going to shoot me for treason?" Thomas sighed. His skin was the color of the mud on the battlefield.

Andrew fumbled in his pockets. "I brought some cooked meat for you. Some wine too. Here, drink. It will make you feel better."

"Does our friend know you're dipping into his supplies?" Thomas managed a dry smile as he fished into his pocket and pulled out a wedge of dried meat, hard with greenish crumbles of salt. He placed it on the boulder beside him. Then he scrabbled out a meager handful of dried peas and spilled them alongside the meat. "Here, take this to your friend with our compliments, mine and Steven's. Tell him that this is the only food we've had for the past six weeks. Ask him how he likes it, will you? And tell his fancy Turkish whore not to cook it. We eat the stuff raw. Advise him to take it with water—from the least fouled puddle he can find. That's the appropriate drink to wash it down with." He stabbed at the peas with his thumb, scattering them. "I'll not be needing this, or your wine or your meat, though God knows we could have done with something yesterday or the day before. It's as well you came now, or I'd not have been here to say good-bye."

Andrew cast about lamely for excuses to offer. Finally he said, "Don't talk like that . . . I brought you food last week. I do what I can."

"Why shouldn't I say what I want? I'm not going to die in comfort, so it might as well be in truth. But I'm sorry to offend you. Might it spoil your breakfast if you look at mine?"

"The way you talk, a man would think I live in luxury up there. Believe me, it's been half rations for us all."

Thomas turned his face away, his expression a combination of disgust, fatigue and illness.

Puppy-eager to make amends, Andrew bent over him. "Here, let me make you more comfortable." He grasped Steven's collar, holding a lapel in each hand, and tugged. Thomas's weak hands beat him away.

"Leave him be," he ordered. "Let him stay where he is."

"You can't leave him there."

"And why not?"

"Well, he's dead." It sounded stupidly inadequate.

"He may be dead, but he is still my brother. Where he goes, I go, too. At least I take care of my own."

There was nothing to be said to that. Andrew straightened up and glanced back toward the stone huts. Lord Longworth would be expecting him at breakfast, and Lord Longworth did not like to be kept waiting. He would have to go soon.

To Thomas he said, "At least let me take off his coat. I could spread it over the both of you."

Thomas's grip tightened protectively about his brother's shoulders. The dead head lolled forward. "We'll manage."

"Are you going to eat the food I brought you?"

His cousin ignored the flask of wine and the chunk of meat in its wrapping of cabbage leaf. His gaze traveled beyond Andrew to the water-streaked sky. The whites of his eyes seemed as hard as roughly glazed china. "We could have done with your help earlier."

"Thomas, that's not fair!" Andrew squatted to bring himself level with his cousin's face.

"Watch out for the shit," said Thomas uninterestedly. "We were sick in the night."

Andrew pulled the hem of his greatcoat out of the puddle of bloody excrement and scrabbled some stones over the mess. "Look, Thomas, I haven't been able to come and see you because I've been busy. Lord Longworth keeps us on the go the whole time. He's forever having conferences with the other commanders, and we have to be there to write down everything that is said, and then later to read it all back to him and change the things he said into things he should have said so the record is just the way he wants it. I'm probably a lot busier than you are. Last night, when the storm got bad, I came to find you, but the wind was so strong I couldn't. I got lost a dozen times and finally gave up. The only reason I'm here now is that Lord Longworth was so dr...sick last night. He won't be having his usual early start."

Thomas was looking past him. His face had softened, and when he spoke, his voice was very slow. "There was a terrible storm once, long ago when we were very little. It came up suddenly. Steven, Charlotte, and I were playing near a haystack making animals out of little bits of straw. Steven was making spiders and bugs to tease Charlotte with, and she was so angry with us, I can still remember the look on her face. Isn't that funny after all these years, to remember a thing like that? She was mad as hell with us because we wouldn't take her home. She said she was cold and it was going to rain and her new dress would be ruined. And then it hit. First there was the rain, so heavy that each drop seemed to hold a whole cupful of water. Then the wind came howling down out of the sky as though God wanted to clean everything off the ground. The only thing to shelter under was an old farm cart with a canvas haystack cover piled onto it. We dived between the wheels. To us it was all a game, but Charlotte was frightened. She was crying so loudly that her voice got all mixed up with the wind and you couldn't tell which was which. Funny little Charlotte. She never did like playing with us." He closed his eyes and rested, his face still leaning against his brother's dirt-gray hair.

After a time he said, "God, I wish I was home again."

"You will be soon," said Andrew. "You'll be better soon and then, when the war is over..."

Thomas nodded. "I'll be home soon."

Andrew straightened up again. He could see figures standing in Lord Longworth's doorway. "I have to go now."

Thomas nodded. His eyes were closed.

Andrew felt helpless. His offers of help had been rejected. For a moment he considered the idea of transferring Thomas into his own bed where he would be protected from tonight's frost. It was quite impossible, of course. Even if he got Thomas to agree, the other officers would find plenty to say about sharing their hut with a sick man, and a private at that. Thomas would be pitched out into the cold, worse off than he was here.

"Take my coat," he said, fumbling with his buttons.

"Don't be silly, cousin. I'm warm enough, and besides,

someone else will have mine before today is over. Why should they get yours as well?"

"If you're sure . . . you're warm enough . . ." How could he say good-bye?

Thomas helped him out. "Give our love to Mother and Father and to dear Charlotte. Tell them that we were talking about them and thinking of them right up to the end. And please say good-bye to your family for us both."

Again his voice held reproach. Andrew felt bitter at his own impotence. He had tried to reason with his cousins; he had tried to help them. He had argued with that bastard as much as he dared. If he'd spoken more strongly, he might have been shot, though he *was* the son of Lord Longworth's oldest friend. Andrew might disagree with many of his orders but he had to carry them out, no matter how he loathed doing it. The twins seemed to think he was in the position of being able to wage his own private war against their commanding officer. Well, there was little point in repeating himself now. He reached down a hand which perhaps Thomas did not see. "Good-bye for now," he said with false cheer.

There was no reply.

Andrew cursed all the way back to the stone huts. The boys had been more eager to come to war than he had. They craved adventure. At home evening after evening had been crammed with excited talk about this campaign and what a marvelous adventure it would be—the high point of their lives. Instead they were dying in miserable squalor.

Picking his way swiftly, Andrew thought about his own family, his parents and three young sisters. And Violet. Strange how all these years he had taken her for granted, loved her, played with her, adored her, been amused by her, but never thought much about her at all. Yet in all these long months he'd been away, he had thought of little else. His relatives were the blurriest of pictures now, but Violet's face was so sharp in his mind that he could see her as if she was here: how her crinkly dark hair grew in a widow's peak on her brow; how her lashes were thick and straight to the tips, when they curled suddenly; how her lips were full and outlined with a faint, pale ridge of skin; and how soft and yielding she felt when he wrapped his arms about her and she laid her cheek on his shoulder in surrender. Her letters were tucked under his mattress, letters worn along the edges but still as loving and neat

13

as she was. Thinking of her brought on a raw, familiar pain, and he hurried faster, forcefully turning his thoughts to more mundane things.

Two

The house Andrew Fielding looked forward to returning to was the grandest house he had ever lived in. It had been built fifty years ago in a style which had looked severe at the time but now appeared gracefully, warmly elegant. It had tall windows, high doorways, and a steeply gabled dark slate roof which was raised in square-shaped blisters all along the back where the servants' bedrooms looked across the roofs of London. In its time the house had been a showpiece, set off by three acres of trees and dark velvet lawns which merged into Hyde Park on their western boundary. There was a painting in the parlor of how it had looked, a sandstone block with chimneys sitting at the top of a wide avenue of dignified shrubs and flower beds. In the years since the artist had propped up his easel, the house had lost much of its land and now huddled close to brick and stone neighbors. Clarence Street lay down in front of the crocodile-ridged steps, drawing traffic toward the park entrance. The original three acres had shrunk to a small backyard where lines hung heavy with towels, and washtubs were turned on their backs against the warm brick walls of the carriage shed.

Five years ago Matthew Fielding had bought this house as a surprise for his wife, who covered her initial disappointment well, considering that she had ached for years to own one of the smart new town houses in Nightingale Square or an ivy-covered villa just off the Mall. Soon she saw that Matthew was right. This was a perfect house, neither too plain nor too ostentatious, absolutely correct for a wealthy family moving up in society. The rooms were spacious and plentiful, with health-ily cold and bare servants' quarters and a cool, dry cellar. The only point Grace made in criticism was that it was so far out, by which she meant far away from the palace and the cluster of royal dwellings surrounding it. But Matthew was quick to retort that Mayfair was already being spoken of as the best section of town. "If the city depresses you, we could always move back to Sydenham," he offered, teasing her.

She cheered up when Matthew placed the decorating and furnishing entirely in her hands. To help her, Grace had her old friend, Lady Alice Longworth, who was eager to assist, being idle since her husband had taken his company to the Crimea in 1853. The two women transformed the house into a brilliant example of what was currently stylish and tasteful. Thickly patterned carpets were spread on the floors, and the walls were hung with richly embossed wallpaper. All the ceilings were repainted white with ornate gold-plaster trimmings. Every mantelshelf was laden with fancy knick-knacks and so many ormulu clocks that one could tell the time from any place in any room without moving one's head. When the dozens of flouncy-edged mirrors had been hung in place, and the parlor and morning rooms had been stocked with tapestry and brocade armchairs and sofas stuffed to the point of bursting their buttons, the house was complete and Grace was well pleased with it.

Now, at two o'clock on a Wednesday afternoon, Grace was in the morning room seated at her desk. While she waited for her afternoon guests, she frowned lightly over a tentative guest list she was drawing up for a dinner party to be held in four weeks time. Matthew Fielding was in his study, reading *The Times* and waiting for his lawyer. In the kitchen Violet was setting out cups and saucers on oval silver trays, ready for the ladies who would come to call for their gossip and refreshment. Bess, the buxom cook, was at the door, loudly arguing the price of lemons with a fruit vendor. Her grating voice made Violet wince. She wished that Bess's husband Myers, the butler, would return from his inspection rounds and make her tone her language down. Still Bess's anger served a good purpose. There wasn't another house in the whole of London that could eat as well for the same money.

As usual, in the quiet lull between luncheon and afternoon tea, the three daughters of the house were in Victoria's, the eldest's, bedroom, chattering and laughing as they waited to have their hair done. It was not going well. Their governess, Miss Nancy Boswell, was still working on Victoria's hair. Her hands were troubling her badly today.

"Please can you go faster, Nana?" begged Albertina from

15

behind them on the window seat. "We shall never get to the park at this rate."

Miss Boswell did not appear to have heard her. Her wrinkles were set deeper than usual as she concentrated on fastening a hairpin into the dark, glossy hair.

Victoria said gently, "We have plenty of time."

"Keep your head still, please, Victoria."

"I'm sorry, Nana." She moved the tortoiseshell mirror until it reflected her face at a more flattering angle. The squarish face that stared back so earnestly had even features, wide-spaced brown eyes, and a rather pointed nose and chin. (Like a witch's, Albertina sometimes said unkindly.) Long ago she had decided that her best features were her clear skin and her hair. It would have been nice to have golden waves like Albertina's, but her own was beautifully thick and rich like her long, curling eyelashes.

"Hold the pins up higher, please. And stop staring at yourself. All that peering into a mirror is going to make you vain to the point of illness." Another moment and Nana seemed satisfied.

"There, now, you may put your bonnet on, dear." Her governess patted her shoulder to dismiss her. Victoria turned to the window in time to see Albertina pull her head in from where the sash hung wide open. Miss Boswell drew in a sharp breath. "Albertina Fielding! You know that is strictly forbidden. Your mother would faint in horror if she knew that you were leaning out over a public street."

Albertina flushed. A sulky expression soured her exquisite face. "Victoria has a much better view from her window than I have. My room only overlooks dull backyards. I never get to see anything interesting from there."

"You had first choice, remember?" Victoria folded and tied the cream ribbon, perking out the loops to make a soft bow under her chin. "You wanted that room because it was bigger and had prettier wallpaper."

Grimly Miss Boswell persisted. "One of these days you will take a tumble right onto the steps, and what a fine time we shall have cleaning up the mess. You would be broken into pieces, and I do mean broken. If I catch you leaning out of windows again, your mother will hear of it, yes, and your father too. Now come here and let me dress your hair."

Albertina subsided into a mound of blue poplin ruffles. She

raised her chin and said, "I would like you to be more careful today, Nana. Yesterday you almost combed a slice out of my ear." She held up the tortoiseshell mirror. "Look, you can still see the red mark."

Victoria, who had picked up her prayer book and opened it at the Third Psalm, which she was learning, glanced at her sister in disgust. Albertina was such a *baby*! Though she was a head taller than Victoria, and more developed in every physical way, she often acted as though she were younger than the nine-year-old Birdie. And *she* was the one who was in such a hurry to get to the park! "Let me brush her hair for you, Nana," she said resignedly. "Your hands must be very tired."

"I would be grateful for that. I need to fetch more pins from Birdie's room."

As soon as Miss Boswell had gone, Albertina complained, "It's terrible having to go through all this torture every day. Nana doesn't seem to realize how much she hurts. I hope that the new maid Aunt Brownie is bringing can do hairstyles."

"Please try not to be so harsh with her," soothed her sister. "She is so tired lately, and she cannot help it if her hands are sore."

Albertina pursed her mouth.

"And she *is* good at it, even if she takes so long. Her hair styles are lovely."

"With half the pins skewered through the scalp," said Albertina dryly, and both girls giggled, breaking off abruptly as their governess returned.

"Shall I brush your hair, too, Birdie?" asked Victoria.

Her younger sister was taking no notice. She was in a corner teasing Flounce, her golden cocker spaniel, with a scrap of biscuit. She hid it in the folds of her tartan-printed skirt, then produced it, only to snatch it away again. Flounce patiently attempted to snare the morsel, while Birdie burst into high peals of laughter.

"It's cruel to tease him like that," observed Albertina in a lofty voice. "He is your dog and he trusts you."

"He doesn't mind. He *likes* this game, don't you, Flounce? Here, have a taste. No, no, not so much. Down, boy, there's a good dog." She broke off a tiny crumb which he slapped from her fingers with his rough tongue. His squeaky whine begged for more.

"If you come here now, Birdie," said Victoria, "I can brush

17

your hair ready for Nana to pin up."

Flounce took immediate advantage of Birdie's shift in interest to grab and gulp the biscuit.

Birdie stamped her foot in annoyance. "Bad dog, Flounce! *Bad* dog!"

Miss Boswell intervened. "Come here now, Beatrice. Albertina is wriggling and fidgeting so much that I can only assume that she does not want her hair done after all. I shall do yours now instead."

Quick as a cat Albertina twisted to catch hold of Nana's arm, while Birdie watched with interest.

"*Please*, Nana," wheedled Albertina, knowing full well that she would not be allowed out of the house with her long hair hanging loose. She couldn't miss this visit to the park, their very first outing unchaperoned.

Finally the three girls were brushed, curled, bonneted, and standing in a row on the floral carpet, ready for their governess's inspection. Not a detail escaped her. Here she tucked in a curl, there she twitched out a ruffle. She teased Albertina's bow a fraction more and brushed a few sticky crumbs from Birdie's tartan. Her twisted hands made hollow whooshing noises on the shiny fabric.

"Young ladies always keep together and look after each other," she reminded them, frowning. "And young ladies always stand up straight, and I do mean straight, Albertina. Do try to look more dignified. Slouching is so unbecoming, and it makes you appear no less tall."

"It's not fair," Albertina said. "Victoria is a whole year older than me, and yet look how *enormous* I am beside her. I feel like an elephant!"

"And I don't think it is fair that everybody notices you and thinks that you are the older one." Victoria spoke kindly but insincerely, for she was very proud of her daintiness. I may not have her doll's face, thought Victoria, but I do have something she wants.

"Envy, jealousy, malice, and pride. They shall never in my heart abide," Miss Boswell lectured. "Look after each other, girls. Remember all I have told you."

"Yes, Nana."

Their demure tone and downcast eyes did not deceive their governess. As she waited near the window to watch them leave, she fretted over Mrs. Fielding's decision to let them go out alone. Still it would have been a shame to waste such a beautiful day when there had been so few outings this spring.

She heard the girls' boots go clipping down the stone steps. Their bonnets and swaying hoopskirts came into view. She noticed with maternal pride how well they walked, how gracefully. Victoria, in the center, held a mittened hand in each of hers.

On her way out of the room, Miss Boswell paused at the mirror and patted her netted gray hair. The light was unkind to her round wrinkled face, but she sighed without caring and said, "Oh, Robert, what would you think of me now?" The pink marble clock on the hallstand told her it was two forty. There was time for a nap before Miss Beatrice brought the new maid at four. She placed a hand on the cold stair rail and leaned over. Myers was in the downstairs hall greeting afternoon callers. More subdued voices could be heard in the parlor. Being ill had some compensations, she thought. She *was* spared the afternoon teas.

Alone in her room, she locked the door. As she drew the curtains, she noticed Lord Benchley's carriage coming down the street.

Miss Boswell was not interested in the lawyer's arrival. She jerked the curtains to, and unlaced her short boots and lay down, cushioning her feet on the folded coverlet. In a few minutes she was deep into a dreamless sleep.

Three

Lord Henry Benchley swore angrily as his carriage wheels struck another loose cobblestone. He closed his eyes, for the breeze was stinging them and making them watery. He had not intended to drink so much, but once again he had not stopped until the bottle was empty. Why did he do it, when he knew the next day he would suffer agonies? His head was ringing with the din of iron on stone, and every slight bump gave him a new jolt of pain.

"Damn it, man, slow down," he said irritably, glaring at the thin, stooped back of his elderly coachman.

"We are nearly there, sir," replied Tom Booth helpfully.

"I can see that," he snapped. "I *have* been here before."
Soon Matthew would pour him a hair of the dog, a good, stiff
glassful that would rinse the foul taste from his mouth and
clear his head for business. It looked as though they were in
for another trying day and he would need to be agile-witted.
Those damned men from Liverpool were arriving later, and
things could develop into nastiness unless he managed to deflect
them in the right direction. So much depended on him. And
what a bloody mess they were in!

He had warned Matthew so often, told him what could
happen if he grew greedy and impatient. "Take it slowly," he
had advised. "Sell your shares to the small people, the little
investors. Sell in batches and spread them thinly. Pay a nice,
healthy dividend for the first few quarters. That's your advertising. They tell their friends and you pull them in. It's easier
than fishing. All you do is bait the hook to start with, and then
the orders roll in on their own. Then, when things get tight,
they will be patient. They'll trust you, you see? All you need
to do is toss them the odd dividend and you'll be able to keep
their confidence indefinitely."

But, no. Matthew had to get greedy, and off he went selling
huge blocks of shares to money-fattened businessmen who
could spot an irregularity on a postage stamp at twenty paces.
What in hell did Matthew hire him for if not to give advice?
And then he goes and tosses that advice away! So here he was
in the squeeze, and Lord Benchley was expected to come up
with some miracle to pull him out of it. He swore and shifted
his enormous bulk uneasily.

It was a bad business this time. Those Liverpool chaps were
shrewd. They were not about to be put off by any fancy double-
talk. They wanted facts and figures, plain facts and accurate
figures. *Now.* Determined, they were, too. At the first whiff
of trouble they had come baying down like a pack of hounds
scenting a fox. Lord Benchley's full lips tightened. He had a
whole briefcase full of facts and figures for them right here at
his feet. That should take the heat off for a while. With any
luck, by the time they had sorted them out and come yipping
back, things should be on the upswing again.

He noticed his carriage turn into Clarence Street. He sat up
straighter when he saw the Fielding girls out with their dog.
What charming young delicacies they were! It made him feel
better just to see them. Young Beatrice was a delight with her

impishness. He had never fancied Albertina quite so much. She was too knowing, too confident for her age, though she was indisputably the handsomest. Victoria was the one he liked best of the three. Seventeen she was, but still a child to look at. Her father said that she had a mind of her own and a will to go with it, but that was hard to believe. She was so soft-voiced and demure. He approved of the way she kept her eyes downcast, whereas Albertina would stare a man straight in the face with that hard look of hers and unnerve him. And Victoria was old enough to be wed. Yes, quite old enough. Gazing at her as she strolled toward him with bonnet bobbing and pink sprigged skirts swaying gently, Lord Benchley resolved that if the day went well, he would ask Matthew for what he had been thinking of for some time now. Matthew was in the position where he might well feel he should show a little gratitude for all the effort Lord Benchley was expending on his behalf. And why shouldn't he ask for her? His law business was building up nicely, he had property, and there were regular rents coming in, not to mention the prospects when his uncle died. Most important, he had the influence and connections to do Matthew and his family important favors. Yes, Matthew could do much worse than acquire him for a son-in-law.

He touched the rim of his top hat as he drew opposite the girls. The sisters bobbed serious little curtsies in return. Delightful, he mused, utterly delightful. Yes, it could well turn out to be an excellent day. A wife was just what he needed. It was undignified having to resort to prostitutes twice a week. A man should not have to be degraded in that way. It was humiliating. His headache returned in full force as he recalled last evening. "Is *that* all you can do?" the dirty little creature had said. "It don't hardly seem worth while to come all the way down to the East End just to do *that*!" And she had fallen about laughing; and him there like a fool with not a shred of clothes on, with her bursting into new laughter every time she looked at him.

Still one couldn't expect good manners and considerate behavior from such a low class of person. A well-bred wife would never insult her husband. She would do as she was bidden and show no disrespect. And she would not be able to shout for her pimp to rescue her. He could still hear the shrill laughter that had changed without a break into a scream of fear.

Lord Benchley shook his throbbing head. Stop it, he thought

sternly. Don't ever think of that again. Do your best by Matthew this afternoon, and he will count it a small favor indeed to marry his daughter to a lord of the land. His face bent to accommodate a smile. Victoria, he thought smugly. Yes, a demure child bride would suit him very well indeed.

Four

Hyde Park was the airing ground for the entire west section of London. From Mayfair, Knightsbridge, Chelsea, Fulham, and places even further afield, people gathered to enjoy the lake, the trees, and the wide, gentle slopes.

They walked, rode in omnibuses, or hired cabs pulled by sweating horses, or drove carriages and landaus. They pushed prams if they were nannies or heaving barrows with goods for sale if they were vendors, for the edges of the park were not crown land and business could be conducted there with a carnival spirit.

If you had a penny in your pocket, there was always something interesting to do, or something good to eat. You could watch a Punch and Judy show, listen to the buskers, or hire a boat to row across the lake. You could eat strawberry ices in the jasmine-covered kiosk, and gasp as the cold sweetness slid down your tongue, or you could burn your fingers on the floury roasted chestnuts that sold a heaping handful for a penny.

The girls loved the park. Because they lived so close, they felt almost as though it were theirs, and they had a special affinity for the people who used it. It was as if they were all guests at a gigantic, continuous garden party. As they approached the park entrance, they quickened their pace.

As soon as they passed through the gateway, Albertina let out a whoop of glee. She tore her hand from her sister's grasp and pranced on ahead, skipping out an impromptu dance and bunching up her skirt at either hip, the better to kick up her pale blue boots.

"Albertina!" called Victoria in alarm.

Her sister laughed up at the sky. "I'm happy! I'm so happy!"

"Albertina! *Stop it!*"

Albertina turned so abruptly that her skirts swirled and her boots were visible almost to mid-calf, a sight that made Victoria

22

blanch. Albertina swept a deep, joyful curtsy. "You called, madame?" she lisped in an excellent imitation of Miss Boswell's school-French accent.

Victoria hurried to her side. "People are staring at you," she hissed angrily.

Albertina glanced about her. Near them in the shade stood three young gentlemen. They were dressed for riding, in cutaway jackets, brown saddle trousers, and high spurred boots. All three stared and smiled at her in open amusement.

Albertina flushed. She had been enjoying herself so much that she had forgotten the existence of the rest of the world. For a moment she froze in embarrassment, then her impudent nature surged to her rescue. Impulsively, in defiance of their grins, she stuck out her chin and made a deliberate and mocking curtsy in their direction.

Gravely they replied with bows.

Victoria was scandalized. She hustled around until she stood between her sister and the young men, her back to them.

"If you don't behave properly, I shall tell Nana as soon as we get home," she warned.

"You would, too, wouldn't you?" Albertina shot back at her, her blue eyes cold. "You always want to spoil my fun."

"Yes, I do, when this is your fun." She seized Albertina's arm and tugged her along. "You know what Nana tells you, and she tells you every day. I can't see any fun in attracting the worst attentions of young dandies like them."

"What harm have I done?" Albertina asked when they had gone a few yards.

"What harm? You don't even know who they are, let alone whether they are gentlemen. They are probably discussing you right this moment, and fortunately we do not know what they are saying. Of this you can be sure. Nana would be horrified if she could overhear their conversation."

Albertina peeked back around the rim of her bonnet. Victoria immediately gave her arm a sharp jerk, but not before she saw one of the dandies wave at her in a very familiar way. Victoria was right, she thought in dismay, and right then most of the shine went off the afternoon. A moment ago she might have been silly enough to wave back, but the disapproval had sobered her. "It's so unfair," she cried. "There are no young men for us to talk to any more. Everybody we know is away in the horrid Crimea and we have to suffer for it. We don't

23

have fun the way we used to, when Andrew brought his friends home every weekend."

"I don't really think that Andrew and his friends are having much fun either, away at the war," Victoria said gently.

"Oh yes, they are," chirped in Birdie who has been quiet but round-eyed during the encounter with the gentlemen. "Andrew has a rifle to shoot with. And two pistols!"

"I'm positive that it can't be as bad as the papers say," declared Albertina, relieved to change the subject away from herself for once. "Nana always says that they exaggerate to make the stories sound more exciting, just like storytellers do. Anyway, judging from what Mrs. Duberley writes, they are having a jolly good time there."

"Albertina! You're not supposed to read her letters!"

"I do when Father forgets to cut that part out of *The Times*. If he forgets, why shouldn't I? What she says is far more interesting than all that miserable stuff about the wounded and dying. She notices more cheerful things. Do you know what I would like to be? I would like to be Mrs. Duberley, living on her ship in the harbor and being entertained by all those gallant officers. What fun she must be having!"

Victoria thought for only a moment, then said, "And I would like to be one of Miss Nightingale's nurses, helping to save our poor soldiers and bringing comfort to the dying."

"Don't let Nana hear you talk like that. She says that nurses aren't quite respectable."

"I'd like to be a soldier and shoot the enemy until they're all dead," offered Birdie.

"If Aunt Brownie wanted to be one of Miss Nightingale's nurses, then there could not possibly be anything unrespectable about them" said Victoria. "You do get some funny ideas, Albertina. Now then, what shall we do first?"

Albertina wrinkled her dainty nose. "Could we go to see the horses? I have a pocket of sugar lumps to give them. I sneaked them at breakfast when Nana wasn't looking, and they're beginning to go all crumbly in my pocket."

As they moved along the broad, pebbly path, bordered by red-flashed tulip beds, Birdie jerked at her sister's hand. "I want to ride a pony."

"I'm sorry, dear, but Mother says no and Nana says no, so I have to say no as well. But cheer up. You can have some sugar lumps to put on your palm for them, can't she, Albertina?"

Birdie scowled and jerked at Flounce's lead. "I don't like doing that. They blow on your hand and it tickles. I know what I want," she said suddenly. "I want some cherries. Look, there's our cherry man!"

She pointed to where the barrow was being set up near the iron fence. A red and green striped banner fluttering from the railings proclaimed that the cherries were now on sale. People were beginning to drift towards it. These particular cherries were famous for their juicy sweetness.

Victoria said, "We shall be coming back this way soon, dear. First we shall visit the horses. We are almost there, now."

Birdie stood firm. "I want some cherries *now!*"

"Please be patient, Birdie. When we get back, there will still be plenty left."

"But I'm hungry *now!*" An ugly warning whine underlined her demand. "Nana gave you some money for me to spend, and I want my cherries now."

The other sisters looked at each other and shrugged. Victoria untied the purse from her belt and loosened the corded silk strings. Taking out a heavy brown penny, she pressed it into Birdie's hand. "Be careful not to drop it. You may skip on ahead and buy some. Here, let me hold Flounce for you."

Much later they stood on the banks of the Serpentine, knowing it was time to start out for home yet reluctant to leave and put an end to such a beautiful afternoon. Birdie was throwing snapped-up twigs at the ducks. Flounce lay beside her. The water was alive with activity. Rowlocks creaked and backs strained as the white and orange rowing boats lurched across the lake. Other boats, awaiting customers, nudged each other at the tiny jetty. A family of swans slid under the trailing willow veils while everywhere near the banks flapped the ducks, hundreds of them, all competing noisily for offerings of food scraps.

"We haven't seen anybody we know yet," complained Albertina in response to Victoria's suggestion that they go. "We can't go until we see *somebody.*"

Victoria laughed. "Your wish is granted. Isn't that Mrs. Palmer coming now? It certainly looks like her carriage."

"She hardly counts as anybody," retorted Albertina, who

25

had been rather frankly criticized by Mrs. Palmer on several occasions.

"She has seen us, too. Look, she's waving."

The girls dropped polite curtsies to their mother's friend.

"Oh, mercy," groaned Albertina. "She's going to stop and talk to us." For Mrs. Palmer now was tapping her driver on the shoulder with her ivory walking cane. "We should have pretended not to see her. Oh, do let's go quickly. She will keep us here for ages asking those horrid snooping questions."

They glanced about hurriedly for Birdie but heard her shriek before they saw her.

"Flounce is gone!" she sobbed. "I was looking at the ducks, and he just went away!"

"Oh, you stupid creature," snapped Albertina. "You were supposed to be holding his lead all the time."

"It won't help matters if you upset her even more." Victoria scanned the park worriedly.

"Somebody has stolen him!" wailed Birdie.

"It would serve you right if they had."

"Please stop it," begged Victoria. "If he has gone anywhere, it will be home. Cheer up, Birdie, do. He has probably gone to see what Bess has fixed for his tea. Oh, no! Is that him? Oh, it is! Oh, *Flounce!*"

Their dog was further along the bank with his head and shoulders in a double-handled wicker picnic basket. He was obviously finishing off somebody's lunch. At the same moment the girls saw him, the owner of the basket noticed him, too. Before they could get there, the stringy youth had picked up a solid stick and dealt Flounce a series of thumping whacks on the hindquarters. Yelping, Flounce tried to struggle under the handles to escape the blows but succeeded only in getting his front legs through. The handles held him fast. Unable to free himself, he staggered away, thoroughly frightened and uttering yelps that split through the noises all around him. Suddenly the basket bumped on a curbstone, tipping him over. The girls saw a tangle of yellow wickerwork, at first down the bank and then faster, until with a splash and a shower of dirty water the whole bundle landed in the Serpentine. Ducks scattered in panic. There was a thrashing turmoil in the water where Flounce had disappeared.

Birdie burst into hysterical crying.

"Why, he's going to drown!" said Victoria in horror.

She picked up her pink sprigged skirts and scrambled awkwardly down the bank. She had no idea how she might rescue Flounce and was oblivious to the people watching. It was not important that she was wearing a new dress or that she could not swim. All she knew was that Flounce was wedged so tightly into that basket that he couldn't possibly escape death unless she rescued him. She didn't even see the young man until he had pushed her aside and, careless of his high polished boots, had waded out into the water. He bent over the broiling place and plunged his arms in deeply, not seeming to mind the splashes that showered over him.

Up came Flounce, still kicking and still imprisoned. Water streamed from the holes in the wickerwork and poured down the young man's riding habit. He carried the struggling load to the bank and dumped it, then strained at the handles until they snapped off. Flounce rolled onto the grass. Water ran from his plastered-down coat and oozed from his mouth. His skinny tail thumped hesitantly. Though subdued and frightened, he was very much alive.

"Thank you," said Victoria, overcome. "Thank you so very much. He is my little sister's pet, and her heart would break if anything should happen to him. But, oh dear, you have ruined your clothes."

The young man smiled, despite his splashed face and the dirty water running from his hair down his forehead. "I'm not quite the dashing figure I was a few minutes ago, but never mind. The clothes will clean and the boots will dry."

"It was so brave and good of you... so kind..." Victoria felt that a few words of thanks were not enough, but she had not been given any instructions from Nana to cover this type of emergency. "Do not speak to strangers" hardly applied now, and what else could she say but "Thank you"?

She looked into his face. Merry eyes crinkled at her, and slightly uneven teeth gleamed below a drooping sandy moustache. Surely she knew this face! She was about to ask him, when, as if to prompt her memory, he clicked the heels of his muddy boots together and gave her a formal military bow.

With a pang of shame and dismay she recognized him. It was one of the dandies Albertina had flirted with earlier. What fools he must think they were, behaving so shamefully and then letting their dog get into disgraceful mischief. No wonder he was grinning! She longed to snatch up Flounce's lead and run, but that would be terribly rude. No matter who he was, or how little she wished to speak to him, he had saved Flounce—and ruined his clothes in doing so. She looked helplessly up to where Albertina was comforting Birdie. Quite a crowd had gathered. Uncomfortably Victoria noticed Mrs. Palmer, prominent among the staring faces, sitting tall in her carriage for a better view.

"You've ruined my basket!" The stringy, red-faced youth stood accusingly before them, shouting so that everybody could witness his indigation. "Twelve pence, that basket cost me just last week. And look at it now! What use is a basket like that? Who's going to pay for it, eh?"

Victoria felt stricken. In her purse she had exactly two pennies, and her sisters had nothing. If only Nana had come with them, none of this would have happened. But even if it had, Nana would know what to do. She would be able to deal with this obnoxious young man. He was still shouting, obviously enjoying the attention.

Calmly the other young man, the dandy, interrupted and stopped the tirade. Without even attempting to haggle over the inflated price, he handed some money to the youth. "Take this and go," he ordered in a level voice. "You are upsetting the lady."

"*She* should be upset!" retorted the youth. "Ha! It's me who lost my basket." Still grumbling, he picked up the remains of his basket and stormed away.

"I...I don't know how to thank you..." Victoria was shaken and very close to tears.

He was smiling at her again in that impudently merry way as he rubbed his hands on a damp handkerchief. "Please don't thank me. It has been my lifelong ambition to help a lady in distress. And though I've met many ladies, none of them has ever seemed distressed when I was near. Until today, my timing was all wrong."

She had to admit that he was perfectly charming, and quite the gentleman, but she had a nagging feeling that he was mocking her and that all this would be a subject for jokes and gossip with his two dandy friends. Hurriedly she said, "I shall have to repay you, only I haven't enough money with me now."

"Think nothing of it." He pushed the handkerchief into his pocket. "It was I who broke the basket. I should pay."

"Oh, no!" she insisted in horror. "That would not be correct

28

at all. It would not be proper for me to be in your debt." She rushed on, for he seemed to be grinning more broadly. "You must call at our house. I shall tell Mother all about you"—she had a horrid, sinking feeling at the thought—"and she will want to repay you and to thank you for your trouble. Please come, I shall insist on it."

"And will you be there? I shall come if I can see you."

Blushing, she picked up the leash.

His voice was quiet and kind. "I'm sorry. Please forgive me. The last thing I would wish is to embarrass you. But I would like to see you again, with your mother's consent and in proper circumstances, of course." He reached over and took the leash from her. "Perhaps I could accompany you home?"

"Oh, no!" Aware that she sounded discourteous, she tried to qualify what she had said. "It's our Nana, you see. She . . ."

"I understand. She would not like you to appear with a strange young man in attendance. I had a Nana of my own, once. Well, then, I shall call on you next month. I shall be away for several weeks but will visit your mother on my return." He handed the lead back. Teasingly but warmly he said, "You had best tell me where you live. Otherwise I shall be forced to follow you home, and that would look very bad to your Nana."

She told him her father's name and their address, and he repeated it, then said, "Lawrence, Captain Charles Lawrence at your service."

He looked expectantly at her, waiting to hear her name. All she could do was to duck her head shyly and say, "Thank you, Captain Lawrence, and good day to you."

Smiling, he watched her walk to her sisters.

Five

As they approached the house, the girls made a very different picture from the one Miss Boswell had seen from the bedroom window earlier in the afternoon. Their buoyant mood had been completely deflated.

Birdie's pretty tartan was dirtied where Flounce had jumped at her. Albertina's dress was muddy too, but she was more worried that her scrap of harmless fun might be blurted out by

Birdie, who would be certain to begin accusing the others the moment she herself was scolded.

Victoria, who looked the most composed, felt the most dismal. She had been in charge, she would be held responsible, and this would be their last outing alone. There was no escaping a scene either. Mrs. Palmer had seen the whole humiliating spectacle, and it would be only a matter of hours before an embroidered version of the story would be recounted to their horrified mother in her own parlor.

If only Andrew were here! He would show everybody the funny side of what had happened, teasing and laughing until even Nana would be amused. And because he could never resist a warmed-up audience, he would follow with an account of an even more outrageous escapade of his own. He knew how to make Nana smile.

Miss Boswell was not smiling now. As the girls drew near, she came hobbling down the steps to meet them, frowning and dismayed.

"You may explain this later," she said curtly. "You *will* explain later. Right now, you must hurry in to see your Aunt Beatrice. She and Miss Manfred are leaving soon. No, Birdie, you cannot go in looking like that. Let me have Flounce, and I shall take him around to young Will to be bathed. Would you two please take Birdie upstairs and ring for Joan to change her dress? Hurry along. Your mother has been waiting for you, and Miss Manfred is anxious to go."

Their aunt sat on the best velvet-covered divan, surrounded by the elegant gloom of the parlor. Beside her sat Miss Eunice Manfred, her constant companion, a buxom, coarse-featured woman who had lived with Beatrice for eight years. Victoria had deduced many years ago that Miss Manfred was disliked in the Fielding household but couldn't understand why because she was a friendly, jolly person, completely devoted to Aunt Brownie. She had been puzzled when her mother had recoiled in horror at the suggestion that the girls call her Aunt Eunice. Victoria would have like that. It seemed odd that they weren't allowed to kiss or hug her when they liked her so much.

"Darlings!" Aunt Brownie laid her gloves aside and stood up with arms wide open. "How very pretty you look today."

"Hello, Aunt Brownie." The girls kissed her in turn and shook hands with Miss Manfred.

Beatrice pulled Birdie up beside her. "And what did you do at the park? Did anything exciting happen?"

Birdie said suddenly. "Flounce ran away and stole somebody's basket. When the man hit him, he fell into the pond and chased all the ducks away."

Grace's eyebrows elevated in alarm. She turned to Victoria. "Is this true?" she asked coldly.

Victoria told them about it. Her mother pressed her handkerchief to her mouth when Mrs. Palmer's name was mentioned and frowned worriedly when Victoria told her all about Captain Lawrence and his help. "How dreadful," she murmured. "How terrible."

But Aunt Brownie threw back her head and laughed. "Nonsense, Grace, no harm has been done. It must have been amusing to see Flounce with the basket tight about his middle. My, but he has learned a sorry lesson today."

"That will teach the rascal not to be greedy," laughed Miss Manfred.

"But how shocking that a strange gentleman should have to give them *money*," Grace said. "He *was* a gentleman, was he not?"

"And a truly kind and gallant one, by the sound of it," put in Aunt Brownie. "In the military, did you say? Perhaps he knows Andrew."

"I think I know some Lawrences. At least, that name sounds familiar," said Miss Manfred.

"I persuaded him to come to the house to have his money repaid. Was that the proper thing to do, Mother?"

"Yes, dear. Of course. We shall have to thank him."

Miss Manfred nodded her head, making the heavy bun bob up and down on her neck. "I should think so, too, for otherwise it sounds as though he did an impertinence instead of a favor," she commented bluntly.

Grace's face stiffened.

Aunt Brownie said, "How very thoughtless of me. I've not introduced Millie, and she will be out there in the hall wondering what we are saying about her. Birdie, would you be an especial darling and ask her to come in, please?"

The new maid resembled a wading bird, with her angular, beaky face, gray dress, and long skinny arms and neck. She bobbed awkwardly to them all and grinned shyly at Beatrice, who stood up to introduce her as though she were somebody important.

"Girls, this is Millie Hamwith. Your mother has kindly agreed to employ her, and I believe that she is going to be your very own personal maid. She has been staying with me while I showed her some of the things she might need to know, and she has learned so quickly that I am sure that you will be pleased with her. I know that I shall miss her."

The new maid bobbed them a curtsy, looking self-consciously ill at ease.

Albertina poked Victoria in the ribs. "Ask her if she can dress hair," she whispered tactlessly, for Nana stood at the buffet near them, pouring herself a cup of tea and staring thoughtfully at the new girl.

Victoria returned the poke and said, "I hope you will be happy with us, Millie."

"Thank you, Miss Albertina." She had a nasal voice.

"I am Victoria," she smiled.

Millie looked confused and upset. "Then I got it all wrong an' I learned it real good, too. Miss Victoria, Miss Albertina, an' the littlest one Miss Beatrice, like her auntie."

Victoria said, "I'm the oldest one, so you have got it right. I have not grown up yet, as my sister has."

Their aunt consulted her pocket watch. "We must be going now. Eunice and I have some visiting to do. Be a good girl now, Millie, and remember everything I told you."

"Are you sure I cannot persuade you to stay for dinner?" asked Grace. "Miss Manfred wouldn't mind, would you, Miss Manfred? We so seldom have just the family alone together."

"*We* would love to stay," said Beatrice, deliberately misunderstanding. "But no, thank you, dear. Do you think that Mrs. Myers might have that basket ready for me now? It is too generous of you, Grace. You have no idea how much your gifts of food are appreciated. There are so many needy folk and far too few people willing to share what they have. You know, I tell everybody I meet how kind you are. Just yesterday I was remarking about your kindness to Lady Astwith, wasn't I, Eunice?"

"Indeed you were. Most impressed she was, too."

Grace blushed with pleasure. "Garth has probably loaded the hamper for you already. Victoria, would you please go and tell Garth that Miss Beatrice is ready to go now? And you might ask Bess to come to the morning room to meet our new maid."

Victoria was glad of an excuse to go to the kitchen. It was an enormous room lit by windows set high on the whitewashed walls and paved with black stone tiles which felt heavenly cool in summer but in winter seemed to draw the warmth from one's body right through one's shoe soles. Against one wall stood the range, huge and lustrous black, with the glow of coals orange inside.

The kitchen belonged knife, spoon, and chopping board to Bess Myers. In fact, through her husband the butler, she ran the whole house, and anything she wanted done was carried out without argument. Her build was appropriate to the most important woman of the household, for everything about her was a bit larger than life-size. She was a striking six feet tall, with bosoms like feather pillows, clouds of frizzy blond hair, a booming voice, and exaggerated likes and dislikes. One of her dislikes was children (apart from the Fieldings); with supreme effort of mind over passionate body, she had never conceived any of her own. All her syrupy affection was directed at her husband, of whom she was possessively watchful, and at her large family of cats.

At this moment Bess was bending into the oven, maneuvering a long-handled spoon to baste the roast. Garth watched idly. He was a narrow-eyed, heavy-browed, garrulous man and he stood up when Victoria entered.

"Are they ready to go then?"

"Yes. They are saying good-bye to Mother."

Bess placed the basting spoon in its container on the rack. "Don't forget the basket."

"Mother has the new servant girl in the morning room, Bess," said Victoria. "She would like you to come and meet her."

"I should very much like that," Bess replied in a hard tone. "I've a few things of my own to say about her. A ragamuffin, I'm told. We shall see, indeed."

Victoria followed her at a distance.

In the morning room it was Miss Boswell who said, with a strange note of triumph in her voice, "Mrs. Myers, this is our new upstairs maid, Millie Hamwith."

Bess glanced at the new maid briefly as if to say that she was not even worth contempt. "So this is her, is it? Hmph, she looks cleaned and scrubbed enough, but a bit of soap and a rough cloth can make anything look clean. What I'm wondering is, has all this household gone out of their heads? Do you know where she comes from, ma'am? I'd not want to go there, ma'am, and I'd not trust anybody that came out of there either, that I would not!"

Victoria was shocked both by Bess's angry tone and by what she was saying, and she wondered why her mother did not put a stop to it and why she and Miss Boswell were sitting by so calmly as if they had heard all this before. Nana was even smiling, and Mother said pleasantly, "Miss Beatrice has given her full assurances that Millie comes from an honest, decent family, and that assurance is quite enough for me."

Bess gave a snorting laugh. "And her coming straight from St. Giles? Hmph! Fish might swim, and birds might fly, but I'm not such a fool as to believe there's an honest man or a decent woman in the whole of that district. Stealing and robbing, that's what they have there."

Millie, whose eyes were growing enormous, chirped up, speaking earnestly to Bess. "Beggin' your pardon, ma'am, but my fam'ly is honest, an' decent too. We all works 'ard, we do."

Victoria had many times seen the maids going about their tasks in tears brought on by Bess's tongue, and she felt like applauding the plucky little waif for standing up to Bess so daringly.

Millie continued. "It's sober we are, too. You'd not find a drop of evil in our 'ouse. It's decent we are, decent and sober, not like some."

Victoria gasped, and Miss Boswell burst out laughing. It was an open secret that Bess loved brandy and kept a bottle of it in her linen press. On every night off her voice could be heard singing wild sea shanties in the kitchen. Millie could not have known, but if she had wanted to sting Bess, she could not have aimed better.

Bess was furious.

Grace remained imperturbable while Bess ranted on in the same theme. Sitting quietly, hands folded, she allowed the cook to have her say. Bess's position gave her the right to speak her opinions; she would be responsible for the child, after all. Besides, Grace herself had doubts about hiring this girl and had only done so after constant pressure from her sister. It would do Millie no harm to see what she was up against should she ever feel tempted to steal.

Victoria understood nothing of this and longed to comfort the girl, who now appeared to be withering under Bess's prolonged attack.

At one point Miss Boswell tried to interrupt, but she was cut off quickly as Bess's voice increased in volume. "This has nothing to do with you, Miss Boswell, and I'll thank you kindly to mind your own business." The cook had no time for hired help who did not "help" in any way but who sat instead at the big table and were waited on by other servants. Miss Boswell neither made her own bed nor emptied her own chamber pot. In Bess's eyes Miss Boswell did no work at all—nothing worth mentioning, that is.

When the tirade of dark forebodings had finally diminished, and the small group had been informed of how everything would be stolen, the house burned down, their very throats slashed in the night, Bess stopped. There followed a full minute's complete silence.

Finally Millie ventured, "If I'm not goin' to please you then, ma'am, might I beg leave to go 'ome now?"

"Of course not, dear," smiled Grace. "You are going to stay with us, and we all hope you will try hard and be very happy, don't we, Bess?"

"Hmph!" snorted Bess. She was satisfied and well pleased with the long hearing she had received. "If we are to have you, then you'd best be coming with me. You can start right in on your duties. Mind that you do as I say right sharpish or I'll fetch you a clip about the ears. Come along, now!"

"She will have to learn Violet's work, and Joan's also," Grace said. "Every time they have a day off, Millie will be able to take over their duties."

"I'll keep her busy, ma'am," promised Bess.

Six

At five thirty Myers entered the study carrying a lighted taper protected by a thin metal cone. Everything about him exuded an air of quiet dignity, and he went about the business of lighting the lamps with a series of practiced gestures. When all four lamps were lit, he extinguished the taper by squeezing the lighted end between thumb and forefinger. Placing the cone on the mantelshelf, he drew the curtains, bringing evening into the study. He addressed Matthew as though the two of them were alone.

"Would it be your pleasure to have the fire lit, sir?"

"No, thank you, Myers."

Matthew moved the lamp on his desk a trifle to the left so that it would not illuminate his eyes. He was tired of being watched so closely. Even though Lord Benchley was doing most of the talking, it was he the three men were contemplating, like dogs who know which cupboard the bones are in. It was himself they were after. They had been here for almost three hours now, and Matthew was coming to the end of his patience. Surely it was time they took their papers and left.

He composed his face carefully and folded his hands across his chest, fingers interlaced together. Matthew was a strong-looking man, so tall and broad that he even looked tall beside Bess. He had straight, classical features, a square chin, a broad nose, a smooth rectangular brow, and a well-cut head of peppery gray hair. Only his thin, indecisive mouth and weak blue eyes looked out of place and made people meeting him for the first time wonder at his character. Enigmatic in its contrasts, his face was an unusual blend of strength and weakness.

He was trying not to frown. In all fairness he could not blame these Liverpudlians for wanting to know about their money—not that they would miss it, by the looks of them. Between them, they'd only sunk in around twenty-five thousand, and to a well-to-do businessman that was nothing.

It was difficult to say just where the money had gone. Those two factories had taken a big chunk of it, and they had done damned well until the war had come along. Overnight his good labor supply had been drained into the army and with it had gone his profits. They'd tried women on the job, but the work was too heavy, and women couldn't stand the heat for long. Production had dropped off so severely that even with the lower wage bills they barely broke even. If he had to sell the factories now, he would be hard put to find a buyer. Nobody would want to buy a sinking business. He'd be lucky to get back a quarter of what he'd put in. And what use was that? This house gobbled money the way a furnace gobbled coal. They had to live well. It was important to keep up appearances, wasn't it?

It was difficult to concentrate. Evans, the short, bristly haired one, was answering Henry's question. "Yes, Lord Benchley, I could say that I am quite satisfied with the dividends."

"We *were*, up until this past twelvemonth or more," qualified Brookes, the stout, older one.

And he's the one who's causing the trouble, thought Matthew. He probably needs the money even less than the other two. They all smell of money, but he's positively stinking.

For the third time that afternoon Lord Benchley explained that the war had affected everybody adversely. "The war will end soon. Oh, yes. No skeptical looks, please. I have it on the best advice, and my informants are infallibly reliable, gentlemen. The war will end soon and, when it does, business will boom again and your dividends will climb accordingly. You may even find that you are gaining double what you received before. Surely that will amply compensate for this quiet time . . ."

"I shall be delighted to believe that when proof is offered me," said Brookes.

Lord Benchley continued as if there had been no interruption. "As soon as the contracts begin flowing again and the labor pools build up, everything will be apple pie and cream again. After all, gentlemen, who are we to complain about the loss of a few shillings here and there when the whole country is suffering?"

Donner, who put Matthew in mind of a vulture, took a sharp look around the study. He spoke in a sour, rasping voice. "I'd not think it a sacrifice to dwell in the likes of this house."

"Aye," said Evans, "that I would not."

Matthew made a rare contribution to the talk. "It's my wife's house."

Brookes looked frankly disbelieving, and the other two men

exchanged doubtful glances. Lord Benchley shifted his bulk in the chair and smoothed his muttonchop whiskers before continuing. "Well, gentlemen, if you are satisfied, as you surely must be after this frank exchange, could we now perhaps be saying good day?"

"Not quite satisfied yet," said Brookes. "You talk as though the war is depressing the whole market, but my shipping shares have climbed fifteen percent in recent months, while all we have seen from you in the past year has been a miserable two-percent dividend. It does not look good, and might I be frank in saying that it does not look aboveboard either. I must ask you again, where is my money?"

"Of course your shipping shares have risen!" Lord Benchley said quickly. "The climate of war is greatly favorable to shipping, just as it is to arms' manufacture and government contracts. I must congratulate you on your astute business sense. You are one of the fortunate few who are able to profit handsomely from England's misfortunes. But when the war is over, what will happen then? I suggest to you that these things will even themselves out." He patted the sheaf of notes confidently. "These shares will soar in value while the others will fall to their proper level. This is one of the basic laws of business, gentlemen. There is no need for you to panic. Your money is safe."

Brookes was purpling as he digested Lord Benchley's remarks. The upstart lord was all but calling him a racketeer. Why, he was as patriotic as anybody. The cheek of it, being robbed and insulted as well! He hammered the words out purposefully. "I want to know exactly where my money is. I want an accounting of how every single penny has been invested. We all want to know."

Damn the man, thought Matthew. Rage was brewing up inside him though he sat quietly with his face arranged in an expression of calm confidence. The other two would have been quite happy to accept Henry's word, but this one was so bloody suspicious and so damnably persistent!

Henry sighed wearily and took on the attitude of a tutor trying to explain something for the tenth time to a dull-witted pupil. "I suggest that you take this folder and peruse it at your leisure. Everything you want to know is set out plainly there."

"And I suggest that *you* take the folder and . . ." Brookes began, then hurriedly controlled himself. He must not lose his temper. The fact that the dodge was so obvious, yet so unchallengeable, infuriated him. But even in his anger he could not help admiring the lawyer. He wished he had someone half as clever working for him. He continued more reasonably. "We want to see tangible evidence that there are actual properties that we have invested in."

"Perhaps we are looking at one now." Donner's gaze was drifting around the study again, silently pricing every item.

Matthew tried to look hurt, misjudged.

Henry laughed. Spreading his pudgy hands, he smiled in supplication. "Come now, gentlemen," he said with merry slyness. "Surely you are not implying that there is something improper in all of this?"

"No?" Brookes's gaze was as hard as a hanging judge's. He stared first at Lord Benchley and then at Matthew.

Matthew leaned both elbows on the broad desk. He's on to me, all right, he thought, feeling ill. He knows every detail there is to know about his precious investment.

For the first time in the interview the lawyer's voice grew sharp. "Mr. Brookes, I am growing weary of your attitude. More than once I have described the situation to you, using plain terms and complete frankness. If you are still not satisfied, there is one further course open, and perhaps you may care to consider it. We could sell your shares on your behalf. Of course you will appreciate that to sell on the present depressed market, you must prepare to sustain a heavy loss. But if you no longer wish to remain in our clientele, we shall make immediate arrangements to dispose of your interests and salvage whatever we can."

Matthew held his breath, but the bluff worked.

"There's no need for that," said Donner.

"I'm not wanting to sell," said Evans.

"Very well then. Mr. Brookes?"

Brookes stood up. His eyes were hard and cold. "We shall see. Our lawyers shall see." He scooped up the folder of papers. "Good day to you both."

Matthew rang the bell for Myers to see them out. Though he came immediately, the businessmen were already collecting their own hats and coats from the hallstand and declined his offers of help as they left.

In the study Lord Benchley was pouring two large whiskeys. His hands were shaking; his headache had returned with the sudden release of tension.

Matthew's hand gratefully encircled the glass. "They will be back, Henry."

"Yes," said the lawyer, spreading himself in a more comfortable chair. "Ah, that feels better. Yes, friend, we must prepare for their return. Those documents will buy us time, but that's all."

"What was in them?"

"No more or less than you heard me tell. Nothing to hang us with, but enough to keep them busy for a while."

"That won't satisfy them."

"No. A lot depends on their lawyer. He may well advise them not to push us. If they do, they are bound to lose money."

"But what will it do to me? If they push, I shall lose everything. It will completely break me."

"I've told you not to worry. What do you pay me for?"

"You were magnificent. I don't know what I should have done without you."

"Don't worry." The yellowed teeth glinted under the gray moustache. "You will receive my account as usual."

"Worth every penny of it. Henry, I don't know what I can do if they press me. It will ruin me. You know that."

Lord Benchley downed the last of his drink and wiped his mouth with the back of his hand. "Stop worrying. You don't have to see them again. In fact, I forbid you to see them alone. If they come, have Myers give them an appointment and make certain you get me here too. But my advice to you is to leave the city for as long as you can and try to drum up more business in the country. Only don't panic. Do the same thing all over again. Keep it small. Go to small traders, shop owners, small farmers. Nobody like that would try to lynch you."

Matthew shuddered. "I couldn't do without you, Henry. You are a real friend in every sense of the word."

Henry eased himself to his feet and refilled both their glasses as he prepared to ask his favor. A moment like this could not be bettered.

Matthew pulled out his watch. He kept no clocks in the study because the noise of the ticking distracted him. "Good God, is that the time?" he exclaimed. "They will be waiting dinner for me. Henry, you must stay and dine with us, I insist on it."

"Here, have your drink. I shan't stay for dinner, but I'll keep it in mind for next time. Tonight I shall work on some fresh ideas for sorting this mess out. There are one or two avenues which might be promising. However, before I go, there is something I would ask of you. It is extremely important."

"A favor?"

"A big favor."

Matthew laughed. "Anything you want, Henry. Ask and it shall be done. It's as easy as that."

Seven

At dinner that evening Millie helped to wait on the family, watched by Myers and instructed by Violet in whispers. While Violet set the dishes out and helped the family to roast meat, Millie held the silver vegetable bowls with a starched napkin and offered them at the right-hand side of each person in turn, according to importance. Mr. Fielding was served first, then Mrs. Fielding, then Miss Boswell, followed by the girls in order of their age. Violet, the shy downstairs maid, had laughed at the way Millie exclaimed over the steaming platters and the cool, jeweled dessert. "Thee won't just be serving it, Millie love. Thee will be having a taste of everything when we have our supper in the kitchen later."

"Us? Tastin' this food?"

"Bess has a grand pot of rabbit and tatie stew for us to fill up on first, but afterward there's always a morsel of everything left to finish up on," she said. "Unless the lawyer lord comes to dinner. Then thee'll be lucky with the smell of a bone!"

"Oh," sighed Millie. "This is like livin' in 'eaven."

"Bess likes for her cooking to be praised," advised Violet. "Thee will do well to remember that."

"Oh, but I will," Millie said earnestly. After her first encounter with Bess she had decided to win the cook's approval no matter what it took. Her family was relying on her wages, very proud of the chance she'd been given. Anyway, if what

41

Violet said were true, Bess wasn't nearly as bad as she made out to be. "Thee has to understand that she always cracks down on the new ones," said Violet gently. "If thee gives satisfaction, and thee keeps away from Myers, then Bess will come around."

"Myers! Do you mean . . . ?"

Violet smiled. "I mean that he's a bottom pincher when he takes his white gloves and fine manners off. Only, if he pinches thee, don't let Bess know. She adores him and thinks that every woman that comes into the house is trying to steal him away. So put him off, and don't let Bess see. She'll blame thee and turn thee out."

Eventually Myers dismissed Millie and Violet. He remained in the dining room to serve the port while they took the last of the dessert plates away to the kitchen where Young Will was scouring the pots. Millie felt tired and ravenously hungry. It was now almost ten. The Hamwiths would have eaten three hours ago at least and been fast asleep by now. She wondered if they missed her tonight, and the first pang of homesickness caught in her chest.

Myers poured port for three, carefully twisting the decanter so that not a drop would spill or splash up the sides of the tiny crystal glasses. He arranged them on a silver tray no bigger than a saucer and offered them first to Mr. Fielding, then Mrs. Fielding, and finally to Miss Boswell. With a flourish, he placed the cigar box, ashtray, and a taper at his master's elbow. "Is there anything else you will be wanting, sir?"

"Not until later, thank you."

Myers' departure was the signal for the young girls to leave and go into the morning room. Tonight, when they pushed back their chairs, their father waved them to sit down again.

"I have something to tell you," he said importantly.

Everybody looked at Matthew except Grace, who had exchanged a word with her husband before dinner and was now watching her eldest daughter to see how she would take the news. Albertina was nervous. Father hadn't seemed at all jolly tonight. He must have heard about the disastrous afternoon.

Matthew surveyed the double row of faces turned toward him. "I have something important to say to Victoria, but I would like you all to share this news with her."

Victoria smiled. The feeling of relief was lovely. Andrew was safe. "Yes, Father?"

For the first time Matthew wondered how his daughter

would feel about the marriage. She would miss out on all the fun of the coming season, with the balls and parties and other young folks' nonsense. And she *was* very young. But, on the other hand, she was making an excellent match. No number of parties and balls would help her to find a better catch than Lord Benchley. Victoria was a sensible child; she would realize that.

"I must congratulate you, my dear. You have made yourself an impressive match and will soon be married. I have made all the arrangements for you." He sipped at his port.

Victoria was surprised. She had realized that a marriage would probably be arranged for her one day, but she didn't expect this for two more years at least. Who could it be?

Albertina glanced at her sister. Victoria seemed remarkably composed. She must have a secret admirer. How romantic! But who could he be?

Matthew was savoring his little drama, aware of the speculation. He leaned back and drew on his cigar.

Finally Victoria had to ask. "Please, Father, will you tell us who this man is? I am curious to know."

"You have been paid a great honor, Victoria. Lord Benchley has paid you the supreme compliment of asking for your hand. Naturally I was delighted to accept on your behalf. He has fine prospects and a secure position in the world. You could not possibly do better for yourself. Frankly, my dear, I did not hope for you to do as well."

Victoria heard him only as far as "Lord Benchley," and the unguarded gasp from Albertina that followed. Father must be joking! He couldn't possibly mean it! Lord Benchley was so ugly and so *old*! Why, he must be at least twenty-five years older than she was.

She looked at her father in desperation. He was beaming now, enjoying his cigar and obviously well pleased with himself. Her gaze swung in panic to her mother, but Grace, who had noticed her daughter's horrified reaction, was addressing the table in a voice that betrayed her agitation.

"We are so *thrilled* about this, of course," she gushed. "It really is *such* a compliment to us all. Just think of it. Fancy a real lord wanting to marry Victoria."

"I'm glad he doesn't want to marry me," whispered Albertina to Birdie.

"Stop that silly giggling please, Birdie," said Grace. "With

43

a proper lady for a sister, you will have to show some respect. She will be just like Lady Longworth."

"With a husband a million times more horrid," said Albertina under her breath. "Oh, poor Victoria."

Victoria felt as though she were going to be sick. Her father, who was smiling, looked fuzzy.

"Well, Victoria?" he beamed. "Not struck dumb, are you? What do you think? It's quite an honor for us all, isn't it?"

"Yes, Father." The words almost stuck in her throat. If only Birdie would stop that hideous giggling! Suddenly her chest hurt and her mouth tasted bitter. She pushed her chair back and rushed from the room, as Birdie's shrill laughter pursued her.

Matthew Fielding nodded sagely. "She's overcome, poor thing. The excitement is too much for her."

Victoria rushed into her room and stumbled against her washstand. Embracing the cool china washbowl, she vomited again and again until she felt empty and exhausted. In the darkness she poured herself a rinse of cold water, then groped her way to the windows and flung the shutters open. The chilly night air burned her face and neck, but her shivers were from weakness. Leaning against the window frame, she breathed in deeply.

Her parents were always pressing Lord Benchley to stay and inviting him to their parties. Up until now she had assumed that it was because he was a lord and because he was such a great help to Father in his business. But that wasn't it at all. She was being thrown at his head, and she hadn't even suspected it.

Albertina had nicknamed him Lord Belchley, and since then they had all taken part in making up horrid rhymes about him. Now she was going to have to *marry* him? Not once in her childhood dreams had she ever imagined anyone like *him* as a suitor. She had built up a very clear picture of whom she would marry. Tall and handsome, he would be, with dark wavy hair and a moustache like Andrew's. And a deep, resonant voice which he would use to pay her thrilling compliments. But it was no use having dreams now. Her future was settled. She had been promised, and her father would never go back on his word.

She shivered. Her eyes, still staring into the dark, began to sting, and her throat ached with the pressure of unshed tears.

The breeze chilled her, but she felt colder still to think of how, very soon, she would have to leave this house, this room, her parents, her sisters, Nana, everyone she loved, and go to a strange house to be a wife to a man she hardly knew and didn't like at all. She would have to sit across the table from him at *every* meal, kneel beside him at morning prayers, attend church with him...Then the horrible thought struck her...There would be much more to it than that! She would have to obey him. She would have to be pleasant to him always. Why, she might even be expected to *kiss* him sometimes! How *horrible*! In utter misery she flung herself on the bed and burst into sobs.

Presently the door opened, and Miss Boswell entered. She set the lamp on the dresser, closed the door and the shutters, and returned to the bed where Victoria was muffling her crying in the rumpled bedclothes. Full of concern and bewildered anger at her employers for even contemplating such a marriage, the governess sat down and stroked Victoria's shoulders.

"There, dear. Crying will not help. There, now."

Though Victoria could not hear what Nana said, she was comforted by her presence. But the sobs continued.

Miss Boswell felt hopelessly inadequate. This trouble was too big to be coaxed away with kind words or the promise of a treat. And apart from offering consolation, there was nothing she could do.

Finally the sobs diminished. Victoria turned her swollen face toward her governess.

"Oh, Nana, what can I do?"

Miss Boswell wiped the back of her hand against the wet cheek.

"Dearest child, please listen wisely. You must accept this. Your parents have decided what is best for you, and you must do as they direct. There is nothing that any of us can do to change it. No, dear, please don't cry. I know how terrible you must be feeling and I sympathize with all my heart. Most parents choose like this for their daughters. They are thinking of your well-being. Believe me. There are countless girls in your situation who must marry men their parents have chosen. You are more fortunate than most."

Victoria sat bolt upright. "More fortunate? Oh, Nana, how can you say such a thing? Why, there cannot be another girl in England who has to marry a man as...as *revolting* as Lord Benchley!"

"That is an exaggeration, Victoria," said Miss Boswell, who looked at Lord Benchley from quite a different perspective. "I really do think that all the laughing and poking fun has made him appear much worse than he really is."

"No, Nana, no. He is horrid. He is fat and old and ugly."

"Well, he *is* fat, that cannot be denied, but he is certainly neither old nor ugly. He has really quite a pleasant face."

"Only if you think a toad looks pleasant," Victoria rejoined sharply. "Why did Father say it was a splendid match? Lord Benchley is rich, but not so wealthy that he doesn't have to work. Elizabeth told me that he lives in a poky little house, smaller even then the one we used to live in. She says that his cook is so inadequate, his dinner parties are a scandal."

"Miss Elizabeth is not always as charitable as she might be. You should know better than to take her word. Lord Benchley lives modestly, I believe, but he doesn't make a grand show on borrowed money like some people do. He is wealthy enough, and has fine prospects, just as your father said. You will be duchess of Lanark one day, when Lord Benchley's uncle dies."

"If that's why they want me to marry him, it is a very poor reason indeed. Lord Benchley's uncle is only a few years older than he is! Elizabeth said that *he* will never be a duke. Oh, Nana, why couldn't they have chosen somebody like Mr. Barnes? He has that magnificent country house, and since Elizabeth married him, she's had all the clothes and jewelry she could want—and her own carriage and pair, as well as a hunting horse!"

"*And* the six children the first Mrs. Barnes left when she died, poor soul. No, you'd not be wanting to be in her place, trying to manage those young rascals. I doubt that all their money and Mr. Barnes's good looks will stop her from aging before her time. Lord Benchley is a better proposition. And as his wife you'll be received into the best houses in London. Even the palace!"

"No doubt that will please Mother. She would dearly love to be invited to palace receptions. But, Nana, you know that society means nothing to me. All I want is to be happy and to be loved."

Uncomfortably Miss Boswell said, "You will change your mind later."

"I doubt it," Victoria said passionately. "I don't care a fig for fine society. These ladies who call here, why, all they do in their whole lives is sip tea and nibble cakes and prattle on about nothing at all. Oh, Nana, I wanted to marry someone young, someone whom I could love and be happy with."

"No, my dear," Nana remarked after a pause. "It is your one great advantage. You have not fallen in love. Oh, yes. I know all about Elizabeth's young man. It was very sad when her parents would not let her marry him and made her wed Mr. Barnes instead. Imagine how she must have felt! It is a terrible and painful thing to have to marry one man when your heart lies elsewhere. You have been protected from that. We have watched over you, so now you will be able to go to your husband with a whole heart. You must believe me and take comfort."

Victoria thought of her imaginary suitor and pictured how he looked to her in her daydreams. Surely she loved him just as she would a living person. Suddenly the picture blurred and there, fixed in her mind, was a tall young man with muddy clothes, laughing eyes, and the sunlight glinting on his thick, sandy hair. She pushed the thoughts away. Captain Charles Lawrence might be a presentable young man, but he was definitely not someone to fasten dreams to. No, Nana was quite right. Her heart was whole.

"Why do you suppose Lord Benchley wants to marry me?" she asked seriously. "It seems so odd, for he shows no sign of liking me or wanting to be friends."

"I don't know, dear. Perhaps he is a man who likes to keep his feelings hidden."

Victoria sighed. "Then he is dull as well. I wonder why he didn't ask for Albertina? She is much prettier and gayer than I am."

Miss Boswell thought grimly that Mr. Fielding would never marry his darling pet off to someone as unappetizing as Lord Benchley, but she said with a smile, "Not prettier than you, my angel. More lively, perhaps, but not more beautiful. Oh, my dear. I pray that this feeling of disappointment will pass quickly so that you can be happy again."

Victoria snuggled back into the lace-frilled, feather-down pillows. She was looking much better now. The angry red had faded from her skin, and her eyes were clearing.

"Why did you never get married, Nana? You would have made a wonderful mother."

A familiar old pain squeezed Miss Boswell's heart. All these years and it still hurts when it catches me unawares, she marveled.

"Tush now," she said briskly. "I have had as good a life as a lady could want right here with you. You four children have been enough to worry anybody's soul to tatters."

Victoria smiled. "Nana, could you possibly come with me when I leave here? It would make such a difference. I wouldn't feel so lonely then."

"I shall—provided Lord Benchley agrees, of course. But not right away, dear. Birdie will need me for some time yet, but your mother has said that when you have a little one of your own, I shall be able to come and look after it for you. I'm not too old to take good care of a baby; these hands could still do a fine job."

"I shall be prompt about having one then," Victoria decided. This was a subject which had mystified all the children, and she wondered whether to ask her governess about it now, while she was in such a confiding mood. She had asked lots of questions in the past which Nana had refused to discuss. But while Victoria was wondering if she should broach the forbidden subject, Miss Boswell was taking matters in hand. She helped Victoria off the bed and, with the aid of a whalebone buttonhook, unfastened the back of her gown.

"It would be a good idea if you went off to sleep now," she said. "This has been a long and difficult day." She kissed Victoria's forehead. "Good night, dear. Don't forget your prayers. I shall come back for the lamp later." She took the washbowl and quietly left.

Victoria slipped out of her underclothes and pulled the long white nightgown over her head, fastening the buttons at the throat. She climbed into bed and for a long time lay on her back, staring into the darkness, trying to focus on the good things about what was going to happen. She was going to be a lady; she was going to be able to start a family of her own. Only she didn't care about being a lady, and she wasn't nearly ready yet for a family.

Much later, when Miss Boswell returned with the clean washbowl, Victoria was asleep. She was tossing irritably, she was frowning, but she was asleep.

Miss Boswell kissed her tenderly on the forehead. "Be happy, my angel," she whispered.

Eight

Bess stood at her six-inch-thick chopping board, dicing onions with a wickedly sharp knife. At her elbow were three bowls of peeled vegetables, one of potatoes, one of carrots, and the third containing shiny, opaque onions. Young Will, who had just finished peeling them, was drying his hands on a scrap of towel.

Myers was seated at a trestle table with a mug of tea fitted to the curve of one brown, rough skinned hand. A brown and white copy of the *"English Woman's Domestic Magazine"* was propped up on an empty cider jug in front of him.

"Don't have him read out the recipes if you don't mind, love," Bess said, over her starched white shoulder. "There's a new concoction I'm stirring about in my head and I don't want anything to disturb that."

"What'll I be readin' yer then, Bess?" asked Young Will. "There's summat 'ere called 'Beside the River.' Would you fancy 'earin a bit o' that?"

"'*Be*side the River', it is. No, thank you, Will. I read that last night." She sliced another onion in half. I've not had a peek into Cupid's postbag yet. See if there's anything interesting in there. Sometimes the letters are good for a laugh."

Violet, who was pasting and polishing the silver at the far end of the table, chirped up. "Thee might find my letter in there this week. I've been waiting some time now."

A bell jangled on the board above the door. Everybody in the room automatically looked up at it. The morning-room bell was jiggling on its brass ring. Myers shoved his stool back as he pushed himself up. "I'll go," he said, pulling his white gloves from under his epaulette tabs.

At the doorway he almost collided with Millie, who was rushing in, pink-faced and breathless.

Bess looked at her with frank dislike. "I thought I told you never to hurry about like that unless there was somebody sick or hurt."

"Or if the 'ouse is on fire," supplied Millie cheerfully.

Bess glared at her. "Which is it then?"

"Nowt like that, Mrs. Myers. Joan is 'elpin' Miss Boswell an' she said I ought to come back 'ere an' see what needs 'elpin' with." Millie twisted her hands together eagerly.

"And that's enough of that bloody 'Mrs. Myers' stuff. My name is Bess and I'll thank you to call me by it. Do you hear? There is only one Myers here, and that is my husband."

"Yes, Bess."

"That's better. And as for Myers, let me tell you . . ." But she broke off as her husband came in with a wide swing of the door.

"Yes, Bess? What was it?"

Bess shushed Millie impatiently and stared at her husband.

Myers straddled his stool. "One extra for dinner tonight," he said.

Millie was immediately alert. "One extra?" she repeated. "Will that be 'im?"

"And who is ''im?' supposed to be?" asked Bess.

"You know! Miss Victoria's intended. Will it be 'im what's comin' to dinner?"

Bess waved the wide-bladed chopping knife so close to Millie's face that the young girl stepped back in alarm. "You listen to me for I'll only tell you once. What goes on with them out there is none of our concern. They do what they please, and there's to be no grubby little guttersnipe nosing into their affairs, not while Myers and me run this place. Do you hear?"

"Yes, Bess."

"Don't just stand there, girl," the cook said angrily. "Get to and help Violet—and try to hold your tongue while you're about it."

Violet patted the chair beside her and smiled reassuringly, inviting Millie to sit down. Millie took a cloth and copied Violet, wiping paste from the jar onto the silver, then rubbing hard to get a rich shine.

"Mind that you get in between the prongs," instructed Bess.

Violet pulled a little face and Millie smiled conspiratorially, for she had liked Violet at first meeting and then more all the time. Violet was dainty and sweet with a shy manner and a beautiful smile, and large, thick-lashed blue eyes. She had black, crinkly hair that frizzled on her forehead and was netted into a puffy-looking bun below her cap. Millie, who had

50

straight, mousy hair which resisted all efforts to curl or confine it, envied Violet her hair more than she envied her her smile or her eyes. She is like a violet, she thought. You wouldn't think her pretty until you look hard at her, and then you can see how beautiful she really is.

Below the level of Will's labored reading, Violet whispered, "Do be doing them carefully, Millie love. She'll be checking it all to make sure they're done properly."

"Why is she so angry?" Millie whispered back. "I didn't mean anythin' by askin' questions."

Violet dipped a corner of her cloth into the paste pot. "She's upset, and I don't blame her at all. It's about the wedding, Miss Victoria's wedding."

"Why? Ain't a weddin' summat to be 'appy on?"

"Not this wedding. This is no happy thing."

"Why, then?"

Bess glared at them suspiciously. "Stop that gabbing, the pair of you, else I shan't be able to hear myself think. Millie, you can leave that now. Fetch a bucket and cloth and wash down the hearth."

"But I done that this mornin'," protested Young Will, looking up from his reading. "Ain't I done it good enough?"

"You did it beautifully," Bess assured him. "I just want it done again. No, you stay with your lesson. Millie can do it and then give it a coat of blacking for me. Mrs. Fielding wants her kept busy, and busy she shall be."

Bess paused on her way to the stove. Suddenly she set down the bowl of onions and said, "Violet, what's that sticking out of your pocket, my young lady?"

Violet gasped and put her hand over her breasts.

"Give it to me." Bess put out her hand.

"Please, Bess. It's my own business. Please."

"In your uniform in working hours, everything is my business, and nothing is yours except what concerns your work. Give it to me."

Violet began to cry. Millie paused at the doorway. A cloth fresh from the clothesline hung from her hand.

Bess pulled Violet's hands away and tugged the paper from her pocket.

"Please, Bess, give it to me," cried Violet.

Bess turned her back on the girl, who subsided, sobbing. She unfolded the letter and began to read it aloud. " 'My own dearest, I miss you so much and think of you every day. When I wake up in the morning, you are the first thing I think about. When I am doing my work, I think about you all the time . . .'" She broke off with a snort. "No wonder your work is slipping, my girl. 'When I go to bed, I lie awake and think about you until I fall asleep. I wish the war would end and you would come home . . .!'" Bess crumpled the letter and glared at Violet, then shook the paper under her bowed face. "This is to *him*, isn't it? This letter is to Master Andrew!"

"No, Bess! No!" cried Violet in terror. "It's not!"

Myers stood up. Very seriously he said, "Then you'd best be telling us who it is to, then."

"It's not to him!"

"Then who is it, girl?"

Violet burst out frantically, "It's my cousin, my cousin Alf. He's in the infantry! Yes, it's for my cousin Alf."

"I don't believe you," said Myers quietly.

"No," said Bess. "You were always hanging about Master Andrew when he was here, always mooning over him . . ."

"I was not!"

"Don't interrupt! Not only were you mooning about over him, but Myers actually saw you coming from his room one night."

"He wanted his hot-water bottle refilled! That's all, I swear to thee!"

"So you said at the time."

"It's true, Myers! It's true, Bess, I swear!"

Bess said suddenly. "It had better be true. And this had better be to your cousin, though why you should write like this . . . It doesn't seem right."

"We're all so worried about him," pleaded Violet. "He's sickly and takes cold so easy, we're all worried and anxious about him. I mean, from what the papers say, it's so bad out there, men dying off like bugs in the winter . . ."

Bess said, "If there *was* anything between you and Master Andrew, you'd lose your job like that." She snapped her fingers at Violet. "You do know that?"

"Thee told me before," said Violet miserably.

"And suppose I was to find out that you had posted a letter to him already, then Myers would have to tell the master and you would be out the door right sharpish. You do know that?"

Violet nodded.

"You'd be gone before he was back. I'd not like to lose you, but I'll not stand any nonsense, and I'm sick of your moping about. From now on you can worry about your job. Now get about with it." She chopped some lard into a heavy black pan and tipped in the onions. They began to sizzle and spit immediately. As she stirred them about with a wooden spoon, she watched Millie filling a bucket at the spigot nearby and sighed inwardly to think of what a complicated and unending task it was to keep the maids up to a high standard. She knew what was going on with Violet, and the sooner Master Andrew was married off the better. It must be all of six years she'd been mooning over him. Not that it would do her any good, for Master Andrew had more sense than to encourage her. And as for this Millie, she didn't seem the thieving type, but there was something odd about her all the same, and Bess didn't like it.

She pushed the onions to the side of the pan, approving their translucent gold color, and tipped in a small dish of shredded bacon, pushing the tiny ribbons of meat down hard against the hot surface.

"That smells good, love," said Myers.

Bess turned to smile at him. At her feet Millie wrung and wiped. Suddenly she began singing quietly to herself and Bess knew then what was different about her. She was unsquashable. Bess had given her a stinging tongue-lashing not a quarter of an hour ago, and already she was actually singing. Violet would be subdued for several hours now, but Millie was acting as though the incident hadn't happened. This one doesn't *think* like a servant, Bess realized. Millie would probably make herself at home in the palace! Well, she would have to keep the pressure on this little baggage. One sign of warmth on Bess's part and she'd be slacking off right away.

"Mind you do the corners," said Bess. "I want a good job done."

Millie rubbed with a will. She enjoyed this kind of work—straightforward work she knew—which could be done without any thought. The warmth from the stove made her face feel flushed. She longed to watch what Bess was cooking; it smelled so gorgeous that her stomach knotted happily. Right then Millie resolved to try to watch Bess, to see how she cooked a dish from start to finish. Then she might be able to buy the ingredients and attempt to duplicate the recipe for her family on one

53

of her days off. Wouldn't they be impressed and thrilled if she could manage that! But she would have to do her observing when Bess was in a better mood. She wondered why the cook was so upset. What could be the matter with Miss Victoria's wedding that Violet could describe it as 'no happy thing'? Surely Miss Victoria would be having a fairy-tale wedding with a handsome groom and everybody smiling? Rich folks are peculiar, Millie decided. She had first thought that at Miss Beatrice's. With four bedrooms in the cottage, Miss Beatrice and Miss Manfred crowded into the one and left the others unused. Fancy not wanting a room of your own, Millie had thought. Rich folks were odd, and nothing like us. We know what to want, and how to be happy. She rubbed the hearth harder, singing absently to herself.

"Will you stop that caterwauling?" snapped Bess. "I'll be getting one of my bad heads if you keep it up."

"Sorry, Bess." Millie's voice was apologetic but she smiled to herself. It was fun to be working in a place where so much was happening, where it was warm, where you had a bed of your own to sleep in, and, best of all, where there were such delicious things to look forward to at supper.

Nine

The morning was dreary and cold. Victoria awoke to hear rain splattering against the windows and the sound of shouting in the downstairs hall. At first she lay quietly, wondering what the matter could be. Then with a sudden gasp of excitement she flung back the bedclothes, tugged on her green silk wrapper, pushed her braids back over her shoulders, and rushed out of the room, banging the door behind her.

Hanging breathlessly over the stair rail, she could see Father in the downstairs hall hugging Mother, who was laughing in happy, tremulous little choking sounds. Birdie was there too, jumping about in glee and shrieking. Myers was, positively grinning, and Nana held the newspaper in both hands, trying to read it through the tears that were welling from her eyes.

Victoria paused only long enough to be sure, then rushed to her sister's room and leaned right over her. "Wake up,

54

Albertina! The war is over! It's in the morning paper. Andrew will be home soon."

"That's wonderful. Now go away," said Albertina sleepily.

At breakfast everybody was jubilant. Even Violet was smiling and sparkling as she stood at the buffet, pouring tea and coffee from tall silver pots. Matthew tried to inject a practical note. He pointed out that as they had not heard from Andrew in more than a month, it was impossible to know where he was or what he was doing. And, as he was Lord Longworth's aide, he would be one of the last to leave when the army did pull out. He warned his family not to expect their brother for some time yet.

Grace would not look at it that way. Blithely optimistic, she decided that he would be home at any moment and sent for Joan and instructed her to air Andrew's room and press all of his clothes.

Victoria forgot her wedding in the excitement of thinking how very wonderful it would be to have her brother home. She had missed him so much. But after the first rush of intoxication she did remember her wedding. Suddenly she wondered where she would be living when Andrew came home. Father had said nothing about a date and neither had Mother. Victoria herself had not asked; she tried very hard not to think of it, in the same way as she refused to think about death. If she could pretend it were not going to happen, then she could better enjoy each day she had left here. But now she had to know. I'll ask Father to please let the wedding wait until Andrew comes home from the war she decided. It's such a tiny favor, surely he'll agree.

At morning lessons the girls were too elated to concentrate on Latin or to study sonnets, so instead Miss Boswell gave them an impromptu geography lesson. On the big globe she showed them where Versailles was. But Birdie heard nothing the governess said about the Treaty of Paris.

"I want to go down to the morning room and wait for Andrew," she declared. "Somebody has to be watching out in case he comes home today."

Finally Miss Boswell capitulated. "Very well," she said, knowing that Birdie would tire of keeping watch by lunchtime. "Albertina, we can have a music lesson. Have you been practicing your scales?"

Victoria took the chance to slip out of the room and tiptoe

downstairs to the study. The door was shut. This door always seemed more forbidding than any other, for it was a strict rule that when Father was working, he must not be disturbed. She took a deep breath and rapped her knuckles against the dark wood.

Matthew was adding up long rows of figures in a ledger. He glanced up when Victoria entered, and she realized from the blank, unseeing look that he gave her that she was breaking his train of thought. "I'm sorry to disturb you," she offered timidly.

"Well, child?" he sounded impatient.

Her courage was slipping away. "Father, could we please postpone the wedding?" she blurted.

"What in land sakes for?" He slapped the pen down, splashing ink onto the ledger. Dabbing with the blotter, he asked, "What has prompted this extraordinary request, when everything has been settled?"

"When it has been settled *for*?" she ventured.

He consulted his desk calendar. "We decided on a date the other evening, but you dashed off before I could tell you. That was an exciting evening, wasn't it? She nodded wordlessly. "Ah, here we are. May thirtieth. That's seven or eight weeks off."

She forced herself to say, "Please, Father, could we put the wedding off a few more weeks, just enough to make sure that Andrew will be home in time? I do so want to be here when we all welcome him home, and it won't be the same if I'm married. Besides, I'd like him to be at the wedding too."

"Is that all that's troubling you, then?" He sounded more sympathetic now, and at the warm tone Victoria was ashamed to find herself bursting into tears. "There, now!" he said in alarm and was suddenly around the desk and dabbing at her face with a handkerchief that smelled comfortingly of cigar tobacco.

He smiled into her face. "Ah, yes," he said with satisfaction. "You're a real bride after all. You had me worried there for a minute and I don't mind admitting it. I thought that you were not anxious to be wed and settled into your own home. I thought there was something amiss with you, that you were like your . . ." Lamely he patted her shoulder. "Don't worry, pet. All brides cry. It's nature, that's what it is. You are lucky to be getting the likes of Henry Benchley. A fine man he is.

There's never been any scandal about him, so you'll never have to fear trouble from gambling or other wo-...." Oh, dear, he was having a bad day! So many worries about the money business that he couldn't even remember who he was talking to. Hastily he said, "If it's Andrew you're worried over, then worry no more. His regiment is absolutely certain to be home by then." He sat on the edge of his desk. "By the way, you won't be seeing Henry for a fortnight or more. He's had to go on a business trip for another client, and I shall be meeting him in Leeds at the end of next week. We have some business in the Midlands to keep us busy for a few days."

Victoria still looked miserable, and Matthew interpreted her despondency as disappointment with the last piece of news. "Cheer up, lass. He'll be coming to dinner especially to bring you your betrothal ring, all in good time. Oh, yes, he wants you to think about what you would like as a wedding gift."

"A gift?"

"Yes, your wedding gift from him."

"I want nothing from him! Nothing at all!"

Matthew looked surprised. It didn't take much to set her off in a crying bout, she who always used to be so calm and even-tempered. "There's no cause to cry, dear!" he protested. "You must think about what you want. It's the custom, and a good one. Ask for something fine. Henry can afford the very best, you know." He chuckled and patted her under the chin. "That man could live well on my fees alone. Run along now and let me get back to this chaos. You'll be a real lady soon, won't you?"

That didn't do me much good, thought Victoria dismally as the door shut behind her. Andrew may not be here after all, despite what Father said. And he thinks I'm *delighted* about the wedding! How can he be so blind?

Myers was at the front porch, admitting Lady Longworth. There was somebody with her, a young woman in a navy blue and white dress. She had gold hair in a bun very low on her neck, with hair brushed straight back from her forehead in a style not at all flattering, contrasting with Lady Longworth's usual confection of curls and ringlets. Victoria watched from the shadows as Lady Longworth shook her dripping umbrella and handed it to the butler as if she owned the house and Myers with it. Victoria stood perfectly still but was seen at once.

"Victoria!" Lady Longworth called imperiously. She was

57

a tall woman with jutting bosoms and a voice that rasped like a nail file. The girls avoided her when at all possible.

Dutifully, if reluctantly, Victoria came forward at once. "Good morning, Lady Longworth. It is not such a pleasant day today is it?"

Lady Longworth ignored the pleasantry. "This is Noelle, Victoria. Is your mother in?"

Surprised, Victoria looked closer at the somber-faced girl but hardly had time to form an impression before Lady Longworth had tugged at her daughter's arm and led her toward the morning room.

Lady Longworth's entrance was characteristically sweeping. "Grace!" she cried, holding her arms open wide. "Isn't it simply *wonderful* news? Isn't it simply *marvelous*!"

"We are all so thrilled that we can hardly think straight," said Grace. "Why, but it's Noelle, isn't it? How lovely to see you, my dear. Do you remember me? I met you at your house perhaps a year ago. It was last June, when your mother and I were planning that reception for the duchess of Preston."

Noelle looked at the floor and shook her head.

"She hasn't a good memory," said Alice. "Sit down here, dear, and don't fidget. She is thrilled about the end of the war too because she has been looking forward to meeting your Andrew. Haven't you, dear?"

Noelle glanced shyly at Grace and nodded. She looked almost unhappy.

Grace rang the bell. When Violet entered silently, she said, "Could we have coffee for two in here, please, Violet, and would you fetch one of the girls to escort Miss Longworth upstairs? She can have tea with the others in the schoolroom." To Alice she said, "The girls would like to meet her, and it is cozy in the schoolroom with the fire going. Quite the warmest room in the house, I always think."

"Perhaps Noelle should stay with me," suggested Alice. "She is very shy."

"Of course," said Grace, adding craftily, "Confidences can wait until another time, then. . . .Oh, dear. Your dress is quite damp at the hem. Do sit yourself here by the fire."

She waited until Violet had brought the coffee and Millie had escorted a reluctant Noelle out of the room. Confidences took precedence over shyness.

Alice sipped gingerly at her scalding coffee. "What is the pressing news?"

Grace smiled. "Victoria is to be married at the end of May."

"What?" cried Alice, forgetting herself for a moment. Her eyebrows steepled and she asked coolly, "And how has this come about?"

"Don't be offended at the suddenness, dear," said Grace. "You are, of course, the very first person outside this house to know. And, I might say, it is just as much a surprise to me as I can see it is to you. I had no idea either."

Placated, Alice said in a more friendly tone, "And who is the bridegroom to be, if I may ask?"

"Of course you may." Grace laughed. "How could I keep a secret from you? It is Lord Benchley, of all people."

"Oh, my dear, what a catch!" Alice was gratifyingly impressed. "Henry Benchley is received everywhere, simply *everywhere*! I have never been able to understand why, but he is. I rather think that it might be because, although he comes from such a fine old family, nobody *ever* feels inferior to him."

Grace did not appear to notice the slight. "We are pleased about the match," she said.

"Well, naturally. So would I be. Extremely pleased. But how did you manage it? All manner of people have been trying to match him off for the past twenty years, but without success. I was told once that he had been rejected twice and was afraid of a third refusal. Quite understandable, I should think."

"He asked for Victoria. He asked Matthew quite formally and very properly, and of course we were so flattered that we accepted at once."

"Naturally. So would I have." Alice flicked out a lace handkerchief and asked a little too casually, "And how does Victoria feel about him? There must be thirty years between them, surely?"

After only a slight hesitation Grace said, "She was rather surprised but very flattered. Who would have thought that she would marry a lord? It is a wonderful compliment to us all."

"Naturally. I would think so too." The cold green eyes saw a great deal more than Grace would have realized, or wanted.

As if she needed defending, Grace said, "Victoria is a sensible girl and will soon grow accustomed to being married. Oh, just think, Alice! Her son will be the duke of Lanark!"

59

"It is exciting, very exciting. And now, dear, you will have to turn your attention to Andrew. Don't you think it is time he thought about finding a suitable bride?"

"Soon, perhaps," fluttered Grace. She dreaded this subject, which Alice broached with uncomfortable regularity. This time she attempted to put her off. "I would rather like Andrew to choose for himself, since he is my only son."

"Nonsense," said Alice promptly. "Andrew is a splendid boy, but like most young men he would chose for his own taste rather than for his future—and that could be disastrous."

She never kept up the topic for long, and Grace was relieved when she said, "I have something rather grave to confide in you, Grace. It is the least I can do since you have confided in me."

Immediately Grace laid her cup and saucer aside. Alice's confidences were always interesting and invariably concerned the weaknesses and misdeeds of someone in their circle—or, better still, someone royal.

Alice took a few last sips of coffee, then sighed. "This is such a tedious business, really. I do hate to bother you with the details."

"Really, Alice, you know that you can tell me anything. After all, what else are friends for?"

Alice smiled.

"It is to do with the war," she began.

Grace leaned back in the pale pink brocade wing chair and tried to hide her disappointment. She had been hoping for spice, and there was none of that in the war.

"I do hope that you are listening, dear, because this is important. Did you know that there was to be an inquiry into the conduct of the war?"

"Conduct?"

"Yes, dear, conduct." Alice tapped her fingers on the rim of her saucer impatiently. "The inquiry is going to examine the way things were run, the planning, how the officers behaved, and so on."

"I've heard nothing."

"Surely you must have. That dreadful man, William Russell, has been urging the government for months now to hold this inquiry, and now the disgraceful fellow is to have his way."

Grace looked perfectly blank.

"Grace, dear, you *must* know what I am talking about. There cannot be a soul in the whole of London who does not know. Don't you read *The Times*?"

Agitated by the note of irritation, Grace said hastily, "Oh, of course. The man who writes to the newspaper describing the fighting."

Alice sniffed, dabbing her handkerchief to her nose. "What he *really* does is stir up trouble for innocent people," she said. "I don't know how they have the gall to print what the brute says."

"We don't see much of it," apologized Grace. "You see, Matthew reads *The Times* first and he often cuts those sections out. He's afraid of upsetting the girls because of Andrew, you understand. The girls are so sensitive and so easily alarmed that he fears too graphic accounts of the fighting might frighten them."

Alice tapped her foot, waiting to swerve back to the main issue of the conversation. "This Mr. Russell has caused endless trouble. Poor dear Wilton has written to tell me all about it. They treated the ghastly fellow so courteously, offered him such kindness, and then the brute goes and writes this dreadful inflammatory stuff about poor innocent officers who are only doing their patriotic duty and who are the very last people who should be hounded by the press."

Grace looked surprised. "That doesn't sound at all nice. I do hope that there has been nothing said against Wilton or Andrew."

"He says nothing directly, he is too cunning for that. If he said something openly, then Wilton could call him out and demand satisfaction. And I assure you, my dear, he would certainly get it! No, the fellow is too sly by far. As Wilton puts it, rather wittily, I think, this brute Russell stabs them in the back with his pen."

"How very clever . . . I mean, how well put. Wilton always did have a witty way with words."

"Yes . . . but you can see the difficulty. This man favors the cowardly approach, and though he has made it clear that many of his accusations are directed at poor Wilton, there is nothing Wilton can fight. At least, not yet."

There was a silence until Grace, who was not sure at all what the point of these revelations was, said, "Alice, dear, I'm certain that you're worrying over nothing. Don't you think that

61

if things were said against Wilton in *The Times*, Matthew would have noticed and made some comment? Of course he would. And if he has not noticed, then I feel certain that nobody else has."

"You are quite wrong, my dear, though I do wish most fervently that you were correct. Mrs. White-Landfell called to see me yesterday. She told me that Russell has caused quite a ruckus, that confidential reports sent by this scoundrel to Parliament have been dreadfully damaging. It is all so ridiculous. Who would believe a blackguard like Russell against the word of honorable men like my Wilton? And yet this is what is happening or they'd not even consider an inquiry. If you ask me, Lord Palmerston and those fellows are looking for someone to blame the terrible defeats on, a scapegoat, if you like."

"I still don't see why you should be worried, Alice. They won't be blaming men who were right there where the fighting was. Gentlemen like your Wilton will be praised, not criticized. You will see, dear."

Alice sniffed. "If Wilton was to come home in triumph, all of his sacrifice would have been worthwhile. Instead, because the war was lost—not through any fault of his, mind you—he faces possible disgrace and certain shame."

"It cannot be true. I cannot believe you."

"It's true. Wilton said so, and Mrs. White-Landfell confirmed his suspicions. She told me to warn Wilton."

"But why Wilton?"

"Oh, there will be others—cowards or those officers who gave their men the wrong orders, but Wilton I cannot understand. He stayed. He is one of the loyal ones. If anybody should be held responsible for our failures, it should be those who deserted their commands." Alice flapped her handkerchief indignantly. "Why aren't those men the ones to be accused? Why should it be my poor, brave Wilton?"

"Please calm yourself, Alice. Remember your heart."

"How am I to keep calm when my poor husband is to be persecuted?" Alice began to sob.

Grace knelt by her chair. "Please, Alice. I feel so sorry for you. Is there something I can do to help?"

"There is something," wept Alice.

"Do tell me what it is," urged Grace. "I cannot bear to see you so upset."

Alice dabbed at her eyes furiously. "When they launch the inquiry, they will be calling on men who have worked with Wilton to give statements, evidence which could perhaps put him in an unflattering light. I would like you to persuade Andrew not to say anything which could harm Wilton..."

"Alice!" gasped Grace. "How can you suggest such a thing? Andrew would give Wilton his loyalty as a matter of course. He owes his position to him! He would never..."

"Yes, dear," cut in Alice. "I know that Andrew feels indebted to Wilton, and so he should."

Grace nodded.

"But these men in Westminster can be devilishly cunning. That is why I was warned. If Mrs. White-Landsfell came especially to tell me what to do, it would be foolish to ignore her. She knows everything that goes on in Westminster. It is whispered that Wilton, because he was in charge of supplies, will be the prime target of the vicious accusations. Andrew will need to have all his wits about him if he is not to be tricked or beguiled into giving them the answers they want. They have ways of twisting the simplest and most innocent answers to their own meaning. And Andrew is such a helpful and well-meaning lad, it might not occur to him that he is being used."

Grace nodded.

"I feel that it would be best if Andrew could be persuaded not to help with the inquiry at all. Wilton says that he could plead illness as an excuse not to testify. Once he is there, there is no way of knowing what they might wring out of him."

Grace nodded.

"Wilton thinks the world of your son, you know. He feels that Andrew has a great future in the army. I know that he already looks on him as a son, and would be so proud if..."

"You can rely on Andrew," said Grace quickly. "He is a good and grateful boy."

"I know," said Alice. "I know he is."

Albertina stood beside Grace as they bade good day to the visitors. As soon as the door closed behind them and Myers had glided past on his way back to the kitchen, Albertina burst out, "She was weird, Mother. She was really strange!"

"Noelle?"

"Yes. She just looked at the floor and wouldn't talk to us, but she ate all the cream cakes, just popped them into her

63

mouth and swallowed them without chewing. We tried to talk her after the cakes were all gone, but she didn't say anything except that she was looking forward to meeting 'young Mr. Fielding!' Why would she want to meet *him*? She said it in a strange voice, too, the way Birdie talks when she's quoting poetry. Will she come again?"

"I don't know," said Grace, "but I rather think she might..."

Ten

Now that the wedding was only five weeks away, the mood of excitement was infecting everybody. Birdie chattered of nothing but bridesmaids and decked Flounce out in scraps of lace and ribbons, then made him "sit and stay" while she read made-up marriage vows over him and one of her dolls. Miss Boswell hobbled about after Mrs. Fielding with a notebook and pencil for note-taking. Myers kept the servants busy. He decreed that the whole house, from the attic storeroom to the coal cellar, was to be thoroughly scrubbed. Buckets, brooms, and stepladders cluttered the hallways, and all the rooms smelled of lye soap and wax. The maids had no time to gossip, Young Will had no time for his reading lessons, and Old Will grumbled because he never seemed to find the time to sit on the back steps and enjoy a pipe. Bess filled a dozen pages in her menu book writing out special suggestions for the reception. She had been annoyed to hear of the caterers whom Lady Longworth had recommended but was mollified when she was told that they would be providing only the basic foods: hams, roast meats, and baked vegetables. Her menu of salmon aspics, stroganoff, curries, oysters and caviar, fried chicken, and assorted cakes and trifles, would be the main fare.

Every day now visitors flocked to the house. Grace was thankful that Matthew was either away or too busy to be annoyed by the gaggles of women who clustered in the downstairs rooms.

Alice Longworth came every day. She did not wait for the "proper" hour of two o'clock but came at noon to begin helping Grace. Bonneted and shawled, she would sweep into the morning room and take command. She had the final say on the guest list, she recommended the tradespeople, she knew who made the freshest and most tasteful flower arrangements, and who could supply the best champagne at the lowest price. Grace was relieved to have her assistance. Alice seemed to have such a perfect eye for detail. It was she who suggested the scalloped name cards on the pews, and it was her idea to have a bower of white roses above a tiny round table to frame the wedding cake. It was the least Grace could do in return to invite Noelle to be a bridesmaid.

Victoria tried to keep out of her way. Unlike Grace she did not appreciate being managed, but she listened politely to all the advice and tried to smile at the personal remarks. Of course every lady who called wanted to have an intimate word with the bride-to-be and to offer good wishes—which to Victoria sounded so insincere that she could hardly accept them graciously. She heard Lord Benchley described so glowingly so often that she began to wonder if she was the only person who thought him dull, ugly, and fat. To hear the way he was talked about, a stranger would think him a prince instead of a toad, she thought glumly. At the slightest excuse she would slip off to her room to sit quietly on the window seat, but the moments of peace were brief. Inevitably another carriage would roll up, another brace of ladies would alight, and presently Joan or Violet or Millie would be tapping at the door to summon her back downstairs.

Twice a week Madame Soiska came for dress fittings. She was a dour, dumpy woman who could sew pure heaven into the most glorious creations. Promptly at eleven she would stagger up the stairs while Millie assisted her with the billowing, calico-wrapped gowns. For the next hour Victoria had to stand perfectly still with her arms held out from her body while Madame Soiska worked around her with pins and tape measures and long, looping basting threads. It was excruciatingly uncomfortable and her arms ached, but if she fidgeted, Madame would bark at her through a mouth clamped over a row of pins. The hour had one real consolation because Millie stayed to help, and she was as lively and chattery as the older woman was laconic. She talked incessantly, and Victoria listened, fascinated first by her accent and later by what she said. It was such a refreshing change from parlor conversation to hear about things that society folk never discussed and probably didn't know about.

Today Millie was telling her all about the work she used to do. Sometimes she sewed gloves at home with her mother. "Not that I was much 'elp. My sewin' ain't up to much." In the season when cress was in the markets, she might buy a trayload to sell in the streets. "A tough lark that was, too, miss. You 'ave to beg folks to buy. On a real cold day my 'ands would be froze clear through. Used to be able to see the bones in my fingers, my skin would be so blue. Some days the 'ole lot would go in a few snaps, an' other days I'd have to trudge from one side o' West End to t'other."

Madame Soiska sniffed, making her face look like a Pomeranian's. She made it clear she did not approve of Millie. "This hem iss done," she said. "Ve take eet off and see the feet of this next one."

As "thiss one" was being arranged over the wide-hooped petticoats, Victoria smoothed the fabric under her finger and felt a tremble of pleasure. This gown was truly lovely. The material was a soft blue silk which looked gray and silver in certain lights. The only ornamentation was the design itself, for the material was so beautiful it needed no other. Swaths of silk clung around the hipline and at the shoulders above fitted sleeves. The bodice was a simple, smooth curve tucking into an impossibly tiny waist. All around the hem the skirt was looped up to show ruffles of the same fabric peeking out from underneath. Victoria admired it in the huge dresser mirror and sighed with delight. While her other gowns all seemed to say, "Look at me. I'm a beautiful dress," this one seemed to whisper, "Look at me. I'm a beautiful woman!"

Victoria caught a glimpse of Albertina going past the open doorway. Impulsively she ran to the door and cried breathlessly, "Oh, do look at this, Albertina! Isn't this the most beautiful dress you ever saw?"

Her sister, who was by now a few paces down the hall, half turned and gave a careless glance in her direction. "It's very nice," she allowed grudgingly, then turned away again.

Victoria ran after her. "Please don't be like that," she pleaded.

"Like what?" she shrugged off Victoria's hand.

"Please don't be so . . . so far away. I hardly have the chance to see you any more, and when I do, it seems as though we're not good friends any longer."

"Why should you worry about that?" said Albertina tartly. "You are so busy these days being fitted for one new gown after another. How many does this make? Twenty?"

"Albertina, that's not fair! It is less than half that many. And I didn't ask for them. It was Mother's idea, and you know that perfectly well. She insisted that I have them. Besides, you and Birdie are having new clothes too."

"Two gowns each, to be exact."

Victoria tried again to take her arm, but Albertina snatched it away and hurried on walking stiffly, head high. Victoria rushed after her. "Please, Albertina. In just a few weeks we will be separated for*ever*, and I really couldn't bear it if we weren't friends when I go.

"Oh, leave me be," said her sister crossly. "I'm sick and tired of all this fuss. Victoria this and Victoria that. Everybody coming to call on you. Everybody fussing over you, telling you how beautiful you look, bringing you presents . . . I could go away and nobody would even notice I was missing."

"That's not true." Victoria tagged after her sister who was now haughtily walking downstairs. "You are much prettier than I am. People have always said so and fussed over you. I'm only the center of attention now because I'm the bride. It will be exactly the same for you when you are married and I hope you enjoy it more than I do! Oh, please be friends again!" Finally, in desperation, she dragged out what she had steadfastly been refusing to look at. "Have you thought how this is for me?" she demanded. "Have you considered that all I will have for company will be Lord Benchley? Would you really like to be in my place and marrying *him*? Do you think a thousand new dresses would make that thought any happier?"

Albertina turned to her sister. They both looked equally distraught. "I never thought about that. I'm sorry, truly I am," she said in a voice thick with shame. It was mean of me to be envious of your beautiful dresses. And we *are* friends. I shall come to see you often when you are married. Old Will shall be tired out from driving me back and forth to your house. Come on, do let's show Mother and Nana your new dress. They'll be in here." She darted into the morning room, without waiting for her sister.

Victoria hesitated, looking back up the stairs. Madame Soiska would be wondering where she was. Then the doorbell rang. Lady Longworth is rather early today, Victoria thought. The bell rang again. There was no sign of the butler, so Victoria opened the door.

There on the top step, in full dress uniform, stood Captain Charles Lawrence. His eyes widened slightly when he saw her. "Princess," he said softly. "I had hoped to see you, to catch a glimpse of you perhaps. But this is far more than I could have ever hoped for or dreamed of."

Flustered, she glanced back into the hall, hoping to see Myers or one of the maids, for she was suddenly and acutely conscious of her loose hair and stockinged feet. The hallway was empty. "Oh," she said in confusion. "I thought it was one of Mother's friends, I thought you were . . ."

"Is something the matter?"

"No, Captain Lawrence. Not really. It's just that . . ." She knew she was blushing. Her face was hot and her heart felt high and tight in her chest.

He smiled at her. "May I please be permitted to come in?"

"Oh. Oh, yes, of course. Please do come in," she said in dismay.

When he brushed past her in the doorway, there was the faint sharp smell of cologne. He stood close, looking down at her and smiling as though he had been looking forward to seeing her. Why, he is very handsome, she thought. She had not really noticed his looks that day in the park. Today, with his uniform on, he seemed different.

"What a tiny little creature you are, princess." His voice was as brown and smooth as his polished boots.

He's laughing at me again, she thought, embarrassed. He's teasing me like Andrew does—paying compliments when he's really making fun.

She led him into the parlor to wait for her mother and offered him a chair, but his attention was caught by a photograph of her, taken two years ago, before Andrew went away to war. In it a serious-faced girl sat very straight on a divan with a potted palm and a drape of cloth arranged behind her. Victoria hated the photograph because it made her look so babyish and sad-faced, but Captain Lawrence picked it up and held it for a moment.

"If I were a thief and come to rob this house," he said thoughtfully, "this is the only thing I would steal. It is a lovely

68

picture, princess, though of course not as beautiful as the original."

What a tease he was, and cheeky too, for he had no right to talk to her like that. She tried to speak calmly. "If you would please wait here, Captain Lawrence, I shall fetch Mother."

After a twirl in the morning room so that Nana and Mother could admire her gown, she darted back up the stairs. To her dismay she found that she was unable to resist peeking back toward the parlor. There he was, standing just inside the door, watching her. He smiled broadly. She sped faster up the stairs, blushing again.

At the top Millie was waiting, wide-eyed and most impressed. "Oooh, miss, what a beautiful gentleman!" she whispered. "is 'e your intended?"

"No, Millie, he's not."

"Oooh, dear! I couldn't 'elp but see the looks 'e gave you. I was sure it was 'im. 'E's right *beautiful*, 'e is."

For a moment she allowed herself to wish that Millie was right, but the thought gave her a sharp pain, as if one of Madame Soiska's pins were jabbing into her chest.

"The old biddy is beside 'erself," Millie was saying. "She 'as two more dresses to fit an' she says she ain't got all day."

That evening, as they were going upstairs to bed, Albertina said archly, "I *was* silly, fussing over all the attention you've been getting. Do you know that I received a very pleasant compliment of my own?"

"Do tell me about it."

"It was from that kind Captain Lawrence. You remember him, surely? He was that rather dashing gentleman who rescued Flounce."

"Of course I remember. What did he say?"

Albertina giggled. "Mother told him that we were very busy because there was a wedding in the family, and right away he wanted to know who was getting married, and when Mother told him, he looked so pleased that she guessed from his expression that he likes me. Just fancy that!"

"Fancy!" said Victoria. She was getting that queer little sharpness in her chest again.

"Mother said that he is ever so nice, with perfect manners. He has been out in the Crimea, too, but was badly wounded last November and had to be sent home. He knows the Barneses

69

and he knows Andrew! Can you top that for a coincidence?"

"I imagine a lot of people know Andrew."

"But he knows him quite well. Mother said that he spoke very highly of him and asked if he might call again, so Mother said to come back when Father gets back. Wouldn't it be fun if he really does like me?"

"Andrew?" Her throat felt tight and hurtful.

"No, silly. Captain Lawrence. What *is* the matter with you? You know, I didn't think he had even noticed me what with all the fussing over Flounce, but he must have if I've made an *impression*. I wonder if he will ask to come calling on me? I'd like that. He is ever so good-looking, don't you think?"

"I suppose . . ." Victoria tried to smother her feelings and share her sister's pleasure. What did it matter to her if a whole regiment of Captain Lawrences came calling on Albertina? She was going to be married and nobody would ever come calling on her now. She tried to say something nice, but the words would not form in her mind, for her head was blocked with all the sick jealousies she had ever felt for her sister, all gathering now, blocking her thoughts. Beautiful Albertina, the prettiest and most confident, with first choice of everything as a matter of course, befitting her father's darling.

Albertina danced down the corridor, one hand held up as if given to an invisible partner. Hating herself for imagining it, Victoria suddenly saw Captain Lawrence as that partner . . .

Eleven

The bed creaked.

"Violet?"

"Did I wake thee, Millie?"

Millie's eyes were shadows. "I was awake. I was worried about you, Violet."

Violet unrolled her stockings and tossed them in the general direction of her shoes. Her arms were striped with a silver line of moonlight as she reached around to unfasten the row of buttons down her back.

"Want me to 'elp?"

"No, thank thee. I can manage fine."

"I was worried that Myers would catch you. After 'im sayin'

'e'd dock your wages if you were late again, I thought 'e might be waitin' up."

"Thee can stop worrying. I had a lovely evening. A real treat it was." She bounced on her bed.

"I'm glad you 'ad fun."

"It was the best evening yet. We'll be wed soon, I fancy, so thee must understand that I don't really care if Myers does catch me. It will help me make up my mind." She stood, flipped back the blanket, sat down, and then slid both feet at once into bed.

Wide awake now, Millie was sitting up attentively. "'As 'e asked you, then?"

"Not yet, but he will. He didn't want me to leave. Oh, he tried so hard to make me stay. It's best for him that he weds me. Yes, it's no life for him being on his own bringing up two little ones. He needs me, and it's up to me to make him ask. Men are shy of doing that. It's a big thing for them."

Millie was incredulous. "'Ow can you get a fellow to ask you that?"

Violet snuggled her head into the thin pillow. Her voice sounded less buoyant now. "I'm not giving him any," she said frankly. "If thee wants a man, that's the best way to do it. The more he's fooled around, the easier he is to get that way. And my Ted has had more than his share of women, I'll be bound. No, I've made it plain as pudding that he'll not get any from me. Thee must remember that, Millie. Give it to them only if that's all thee wants, for once you do, they'll be giving thee nowt else, not even the time of day."

"Men ain't all like that."

"No? Has thee ever tried to marry one?"

"No, I ain't."

"Then thee will learn. The finer they be to thee at first, the worse they be later. I've seen a lot of it, Millie. Not from myself, for in a way I've been lucky not to want to bother with men, but I've seen dozens of maids come through in the ten years I've been with this family, and most of those maids have men troubles, and always the same reason. I tell thee truly, men are all the same. If thee learns about it now, it will save trouble later."

"Your Ted, is 'e like that?"

"Probably worse."

"Why are you wantin' to marry 'im, then?"

"I ask thee," said Violet patiently, "who else is wanting to marry me? He'll be good to me, and I'll be good to him, and that counts for a lot."

"Don't you love 'im?" asked Millie, disillusioned.

"Oh, I like him well enough."

Millie cupped her face in her hands. "I'll not wed any man unless I loves 'im."

Violet collapsed into laughter which she muffled with the edge of the coarse blanket. When she could, she whispered, "Thee will be believing in fairies and goblins next. Love brings trouble, not happiness."

"That's sad."

"That's the way of life."

"Have you been in love, Violet?"

There followed a long, poignant silence. Millie wondered whether she had overrun the bounds of their tentative friendship. Then Violet said quietly and dryly, "I was in love for years and years and years. All my life it seems."

"To the same man?"

"Yes, the same one."

Millie was bolt upright with indignation. "Then why ain't you marryin' 'im? If you loved someone that long, ain't it plain that 'e's the one for you?"

Violet did not reply but sat quietly, and it was some time before Millie realized, sensed actually, that she was crying.

Instantly she was out of her bed and embracing the older girl. "I'm sorry. What a clumsy nit I am sometimes! Is it the young master I 'eard Bess scolding you about?"

Muffled thumps came on the wall from Joan's room next door.

Millie lowered her voice back to a whisper. "Please, Violet. You've been good to me an' I'd 'ate to spoil it, so don't tell me nowt you don't want to. I ain't nosy, honest I ain't."

Violet rubbed the back of her hand across her wet face. "I know thee didn't mean to upset me. But ever since I came here, Master Andrew and I have been...Well, I don't know how to tell thee. We took a liking to one another right off, only later it was more than that. We were both fourteen when it started to be loving between us, and I suppose it's true to say that we loved each other ever since." She chuckled to herself. "Bess has suspected all this time. He changed me, everything about me. The way I talk, the way I look, all that

72

is the way he likes it. Bess used to try to catch us together, but Master Andrew was too clever for her. Many's the time when he would wait to hear her snoring, then slip in and spend the night with me."

"Was that letter . . . ?"

"Yes. I was halfway through writing it. That's something else he did for me, taught me to read and write. I want him to know about Ted and not to come home expecting me to be here."

"But why go to Ted when you loves 'im? It don't make no sense at all."

"If thee thinks about it, it will. I *love* him, Millie. Soon he must get married, and I don't want to be here then. Or I could start a baby to him. . . . We couldn't go on being lucky forever, could we? Does thee know what would happen then?"

Millie shuddered. Miss Beatrice had told her what fate awaited servant girls who fell pregnant. No, Violet was right. In silent sympathy she patted her friend's hand.

"He says he loves me and he would look after me, but he doesn't mean it," Violet said flatly. "He's not even answered one of my letters. If it's not safe for him to write to me just the once, then he'd not be able to protect me if I did fall with a baby. It's not his fault; he can't help who he is. If he was a butler or a garden hand, I know he'd marry me in a snip. No, Millie love. This way is best. He's been away two years and in two years all feelings get less. If I'm gone when he comes home, it will be much easier for us both. If I see him again, everything will be back strong as ever, and how will I ever escape then? Can thee tell me that?"

"I wish I could 'elp you, Violet."

"Thee is being a friend to me, and a friend is what I need. Don't thee be sad for me though. I've had so many lovely times to think about, and they'll warm me the rest of my life. Ted is a good sort. We'll rub along happy enough. No, if thee has any pity, save it for poor Miss Victoria. She's the one who needs all the pity in the world, poor wee thing. She's not known the happiness I have. Beside her, I'm lucky!"

Twelve

Of all the rooms in the house Victoria's favorite was the conservatory. It was a peaceful room, cool and green in the summer, warm and green in the winter, lush with sturdy, thick-leafed bushes and misty with hanging veils of fern. The smells of spaghnum moss and decaying leaf mold mingled with the spicy perfume of a dozen different varieties of tiny starred flowers, giving the air a luxuriously heavy languor.

The conservatory was Victoria's own special domain. Several years before she had asked Old Will to teach her about the plants. Soon she could tend the conservatory on her own. She knew how much to water and how often, which plants needed trimming and which ones liked to wear their dead leaves like wrappers around their stems. In spring and autumn she moved the ferns that appreciated warmth from the sunny side in the summer to the side where the heaters exuded warmth in winter. All the plants were tended with the love she would have given a pet, if she had one. She spoke to them tenderly as she fed them tiny spoonfuls of ground fish meal, sprinkling the salty-smelling powder at the outer edges of the soil so as not to burn the delicate roots.

Now that she was leaving, her job was being passed on to Millie. Because Old Will had no time to train her, and because Victoria preferred to do it herself, she was there with Millie today, showing her how to trim the larger plants with a knife. Millie watched carefully and held a flat oval basket for the leaves to be put in.

"Plants are filled with a kind of blood, like ours," Victoria told Millie. "So if you do cut, you must do it cleanly, near the main stem. Then the plant will recover quickly."

"Blood in a plant!" said Millie, disbelieving. "Pardon an' all, miss, but might you be pullin' me leg?"

"Not at all. Look at this." And Victoria squeezed a cut stalk so that a translucent drop of sap oozed out onto Millie's hand. "See? All living things are filled with blood. Miss Boswell taught us all about that."

"Just fancy!" Millie exclaimed, rubbing the back of her hand in distaste. "But it's nowt like our blood."

"No."

"Me Mam coughs up blood. Spits it up reg'lar, she does." It was said casually, as Millie laid the severed leaf on top of the others.

"How dreadful."

"Oh, she don't do it all the time," said the maid cheerfully, as though coughing up blood was a party trick her mother kept for special occasions. "Only when 'er chest gets rotten, then she coughs a lot. Cain't sleep at nights sometimes for the noise of 'er 'ackin' away. Sounds like 'er 'ole insides is scrapin' up."

"What does the doctor say?" Victoria wiped the blade on a cloth and replaced the knife in its leather sheath.

"We don't 'ave no doctor. 'Oo'd want to come doctorin' to the likes of us?"

"Who looks after you when you're ill?" asked Victoria, adjusting a cloth tie around the stake.

"We looks after each other real well. An' Miss Beatrice, of course. She keeps an eye out for us. When me brother cut 'is leg last year from fallin' off the wagon, she showed me 'ow to clean it an' wrap it up. Real bad it was, too. All the folks in the buildin' thought 'e was done fer, 'e'd lose it for sure, but now 'e 'ardly 'as any limp or nowt."

With that, Millie went out to refill the watering cans, leaving Victoria to ponder the gulf between their lives. She was deep in thought and lifting down a bowl of maidenhair fern which needed repotting, when a voice interrupted her wonderings.

"Good afternoon, princess."

She turned, so startled that she almost fell off the low stool. There, right beside her, so close that she could have reached out a shaking hand to touch him, was Captain Charles Lawrence, resplendent in his red-coated uniform, with an expression of mischief and pleasure on his face. He bowed, no more than a slight inclination of his head. His smile warmed her; she could feel herself blushing.

"What are you doing here? How did you get in?"

"You never seem very pleased to see me," he observed, still smiling.

"You frighten me. You take me by surprise. I almost dropped this fern and it's one of my favorites."

"Let me take it, princess." He set the bowl on the table and

75

drew her down to the seat to sit beside him. "How are you?" he asked.

She was so taken aback by the way he had breezed in and so confidently taken charge of her that she said nothing, merely stared at him.

Understanding perfectly, he laughed outright. "Your eyebrows look like two dark birds all swooped up like that. You *are* pleased to see me, aren't you?"

She nodded, bemused.

"I hoped you would be, princess. I thought you might. You see, I have such good feelings about you that somehow I know nothing is going to go wrong. Do you know what I mean, princess? I shouldn't call you that, should I, when I know your name? But, confidentially, princess suits you very much better." His eyes were crinkling at her and he seemed very pleased with himself, as though he were bursting with a splendid secret that in a moment they would share. "I have been in to see your father," he confided.

"Oh?" Why would he be wanting to see *Father*?

"Yes, this very minute. We had a long talk together with an extremely satisfying outcome, from my point of view—I hope from yours, too. Now listen to this! He has given me full permission to come calling on you. So now, my proper little princess, you may talk to me without anybody being outraged." He laughed happily. "What do you think of that?"

She said nothing.

He rushed on eagerly, "I was just on my way out when I caught a glimpse of you in here, so I just had to come in and tell you the good news. It *is* good news for you, isn't it? Please do look at me! Am I being too direct and upsetting you? If I am, I do apologize. I haven't done much courting. I've had this queer idea all my life that when I met the right girl, I would know straight away, and I suppose that's why I'm rushing things. You see, I've been waiting to meet you for so long. The first time I saw you was months ago, when I had just returned from the war. You and your sisters were in the park watching the skaters. You were all muffled up in a long coat with a furry hood, and you looked so sweet that when I went back home I thought of nothing but your face all evening. I went to the park again. I saw you many times but you never seemed to notice me. It was a temptation to follow you home, but I was afraid that your Nana might notice me and of course that would put an end to my prospects. When your dog fell into the lake, it was a stroke of luck. If it had happened one minute later, I'd have been on my way home and some other lucky fellow would have had the privilege of rescuing Flounce." He paused and grinned at her, suddenly self-conscious. "I'm really rather a quiet chap. It's just that I've been looking forward to meeting you, and now there's so much to say."

Victoria was in a state of pleasurable confusion. She had never imagined hearing such a speech, and the straight sincerity of it won her over completely. However, she had a nasty feeling that some horrible mistake had been made. "Captain Lawrence," she began.

He took her hands. "Please call me Charles."

"Charles."

He beamed. "That's better. Your father said I must have your permission before I come calling on you. Do I?"

It was clear he thought she was Albertina and didn't realize that she was the eldest, and that it was she who was getting married. A flash of rage seared through her as she realized the import of what he had just said. Father would promise *her* to Lord Benchley without asking how she felt about it, but for Albertina it was to be quite different. *Her* suitors had to have her special permission before they could come calling. How unfair it was! She was given to the first man who came asking, but for the beautiful Albertina there was to be a proper romance, love, and a choice of suitors.

"I *am* doing this badly," Captain Lawrence was saying. "I haven't told you my prospects yet, and you must not give me your answer until I have. I recited them all to your father, so I quite forgot that they should be told to you. Princess, I'm afraid that I'm only a second son, but I am from a good family. The Lawrences are landowners in Devonshire, and well-to-do, if I might be frank and admit it. Naturally all the property goes to my older brother Derwood, but when I marry, I will be given a lump sum of thirty-five thousand pounds and an allowance of four thousand pounds a year. It's not much, I know, but enough for a small country house with modest upkeep and a little town house as well. With the money I earn, life should be comfortable. Your father said that you could do better for yourself, princess, but he did say it was up to you. Oh, don't look upset. Of course I'm not proposing to you, but it's only fair to tell you all this so that when I *do* propose, you will know what it means. Now, do I have your permission to come calling?"

Something of her fury and dismay must have shown on her face, for Charles said very quietly, "My clumsiness has offended you, hasn't it?"

"Truly, you have not offended me."

He held her hands flat between his. Weakly allowing it, and hoping that nobody would come in and find them together, Victoria tried to order her thoughts.

"Charles," she began.

It was a poor beginning, for he smiled adoringly at her and she thought that she had never known a worse moment than this. Not even with the news of her engagement was broken to her had she felt so dreadful.

"Charles, there has been a serious mistake."

Her hands fell under their own weight as he drew away.

His voice was hurt and surprised. "You don't like me at all?"

If only she could turn away from his eyes, it would be easier to tell him. She broke a wiry spray off the fern and picked the baby leaflets off it, one by one.

"The mistake has nothing to do with what I think or how I feel. It's something else. You think that I am Albertina, and I am not."

He took her hands again, crushing the remains of the fern with them. "Don't tease me, princess. If you don't think you could come to care for me, then please don't be afraid to say so, for you must be honest. If I have been over-confident, then it is my own fault. I thought I saw something in your eyes, heard a hint of something in your voice . . . that is why I thought you would welcome me as a suitor."

"Please listen," she burst out desperately. "It's true. I am not Albertina. She is taller than I, and has light-colored hair, and people are always confusing us, believing her to be the oldest of the three. But I am Victoria. I am the oldest."

He flinched. "And you are engaged to be married?"

She nodded miserably.

"When is it to be?"

"The thirtieth of May."

"So soon? That's almost no time at all." He gazed unseeing down at her hands, stroking her fingers, absently brushing away the crushed leaflets. Victoria could feel tears slipping out and wanted to rub them away, for they made her cheeks burn, but she left her hands where they lay in his possession. She felt tired. She also felt an unreasonable and quite improper urge to lay her head on his scarlet-jacketed shoulder, against the gold-braided epaulettes which a few minutes before had seemed so jaunty. With his shoulders bowed, they now seemed somehow pathetic.

Finally he said, "Tell me all about him."

Victoria shrank. "Lord Benchley?"

"A lord, is it, then?" Charles sounded sad and angry at the same time. "No wonder your father said that Albertina could do better, with you marrying a lord. Has he money?"

"Enough, apparently."

"Which probably means ten times what I could offer you. How old is this Lord Benchley, then?"

"Quite old, I should think. Forty or fifty, perhaps more. He is a friend of Father's, you see. They arranged it between them."

He still held her hands, but loosely now as if waiting for her to claim them back. "I must ask you. Do you love him?"

She bit her lip, knowing that evasion was the proper course here. Then she decided to be honest. "I don't like him at all, and I dread being married to him." That sounded so ungracious and disloyal that she added hastily, "Father says that he will be a good husband, and I suppose he should know."

"So this marriage is a business arrangement? He has helped your father in some way, and in return he is marrying you?"

"I hadn't thought of it like that, but that is probably how it came about. I don't understand why he wants to marry me. He doesn't seem to like me. I don't understand any of it."

"I can understand." He had lost his listless, defeated tone and had become tense and alert. "I hate him already! Princess, we cannot let it go at this. Not after all these months of hoping to meet you. Could you refuse to marry him?"

"Defy my parents?" Belatedly she realized that she should not have given him any hope by allowing the conversation to drift in such a dangerous direction. "Charles, I don't see how I can. They are only thinking of my well-being, and all the arrangements have begun. I thought of defying them, right at the start when they first told me. I was so unhappy I wanted to escape any way I could. But Nana had a talk with me and told me it was all for the best. . . . Only now I feel . . . Oh, Charles, you must go away, you must. And if you think of me at all, think of me as being married already."

He smiled as he wiped a tear away with his finger. "Don't cry. If you *were* married already, I would be trying to find a way to steal you away from your husband. No, don't look so horrified. I'm only trying to make light of one of the least amusing situations I've ever been in. Listen, princess. You say you don't love this Lord whoever. Could you care for me?"

She bowed her head, for he could not possibly expect her to answer a question like that.

"I'm in love with you," he pressed. "You know that, don't you?"

She nodded without looking up.

"Is there any hope for me?"

"Charles, you are asking the impossible," she begged miserably. "I cannot answer. I cannot change things. I must accept what is to be. Don't you realize that you are being cruel to me by asking me to consider an impossible alternative?"

"No, princess, not impossible at all. Now listen. If you were not engaged, would you be able to give me hope?"

"Yes, I would." And she looked shyly at him through her tears.

"Let us see what can be done, then, shall we?" He gave her hands a final, confident squeeze and strode out, pausing to wink at her from the doorway, which made her laugh despite her strong misgivings.

Millie came in so promptly that it was obvious she had been hovering outside the door. She set the watering cans on the table and looked at Victoria shrewdly. "'E's a fine young man, 'e is."

Victoria dabbed at her face with her handkerchief.

"'E do look smart in 'is uniform. 'As 'e been to the fighting then, same as the young master? 'E's gone in to see your Father, 'e 'as. 'E rapped on the door ever so sharpish an' went right on in."

Victoria had an unhappy feeling that the interview would be neither pleasant nor successful, and when she heard an outraged bellow some moments later, she realized she was doubly correct.

Millie's jaw dropped comically. "'E's roarin' at the young man, then, miss!"

Victoria said nothing, merely sat there waiting disconsolately to be summoned to the study. When the summons came a few minutes later, only her parents were there. Mother was seated in a chair near the window and Father stood with his back to the fire. Matthew looked angry and Grace looked distressed.

"What did that young buck say to you?" demanded her father without preamble.

"He was mistaken. He thought I was Albertina."

"You are not answering my question!" roared her father. "I asked you to tell me what he said to you. Tell me!"

"Matthew, please be gentle," pleaded Grace.

"What did he say?"

"He asked permission to call on me," said Victoria. "He said he loves me. He told me his prospects and asked if he might pay attention to me."

"And, young lady, what did you say to him?"

"I told him he had made a mistake. I said that I was going to be married soon."

"Come, now, you must have said more than that."

She realized the enormity of her indiscretion. Charles must have told Father what she had said, or enough of it to be able to ask him to change his mind about the wedding.

Bravely she said, "He asked me if I loved Lord Benchley and wanted to marry him, and I told him the truth."

"Which is? Come on, let's be having it out."

"I do not like him and I dread the thought of marrying him."

Grace's face went white and Matthew's took on the color of fine old port. There was silence until he burst out, "You had no business to say that, no business at all. And he had no business to speak to you."

Victoria was growing angry too, now. "You gave him your word that he could speak to me. That is, he thought it was to me, since he had Albertina and me confused."

"But to *encourage* him! What if it should get around that you had said that about Lord Benchley? There would be a dreadful scandal," fluttered Grace.

"He has turned your head, that's plain," said Matthew, calming down a little. "Even so, you should not have said those things. You are suffering from prewedding nerves, that is all. Of course you want to marry Henry. You said so just the other day."

"He can offer more than this nobody captain," enthused Grace. "*He* is only a second son, and not a particularly distinguished one at that. Perhaps it is just as well that we shall not be seeing any more of him. Now run along, Victoria."

Despite her father's words, Victoria though of little else but Charles. His bravery in going to speak to her father impressed her deeply, and she was equally compelled by his straightforward manner in declaring his affections. She now began to think of Charles as more handsome than he really was, more articulate, more clever, more brave. If the picture needed any extra polish, that was provided by Millie's worship of him and the fact that Albertina wanted him for herself. She began to fantasize about him.

Then reality invaded her play world. One evening after dinner, when she was seated beside Lord Benchley on a parlor sofa while Mother chattered and Albertina played Chopin rather badly, Victoria let her thoughts drift toward Charles, as they always did unless she anchored them firmly.

Quite suddenly Lord Benchley took her hand. It was the first display of affection he had shown her, and it took her by surprise. The gesture, one of ownership rather than affection, repelled her so violently that she had to actually force herself to leave her hand where it was. It seemed to want to act independently and pull itself away, as though not only her heart and mind, but all of her body rejected him.

That night as she lay in bed, despair assaulted her. She was only beginning to realize what marriage was going to mean, and she lay awake for hours wondering how to escape. The Fieldings at Sydenham might shelter her if she could make her way there, but Victoria doubted that they would support her. There was nowhere else she could go. It seemed that her only way out lay in refusing to marry him. In the darkness it seemed easy. After she had thought about it for some time, she could even imagine her mother and father saying that since she felt so strongly, then of course she could back out. They might even offer to go ahead with the wedding plans and merely change the name of the groom!

Next morning it was all dust and nonsense again. She sat opposite her parents at breakfast, knowing her dreams were hopeless. It would be futile to defy them or ask for their understanding. She had been right when she told Charles that she was as good as married already.

But help came.

All afternoon Millie had hovered about. Though Miss Boswell had given her messages and errands to run, she had popped back quickly and hovered in the background again. Victoria thought it odd, but it was not until late afternoon when Victoria came upstairs to dress for dinner that she found out why. On the pretext of coming to help with the buttons, Millie followed her and shut the door behind them with an air of great mystery.

She whispered (though there was not the slightest danger of being overheard), "I seen that gentleman, miss."

"Oh!" She could see by the look on Millie's face that she was referring to Charles. "He came *here*?"

"Oooh, no, miss. Well, sort of, I suppose. I was out sweepin' the step in front an' there 'e was. I seen 'im down there at the corner, like. 'E seen me right off an' waved like this. She beckoned with her skinny arm. "I looks all around, of course, only nobody seen me. So quick sharp I trots down the street to 'im. 'E gave me this an' said to be sure to give it to nobody 'cept you, an' be sure an' tell nobody." With bony fingers she undid the shoulder fastening of her apron and slipped Victoria a sealed package.

Millie stood by the door while Victoria broke the seal and spread the stiff paper on her lap.

"Dear Princess," he had written. "I have looked for you every day in the park, but each evening have had to return home without even the glimpse of you that would have made the day perfect. I can understand why you have not been out, and I hope that my attempts to free you from your engagement did not cause any friction between you and your parents. Your father impresses me as a fine man who genuinely believes that he is acting in your best interests. I tried to point out that happiness is much more important than a greater degree of wealth and a *NAME*, but he sought to disagree with my reasoning.

"I must see you again. Just once. Please do not deny me that. No doubt your family keeps you busy during the day and it would be dangerous for you to venture out alone at night, but could you possibly meet me early in the morning? I shall wait for you at daybreak just inside the park gates. I shall go

83

there every morning until the day you are married, for only then will I give up hope. Please see me."

It was unsigned.

Victoria read the note twice, the second time slowly while she decided what to do. Then she said as she began to change her clothes, "Who do you share a room with, Millie?"

"Violet, miss."

"Good. She wouldn't say anything. But best she doesn't find out. Is she a heavy sleeper?"

"Oooh, yes, miss. She likes to talk an' takes 'er time about droppin' off, but she 'as to be roused real fierce in the mornin', she does." She took Victoria's discarded dress and put it on a hanger.

"Good. Now listen carefully, Millie. Come over here and pay attention. It doesn't matter if anybody comes in now. Tomorrow morning do you think that you could come down here very early, before it starts to be light, and help me to dress? I'm going to go out for a little walk."

"Are you off to meet 'im, then?" Millie's face paled still more with excitement as she helped Victoria slip on a lemon silk dinner gown.

"Yes, but it's best that you forget you know that."

"Oooh, miss, 'ow *romantic*!"

"It won't be in the least bit romantic if I get caught, so remember that and say nothing," said Victoria sternly.

"I won't say one word to anybody," promised Millie.

"Mind you don't," smiled Victoria, turning her back so that Millie could do her up. She turned her head from side to side to check her hairstyle in the mirror. "You had better go and help Albertina with her dress now, and be very careful not to say anything at all to her."

"I'll 'old me tongue!" said Millie happily.

Victoria smiled as she watched her go. She sat on the window seat and leaned her arms on the broad window ledge. Cupping her face in her hands, she gazed out toward the park. The world had never looked more beautiful than it did at this moment. The sky positively blushed with its sunset. Half-furled banners of cloud draped the horizon, shot through with rich pastel colors where the sunlight touched them. Higher in the sky she could see the first stars of the night, faint points of brightness, each one no bigger than a tiny chip of silver.

She reached down a hand to touch Charles's letter where

it lay on the seat beside her. This was the first real secret she had ever had, and she savored the tight feeling of repressed excitement it gave her. She would have been content to stay there dreaming until the dinner gong summoned her, but she was roused sharply by her mother's tap on the door, instantly recognizable. Hastily she turned around and straightened her dress, thrusting the letter deep into the folds of her skirt.

Grace frowned as she noted Victoria's high color and the odd glitter in her eyes. "Are you feeling quite well, dear?"

"Yes, thank you, Mother."

"Are you certain?" Grace put her palm to Victoria's forehead. "You feel cool but you look feverish."

"I was romping with Flounce earlier on."

"I must warn you to be careful, dear," Grace said. "Exercise is not good for a young lady. It brings on hot flushes and could cause you to catch a chill. We don't want you indisposed now."

"No, Mother." Victoria moved her hand slightly, and the letter made a rustling noise. She froze.

"I think that Nana could do your hair again tonight," said Grace. "Your dress will do. That yellow silk becomes you, and it goes well with my peacock. I think a pair of yellow roses in your hair, high at the back . . ."

"But, Mother . . ."

"The duke and duchess of Woolbridge are coming to dinner especially to meet you, and you are to look your best."

"But they have already met me," sighed Victoria. The duke and duchess were even older than Lord Benchley. He was deaf and noisy, and she had a haughty face like a camel's.

"They want to meet you properly, to notice you," said Grace in exasperation. "They are Lord Benchley's dearest friends and you will be seeing them often. Mind that you make a good impression. Talk to them. Make conversation, but stick to safe subjects."

"Yes, Mother."

Although Victoria tried to be pleasant, the evening was a dreary torment for her. Lord Benchley behaved exactly as he always did. Nobody could have guessed that he was her fiancé. He stared at her with his small dry eyes and damply kissed her hand, then sat beside her at the table and, as usual, ignored her. She reflected on the drabness of their future mealtimes together, and once again agonized for a way to escape.

Perhaps tomorrow would provide the answer . . .

Thirteen

Clarence Street was hushed in the gray predawn and wrapped in a spun-cotton packing of fog. Damp wisps clung to the door pillars and lampposts, and puffs of fog made ghostly blurred shapes out of the solid brick houses. Before they had gone twenty yards, Victoria and Millie had lost sight of the house.

They pattered along quietly, their breath trailing a silent mist. Millie was shivering. She wore her brown uniform dress and a look of unhappy determination. Victoria had tried to stop her from coming and there might have been an argument if it had been possible to speak in the house. She wanted to go alone. If she were caught, nothing worse could happen to her than was already going to, but if Millie were caught, she would be instantly dismissed for her part in the escapade. But the maid was determined. Now that the thrill of romantic excitement had worn off, Millie no longer thought this was such a splendid idea, but she was not going to abandon her mistress to Lord-knows-what dangers in the park. What if the young gentleman didn't show?

But Millie stopped discreetly at the gate as soon as she saw that he was there, standing under the elm tree where she had first seen him with his friends. He came striding out. She stopped the width of the polished cobblestone drive away from him, suddenly shy. He looked unexpectedly glamorous, scarlet and mustard and gold braiding against all the whites and grays. In a few strides he had covered the distance between them, and before she could draw a breath to utter the polite greeting she had rehearsed, he had taken her in his arms. Roughly he pushed back the hood and pressed her head against his jacket, kissing her tumbled hair. His breath on her forehead was sweetly warm after the cold morning air. He smelled of cologne and damp wool, and she could feel his heart quite plainly, thumping near her cheek. It amused her. In the mood she was in, light-headed with happiness and trembling all over from nervous excitement, it seemed amusing that she could feel his heart beating.

"What is it, princess?"

"I'm laughing because I am happy." As she spoke, she noticed the steady pulse in his neck. Reaching up on tiptoes within the circle of his arms, she touched her lips to the place. It's amazing, she thought. It feels completely natural to be in his arms. "I love you, Charles," she heard herself saying. She had whispered the words so often to her uncaring pillow that now they slipped out almost on their own.

He took a deep breath and his arms tightened hard. She caught a glimpse of his face; his eyes were filled with pain. That puzzled her, made her suddenly concerned for his feelings. Then his mouth came swiftly over hers and her thoughts were blotted out. It was clumsy at first, the kissing. Then he moved her head, taking firmer possession of her. She had dreamed of kisses like Nana's or Mother's, chaste, gentle, tepid, affectionate. But Charles's kisses were a passionate invasion that left her boneless, with no will of her own. Finally he held her off at arm's length. She was so limp and breathless that her knees buckled under her, and he had to scoop her to him again to steady her.

"Be careful," he said. His eyes were merry again and she wondered if she had imagined that strange, hurting look. He was smiling and admiring her brazenly, and it felt glorious. "Princess, you're blushing!"

"It's the way you're looking at me. I'm not used to that."

His eyes were suddenly careful. "If you wanted, you could get used to it. I could look at you this way forever. Would you like that?"

Would she like it? Oh, if only this moment could go on forever!

"Will you come away with me?" he was asking from the other side of her dream. "Would you leave everything and just come with me? You can trust me to look after you. I shall make you happy, please believe that. You would never regret coming with me." He spoke rapidly, aware that the lightening dawn was eroding their time, that very little was left. "Please trust me," he urged. "Please know that I love you."

She looked down at her feet and scuffed at the moss with the toe of one slipper. How could she even consider marrying Lord Benchley when she had this choice? Far at the back of her mind she seemed to hear Miss Boswell's voice saying, "It is a terrible thing to marry one man when your heart lies elsewhere. You at least will go to your husband with a whole heart. Take comfort in that and be grateful." Be grateful? This is what she had to be grateful for. Charles loved *her*, not some business arrangement. Her heart belonged to Charles and she knew with absolute conviction that she must follow it.

"Will you?" There was no pleading in his voice. He asked with dignity, giving her a real choice.

He misunderstood her silence. His eyes dropped, and he squeezed her hands together so hard the bones in her fingers were driven together, wringing out his disappointment.

She understood immediately. "No, Charles, please. I was hesitant because I am going to have to hurt so many people. But it must be done. I have no choice. I love you. I can't marry anyone but you. I don't want to hurt anybody, but I must come with you."

He looked disbelieving for only a second before he drew her to him again, laughingly kissing away her tears. "Don't cry for something that has to be," he whispered.

She began to kiss him, and then they were both kissing and laughing, the one mixing up with the other, until he realized the time with a nasty jolt and pressed her cheek to his coat again so that he could talk to her.

"How much time will it take for you to get ready?"

"Three days?" she asked. "Would that be all right."

"Three years, it will seem. Bring a few things with you, only one or two dresses and things, for I can buy you more, and come here, at this time, three days from now. I shall have a carriage ready to take us away. Remember, not a word to anybody."

"They will worry dreadfully . . ."

"Do you think I would let them be worried, princess? No, there will be a messenger ready at a signal to take a note to them from me to tell what has happened. They will know all about it before they have even noticed you're gone. And once we return to London, safely married—doesn't that sound like heaven?" and he kissed her hair, "I shall go to your parents and tell them that we are sorry to have deceived them and that we love each other so much that nothing could stand in our way. They will understand. And once they see that the world hasn't stopped, they'll forgive us."

It was time to go. One last kiss, which they were both reluctant to end, and he stood back in the shadows to watch her walk away. Millie was waiting at the archway, shoulders hunched, rubbing her bony arms in a futile effort to warm them.

"You're goin' to go with 'im, then, miss?"

She realized that Millie had seen and heard everything.

"I'm so 'appy for you, miss. 'E's a fine an' beautiful gentleman, 'e is."

Victoria smiled. She felt warm and safe, as though nothing could hurt her, ever again.

Part Two

*Summer
into
Autumn*

One

The back gate opened to admit a tall, thin man who was dressed somberly in a heavy gray overcoat, despite the warmth of the afternoon. Dark hair wisped onto the gray collar and a ragged moustache hid his mouth. Under pale skin he was wasted, and warm eyes seemed the only living thing in his face. Millie and Violet stopped their work in the cramped backyard and turned to face him. That's no tradesman, thought Millie, puzzled, but Violet cried out with the sound of a startled bird. Suddenly, Millie realized who the young man was. His gaze was fastened on Violet.

Dropping the carpetbag that had been weighing down one shoulder, he held that hand out to Violet. He didn't speak, nor did he smile, but the look on his face pushed instant tears into Millie's eyes. At his feet Flounce bounded and barked frantically, but the man ignored him. He took another step toward Violet, still holding out his hand.

Wordlessly he moved toward Violet, his hand outstretched to draw her toward him. Millie felt like rushing behind her friend and giving her a push, for she stood there stunned and helpless. Millie could hardly credit what was happening, but it was plain that he was going to sweep Violet right into his arms, right there in broad daylight, not minding that he was the young master and she only a servant, all bedraggled and damp with soapsuds.

Just as he was about to touch her, the door crashed open and Old Will's cracked high voice said, "It's Master Andrew!" Within two seconds Bess was dashing down the steps, striped skirts billowing and arms out stiff as a scarecrow's to wrap him in a hearty hug of welcome. It was she who laughed and cried and exclaimed over him. It was she who gave him two kisses, one on each cheek perilously close to his grimacing mouth. He barely had time to throw Violet a wry glance as Bess hustled him indoors.

Shaken and white, Violet sat down on her stool and covered her face with her red, water-wrinkled hands. Millie fled to her in a rush of concern.

"Please don't cry," she said. "'E might come out again, an' you don't want 'im to see you cryin'."

"He's seen me cry before," said Violet in a strangely quiet voice. "Thee mustn't worry, Millie love. He'll not be coming back out. They've got him now. Once they get him, there's nothing for me. He belongs to his family now."

"'E didn't come in at the front door like 'e should," said Millie in awe. "'E came round the back way just 'opin' 'e'd see you. That was why, weren't it? The way you was talkin', I thought 'e didn't really love you. But 'e does, all right."

Violet's rough, trembling hands pressed hard at her chest, just below her throat. The pressure seemed to thicken her voice. "I wish I hadn't seen him," she said hopelessly. "He shouldn't have come home so soon. I should have been wed by the time he got home."

Millie felt slightly irritated at the way Violet was ruining the heady romantic dream. "Well, 'e's 'ere now an' no mistake."

Violet raised her head. "What shall I do?" she asked.

"'Ow should I know?" said Millie shortly. "I ain't never 'ad nobody look at me like that, an' I know I never will. It'd be grand to 'ave your problem, Violet. That's better, smile."

"Does thee really think so?"

"That 'e loves you? Plain as me nose."

"He's been away two years," Violet said, plunging her hands back in the water in a businesslike way. "Not one word did I hear from him, not one."

Millie lost her patience. "And what if you 'ad? Bess would 'ave got 'er 'ands on the letter an' next thing, slam, you'd be out on the street. Don't you think 'e realized that? 'E loves you right enough."

Violet was sitting, slouched, with her arms in the water and her chin resting on her chest. Suddenly she burst out crying.

Urgently Millie grabbed her by the shoulders and shook her firmly. "Stop it, stop it," she hissed. "Bess will 'ear you wailin' like that an' she'll fetch 'erself out 'ere to see what's happenin'. Stop it, Violet."

But Violet clawed at Millie's sleeves. "He's been hurt," she cried distractedly as if she had only just noticed. "Didn't thee see it? He's been hurt!"

"What do you mean?"

"He was limping and holding himself not quite straight, as if he was sore inside. I tell thee, he's hurt bad. He's been sick too. He's pale, too pale for him, and thin, not like he was before. Oh, Millie, he's come home hurt and sick and I've not said as much as 'Welcome home' to him. Oh, Millie, what can I do now?"

Tenderly Millie folded her hands around Violet's hot face and laid her cheek against her cap. "Poor Violet," she whispered.

Two

Victoria glared at her sister's mauve-clad neck with ill-concealed impatience. If only Albertina would cease her mindless chattering and go away, she could get on with her packing. Lately Albertina seemed determined to cling to her with gloating persistence. Her entire conversation concerned her conquests in the coming "season" of balls and parties (from which Victoria, because of her marriage, would be excluded) and plans for the redecoration of the bedroom which would be hers once Victoria had gone.

Albertina frowned prettily at her reflection in the gilt-edged mirror. "I rather think I shall wear my hair in a bunch on one side, like this, with perhaps a rose tucked artfully in the back, as if I had nonchalantly put it there while strolling in the garden. What do you think of that?"

"That sounds lovely, dear." If she could manage to sneak another carpetbag from the trunk room in the attic, it would be easier to pack her things. Her bag held such a tiny amount and all her dresses had full skirts with yards and yards of fabric. Her favorite apricot poplin with the black velvet laces at the waist and sleeves took up the whole bag all by itself.

"Elizabeth writes that *everybody* will be there," said Albertina with satisfaction. "The last time the St. Claires held a garden party it was such a success that this time nobody wants to miss it. What a pity that it is so soon after your wedding that you won't be able to go! Mother says that even though you are not going on a honeymoon, it wouldn't be at all proper for you to appear in public until at least six weeks after the wedding. It's almost as bad as being in mourning!"

"I suppose so." Of course! She could wear her poplin dress and pack two others instead. Three dresses wasn't much to start a new life with, but it would have to do.

"I hope I won't get married for *ages* yet," crooned her sister, tugging at a ringlet.

Victoria had listened to more than enough of this. "Aren't you going to change for dinner?" she asked, carefully casual, for nobody could stay more firmly put than Albertina when she suspected that somebody was trying to get rid of her.

With a critical turn of her exquisite chin, Albertina said, "Yes, I think that this way will suit me very well, and have me most gratifyingly noticed as well."

As if to rescue Victoria, Millie rapped on the half-open door. "Miss Albertina? I was lookin' for you to dress your 'air. If you'll be comin' now, I'll be much obliged. Be back in a minute, Miss Victoria."

"Thank you, Millie."

Victoria waited for a full three seconds after her door closed, then dashed to the wardrobe. She flung the doors wide and hooked out the blue floral tapestry bag. It was stuffed with the apricot poplin dress. Victoria pulled the dress out and hastily smoothed it onto one of her padded sateen hangers. Underwear, stockings, she calculated mentally. Oh, and a nightdress! She could hardly sleep in her vest and camiknickers. Flipping the corners of her folded underthings, she found her prettiest nightgown near the bottom of the drawer.

A tap on the door made her jump in fright. Andrew's voice asked permission to enter. Quickly she kicked the bag to the back of her wardrobe, calling, "Come in!" and feeling surprised and pleased that Andrew was seeking her out. Since he arrived home the day before yesterday, she had not had the chance of a moment alone with him.

He lounged in the doorway in his old casual attitude, his eyes lingering on the disarray of half-opened dresser drawers. "Not planning to escape, are you?" he said a little too lightly.

She covered her startled reaction by pulling him in and closing the door, even managing a laugh. That, and the ease with which she lied, astounded her. "I was sorting through my things. I have so many dresses to give away that Aunt Brownie is going to need several trips in her carriage to carry them all off with her. Do sit down Andrew." She plumped a cushion and arranged it invitingly on the window seat for his back. "There now, make yourself comfortable, for now that I have you all to myself, I have no intention of letting you escape."

Settling awkwardly with his stiff leg, he sighed and cast his eyes about her room. "I used to imagine you here when I was away. I'd be in my dugout huddled in a few overcoats with a bit of rag over my boots to pad them for a pillow, and I'd think of you fast asleep in your huge fluffy bed. This room is exactly as I used to picture it. Nothing has changed, not even you. I wondered if you would get new wallpaper. Remember all the ruckus because you loathed this stuff with the pansies, and both you and Albertina wanted the other room?"

"She won, of course. She always does."

Her voice was so clear and free of envy that he glanced at her hard and swiftly. "Don't you mind?"

"I did, but not any more." She smiled at him, thinking that it was impossible to feel one twinge of wistfulness when in a few hours she would be marrying a man whom Albertina had set her sights on. No, if anything, she felt sorry for her sister. "She changes like the breeze anyway. Now she's decided to move in here when I leave. She's decided that she likes this room best after all."

"That's our Albertina all over." He wore the indulgent expression that Victoria was used to seeing whenever her sister was being discussed. "She's grown up while I was away. She's grown even more beautiful. She's going to be the rage of all of London when she comes out—if she comes out, that is."

"*If*? Why, Father will give her the most magnificent coming-out ball ever. She will adore being the center of attention!"

"The only young ladies who come out are those whose families can afford the expense."

"What a silly mood you are in, Andrew! Still, I'm glad you came to see me, if only to talk nonsense."

He tried to smile, but his eyes were serious and searching. "I actually came to talk about the wedding."

"Oh." She wondered for a minute whether to confide in him. She had been standing beside him when Father had told him about the wedding. Andrew's reaction had been chilling in its implications. "Oh, God, no," he had muttered in a moment of stripped-down honesty. He offered her a dry kiss of congratulation.

"Please don't let's talk about the wedding," she said. "We have such a short time left and I don't want to discuss Lord Benchley. If you cannot think of a more pleasant topic, then I shall invent one."

His eyes held hers. "Shall we talk about Charles Lawrence?"

She was so unprepared that she couldn't keep the sick, white look of fear off her face. So it's true, Andrew thought. Mother and Father do have reason to be concerned. He ached with pity for his sister.

Victoria murmured unsteadily, "Why talk about him?"

"Father told me he had declared himself to you," he said frankly. "It's a shame that this other business was already arranged. He's a fine chap, Charles. But we have to talk about your wedding, like it or not. Because there's some speculation that you might be planning to balk at the altar, I've been asked to chat to you about it."

She nodded, eyes downcast.

"You realize that in the church nobody can make you say the words that will bind you to him, don't you?"

Again a nod, her head bowed.

"*Are* you planning to refuse to take your vows?"

She flared up angrily. "You're not a bit fair to me, Andrew. How would you like to have to marry somebody like that? How would you feel if you were in my place? Of course I've thought about refusing to take my vows! Of course I've thought about escaping—not that it would do any good," she added hastily in case Andrew was of a mind to develop the train of thought. "Do you know that father didn't even consult me? He arranged it all first and told me afterward. It won't be like that for the other girls, just for me. Why, Andrew, why?"

"He has no choice," said Andrew.

Victoria pulled a face of disbelief.

"Haven't you noticed how . . . changed Father is? I noticed it as soon as I came home. Surely you must have seen it too."

"Oh?" She frowned. "We *have* been anxious about him, come to think of it. Before the engagement, I was worried. He never seemed to laugh much any more. He looks tired, too. I asked Nana if he was ill and she said most definitely not."

"He's not ill." Andrew looked solemn. He crossed the good leg over the bad, wincing. "He looks tired for the same reason he was so glad to accept for you when Lord Benchley proposed. I think you're grown up and sensible enough to know all about it, but you must promise me you won't say a word. I only know about this through Lord Benchley, and he only told me because he wants my help in quite another matter. I wish that there was some way out of this for you. But Lord Benchley is quite determined to have you, and there is no way that Father can refuse him."

He leaned toward her, and Victoria could see the network of broken veins in his cheeks where they had been tipped by frost. The expression in his eyes startled her. It was the same look of pain she had seen on Charles's face that morning in the park. In some powerfully strong way he pitied her, and she wanted to comfort him and tell him not to worry, for she *was not* going to be Lord Benchley's bride. But the riddle of what Andrew was trying to tell her prompted her to nestle at his feet and say, "What *is* all this about? You are completely confusing me. How can Lord Benchley possibly have some hold over Father?"

"You must promise not to tell," he said fiercely.

She nodded, frightened now at his face and his tone. "What is the trouble, Andrew?"

"Father is about to be ruined. The only person he can turn to right now is Lord Benchley, and even he may not be able to save him. But if Lord Benchley abandons Father, everything will crash around this family."

She held up her hands in protest. "Please, Andrew, I don't

understand. How can Father possibly be 'ruined'? That means to lose everything, doesn't it, so how could that happen to him? Father is so clever. If he has lost a bit of his money, surely it would be no trouble for him to make some more? Why, Father is always saying that even though it is not quite respectable to be engaged in the pastime of making money, he cares not a fig for respectability, because making money is the thing that he is best at in the whole world!"

"It's a shock for me too. I came home expecting to be able to buy a first-class commission in the army, and instead... Well," he said, pulling himself up straighter on the window seat, "the position, briefly, is this. Some businessmen have made big investments with Father. They gave him a lot of money to spend for them, hoping to turn a good profit. Father spent the money on other things, like this house, some factories that are losing money, and some buildings that were burned down in a recent fire. Now the men want their money back, and Father cannot give it to them. They are claiming he has been dishonest and are threatening to complain to the police."

Victoria was indignant. "How could the police be interested in something like that? Father hasn't *stolen* their money, if they gave it to him in the first place!"

Absently Andrew rubbed the back of his hand under her chin. "Unfortunately the police could be very interested in what has been going on. I'm sorry to say that Father has broken the law. Yes, I know it sounds utterly preposterous, but it is true. If these men press charges, Father could go to prison."

Sitting back on her heels, she stared at him earnestly, trying to absorb this incredible idea. Only bad men went to prison, wicked men who stole things and murdered people.

"I can see that you don't believe me," said Andrew miserably. "I don't blame you, for I was hard-pressed to believe it myself, but Lord Benchley explained it carefully to me. He's been trying very hard to keep the men at a distance in the hopes that business will pick up again, but so far things don't look very good."

Victoria looked puzzled. "Why doesn't Father just sell some of his things so that the men can be paid back? Wouldn't that solve everything?"

"It's complicated. Part of it isn't Father's fault..."

"*All* of it isn't his fault!" she interjected angrily.

"Hush! Someone might hear you. A lot of the property

Father has was bought just before the war and during the first months of it. Prices were high then, and they've gone into a real slump now. To pay the men back, Father would have to sell every single thing we own. This house would have to go, the carriages, the servants, the furniture..." He was exaggerating on purpose. "There would be no money left at all. We would be poor, Victoria, really poor."

"There must have been a terribly large amount of money involved," she said wonderingly.

"There was."

She shrugged impatiently. "Lord Benchley must be making a mistake," she insisted. "If things were in that bad a mess, Father wouldn't be spending all this money on the wedding."

"Victoria, your wedding could be Mother's last chance to make her big impression on society. It could be the salvation of the family. It probably will be mine too, for Lord Benchley is going to help me with something later. He's the only man Father can completely depend on now. He is doing all that he can to help, and with some clever legal work he might be able to clear things up for Father. Tell me, wouldn't you do all you could to keep Father out of prison?"

"Of course I would!" she cried.

"Even marry Lord Benchley?" he asked quietly.

"Ooh," she faltered.

"Look at me. Please. We are thinking of you and of your well-being. Lord Benchley is a good man. You will have a good life with him. Please don't do anything impulsive now, like backing out at the last minute. Our family is in no condition to sustain the blow of a scandal. By going through with this, you will be helping all of us."

His soft voice was all the more cruel for the love it held. In vain Victoria tried to check her tears of anguish. She loved them all—of course she did! She wanted to tell her brother how she dreaded a life spent in Lord Benchley's company, how she wanted to be able to love Charles and spend her life caring for him. Instead she pressed her scalding face against his jacket front and wept miserably, "It's so horrible being grown up. I hate it. It's nothing like I thought it would be."

He embraced her gratefully, knowing that he had succeeded.

Squeezing her shoulder with false reassurance, he said, "You will be happy. Wait and see."

When he had gone, Millie returned. Victoria told her that

100

she would not be going down to dinner, and gave her the special instructions for the morning, overriding her protests with a cold bitterness that clipped Millie short. Then she locked her bedroom door and took her blue-embossed leather writing case from a drawer. She wrote the letter and sealed it, crying so hard she could hardly see.

Three

It was still dark when Victoria awoke. She lay on her side, staring at the shutters, where stripes of gray crept faintly between the painted wooden slats. Sighing, she snuggled deeper into the bed, pulling the warm nest of blankets up over her shoulder with a sleep-warmed hand. And as she had done every morning for the last several weeks, she thought about Charles and sighed again with happiness.

Then, waking a little more, she remembered what had happened. It was over; her dream was totally smashed. Right now he would be in the park standing beside a carriage which was supposed to carry them through the sleeping city to the start of their new life together. She wondered what he would think when Millie gave him the letter. She couldn't have risked going to see Charles herself. Once she was there in his arms, she might not have had the will to return to the house.

Then a nasty thought snapped her wide awake and sat upright in bed. Suppose Charles had resigned his job? Suppose he had left his lodgings and rented a house for them to live in. He might have gone to a lot of expense and altered his whole future on the assumption that soon he would be a married man. All because of her. The thought was like a slap that physically hurt her. What a pitiful compensation a letter would be!

Of course he wouldn't understand. Her letter had stated that she must marry Lord Benchley. How would that sound after her passionate outburst when, with her hands imprisoned in his, she had said, "I have no choice. How can I possibly marry anyone else when it is you I love?"

She threw off the bedclothes and crept carefully to the windows. Gingerly she eased the shutters back, catching her breath when they squeaked. It took a long time to hitch the heavy window sash up high enough to get her head out. Oh, please let me be in time to stop Millie, she prayed silently. Somehow she would call the maid back, get dressed, and keep the appointment herself. Then she could have a long, long talk with Charles and seek his consent. He would see what she must do, and he would tell her that she must go ahead with her parents' plan. That way he would be able to take comfort in knowing that she really loved him and didn't want him to be hurt. They would be able to say good-bye properly.

Below her one of Bess's cats was taking an early morning reconnaissance stroll. There appeared to be a figure moving away toward the park, but the light was so dim that it could be a shadow moving on the cobbled footpath. But wait, here was Millie now, scurrying soundlessly toward her. Victoria opened dry lips to call out to her, but checked herself in time. No, someone else might hear. She recognized the figure below her. It wasn't Millie at all! It was Young Will.

There was no time to speculate about what he might be doing out there, for another figure, this one larger and puffing noisily, followed him out. They were whispering. None of the words could be distinguished but one voice undoubtedly belonged to Bess Myers.

In alarm Victoria pulled in her head. She tried to calm herself and watch what was going on. It appeared as though Millie were being followed, for Young Will set off in the direction of the park. From where she stood, back from the window, Victoria could see the cook standing at the edge of the road.

Time passed. What was going on? Would Young Will see Charles and possibly recognize him? Victoria clutched her shoulders, shivering under the thin silk nightgown. She dared neither to close the window and shut off the draught nor risk going back to the bed for her wrapper.

Just when Victoria was certain that she would scream out loud if something didn't happen soon, Young Will returned, gliding into her line of vision. Bess took a few steps to meet him and Victoria drew as close to the window as she dared, straining to listen. The sky was lighter now and she could see them more clearly. None of the excited whispering was intelligible, and the pair disappeared from view. When Millie finally came by, walking slowly, her head drooping, she did not so much as glance up at the window.

As soon as the gong announced breakfast, Victoria went down. She had dressed herself, then sat on her bed for more than an hour already. Grace, Nana, and Birdie looked up in surprise when she entered.

"It's most out of character for you to be down so early, dear," said Miss Boswell. "Are you quite well? Did you sleep poorly last night?"

"Nothing like that." Victoria smiled, delighted with her newly discovered acting skills. "Today is such a lovely day that I don't want to miss one single moment of it." She bent down, holding her glossy mass of long dark hair out of the way so that Miss Boswell could do up her buttons. "I rang for Millie to help me dress, but there was no reply. Do you think the string on my bell might have broken again?"

Grace ignored the reference to Millie and said, "Could be," before glancing up from the neatly written lists beside her plate. She contemplated her daughter. "Are you sure you are quite well? Your eyes look rather watery this morning."

"Her skin is like ice," pronounced Nana, feeling between her shoulder blades.

"I'm quite all right," protested Victoria impatiently. She detested being fussed over as if she were an arrangement of flowers. All she wanted was to find out what happened to Millie. Smiling widely to prove how marvelous she felt, she whisked her cup from beside her plate and filled it from the silver teapot which stood on the candlelit warmer. "Are you not eating today?" Nana asked.

She did not help matters by saying hastily, "My throat feels rather dry. I'll have something to eat later."

It was the wrong thing to say, for she normally ate a conspicuously large breakfast. Grace laid her lists aside with the air of having made an important decision. "You are certainly coming down with a cold then, dear. Perhaps it would be best if you went back to bed. I shall send up a tray later."

Victoria's nerves were snapping with irritation, and she spoke more sharply than she intended. "My throat is only a wee bit dry, not sore. Please stop fussing, because I am perfectly all right." As if to settle the matter, she pushed her chair back and returned to the buffet. Fully aware that Miss Boswell was watching, she made a point of filling her plate.

Grace sipped her lemon tea thoughtfully. The unpleasant

note in her daughter's voice had jarred her attention away from the guest list. Victoria was definitely behaving oddly these days. Grace resolved to ask Dr. Fry for a small prescription of laudanum to help Victoria. Perhaps a mild dose and a good sleep for a few nights would soothe her.

Suddenly Bess strode in to the room, businesslike and rather pleased with herself. Coming right to the point without ceremony, she said, "Excuse me, please, ma'am, and I'm sorry to disturb you right now, but there is something important I have to bring to your notice."

Grace did not see that Victoria had laid her knife and fork aside and grown extremely pale. She said vaguely, "Oh, dear me, Bess. Could it perhaps wait until after breakfast?"

"The caterers will be here then and you'll be wanting my help with the menu, I was thinking. Otherwise I'd not be here to disturb you now."

"Very well, then. What is your problem?"

"Just this," said Bess with evident pleasure. Turning her head, she barked, "In here with you sharpish!"

In slunk a frightened Millie, seemingly shrunk to half her normal size, her hands twisted together and her face blotched red from blows or crying.

Grace's eyebrows rose. She nodded meaningfully to Miss Boswell, who acted on the hint at once by saying, "Come along, Birdie, we can take Flounce for a walk."

Once they had left, Grace turned to Bess, ignoring her eldest daughter who sat frozen at her place. "Well, Bess?"

"I've told this one the rules quite plainly, ma'am."

"I'm sure you have."

"She went out early this morning. I heard her moving about, and I rousted Young Will to follow her. Right before daylight it was."

"You did the right thing," nodded Grace, and to Millie she said, "You did remember the rules?"

"Yes, ma'am." A tiny wavering voice.

"Then where did you go to?" Grace's tone was stern and kindly at the same time.

Millie rubbed the back of one narrow hand across her mouth and stared fixedly at the floor.

Bess tossed a look of disgust at the bowed head, the wrinkled cap awry over the straggling mousy hair. "She went to meet a man," she announced.

Grace's eyebrows shot up into points.

"Who is this man?" she asked less kindly. "You *do* have to tell me."

Victoria was positively giddy with panic. She clutched at the napkin in her lap, digging her nails into the loose weave, and stared at the girl, willing her to keep silent.

Millie stood with her head bent, her shoulders convulsed with sobs. She mumbled faintly, "I can't tell you, ma'am. I'm sorry but I can't."

"Nothing happened between them, ma'am. Nothing like *that* at least, or so Young Will said. It was worse. You see, ma'am, she gave him something. A package of some kind, Young Will said, and it can't have been from her wages for Myers gave them to her to take home last Saturday and she's been telling us how glad her mum was of them. So it seems to me, ma'am, that she has taken something from this house and given it to that man. She's not sold it, because I stripped and searched her right properly the minute she came in, and she'd no money on her."

Grace said calmly, "I shall want to question Young Will later on, when we have seen the caterers. Keep him away from Millie until I have spoken to him, would you please? Now then, Millie. What did you give to this man? I can understand why you are reluctant to divulge his name, but you must see that you will have to tell me what you gave him."

"I can't tell you, ma'am. But I ain't stolen nowt, not like she said," and she looked at Bess with real hatred. "I wouldn't do nowt like that."

"But you admit that you did give the man something?"

"Yes, ma'am."

"Don't you see, Millie, that you must tell me what it was? If you have stolen nothing, then you have no reason to be afraid. Don't you understand that?"

Millie stood up straight and said, "I can't tell you, ma'am. I wish I could because it would get me out o' this mess, but I can't go back on me word."

Grace's long nails tapped on the tablecloth. "Then I must dismiss you."

Bess managed to keep from smiling outright. Victoria felt ill with shame.

Millie pleaded desperately, "I ain't taken nowt, ma'am. I never took nowt that weren't mine, not once in me life. I wouldn't do owt like that to you when you've been so good to me an' all. Please believe me, ma'am."

"Was it something of yours that you gave him?"

Millie's reply confirmed Grace's suspicion. "No, it wasn't mine."

Grace frowned. Millie was now broken in and she would really be needed in the next few weeks. There was no saving the situation, though. She turned back to her lists, saying impersonally, "Old Will will drive you home this afternoon."

Millie stared at her mistress in horror, then abruptly turned and fled, weeping, from the room.

"This is a good morning's work you've done," said Bess, adding charitably, "She's the best worker I've had under me in many a long year though. We shall miss her."

"Thank you, Bess," sighed Grace. "Please confine her to her room, and of course I shall not need to speak to Young Will now." She continued to study the papers as though nothing whatsoever had happened to interrupt her.

Victoria sat miserably behind her cooling plate of unwanted food. What a coward I am, she thought. What a mean, despicable coward to treat first Charles so shamefully and now Millie. While she wondered whether anything could be done to mend things, Grace spoke.

"I wanted you to stay and hear all that. Soon you will be the mistress of your own house and have your own servants to deal with. Dismissing a servant is an extremely distasteful matter, and unfortunately it grows no easier on the second or third time. However, when you have to do it, resolve to be ruthless, especially in a case like this where there is a suspicion of theft. A dishonest maid is simply not worth having, no matter what her other qualities may be."

"But, Mother, Millie *needs* this job. Her family is so terribly poor . . ."

"I know, dear. That is what makes the task so unpleasant."

"But what if she were telling the truth?"

"There was only one way to judge that, and she failed the test. If she had freely told everything, even if it meant putting herself in a bad light, then what she said would have been accepted and I would not have dismissed her. However, she was not prepared to be frank, therefore it must regretfully be inferred that she is not honest. Really, dear, I know that you

106

liked the girl, but you must not take things to heart so much. She is only a servant, after all."

As the morning wore on, Victoria felt more and more wretched. Twice she went into the morning room where her mother was working, and twice she came away without being able to reopen the subject. Remembering what Bess had said about how delighted Millie's family was with her wages made Victoria realize that she had to do something. A full confession seemed the only way, for she would have to insist that she had forced Millie to help her and threatened the servant to make her keep quiet. Mother would be horrified to think that she could have planned to act so deceitfully but would surely forgive Millie and be impressed by her loyalty.

Once Victoria had fixed firmly on this resolve, the pressure from her conscience lessened and she felt much better. She went happily into the conservatory to rehearse her story before trying it out on her mother.

While she was there, the doorbell rang. Myers's shadow blurred past the frosted glass on his way to the front hall and presently she heard him discussing the weather with Lord Benchley. Suddenly she had a marvelous idea. She could save Millie's job without the possibility of Mother asking awkward questions about why Victoria had changed her mind and decided not to elope. Grace could be relied upon to examine the story from every angle and to fasten promptly on anything which did not sound quite plausible. She sped out into the hall, skirts swaying, and caught up to her fiancé at the door to her father's study.

As she curtsied to him, she used her most dazzling smile. "Good morning, Lord Benchley," she cooed sweetly.

He was mildly surprised by the especially friendly tone, and even more surprised when she swiftly moved in closer and held out a slender hand to be kissed. Victoria usually kept shyly out of reach and had to be coaxed forward by her mother.

She said appealingly, "Father said that you would like me to choose a wedding gift. Is that so, sir?"

"Certainly, my dear."

She retrieved her hand and rubbed it on the back of her skirt. "I have decided what I would like, but it is something rather big and expensive, so perhaps I could tell you so that you can consider it first."

"You may have anything you wish," he said absently.

"I shall be lonely at your house, with servants who are all strangers to me. Might I please have a maid of my own?"

"Of course, of course." He ran a pudgy hand over his moss-thick hair. Mrs. Foster had discussed this with him weeks ago, and it had slipped his mind. He had been planning to ask Matthew if one of the servants could be spared to go with the bride. Mrs. Foster said she had enough to do without running after a giddy young wife, and furthermore she had no notion of training a lady's maid. It would be easier to fetch one from of the Fieldings' house than to go through all sorts of nonsense. This would settle everything nicely and placate Mrs. Foster as well. He bowed to Victoria and opened the door to her father's study.

Victoria slid through before him. "Father," she said, hoping that her mother had not mentioned Millie's trouble yet. "Father, I have chosen my wedding gift. I have asked Lord Benchley if I could have one of our maids and he agreed. Mother does not want Millie any more, so may I please have your permission to take her with me?"

Something was not quite in place here, Matthew thought. "Why doesn't your mother want her?"

"There was a little bit of trouble," she said airily. "Nothing really important, but Millie doesn't get on well with Bess. I like Millie very much, and it would make all the difference in the world to me If I may take her with me when I go. Please say that I may."

Matthew smiled indulgently, pleased to see her looking so happy when he himself had so many worries. "I'm sure it can be arranged, but . . ."

"I know, I must ask Mother first." Darting around the desk, she planted an impulsive kiss on her father's cheek, then dimpling prettily she curtsied to the men and left the room.

"Delicious," murmured Lord Benchley, half to himself, as the door swung to behind her and he caught a flashing glimpse of lace and embroidered slippers.

Matthew's mind was not on his daughter. "Is there any good news yet?" he wanted to know.

"I'm afraid the situation is still dismal." The lawyer rested his briefcase on the desk and opened it. "Look at these. It's not much, but those factories are not doing the volume of business that would warrant a solid mortgage investment, so this is all I could reasonably expect to borrow against them. Money is tight at the moment."

"I wish I could have a guinea for every time I've heard that in the past few months," said Matthew with a trace of petulance. He looked over the papers and swore at the pathetically small amounts offered. "This is not even enough to pay you for your trouble."

"I'm trying to see if I can get anything from the Morgan brothers. They have the money to spare, and with a chunk of luck and a good push I might be able to sell them a mortgage on this house—perhaps up to two thirds of its value. They will expect a high interest rate, but it should be enough help to get us clear. As I figure it, we will still need seven or eight thousand to be able to offer Brookes and company their shares back at a profit."

"That would be a damnably generous profit!"

"I can't think of any other way to call the hounds off. And that may not be able to work either. They feel badly stung. Don't worry about my fees for the moment. You've given me the dowry and that will keep me going. Yes, yes, I know it's Victoria's but I shall nevertheless deduct my fees from it and delay sending you my accounting for, say, twelve months. Is that reasonable?"

"It's more than reasonable. You are being damned good to me."

Lord Benchley showed his small broken teeth. "Not at all. You are a fine businessman and it is a pity that circumstances have stacked up against you like this. I value your business, and it makes good sense to do what I can to keep you healthy. Things will be really booming soon and there will be money about just for the picking up. And you are the man to gather it. Now then, to save this situation, I suggest that you make another trip, further afield this time."

"Grace won't like that. The wedding is barely a fortnight away."

"Nobody could be more, shall we say, acutely aware of that than I." And he showed his teeth again. I would have thought you'd be glad of the chance to get away from Lady Longworth. I see she still practically lives here. No doubt she will be glad to see her husband again when he finally decides to come back and face his responsibilities. Andrew told me that he simply abandoned hundreds of thousands of pounds' worth of government property. None of his own, of course. I· gather that his portable wine cellar was intact and accompanied him back to his refuge."

"Alice was bleating away to me about some inquiry," mused Matthew. "You and Andrew aren't brewing up something to do with that, are you?"

"Let me just say that I shall be looking after myself as usual, and that I also look after those who particularly interest me, as Lord Longworth does not. He is a blatant swindler."

"And we are not?" Matthew sighed. "Well then, where shall I take myself off to?"

"Edinburgh and Glasgow, perhaps?"

"They're as tight as a case of lockjaw up there," stated Matthew pessimistically. "Last year I recovered expenses but damned little else."

"You should do better this time. They've had a year now to think on it and you should do better now. So go. There's no saying that I can get a mortgage for this place, and it's best if you're out of the way so that Brookes can't reach you."

"I'll leave in the morning."

"Stay away until a day or so before the wedding. Don't worry about the arrangements. Grace can manage with Lady Longworth to run things for her. When you get up to Glasgow, be confident, be sure of yourself. Those clients in the north will be more inclined to put their hands in their pockets if you don't give a damn whether they do or not. If they smell fear they'll fold their arms and stop listening. And take Andrew with you. A war veteran looks good these days, especially one that shows signs of battle, like Andrew. Having him along might be just the touch you need."

Victoria, meanwhile, was looking for her mother. She found her in her sun-flooded bedroom. Madame Soiska was fretting over Grace's gown for the wedding day. It should have been finished a week ago, but the fit did not meet Grace's exacting requirements. On her knees on the padded stool she took everywhere with her, Madame Soiska pinned while Grace watched critically in the mirror.

"What is it, Victoria?" she asked.

"I came to talk to you about Millie, please, Mother."

"That subject is certainly closed, dear." She nodded toward the dressmaker's fussily curled gray hair; domestic concerns were not to be aired in front of outsiders.

Victoria tried another angle. "I asked Nana if she might be allowed to go with me when I go to Lord Benchley's. I shall be terribly lonely there, and it would help to have someone I know."

Her mother nodded sympathetically. "Up a little higher, please, madame. The waistline is still too low. It will wrinkle up when I move unless the seam is in exactly the right place." To Victoria she said, "We need Miss Boswell here for Birdie's lessons, but perhaps someone else could be spared. Not Violet, she knows so much that it would be far too much trouble to train a new parlormaid. I doubt if we could get one up to her standard ever again. Perhaps Joan . . ."

"Please not Joan. I never feel quite at ease with her. She seems so . . . disapproving. Please, Mother, since you don't want Millie any longer, could she come with me? I had been planning to ask her anyway, because she does my hair so beautifully . . ."

"I had hoped that you might have learned something this morning," said Grace.

"That hasn't changed my mind," begged Victoria.

"Under the circumstances it would be most unwise to take her, and since she's been dismissed already, it is quite out of the question."

"I don't believe what Bess said," said Victoria steadily. "She doesn't like Millie and has been trying to have her dismissed."

Grace wavered. It was unlike Victoria to stand up against so much opposition. Look at the way she had meekly accepted Lord Benchley, though Miss Boswell reported that she had been distraught at the time.

And she seemed so fond of the wretched little maid. Grace could understand that. Millie seemed such a chirpy, cheerful little thing that Grace was coming round to liking her, too. It might do Victoria good to have someone like that in her new home. From all accounts Lord Benchley's house was a dull, fusty place with nothing much to recommend it.

"Very well," she said. "Millie can stay until after the wedding. We need the extra pair of hands and hers are useful, I must admit." As Victoria gave her a grateful kiss, she warned, "If that little mischief causes you any trouble, you must sort it out for yourself. Remember that she is a servant and don't make the serious mistake of letting her form opinions of her own."

"No, Mother."

"Off you go, then." She hoped that the advice had been unnecessary.

When Victoria entered the low-ceilinged room, Millie was hunched up on her bed like a wet sparrow, looking bleakly out of the window. She was wearing the drab dress she had worn on her day trips home. Beside her on the bed was an oilskin bundle, loosely tied with cord.

"I don't know what I'll tell me family, miss," she said in despair. "Countin' on me they was. What a mess to be in! I might 'ave known that old cow would find a way to get rid o' me. Givin' me more than me share o' work an' every time I fooled 'er, I did." Her gawky face flushed red with defiant pride. With her hair combed into a neat knot, Millie looked almost handsome. "What can I tell my family, Miss?"

Victoria said quietly, "Tell them that you are going to work for me."

Millie frowned, then her face cleared in a radiation of joy. "Oooooh, miss! 'Ow did you fix that? You didn't tell 'em . . .?"

"No, Millie," she said, feeling ashamed that Millie had uttered not one word of reproach or blame for her own part in her dismissal. "I didn't have to tell them anything. In fact I think that deep down Mother is sorry she had to be so harsh with you. Now, then. You are to carry on working here and help until after the wedding, and then you will go with me to the other house. So you can unpack your things and go on down to the kitchen again."

Millie laughed with real delight. "Oooh, miss, Violet's goin' to be ever so pleased. She was cryin' something wicked when Bess told 'em what 'appened. An' it's goin' to be a real treat to see Bess's face when she 'ears what's 'appened too."

"You'll have to try to get on with Bess," said Victoria. "And you'll have to try your hardest to get on well with Lord Benchley's housekeeper. It might be a good idea to go out of your way to be pleasant and respectful."

"If you say so, miss. I'm so 'appy I could agree to anythin' right now."

"What happened this morning? Did you see Captain Lawrence?"

Millie's face clouded, and she lowered her voice. "'E were there, miss, in a carriage just like you said. Nowt really 'appened, exactly, but when 'e saw I was alone, like, 'is face went all sort o' queer."

"Queer?"

"Yes, miss. 'Ow can I say it? Like summat bad 'ad 'appened an' 'e knew all along it would, but just the same 'e were 'opin' it wouldn't."

Victoria nodded. "What did he say to you?"

"That was the funny part, miss. 'E didn't say nowt. Nothin' at all. 'E took the letter, an' 'e sat there real quiet an' all. I thought 'e was goin' to speak to me, but 'e must 'ave changed 'is mind. 'E just lashed off at the 'orses an' off 'e went. Oh, miss, but it's a shame. 'Im lookin' so smart in 'is red uniform an' 'is face so sad I felt sorry fer 'im."

Victoria sat very still, twisting Lord Benchley's modestly-sized diamond around her finger. At last, when she knew she must leave, it seemed to take an enormous effort to stand up and walk out of the room.

Four

Clara sat beside Birdie that night at dinner, on a chair stacked with cushions that Violet had set for her. She was almost as tall as Birdie, legless under her long, soft cambric skirts of bright blue banded with gold. But she had hard white hands and wrists of porcelain, an exquisite china face—even prettier than Albertina's, thought Birdie—with blank blue eyes and dark gold lashes, faintly drawn brows, and a curving, rose-colored mouth. Her hair was the only disappointment, for it was matter-of-factly sewn loops of yellow sock wool without style or beauty. Birdie didn't mind this though, and every time she paused in mid-mouthful and glanced at her, the breath caught in her throat in a tight knot of delicious happiness.

Dinner was a deliberately cheerful occasion. The distressing business of the war was set aside and everybody turned determinedly to celebration and gaiety. After all, the war was over and the fireworks display tomorrow night would demonstrate the fact.

Martin said, "I read in the newspaper that they are going

to set off ten thousand rockets at the stroke of midnight."

"Ten thousand!" cried Albertina. "How could they possibly do that?"

"I expect they'll have ten thousand matches being fired by ten thousand men, all at the same time," smiled Andrew.

"Will we be able to stay up so late?" worried Albertina. "It *is* the night before the wedding, but it would be dreadful to miss it."

"We will all have a sleep in the afternoon," decided Grace. "Yes, you also, Birdie, so that you won't fall to yawning during the wedding service."

Charlotte's face was alight with excitement. "You are so lucky, Victoria. Just think of it! If they set the rockets blazing on the stroke of midnight, it will mark the beginning of your wedding day. The only thing that happened on my wedding day was when Patch broke into the hen house and killed two of Mother's best laying hens!"

"And put all the others off the lay," said John dryly. "I've not had a fresh boiled egg since."

"And I think that since we are talking of weddings, we should have a toast to the bride's happiness," said Penelope.

Her husband got to his feet. He pressed his fingertips on the damask cloth and said firmly, "We have had a strange day today. There has been the joy of our being together again after such a long time, and the bitter sadness of recalling unhappy things, and those who cannot be here. But we must not lose sight of the reason that brings us together. Let us drink to Victoria, to her health and her happiness, and let us wish her many long years of both those things, for they are the only things of true value in life."

Victoria sat mutely while the men stood to drink her health. Glancing at each one in turn, she noticed that they wouldn't look at her but instead fixed their eyes resolutely on their glasses or on the walls across the room. She glanced at the women. Apart from Mother, who was gazing at her with a fatuously proud expression, the only one who met her eyes was Charlotte, and she was so tenderly pitying that Victoria felt cold all over. Earlier that day Victoria had resolved to single her cousin out for an intimate talk, in order to find out what it was really like to be married, but after this one glance she changed her mind abruptly. It was plain that everybody in the room with the exception of her mother felt sorry for her and was ashamed of what was happening.

Chilled, Victoria raised her chin and stiffened her spine. She was going to marry Lord Benchley and she was determined not to wallow in self-pity about it. So what if he was grotesque and repulsive? She would try to find the good things in him and concentrate her attention on those. So far, she had Millie to thank him for. Albertina had laughed about that, and said that he had to get her a maid anyway, for as a bachelor he wouldn't have a lady's maid on his staff already. Albertina couldn't understand her indifference, but how could she tell Albertina that she didn't want an expensive wedding present anyway? All she really longed for were Charles and her freedom, and they were as unattainable as blond hair and true beauty.

John continued: "There is another toast to be drunk. Charlotte and Martin have some news for you. I ask you all to join me in wishing them health and happiness too."

"What is it?" cried Victoria at once, glad of something to take her mind from the pain.

But the news was dismaying. "We are emigrating to New Zealand in August," said Martin, ducking his black, curly head in embarrassment.

"You can't possibly do that!" cried Albertina.

"We've been planning it for some time," said Charlotte.

"Come on, Martin," urged Andrew, who seemed to have known the news already. "Up you get and let's be having your reasons for running off and leaving us."

Protesting, and with a high blush coloring his cheeks, Martin got to his feet. "We're not really running away and leaving anybody. We love England, and nobody would be more patriotic than we."

"Aye, that be so," approved John.

"But I'm wanting to be a farmer and own a place of my own, something we can pass on to any young ones we might be blessed with." He smiled at the glowing face that was looking up at him encouragingly. "Here in England I could work for years and not be able to hope for more than a small farm at the end of it, but we want something better."

"But that's the far end of the world, lad," said Matthew. "What about someplace closer, like Canada or South Africa?"

"We did think of that, sir. New Zealand was our choice because we have friends there who have the same ambitions we do. They say there is a great opportunity for people like us who are not afraid to work. One of my friends, Mr. Guy Fowldes—perhaps you know him?—is so keen to have us there, he bought the farm next door to his on my behalf. It's not properly broken in for farming yet, but it's good land with black soil and a stream, fruit trees, and two small cabins. As soon as we heard, we arranged passage on the first ship that could sell us cabin room."

"Oh, Charlotte, how exciting for you!" Victoria could picture her cousin in a long print housewife dress with a matching ruffled sunbonnet drawing water from a stone-walled well outside a log cabin while black hens scratched in the dirt around her and a spotted hound lay in the shade beside the honeysuckle-covered chimney, nose on paws, lazily watching over her.

Penelope sighed mournfully. "We shall miss them so much that I dread to contemplate it. First the boys and now them. It is too much and far too soon."

"Now then, puppy," chided John affectionately. "We agreed not to talk like that. It's the best thing for them. We decided not to try to influence them."

"I'm not, I'm not," she sighed even more mournfully. "I'm afraid that I must confess to garnering what sympathy I can."

"You have all of mine," offered Grace, her traces of ill-feeling melted away. "How dreadful this is for you!"

"John is right. Young people must do what they feel driven to. Where would the world be if they all decided to cling around their parents?"

Birdie piped up, round eyes also fixed with fascination on her cousin. "Nana taught us about New Zealand. She said there are people there who kill other people for meat!"

There was a sudden, embarrassed hush which was broken when poor Miss Boswell stated that she had felt duty bound to explain what cannibals were.

"Don't you feel afraid, Martin?" persisted Birdie, quite ignoring Nana's warning hand on her arm.

"Not really. There are only a few cannibals there, and they shouldn't worry us. You see, Birdie, this city, London, is a wicked place too, with all sorts of frightful things happening. Not right around here, but in other parts of the city. What I think is this: if any of the New Zealand Maoris heard stories

116

about the dangerous goings-on in London, they would consider you very brave to live *here*!"

"Oh," said Birdie.

Still flushed, her governess said, "We shall excuse ourselves now, dear, so that you and Clara can be rested for the fireworks tomorrow. Come along, and I shall carry Clara."

"I want to carry her," said Birdie.

She refused to be separated from the doll, even announcing to her father that Clara was going to ride in the wedding coach.

And, after the wedding-eve dinner, Miss Boswell carried Clara up the stairs to the diminutive, iron-balustraded balcony above the servants' rooms. It had been built especially for occasions like this, though in the long, dull stretches between state fireworks displays and bonfire nights, it served splendidly as a courting nook for the maids and garden boys. Old Will, with Young Will helping some of the time, had spent the afternoon carrying the white garden furniture from the conservatory and arranging it for comfortable viewing. Violet had carried up a tea wagon, then trays of glasses, and all was ready for the jugs of hot spiced wine and currant cookies, buttery and crisp.

Birdie leaned over the railing in a manner that drew a sharp cry from her governess. Reluctantly she drew back and came to sit on a chair. "People don't look real when you can only see the tops of their heads," she complained. "They look like hats with funny arms and legs."

"What a beautiful view," breathed Charlotte.

Victoria agreed. During the first few months they had lived in this house, she had spent hours alone here, dreaming, and it comforted her to know that even after her marriage she would still be able to come up here on her visits home and refresh herself with this glorious vista. It was just after twilight, when the sky was as velvety dark as a moth's wing and the stars no more than faint sparks struck from the dying sun.

All day people had been trickling into the park.

"Birdie, do sit down," said Miss Boswell sharply. The steep climb had tired her, and she was in no mood to cope with nonsense.

"Oh, yes," said Albertina. "If you lean over like that, you will give Mother a real turn. Look, it's starting! I do hope the others hurry up."

Two rockets corkscrewed into the sky, trailing a hiss of

yellow mist. It was still faintly light and they could see the spent rockets as they plummeted into the crowd below, beyond the trees.

"I think they're just practicing so far," said Victoria.

"Do sit down, Birdie," fussed Albertina. "You are blocking everybody's view, the way you're fidgeting there. Come here and keep Clara company."

Birdie sat by Victoria and said earnestly, "I wonder what the ducks will think if any of the rockets fall into the pond? They might think that stars are raining on them."

"They might," smiled Victoria.

And then, almost as soon as the balcony crowded with the rest of the family and Millie brought the jugs and plates of refreshment before slipping away, the display began. A violet staccato of crackers pop-popped like barrages of rifle fire, interspersed with much louder explosions deep and dull like the heavy thump of cannon.

Everybody gasped as an enormous fountain of sparks gushed into the night. The crowd of people breathed one collective sigh.

Victoria watched, enchanted. For a while she was free from her thoughts of tomorrow . . .

Five

Violet stepped out of the shadows at the foot of the stairs. Andrew clattered down the last few steps and swept her up off the floor in one easy movement.

Choking on a little gasp of delight, Violet wriggled down until her coarse leather slippers touched the carpet again. She touched his arm where it was still thick with bandages. "Do be careful, Master Andrew. I despair of thee at times."

Chucking her under her pointed chin in the lightest of caresses, he said softly, "What's this 'Master' business then?"

"Thee has been away so long that I grew used to saying your name like that," she whispered.

"Then say it properly."

"Andrew." She turned her head and looked at him under the thick curve of her lashes, and swiftly he put his mouth over hers. Her hand crept up and rested with utter gentleness against

118

his cheek on the smooth-shaven area between his sideburns and moustache.

Face against her high starched collar he said, "I love the smell of you."

"That's Bess's own lye soap," she said with a giggle.

"It reminds me of you, and that's what makes it beautiful, Violet. God in heaven knows I love you. I've missed you so. I feel as though I can't get enough of you."

She tried to be practical. They were, after all, in the first-floor hallway, and there was no guarantee that someone might not come downstairs at any minute.

"I'm worried that this is dangerous, thee giving me notes at breakfast. Bess will suspect. She found a letter I wrote thee once, snipped it right out of my pocket she did."

He laughed and put an arm about her shoulders, treating her like the comrade of many years that she was. Her long brown skirts over layers of petticoat pressed at his legs as he led her toward his room.

She was still practical. "Will they miss thee up there?"

"I told them I had to go out." It occurred to him that she might want to see the fireworks, and that he was being selfish in making her wait on him. "Would you like to go and watch? We could be together later."

When she turned to look up at him, her head was in the crook of his arm. "Young Will will gabble of nowt else for weeks. Truly but I would rather be with thee."

It was always fun, the breathless creeping into his moonlit room, the moment of suspense as the door was bolted, and the almost unbearable suffocation of their first minutes alone together. Normally Violet was completely submissive, allowing him to undress her while she stood patiently with down-swept lashes and solemn mouth. He would pick her up still, pale body and tuck her into bed where she would lie with eyes closed while he undressed and climbed in beside her.

But tonight, she moved away from him and stood at the foot of his bed, leaning on the rail with both hands clasped on the knob, bone white in the moonlight. He sat on the quilt and faced her, waiting. Their relationship had survived so easily partly because of her ability to come out frankly with anything that troubled her. She never stooped to petty, coquettish revenge if she thought he had wronged her.

"Andrew, what we have been doing since thee got home,

it be foolish and dangerous." She bent her face toward his and lowered her voice as if there was a risk of someone overhearing. "I might fall. I could fall, the way thee is taking me without . . . without . . ."

He teased her lovingly, "You can't say it! Oh, but I adore you, Violet. If you but knew how much I have ached to see you and hear your voice."

Her eyes were magnified by their own tears as she pleaded gently with him. "And I thee. But Andrew, thee must listen to me . . ."

"I must, I must," he mocked her, pretending to be cross. "Oh, what a scold of a wife you will be."

"Please don't, for I cannot bear to hear thee talk that way." And a clear teardrop rolled down the curve of her cheek.

"Come and sit by me, you silly thing," he said cheerfully. When she was settled, he folded her against his chest and spoke to her netted hair, kissing the white line of its parting.

"My father wanted me to be in the army and have a commission of my own, but that isn't going to be possible now. I'm forced to look out for myself."

"*That* means thee will have to find a rich wife. I know that well enough," she said dully.

"Listen, you silly goose. I have a chance to get some fine army contracts, but when that happens, I shall probably have to leave home. How would you feel about being with me, staying with me always?"

This was so unexpected that Violet quite simply did not know what to say. After a time Andrew laughed self-consciously. "I had often imagined how you might react when I proposed to you, but I never quite expected silence."

Suddenly she wrenched herself around in his arms and pressed her flaming hot face into his neck. "Thee does love me!" she cried in shame.

"Of course I do! I've been telling you that for years."

"I thought thee were only saying that to make things easy with us."

He laughed and hugged her shaking shoulders tightly to him. "I understand, oh, but I do. I've lain awake at night and heard a hundred times all the bitter things they will say to me for turning my back on them for you. Before I went away, I used to tell myself that this love between us was only of our growing-up time, that both of us would tire of it and make our

120

lives with someone else." But while I was away fighting, I realized that I couldn't stand the pain of knowing you were married to someone else. You have to be mine—no matter what it costs."

She should tell him about Ted. "While thee was away, did thee have any other girls?"

"Yes."

"Oh." It should be easy to tell him now. Why wouldn't the words come?

He misunderstood the "Oh" and said, "I have been with other girls. If I had not, then what I am going to say would mean nothing. I have never loved anybody else but you, nor am I likely to. You are all I ever thought about when I was away. When I had been shot and didn't know how badly, all that worried me was the thought that I wouldn't be able to say good-bye to you."

"Bess keeps wondering who thee will wed. She says on and on that it will be Miss Longworth."

"Then won't Bess be surprised?" he said, remembering the morning Albertina had accused his mother of matchmaking. How much hurt would poor Violet be subjected to before he could take her away?

"Andrew?"

"Yes?" He placed his dry cheek against her damp one.

"This is lovely, but it don't seem real, and I don't feel right listening to thee. Cats is cats and dogs is dogs and they don't marry neither. Thee is a young master and I be just a maid-servant and what thee proposes just don't happen."

He began to unbutton her dress, starting at the tight buttonholes on her collar. "That is nonsense. Look at the queen's own father! He was married for twenty-seven years to a commoner!" This was not true. The duke of Kent had only lived with Madame de St. Laurent for that time, but Andrew felt that he could count on Violet not knowing that. "So you see, if the queen's own father could do that, why must you insist it's impossible for us? Forget your objections. Just think of my dream." He paused to wiggle a button that was stuck on a tangle of thread. "I see a cottage in the country, somewhere near the coast within the cry of the sea gulls where the sky is a clean, deep blue. There will be roses in the garden and bluebells in the woods nearby, and there we shall live together in the most perfect happiness you could imagine." He slipped the dress from her shoulders and slid his hands under her underthings to her silky breasts. "I love you, and I must always know I have you," he whispered as she arched into his hands and her breath sighed in a warm stream against his bent face. "I love you, Violet."

That same evening, as soon as it grew dark, Charles Lawrence made his way by horse-drawn omnibus to the park, and then back on foot to the house on Clarence Street. He planned to wait until the family had left for the fireworks display, to follow them discreetly and somehow separate Victoria from the rest of her family so that he could speak to her alone. He knew that something had forced her against her will to change her mind. That much had been apparent in the maid's expression when she handed him the note. If only he had not been too stunned to question her at the time. Soon he would know, and, if Victoria really did love him, she would be prepared to listen. There was no obstacle to their marriage that could not be overcome with determination.

Charles was safe in assuming that the Fieldings would go to the display. Most of London was making progress toward the main parks where the celebrations were to be held. *The Times* had predicted that over a hundred thousand people would be at Hyde Park for the celebrations there. Charles had to push and fight his way to reach number twenty-seven and, once there, had to take himself out of the rushing mass and into an alcove between two window boxes of the house across the street for fear of being swept back toward the park gates again. Smoking a thin black cigar, he rehearsed what he would say to Victoria.

He kept constant watch on the door across the road. They probably wouldn't leave until a few minutes before starting time, for with reserved seats in the specially built stands there was no reason to go early to find a place. The crowd was thinning now, and despite his dark cloak and the dim light he began to feel uncomfortably conspicuous. A roaring from the park informed him that the display was beginning, but still there was no sign of movement at the Fielding house. Rockets whizzed and hissed above him. Looking up, he suddenly saw the Fielding family assembled on the balcony. And here he was, casually loitering in plain view of them all.

It was obvious he couldn't remain where he was. He crossed

the road and as he approached number twenty-seven, there was a luck occurrance which he took to be an omen. While he watched, an assortment of servants came out of the service door together. Charles paused and turned his back. When they had all passed, he strode to the door and tried it. It was locked.

For a few minutes he stood there cursing, wondering what to do next. If Victoria was not coming out, then he must somehow find a way to get in to her. The conservatory, of course. But it offered no possible means of entry and for a moment he thought of giving up and going home. Only the knowledge that this was his last chance kept him steadfast. He decided to wait until the fireworks were over.

At midnight the sky was lit with an enormous glow. Spent rockets peppered the street, one landing in the gutter in front of him. There was a cry from the balcony where a casing had landed. Presently the street thickened again with the outgoing tide of revelers. Soon Charles was glad of his shelter alongside the house for the footpath was a solid mass of people, some running, all noisy, tired and in a hurry to get home. Charles waited and watched. The group he was waiting for came soon. He entered the flow behind them and paused at the corner of the house to see what they would do.

Luck was with him again. Three of the people went straight inside, but the old man limped on to the carriage shed and leaned forcefully on the door bolt. It moved inward, taking him with it. Keeping in the shadows of the main house, Charles followed the servants and boldly walked in at the open service door.

Before him was the kitchen where the bespectacled servant was cupping his hands around a candle flame. Close to him the woman sat at a table with her back to the door, unpinning her hat. The boy warmed his hands at the stove. Charles looked about quickly. On either side of him were closed doors. Choosing the right-hand one, he eased it open and walked into what appeared to be a pantry. Moonlight slanted onto rows of bottles and jars. The air was thick with the earthy smell of potato bins. Something rubbed against his ankle. He reached down and touched warm fur, as a cat began to purr loudly. Charles scooped up the thin body and pushed it out beyond the slit of open door, then closed it almost to with his boot.

He heard the sound of dragging footsteps and a cracked voice saying kindly, "Been keeping rats out of the pantry, have

123

you now?" Whereupon the door closed with a bang and Charles breathed easily again. Presently quietness descended and he decided that the servants must have left the kitchen and gone to bed. He emerged. The kitchen was dark, with only the palest shafts of moonlight melting over weird shapes that hung from the rafters. He found the door leading into the passageway and followed that, recalling his scanty knowledge of the house's geography. A ribbon of light showed beneath the study door, and he paused, realizing that Victoria's father was still up working. He was trying to decide where he should hide, and whether it might be safest to return to the kitchen and wait, when he saw a candle, held by a woman with disheveled hair and a long dark dress. Her face, above the candle, was young and filled with terror when she saw him.

He whispered urgently, "Please don't be afraid. I shan't . . ."

Violet stared at him blankly, then dropped the candle and screamed.

"No, no," he begged, thrusting his hand over her mouth. He tugged her into the room opposite the study and whispered, "I came to see Victoria. I'm a friend. I love Victoria. I want to stop her from marrying that old goat. I must see her." Aware that the girl was nodding her head and murmuring assent, he let her go. "You will help me? Good. Tell them you screamed at something . . . a rat, perhaps. And that you ran in here in a panic."

"Hush!" She touched his chest in a gesture that he took to be friendly.

Voices were now raised in the corridor.

"What in the hell . . . ?"

Light illuminated the room in a thin wedge from the partially open door.

"That was Violet's voice."

"Where is she?"

"Here I be, masters," she said weakly, putting a hand to her hair in a futile effort to arrange it. I'm so sorry to get you all in a tizzy, but I got such a fearful fright so sudden like . . ."

"You've been attacked, haven't you?" demanded Matthew.

"Look at the state of her!"

"Where is the man?" from Matthew.

"It's . . . It's . . ." she began helplessly, but the door was flung wide open and the lamplight shone directly in Charles's face.

"Here he is," muttered the man with the lamp. He escorted an unresisting Charles by the elbow out into the corridor.

"Is somebody hurt?" called Grace.

Her husband ignored her. Staring at Charles with a look of rage that was almost unnatural in its intensity, he fumed, "I swear that you have the cheek of the devil himself. First my daughter and now my maid."

"What *is* going on down there?" called Grace.

Violet began to weep.

Then Victoria—it was plainly Victoria now—called, "Father, is everything all right?"

"Go back to bed, I say!" shouted Matthew, bellowing right into Charles's face as he moved in closer to deal with him.

Charles, who quite rightly decided that things could not possibly be worse for him, having nothing to lose, called out, called out, "Victoria! Victoria!"

Her cry of delight reached them all. "It's Charles!" she said, and dashed for the stairs.

Grace seized her arm, spinning her about. "No, dear," she said in a firm, quiet voice. "You are not to go down there."

"Oh, Mother, I must. Father sounded so angry! He could hurt Charles."

"Your father would not hurt anybody. Not even Captain Lawrence."

"He won't call the police, will he?"

Grace smiled at the horror on her daughter's face. "Of course not, Victoria. There will be no police coming here. Think of what a scandal that would cause!"

Six

Victoria awoke the next morning to find her governess leaning over her, shaking her shoulders and trying to smile as she said, "Happy wedding day, dear."

She tried to struggle up to a sitting position but sank back to the pillows, groggy from the laudanum she had been forced to swallow last night.

She lay still and watched Nana open first the shutters and then the window, admitting a dazzle of sunshine. The older woman moved slowly as though her body was heavy with pain.

Poor Nana, Victoria thought, remembering the hysterical scene last night when Charles was evicted so unceremoniously from the house and flung down the front steps like a common thief. Poor Nana had been roused from her bed, looking strange in her hairnet and curling papers. It was Nana who was made to dose Victoria while her mother held her shoulders and forbade her to move. Then Nana had to sleep in the chair at the foot of the bed in case Victoria should try to flee from her bed and elope with Charles.

Miss Boswell turned from the window. "Come and look, dear. See what a beautiful day you've been given."

Victoria got out of bed and knelt on the window seat to have her very last view of the world from this room. Nana stood behind her, unraveling her twin ropes of hair.

"I do hope that what happened last night didn't upset you too much" she said.

Victoria was tempted to confide in Nana, to unload the great misery that was choking her lungs. Then she remembered what Andrew had said. Closing her mind, she said brightly, "Who could feel sad on a day like this?"

"Sometimes it helps to talk about things," said Miss Boswell, disappointed.

"Thank you for offering." Victoria closed her hand over her governess's fingers.

"You are a good girl."

"Gracious no," Victoria said briskly. "I kept you from your sleep last night and you must be exhausted because of me."

"I feel fine. Come now, young lady. We do have rather a lot to do today."

"Why? Is something special going to happen?" She laughed at the silly joke. "I imagine that poor Mother is in a panic by now. If she's nervous before a dinner party, think what she'll be today."

"*Everybody* is in a panic. You should see the scramble in the kitchen. Even Flounce has caught the fever. He always seems to know when something is in the wind, and he has gone quite mad today. When Old Will was sweeping the yard, he snatched the straw broom from him and tore it into a scatter of straws."

"Oh, what fun! Please help me to dress right now, Nana. I want to go downstairs."

"You are to do no such thing," scolded Nana with a smile.

"First you must get back into bed for your breakfast. Joan will soon be up with a tray. Then you will have a bath. The bride does not appear downstairs until it is time to leave for the church! There, now. It is bad luck for anyone except family to see you and there are loads of people downstairs already. Oh, Victoria, some of the gifts are magnificent. You have been given a complete gold dinner set with gold cutlery and tea and coffeepots . . ."

"It is lovely, isn't it? Mother brought me up a piece to look at yesterday afternoon after my nap. It was very generous of the duke of Lanark."

Albertina's head popped around the door. "May we come in?"

"Yes, but don't excite your sister too much. I shall be back later, dear."

Crowding in behind Albertina were Birdie and Charlotte, still in their wrappers. Following them came Joan, bearing a tray with domed plates and a cut-glass vase holding lilies-of-the-valley.

"We had breakfast trays too," crowed Birdie, bouncing on the edge of the bed.

"Not as fancy as yours though," said Albertina. "Look at that! Flowers on your tray. And Mother said that we all have to be extra-specially nice to you, and treat you like royalty."

"Everybody is having trays!" cried Birdie. "It's like being sick, only so much more fun."

"Look at the way she's eating!" exclaimed Charlotte. "Aren't you nervous, Victoria? On my wedding morning I was so tense and giddy that I couldn't eat a single bite."

"I'm not nervous at all," said Victoria blandly.

"It would take more than a wedding to put Victoria off her food," sighed Albertina. "Yet she never seems to get any fatter. I swell out like a balloon and Madame Soiska has to let out my seams!"

"Do you want all that toast?" asked Birdie.

Victoria pushed the plate toward her.

Millie and Joan arrived, carrying the black-enameled tub with the red-rose design. They placed it on its oval base over a spread of bath towels.

"Oh!" cried Birdie, impressed. "You have to take a proper bath and it's only morning!"

Miss Boswell, returning, heard her. "Everybody will be

127

taking baths. Now back to your rooms with you. Your baths will be ready very soon."

Joan, Violet, and Millie entered in procession to empty pails of hot water into the tub, and Miss Boswell sprinkled the water with perfume. She unbuttoned Victoria's nightdress and set out her bathing slip just as Violet returned with an armful of crisply folded white towels. She put them on a chair and stood there awkwardly, her blue eyes worriedly watching Victoria's face.

After an uneasy pause Violet burst out, "Miss, I be really and truly sorry about what happened last night."

Victoria went white.

"Thee might not know it, but it was all my fault he was caught. Fetched me such a fright, he did, that I couldn't help but scream out. I felt so terrible when I saw who he was."

Victoria had to try twice before the words came. "Don't feel badly about it, Violet."

"He called out to thee. He seemed so nice, he did, and he only wanted to talk to thee. He said that he was going to try to stop the marriage, but he didn't get a chance because of me."

"Nobody could stop the marriage, Violet. Please go and don't worry."

"But, miss . . ."

"Please go, Violet."

Chastened, the maid left quickly. Victoria slipped off her nighgown, pulled on her shimmy, and stepped into the luke-warm water. Nobody could do that. Nobody could stop the marriage now.

When Miss Boswell came to dress her, Victoria was already in her lace-trimmed pantalettes and camisole, covered modestly with her silken wrapper. She was listlessly arranging the toilet articles on the dresser. Miss Boswell guessed at once that she had been crying and became at once determinedly businesslike. Distraction, she decided, would be the order of the day. The bride was not going to be left alone for another minute. She organized Joan and Millie with a few instructions and soon the room was tidy.

The governess shook out a new corset and laced Victoria into it firmly. She adjusted the first of the four hooped petticoats about Victoria's handspan waist and fiddled with the hooked catch. "You are going to look very sweet today, and I want to feel proud of you, and I do mean proud."

On each of the cambric petticoats the flexible hoops were set at different levels, one above the knees, one at knee level, one at mid-calf, and another, stiffer one at the very edge of the hemline to hold the weight of the frills and starched lace around the hem. To add more fullness and soften the effect, a fifth petticoat made of layers of taffeta frills from waist to hem was stretched over the top.

"See if you can kneel," commanded Nana.

The kneeling was accomplished easily, and sitting could be managed too as long as Victoria remembered to sit only on the edge of the seat. While she waited for Madame Soiska and Millie to bring in the gown, Miss Boswell polished her hair with a square of chiffon wrapped around a soft hairbrush. She brushed fifty strokes at each side and fifty at the back, and then carefully gathered the loose hairs to be packed in the dressing-table slit, from where Joan would gather them when it was time to make chignons.

Millie was at the door, asking to come in.

"Gracious, child," exclaimed Miss Boswell, opening the door a crack. "Have you carried it upstairs all by yourself?"

"I can manage easy, I can. Joan popped the flat-iron on back of the stove for fear it might be wrinkled." With the governess's help she spread the long, calico-wrapped gown full length on the bed.

"Where is Madama Soiska?"

"Summat dreadful 'appened to 'er. 'Er little poodle got itself kicked by an 'orse right outside 'er very steps an' 'er just on 'er way over 'ere. Course she were too upset."

"These emotional foreigners," sniffed Nana. "The slightest thing distracts them."

"Is the poor little dog all right?" asked Victoria, plucking at a ribbon on her bodice.

"Killed, they reckon, or that's what I 'eard, miss," said Millie blithely.

"Now stand still please, dear," said Nana hastily. "Hold your arms up high so that we can slip the sleeves on first." She and Millie both gathered the skirt up into soft bunches and, working together, guided Victoria's arms into the sleeves while the skirt dropped into place over the frame of petticoats. Next the hem had to be checked for evenness and any folds tugged out smooth before the buttoning could begin. While Millie folded the calico wrappers to be sent back, Miss Boswell took a whalebone buttonhook and meticulously pulled each of the one hundred miniature satin-covered buttons into its taut satin loop. As she worked her way up the spine, the weight of the gown pressed around Victoria's body.

"I doubt whether I shall be able to breathe properly in this," said Victoria. "It feels so much heavier with the petticoats on."

Miss Boswell frowned. "Try not to think about breathing. It is only when you overconcentrate that a thing becomes difficult—just as when you think about a word too long it becomes impossible to spell it correctly. Think about something else instead."

Then I shall overconcentrate on breathing, thought Victoria. If I do, I shall be so busy gasping for breath that I shall have no thought to spare for anything else.

When the last button was done, Miss Boswell stood back to look at the gown. She smiled in admiration, but suddenly her face crumpled and she turned her head away, fumbling in her waist purse for a handkerchief.

Victoria held out richly encased arms to her.

The governess made a choking noise, a tangled laugh and sob. "No, dear. Tears must not fall on your wedding gown. That would only bring bad luck." She shook her head and managed a smile. "I shall miss you. You look beautiful in that dress, truly beautiful."

Victoria's lips curved in delight. She must look beautiful indeed for Nana to say so and almost weep. Stepping carefully past the dumbly admiring Millie, she faced the mirror—and recognized herself with a gasp of surprise. The dress clung so closely over her breasts and shoulders that she seemed to be coated with wet, white, marvelously intricate icing. From the nipped-in band of her waist the skirt belled out in a snowy riot of wild roses, twining leaves and tendrils, and looping, trailing ribbons all scattered with tiny pearls in an embroidered design.

"Princess Victoria," drawled a voice—warm, admiring, filled with affection.

But it was only Andrew, clad in his scarlet military uniform. She turned to see him, unable to stop her constricted heart from racing madly.

"You do look like Queen Victoria, you know," said Andrew who could know nothing of Charles Lawrence's endearments. "Well then, little sister, if Lord So-and-So doesn't turn up at the church, you won't be left standing there, I can positively guarantee you that. There will be a riot of all the eligible men fighting like gamecocks over you."

"Out, out!" cried Miss Boswell, disapproving of both his presence and the tone of his remarks. She flapped her arms at him.

"Not been crying, have you, Nana?" he teased. "Cheer up! Since you so heartlessly rejected Lord Benchley yourself, you must have realized he would go elsewhere. Never mind, there will be lots of other young bucks at the reception to catch your eye."

"You do go on at times," she scolded in a pleased tone, firmly pushing him out all the same. "Be off with you now. Miss Victoria still has to have her hair done."

Now the pace quickened. Birdie rustled in importantly and sat with a demureness foreign to her nature while Nana curled and pinned, then she watched while Nana arranged Victoria's hair, satisfied that the styles were identical. The bridesmaids came in next, Albertina stunningly confident and Noelle with such a bewildered look on her face that Victoria felt dismayed.

She said frankly, "Don't you really want to be an attendant, Noelle?"

Noelle looked slyly at them all. "Mummy made me," she mumbled in her childish voice.

Victoria sighed in exasperation. They had seen such a lot of Noelle lately, and she was always downcast. If they managed to get her to say anything, it was usually something so stupid that they regretted their politeness, and felt embarrassed for her. Her only animation came when Andrew appeared. Cued by his presence she would utter a string of remarks in a naïvely enthusiastic tone: "Good day, Master Andrew! What an especially lovely day it is today. And how are you keeping? Are you rested from the rigors of the war?" All quite innocent enough but so put on that the effect was to make Andrew hurriedly excuse himself for just-remembered business elsewhere—whereupon Noelle would lapse back into her somnolent state.

"You look very pretty," said Victoria kindly, and not altogether untruthfully, for Noelle did have regular features and large, if dull, gray eyes.

"Mummy says I'm ugly."

Mummy should be whipped, thought Miss Boswell uncharitably. Taking Noelle's limp hand, she said, "Noelle, you

131

have a very important job to do today, looking after the bride. Do you think you can manage it?"

"Oh, yes!" Noelle came suddenly alive. "Mummy made me practice every day how to walk up the aisle."

Then all was ready. Matthew knocked on his daughter's door and presented her with an elbow to escort her downstairs. Albertina carried the long sweep of veil, Noelle clutched the flowers, and Birdie followed close behind. There was a hush in the hall below where the servants, the family, and the helpers for the day all assembled to see the bride. The silence lasted until the last step was negotiated, when Grace stepped forward from the semicircle to kiss her daugher. Then, as if on signal, there was a hubbub of talk, congratulations, and compliments.

Prayers were held in the flower-banked parlor, the servants ranged neatly behind the two Fielding families. Matthew kept the service brief; they were already a few minutes late and had a long day ahead. Victoria stood mutely between her two sisters, steadfastly concentrating on her breathing. Birdie, all copper and gold, kept looking up at her as though she couldn't believe that this angel was really Victoria. Albertina looked straight ahead, composed and self-satisfied. Noelle glanced sideways at Andrew, narrowing her eyes and wishing that he would smile at her and please her mother.

The service was simple. There were several Bible readings chosen by Grace, who was now having stronger misgivings about the wisdom of the match. Every text had the same theme, an exhortation to wives to be obedient. This annoyed Victoria and confused her. Hadn't Mother already given her an exhaustive lecture on the subject just yesterday afternoon? The theme of obedience was being rubbed into her! Surely she could bow to Lord Benchley's wishes on domestic matters, and *that* was nothing to fuss about. Anybody would think I was the most willful and difficult creature imaginable, thought Victoria, hurt.

The service ended with Victoria's favorite hymn, the Twenty-third Psalm. As her voice lifted with the others above Miss Boswell's piano playing, Victoria recalled the first time she had heard the tune. Nana had been able to play faultlessly then, with a caressing touch so hauntingly sweet that Victoria used to creep in and hide, hunched behind the piano, aching with happiness as she listened.

Three coaches waited outside. Grace left in the first with

John, Penelope, Charlotte, and Martin. Andrew and the three bridal attendants went in the second, while Nana stayed with Matthew and Victoria for the third, to help the bride at the other end of the journey.

Old Will, decorated in an elaborate sea-green uniform borrowed from Lady Longworth's groom, sat solemnly on the box. Ceremoniously he whipped up the horses. After a slow start, the carriage began to roll smoothly and they were off with a hail of cheers and cries of good luck from the servants.

A few minutes later Victoria was kneeling on a thin velvet cushion at the altar steps, listening vaguely to the words that changed her from Miss Victoria Fielding to Lady Henry Benchley. She heard the words—solemn phrases and sacred formulas that she had wept over in an ecstasy of sentiment at other people's weddings—but today her mind registered nothing.

Even when the bishop took their right hands and placed them together, binding them with a wide strip of silk, Victoria did not look at the man beside her. She could not avoid seeing him as she had trodden the red aisle carpet. He had turned slightly, but not as though to welcome her. Through the pattern of her veil she could see the annoyance on his pudgy features, the first of many reminders that he did not like to be kept waiting.

Many of the guests in the front pews stared at the couple with intense curiosity. The groom was more than just unattractive. He has lumbered, waddled, and wheezed down the aisle and had to be helped by two attendants to rise from his pew at the first chords of the wedding march. Clever—so clever that it was said he had a touch of fox blood—but while his uncle lived, not rich enough to buy a bride. But the person people stared at was Victoria herself. All had turned to watch her dignified walk toward her groom, and all had been affected by the pure, helpless innocence on her dead white face.

The vibrating tones of the organ marked the bridal party's tread back up the aisle, and the guests fell in behind the attendants as they moved slowly toward the sunlight. Then, in the blinding warm brightness on the stone steps, there were more kisses and congratulations. Her veil pushed back, Victoria tried not to think about anything, just to smile. Everything would be all right, she thought, if she could only keep smiling.

With busy helping hands she was raised into Lord Ben-

133

chley's open carriage for the return journey to Clarence Street. Her skirts were arranged on the seat about her and the luxurious length of starched veil lightly folded and placed beside her. The bouquet was passed in to her by a radiantly happy Albertina. Noelle stood listlessly back, her mouth drooping open. Victoria clutched the bouquet in both hands. A scent of stephanotis surrounded her. Suddenly she wanted to leap out of the carriage and run crying to her parents. She wanted to be in her mother's arms. She needed a hug from her father, to feel the rough serge of his suit against her face and the comforting smell of tobacco. Tears burned under her eyelids. Her parents were standing in the shade of the clock tower, deep in conversation with the duke of Lanark. Miserable, alone, Victoria squeezed the ribbon-wrapped stem of her bouquet and tried not to cry.

The road was clogged with sightseers. Weddings attracted every variety of busybody and onlooker. Grubby-faced children swung on the carriage wheels, expertly dodging the flick of the driver's whip. Tradespeople and hawkers pressed close to stare at the bride. Victoria stared back, unsmiling. Suddenly, beyond a cluster of bonneted women, she saw him. He was standing across the street, outside the bay window of a draper's shop. Like the people around him, he just stood there, blankly staring at her. He did not smile or wave.

The carriage dipped precariously sideways as Lord Benchley climbed in. Delighted by his grossness, the street urchins hooted derisively, pushing at each other and laughing. At this point Charles turned abruptly and walked away.

Victoria held the bouquet to her face. Neither the soft touch of the petals nor the sweetness in her nostrils did anything to alleviate her misery.

Seven

Outside the house carriages paused, dipped slightly, and swayed as their occupants alighted. Miss Boswell and Myers waited in the front hall, he to mention to the gentlemen the spirits being dispensed in the study, and she to whisper discreetly about the room at the top of the stairs which might be of immediate interest to the ladies.

Victoria placed a numb hand on Lord Benchley's arm and they moved into the morning room where, with a bow, he left her into her mother's care so that he could find Matthew in the study. So far today he and Victoria had not spoken to each other at all.

The crowd swirled about them, a sparkling mixture of bright colors and babbling conversation. Everyone commented on the wedding service, the beauty of the bride, the elegant decor of the Fielding home, and the exquisitely arranged platters of food. Three violinists, dressed as gypsies in red and black satin and festooned with coin jewelry, drifted from room to room playing soft but lively airs. This was the very pinnacle of fashionable ideas, having been introduced as a novelty by Princess Charmaine at her wedding to a Hamburg duke the month before. A flock of imported maids, all in black and white plumage, swooped among the guests offering food and wine from silver trays.

Grace looked about her with satisfaction and flipped open her dusky pink ostrich-feather fan. "How does my dress look" she asked Victoria.

"It looks lovely, Mother. That rose pink suits you so well."

"Everybody is here," whispered Grace. "I shouldn't gloat about it, but what a triumph it is! This has never happened before, Alice says." She smiled feverishly. "All of these people will return the invitations! Isn't it wonderful?"

"I'm very happy for you, Mother."

Grace stared at her daughter as if for the first time all day. "Are you tired, dear?"

"A little hungry and thirsty perhaps."

"You mustn't eat down here," Grace reminded her. "And do try to look more cheerful. When the duke comes in, please smile at him. If he honors you by talking to you, do remember to be bright, Victoria." With the faintest touch of irritation at her daughter's apparent ingratitude, she added, "Smile! With that expression you look just like Noelle!"

At that moment Noelle looked anything but dreary. She had found Andrew, and, obedient to instructions, had tucked a limp hand through his elbow and attached herself to him. Andrew felt like a dog with a tin can tied to its tail and tried politely to get rid of her.

"Wait here, Miss Longworth, and I shall fetch you a glass of champagne."

"No, thank you, Master Andrew."

"A glass of fruit punch, then?"

"No thank you, Master Andrew."

There was a gold eyelash on her cheek, stuck to a damp spot below her right eye. Andrew refrained from flicking it away. "I'll fetch you something to eat."

"No, thank you, Master Andrew."

Desperately, "Then what do you say if I find you somewhere comfortable to sit? You must be tired of standing."

She smiled naïvely at him. "I like being here with you."

As the afternoon progressed, the air became heavy with the suave aroma of cigar smoke which hung like fog near the ceiling of each room. Grace left Victoria's side and disappeared to talk with her friends in the dining room. Victoria was relieved to see her go. In the two hours they had stood there together, they had received and spoken to an endless procession of people whom Victoria had never seen before but who Grace obviously knew and wanted to know better. So this was society, real society, thought Victoria, forcing an obliging smile and chattering brightly, answering questions: Where had she met Lord Benchley? Had she known him long? How radiant she looked!, everyone said.

Soon she tired of answering the questions and saying, "Lady Wandwood, I do so admire your hat. I noticed it when you came out of the cathedral and thought then how beautiful it was." Or, "That must be an Italian cameo, Lady Brinkforth? It is so delicate that surely the workmanship could not be English!"

When her mother left her side, she was freed at last from these conversations. She was considering a bold exit when her brother came up. "Could I bring you a drink of something? You look pale."

She clung to the arm reluctantly relinquished by Noelle. "Oh, Andrew, I am so tired of smiling! I'm tired of talking and I'm tired of meeting important ladies and gentlemen! And if I don't rest my feet soon, I know I shall fall down in a faint."

"I know what you mean."

"Could you please fetch Charlotte for me? She is just over there. I need someone to help me upstairs, and no, dear brother, you will not do!"

Violet circled around bearing a silver tray quivering with

champagne glasses. "Master Andrew?" she offered, smiling up at him.

He did not hear her, or see her, for the room was crowded and rather noisy and he had just found Charlotte's coppery curls. Brusquely he strode past Violet toward her.

Shaken, Violet ventured, "Miss Victoria, madam?"

"No, thank you," smiled Victoria.

"Oh." Violet paused there, looking troubled. Victoria was just about to ask if something was wrong when Albertina rushed up, obviously excited and trying to contain her giggles.

"You've missed the funniest turn since the Ladies' Guild Concert!" she blurted out loudly. "Noelle Longworth has been clinging to Andrew all afternoon. Clinging onto his arm, mind you, brazen as you like, and mooning over him! She's all set to marry him, just you wait and see!" Laughing, she stepped back a pace and bumped into the tray. She felt it strike the small of her back and glanced around in surprise to see Violet standing there with a dumb, hurt expression on her face.

"Were you listening?" accused Albertina.

"Please!" cried Victoria, taking her sister's hand.

But her interjection was too late. Albertina's angry glare completely unnerved the maid; aghast, they all watched the tray tip and the champagne glasses nudge each other, sliding and tumbling, slopping their contents over the front of Albertina's beautiful dark lemon silk dress.

"My dress is ruined!" Albertina said furiously. "Why, the clumsy little...witch! She'll pay for this with her job!" Blinded with righteous anger, she allowed Victoria to lead her away.

"My, you do look jolly!" said Charlotte, meeting them in the middle of the room.

"This is one occasion when making light of something will not fix it," Albertina informed her.

Before she could regale them all with an account of the accident, a familiar deep, drawling, husky voice said, "Albertina, *dear*! How ravishingly lovely you look!"

"Elizabeth!" they all said, immediately charmed into a good mood. Elizabeth Barnes's voice could lull cobras.

She was a splendid figure of a woman, tall enough to be noticed and slim enough to be complimented. She smiled, showing a slightly crisscrossed row of lower teeth, and regarded each of them in turn with her close-set warm brown eyes. "And you, Victoria, a fine day for you. Every happiness, dear! Charlotte, you promised on your heart that you would come to visit me and I have waited in vain! And, Andrew! I've saved the best for last! The war has improved you. You went away a handsome child and returned a handsome man. How I wish I wasn't already tied down to Mr. Barnes!"

As usual she waited for no replies. Polite chatter was not her idea of a way to pass the time. "I shall catch up with the rest of you later," she warned them. "For the moment I am going to kidnap Albertina and whisk her away to meet Gilbert and Francis. I have finally lured them out of that wretched study and returned them to civilization. They are waiting in the parlor. I tied them up with the window-sash cord so they couldn't run away. Oh, never mind your dress. They won't notice a tiny splash of water and it will be dry in a trice. A man has never been known to drop his eyes below the level of a lady's décolletage anyway!"

It was all a lot of nonsense, but it made Albertina smile. The party from Sedgewick Hall had only just arrived. As they nudged their way through the crowded rooms, Elizabeth told her about their journey, this time in her serious manner that could be relied on as the truth.

"It was horrifying, Albertina! One of the horses stumbled in harness and had to be shot. It was a new horse, one Mr. Barnes bought only a month ago, so I was relieved. It would have been dreadful to have to be there while one of my favorite old ones was disposed of. And what a ruckus there was! Francis—he's an American and rich! I *do* hope you'll like him!— he insisted on shooting the horse, but of course Mr. Barnes wouldn't let him. Mr. Barnes is an excellent host but there *are* limits, and the poor beast *was* his after all. So Francis was properly put out and sulked all the rest of the way here. Gilbert could hardly keep from bursting out laughing at him! Look, there they are, waiting like lambs for us. Aren't they adorably handsome?"

They were indeed a striking trio thought Albertina as she was introduced, but then Elizabeth had never been wrong about men in her life, and Albertina at this moment was grateful to have her for a friend. Elizabeth was older than the Fielding girls, even a year or two Charlotte's senior, but they had known her ever since they were babies. Elizabeth's family and the two Fielding families had lived in a row of three large cottages in Sydenham.

Of the three men, Michael Barnes was undeniably the most handsome, though it was a pity he wasn't taller. Even the youngest of his six children had now outgrown him, and Elizabeth's shoulder was on a level with his ear, but if she didn't mind, why should anybody else? He beamed and kissed Albertina's hand and said that he was sorry she had not been able to join their last weekend house party.

Albertina recognized the taller of the other two men with a little thrill of respect and awe. She had not expected "Gilbert" to be *the* Viscount Marley. The quickest of shy glances told her that he had an interestingly lean, olive face, thick brown hair and narrow brown eyes, flat as wood, with which he was looking at her with speculative interest.

"This is Gilbert," said Elizabeth, proud as if she had created him herself.

Albertina made a graceful little curtsy as she took his hand and was dismayed to see his reaction. Immediately his expression became bored and disdainful. Albertina's cheeks stung. So he is not amused that I know who he is, she thought. Very well, I shall tell Mother that her precious Viscount Marley is a most disagreeable person! Quite deliberately she turned her attention to the third man, Francis Blake. With the idea of vengeful mischief she gave him an even deeper curtsy when introduced, with a warm smile to go with it.

He smiled back at her in a naturally disarming way that relaxed her. Albertina had not yet developed a veneer that would protect her against disdain or disapproval. Grateful for the show of friendliness, she studied this young man curiously. He was dressed in the latest "country" style, a suede jacket and silk cummerbund gleaming redly about his middle. But his face, on a level with hers, was startingly ugly. It was battered, freckled, and topped with carroty hair as rumpled as an unmade bed. Along one side of his face from ear to chin stretched a curved scar where the skin rippled and puckered. She wondered why he had this flaw so blatantly on show, when a set of muttonchop whiskers like Lord Benchley's would have covered the ruched flesh completely and added charm to his face. Being conscious of her own appearance, she admired him for his disinterest in his. Whatever he looked like, she decided that she was attracted to him.

He patted his holstered guns and said, "I'm mightly pleased to meet you, ma'am."

Albertina astounded herself by replying, "But I feel a little nervous of you, sir. It is a new experience for me to meet a man so heavily armed."

If he thought her unduly forward, he showed no sign of it. "You find it intriguing, I hope?"

She smiled, showing perfectly matched teeth and the tip of a rosy tongue. "I wonder what species of wild animals are endangering you, sir?"

"He uses the guns to keep the women away," Elizabeth said dryly.

"Why do you need two of them?" By now, Albertina was genuinely interested in the revolvers.

Smiling, he slipped one hand into his jacket front and brought out a small gun. The slim brown barrel looked like an extension of his thick, calloused fingers. As he slipped it into her hands, he said matter-of-factly, "These are like pets, or old friends. I take them everywhere."

When Albertina realized what he had given her, she flung up her hands in an instinctive gesture of fright and squealed. The American caught the falling gun easily and put it back into his pocket.

Pleasantly he said, "You would make a splendid Southern belle, but not a Yankee lass. A Yankee lady knows how to shoot a pistol and a rifle as well."

"All Yankee ladies?"

He nodded. "Their mothers teach them. It's as much a part of their education as learning to brew a good chowder."

Elizabeth nudged her. "Don't take any notice of Francis. He's a *terrible* romancer."

A patently false look of hurt enveloped his blunt features. Albertina laughed. She was strongly aware of a feeling of happiness, of being deliciously entertained.

"I believe myself to be an excellent romancer," Francis protested. "There's nothing terrible about me at all."

"You are wicked," decided Elizabeth with evident approval. "I know there are dozens of ladies who could assure us of that!"

"If they are ladies, they would do no such thing!" To Albertina's astonishment Francis winked at her. "I am trying to impress the sister of the bride and you, my dear hostess and lovely friend, you are spoiling my efforts."

"I do beg your pardon!"

He smiled at them both, and Albertina was so filled with bubbling enjoyment that she couldn't help smiling back. But her gaze was drawn beyond him to where Gilbert Belton, Viscount Marley, stood silently. He had not taken his eyes off her face for a moment. As they looked at each other, she could read his expression clearly. An odd feeling of fear possessed her. For the second time in only a few minutes she deliberately turned away from him.

Upstairs in her room Victoria sat at a small table on which stood a goblet of white wine and a plate with a breaded chicken leg, a small veal cutlet, a spoonful of peas, a butterfly-shaped oyster pastry, and a spiral roll of pink ham. She poked listlessly at the cutlet with a small dessert fork, her hunger gone.

Charlotte sat on the straight-backed bedroom chair and tried to think of something to say. Now that she was alone with her cousin, it seemed ridiculous to pretend that something splendid had happened. Her mind squeezed tight with pity for Victoria.

For a long time they sat like that, Victoria staring dumbly at her plate and Charlotte trying to think of something light and pleasant to say. Suddenly Victoria burst out, "Charlotte, I'm terrified! Nobody but me seems to realize that I'm going away forever! Everybody but me seems so *happy* about it!"

"But you're not going far away, dear," Charlotte said quickly. "Lord Benchley lives not two miles from here. I'm the one who is going far away, and it's not nearly as terrifying as you might imagine."

"You have Martin, that's why. I have nobody."

The groom had been closely scrutinized by everybody for the whole of the time he had been on view today. Not once had anyone seen a look of warmth or affection on his face.

Raising her white face, Victoria looked blankly at Charlotte. "You must tell me what being married is really like. Mother said that it will be very strange, but she wouldn't say why. She said I must force myself to endure it even though I wouldn't like it. What did she mean?"

Charlotte ventured uncomfortably, "It will be strange for you to live in another house when you've hardly spent a night away from home before."

"She didn't mean that," said Victoria, sensing in her confusion that even Charlotte was hiding something. "Mother said that it would be fun having a house of my own to run. I've always looked forward to that, Charlotte, planning my own meals, choosing my own decorations, and arranging the furniture as I please. So what does Mother mean?"

"I don't know what your Mother meant," said Charlotte evasively. She could not bring herself to meet those huge dark eyes across the table. "Aunt Grace often says cryptic and mysterious things that I don't understand. Perhaps . . . perhaps she meant that it might be dull living with someone so much older?"

As if in answer to Charlotte's prayer, the door swung soundlessly open. There stood Noelle, her face calm and questioning.

"Come in, Noelle," said Victoria.

"She's looking for Andrew," whispered Charlotte.

Noelle didn't speak. When she was satisfied that Andrew was not lurking in a corner of the room, she drifted away in a cloud of deep lemon.

Charlotte got up to close the door. "Andrew must have escaped," she smiled, glad to change the subject. "Did you see the way she was hanging on to him? I wonder how he managed to lose her?"

Victoria sighed. "Her mother has put her up to it. Lady Longworth has clear ambitions to have Andrew as a son-in-law. She was hinting as much to Mother the other day, and right in front of me, too. Have you ever noticed how, when you are being fitted for a dress, you seem to become invisible and people say the most extraordinary things in front of you?"

"Noelle seems a sweet little thing," said Charlotte.

"Oh, she is, but she is very odd. She never has a thought of her own and parrots everything her mother tells her to say. Her mother never takes her anywhere but here, so we are really the first people she's met."

"No wonder she was clinging to Andrew."

"He dreads her, too, poor Andrew. He only notices girls who sparkle, and I'm afraid that Noelle is very dull-witted indeed. She is not suitable for Andrew at all."

At that moment Andrew was in the conservatory, listening to Miss Manfred's views on his sister's match.

"It has to be," Andrew was protesting. "Victoria is the means to link our family to his."

"Rubbish," snorted Miss Manfred, drawing up her corseted figure to military stiffness. "I wonder who invented these odd ideas about joining families? Some fool who was mad for money, no doubt! When the chains break, the world doesn't stop, does it? Of course not! It's nothing short of a crime, selling a dear child like that..."

"Hush, Eunice!" begged Beatrice in horror, fluttering her ivory lace fan rapidly to cool her flushed cheeks.

"Am I offending you, Andrew?"

"No, Miss Manfred." It was the truth. Andrew admired equally her good humor and candid speech. "Mother would be offended if she could hear you, but personally I agree. It *is* a crime. Victoria should have a choice, but circumstances have conspired against us recently, and this wedding was unavoidable."

"And what are your plans?" asked his aunt smoothly. "You are not planning to take part in this war inquiry, are you?"

He started. "Of course you would be interested in that! You helped to train the nurses for Miss Nightingale, didn't you? I had forgotten."

"Miss Manfred did, and I helped her," she corrected him gently. "Now tell us."

"My plans are not settled yet, Aunt," he said awkwardly, finding as always that it was difficult to lie to that serenely sweet face.

"The inquiry, Andrew?"

"They cannot begin until all the officers are home, and Lord Longworth is still away."

"Taking a cure, I believe," said Miss Manfred. "Westphalia, isn't it?"

"There is no cure for what ails him," said Andrew morosely.

"Don't judge him too harshly," said Aunt Brownie softly. "It is too easy when you are young to see things simply and mistake that for clarity. Lord Longworth may have serious failings, but his wife is a good friend to your mother and, when you decide what you must do, that fact should be put into the balance with all the other facts."

"Yes, Aunt."

"What are you doing shut away in here?" asked Grace, gliding in. "What has driven you away from the other guests? Has someone been flirting with you again, Beatrice? John?

143

Oh, dear, he is *incurable*! You were sensible to rescue her, Miss Manfred. Andrew, might I have a word in your ear, please?"

She drew him out into the hallway.

He faced her. "What diplomatic crisis has arisen, Mother?"

"Will you see what you can do with Albertina?" she asked. "She is in the parlor there, standing right beside Viscount Marley . . . *Viscount Marley*, can you imagine! And she is ignoring him! Could you please . . . ?"

"Excuse me, please, Mrs. Fielding." Myers loomed darkly beside them. "There are two gentlemen here, from the police."

"What?" Andrew put a hand protectively on the middle of her back.

"Tell them to come back in the morning, please, Myers."

"I did, ma'am, but they insist."

Grace glanced apprehensively beyond him. The two men stood at the half-open front door, hatted and cloaked against the evening chill. Behind them, the sky was darkening. The men politely raised their hats a fraction.

Grace's hand was at her throat in a gesture of helplessness. "Whatever can have happened? I do hope it is not bad news. Perhaps Uncle Driscoll has died . . ." She frowned at Myers. "Show them up into Andrew's bedroom. The study is impossible . . . too many people."

"I shall find Father," said Andrew.

Grace had a sudden thought. As he turned to go, she tapped his sleeve with a finger. "Find Lord Benchley, too," she said.

Matthew spent a half hour with the men from the police. Lord Benchley, as his lawyer, remained with him. When they returned to their guests, it was time for the speeches. Toasts were drunk. Victoria's diminutive hand rested under Lord Benchley's large, soft one as they cut the cake.

Everybody cheered.

Eight

Lord Benchley's home was one of a row of terraced houses in a narrow cul-de-sac on the fringe of fashionable Mayfair. Victoria could see nothing from inside the closed carriage, but from her chilly vantage point beside the driver, Millie picked out the house at once. Light showed through the lower shutters and the ice-blue fanlight above the front door. Tom Booth hooked up the reins and scrambled down, ignoring Millie, who was left to find her own footholds among the harness anchors and shafts while Lord and Lady Benchley were ushered down to the pavement. While the carriage was being put away, it was Lord Benchley himself who opened the front door for Victoria and Millie. Once inside the house, he accorded the two women equal indifference. He was reeling somewhat already, sated with too much of Bess's excellent food and a great deal too much liquid refreshment.

The hall was disappointingly bare and so lacking in character that the only thing that tired Victoria noticed was a tarnished brass gas lamp hanging from a chain in the center of the ceiling. A middle-aged woman, very short, plump, and jowly, hurried along the dark passage toward them until she stood directly beneath the light. She wore her gray hair twisted in a braid over each ear, like the curly horns of a ram. She bobbed an unsmiling curtsy. Her eyes stared levelly at Victoria for a brief moment, then flicked on to Millie for a similar summing-up before coming to rest on her master.

"Would you care for some supper, sir?" Her voice was as flat, hard and gritty as the carpet they stood on.

"No, thank you, Mrs. Foster." He turned from hanging up his hat. "She might care for some, though."

"Ma'am?"

"Could I trouble you for a cup of tea, perhaps?" Victoria was annoyed by her own conciliatory tone. After all, she was going to have to give orders to this woman.

"It will be no trouble," she said shortly and with obvious annoyance. "In the parlor or your room?"

"My room, please."

Lord Benchley leaned against the hatstand. "Would you show them upstairs, please, Mrs. Foster? I have some things to attend to in my study." To Victoria he said, "Good night, my dear."

She wondered what to call him. "Sir," as Mrs. Foster had addressed him, seemed appropriate, so she used that.

"Good night, sir."

He smiled and watched them ascend into the shadows behind Mrs. Foster's dumpy figure.

The hallway was narrow, the stair carpet a wide ribbon with

blotchy varnished strips on either side. Mrs. Foster paused at the upper landing where four lamps were arranged on a low, dusty table. She lit one and replaced the finger-smudged glass chimney, then used that to light their way into the bedroom.

It was such a small room that the large black-iron bedstead seemed to take up most of the room. Noting the size of the bed, Victoria's heart sank. As though she could read minds, Mrs. Foster commented, "The drssing room is in there, and Lord Benchley's room is across the hall." Grudgingly she added, "I hope this room pleases you."

Victoria wearily scanned the bare floor, the drab brown walls, the brown curtains, and the dusty-looking furniture. She would deal with it later. Stretching her aching cheeks into the shape of a smile, she said, "This will do very well. Are my cases and trunks unpacked?"

The suggestion was not taken kindly. "Of course not, Ma'am! I've got my own work to do. Your things are in the dressing room. I'll fetch your tea. There will be tea in the kitchen for your maid when you have finished with her." With a formal bob she marched out.

Millie ran a finger along the top of the washstand. "She don't spend much of 'er time dustin', an' that be true!" she said in disgust. "This room ain't been cleaned or aired in months!"

"What do you think of her?"

"'Ard to say right off. She might thaw out real nice, an' again she might not." She dragged a chair over to a clear space. "If you sit down 'ere, miss, I'll undo them buttons for you." She slapped the seat of the chair and a puff of dust rose up. "Never mind, miss, I'll see to cleanin' this room up tomorrow."

"I'm too tired to even care about it now," said Victoria, grateful to have Millie there. How unpleasant it would have been to have Mrs. Foster undress her tonight! "You will need a buttonhook for these buttons. I made certain that one was put in with my nightdress and toilet things. You will find them in the small blue case. Do hurry, Millie. I feel as though my shoulders will split under the weight. What a relief it will be to get rid of all these trimmings. I feel like one of Bess's fancy dessert cakes, all frosting and stuck-on decoration. It will be good to be plain me again."

"I don't reckon I'll forget tonight as long as I live," Millie burbled as she unpinned, unbuttoned, rubbed, brushed, and helped Victoria into her nightdress. "All them ladies looked so lovely, an' them 'andsome gentlemen! Some of 'em was real nice to me..."

But Victoria was not listening. She ached for sleep. In the time it took Mrs. Foster to prepare the plain tea tray, Victoria had been undressed and dressed and tucked into bed.

"I'm sorry, Mrs. Foster. Really I am," said Millie. "Me mistress is fast asleep. She won't be needin' that tea after all, now."

It seemed to Victoria that she had only just plunged into slumber, and her first instinct was to fight whatever it was that was trying to awaken her. The hand grabbed her shoulder again and shook her more forcefully this time.

She stirred. "Nana? What is it?" Rolling onto her side, she blinked to force her eyes open, trying to focus on what had awakened her. Something was wrong. She saw a lamp but it wasn't her lamp nor her dresser. Then she realized where she was.

Lord Benchley stood beside the bed, clad in a voluminous striped nightshirt. Why was he wearing that floppy striped cap on his head? His eyes were shining with moisture, and he swayed on his feet.

I *am* tired, she thought. She was annoyed at being disturbed, yet she struggled to be polite.

"What is the matter, sir?" she asked, nodding. Her eyes were closing again, and her body sagged into the damp mattress.

Lord Benchley made no reply as he swayed, rocking back and forth. After a time he leaned further toward her.

Understanding dawned—and with it impatience and relief. He wanted to kiss her good night! Thank heaven that will be over quickly, she thought. She arched her neck and held up a cheek to help him place the kiss.

When his face was almost upon hers, she caught the full impact of his foul, whiskey-soured breath. Its effect on her was immediate: She stiffened and pulled her head back and away from him. She feared that she was offending him, but his breath was so acid and strong she'd been unable to stop herself.

He stared at her with a strange half smile. Then, without warning, without altering his expression and without taking his eyes from her face, he hooked both hands in her blankets and dragged all the bedding together into a bundle on the floor.

Jolted awake in alarm she shrank away from him, both hands at her breasts in an instinctive protective gesture. This was ridiculous! She had already bade him good night. There was no call for him to disturb her like this. Should she be frightened, or angry? Why didn't he say something instead of behaving in this weird and offensive manner?

His next action alarmed her more. He gripped the hem of her nightgown and yanked the garment up around her neck, narrowly missing hitting her in the face with his closed fist. Still more puzzled than frightened, she pushed down at her clothing, but when his fingers ripped at the waistband of the modest garment she wore under her nightgown, she was galvanized into indignant action herself. Lashing out a foot, she kicked him in the soft midriff. Then, before he could catch his breath, she was scrambling on all fours to the other side of the bed.

Standing on the chilly floor in the gap between bed and shuttered window, the bed a broad barrier between them, she watched him, trying desperately to figure out what was happening. Lord Benchley *might* be insane. No adult in his right mind would want to play childish games in the dead of night, pulling off bedclothes and such. He would probably start throwing pillows next! She and Albertina had given up such babyish rompings years ago. And as for trying to look at the hidden things all decent people *never* uncovered . . . even children did not do that!

"Come here," he said sullenly.

It could be that he was drunk, of course. Nana had told the girls that drink was meant to be taken in moderation, or else it could do strange and terrible things to a man's mind. Perhaps Lord Benchley had accidentally taken too much.

If that was all, then what should she do?

"Come back here," he said.

He actually *expects* me to do as he says, she thought in astonishment. Her mother's words came back to her, along with the Bible texts. "Be a good, obedient wife. A wife should obey her husband. A wife's duty is to please her husband."

"Come back here!"

"No," she said with more force than she felt. "No, I most certainly shall not."

148

"Then I shall make you, my dear," he said unpleasantly.

His tone made her frightened for her safety. Suddenly the atmosphere in the musty room seemed menacing.

Lord Benchley moved toward her, a giant lumbering around the foot of the bed.

She began to panic. He was going to beat her. She had never been beaten, but she knew it was horribly painful. Her husband was going to beat her because she had not wanted to kiss him good night.

"What do you want from me?" she ventured in a quavering voice.

His reply was a nasty laugh. He moved closer, slowly, as if he had all the time in the world to command. He seemed in no hurry to catch her at all, so completely sure of himself was he.

Somehow she would have to escape. If she could reach the dressing-room door, she might be able to block the way somehow, drag the trunks across, and barricade herself inside. Leaping onto the bed, she scrambled for the other side, but he moved with surprising speed and in one pounce seized both her ankles. She gripped the mattress edge and kicked frantically as hard as she could. But with humiliating ease he flipped her over on her back, rendering her helpless. He dragged her across the bed toward him until her legs were half off the bed. When he relaxed his grip on her ankles, she began to kick and struggle, hitting his chest with ineffectual punches. He laughed, panting heavily, and pushed hard against her waist, holding her down and forcing the breath out of her body in one swift movement. There he held her, pinned and helpless. With his other hand he clawed at her undergarment again. The sound of tearing fabric was loud—she could hear it above her sobs, and she cried out when seams dug into her skin before they yielded. In heightened terror she struggled wildly, arching her back and trying to twist her body to prevent him from pushing his bulky body between her thighs.

"What a sweet little thing you are!" he said approvingly.

The words caught her unaware and lulled her into a sense of false security. His warm tone made her doubt her conviction that he was angry with her. But in the very next second she was torn by a wrenching pain. Then she screamed, fighting his hard-pressing hand and harder-pounding body.

Her horror intensified when she opened her eyes. She could

see his face quite plainly, suspended above the rim of his hand. His eyes were closed and his face was congested in an expression of absolute rapture. Quite unaware of her cries, completely uncaring, he thrust on and on, driving the ghastly hurt deeper into her. He opened his mouth and sprayed moisture into her face, and she turned her head away, sobbing and retching into the moldy mattress.

Eventually he pulled away from her with a wet sucking noise. Her legs fell under their own weight to the floor and her heels thudded on the floorboards. He stepped back and picked up her ankles, swinging her body onto the mattress.

She recoiled from him. And though it did not seem to matter now, she pushed her nightdress down over herself as well as she could.

He seemed to find the gesture amusing. "Well, my dear," he said with relish. "Wasn't that a lot of fuss about nothing?"

Not knowing what he meant, and not caring, she turned away, weeping in helpless anger.

He laughed. As a final insult he leaned over and patted her bottom. "Good night, my dear," he said.

Nine

At about the time the marriage was being consummated, the last of the wedding guests was leaving the reception. Grace and Matthew stood in the front hall saying their farewells and accepting the final compliments. It was past two o'clock and the long day's strain was beginning to show on them. Matthew especially looked tired. His shoulders stooped wearily, and he seemed older than his fifty-one years.

When the front door closed and Myers bade them a quiet good evening, Grace leaned against her husband and smiled up at him. "Was it a success?" she asked, knowing full well that it had been a social triumph beyond imagining, but wanting her husband's assurances to make the evening perfect.

His answer was dutiful and sincere. "It was marvelous. You were a charming and elegant hostess."

"I thought that everybody seemed to be enjoying themselves. I certainly did, and that is a sure sign that things are going well." She smiled, remembering the way Matthew had gently held her gloved hand during the service. "I felt like a bride myself."

"You look like a bride." His voice seemed to contain more tenderness than usual. He embraced her, crushing her stained dress against his suit, kissing her full on the mouth.

When she pulled away, she was blushing in delighted surprise. Matthew usually kept his embraces for the privacy of their rooms.

"Go on up to bed," he said. "I have a few business things to do. There hasn't been time today."

"But your study will be in such a mess . . . Surely there is nothing so urgent that it cannot wait until morning?"

"I'm afraid there is."

She looked like a disappointed child, and he knew that she'd been hoping to hold a long postmortem on the reception, sharing the compliments she'd received, discussing the guests and everything that had happened. It had become one of their traditions after a dinner or a party.

"Couldn't you at least come and help me with my dress?" she coaxed. "Joan looked so tired that I sent her to bed an hour ago."

He still had seven hours until the police were due to return. But if there was any last special thing he could do for her, it couldn't be better than this. Smiling, he held out an elbow for her to tuck her hand through. There was no hurry and he was feeling splendid.

At three thirty he crept quietly down to his study, carrying the lamp from the bedroom. Locking the door behind him, he took fresh notepaper from his desk. He had three letters to compose. As he set out the things he needed—pen, ink, wax and taper for sealing—he pondered on the way things had aborted. The greatest crises seemed to be triggered by such little things. Here nobody could be blamed, not even Brookes who saw the expensive wedding as the drop of water that overflowed the jug. It was just bad luck everywhere.

The first letter, to Lord Benchley, consisted of a page of detailed business instructions. Henry knew most of it already and would see that everything was taken care of properly, but there were one or two minor details that might be overlooked. The next letter was for Andrew. As head of the house he would have many responsibilities, and the letter detailed these. The third letter presented the most difficulties, for it was a letter to Grace, and gratitude is never easy to express. Over the years she had done a lot to help him. He attempted to mention as many specific instances as possible. He was aware that she would be partly blamed for what was happening: He knew of her reputation as a spendthrift and social climber. This letter would have to both comfort her and guard against hurt. He wrote leisurely, thanking her for making him a comfortable home, for raising four lovely children in whom he took such pride, for nursing him unflaggingly when he was ill with pneumonia one spring, for showing him true loyalty outside the home and in, and most of all for being sweet and loving no matter what worries she had.

"During the whole length of our marriage it has been a source of strength and comfort to me to know that you were always there to approve of me and to love me," he wrote. "Both of us are aware of homes where love does not exist, and of the bleak lives those people share. My life is not going to be as long as I had hoped, but it could not possibly have been happier. Thank you, Grace, for everything, but most of all for being yourself."

When he had finished, he poured himself a large glass of whiskey and sipped it while he read the letters through, making a few slight alterations as he went. Then he removed the glass from the lamp and lit the taper, turning the sealing wax in the heat of the slender flame. Each letter was sealed with three drops of red wax. He placed them in a row on his desk blotter and checked the time by his pocket watch. It was almost five. In an hour the servants would be rising.

From his watch chain he took a silver key and unlocked the cabinet below his depleted liquor cupboard. At the back, behind a stack of books, was a flat wooden box. Dusting it off with his handkerchief, he snapped open the brass catches and raised the lid. Nestling inside, in a padding of red velvet, was a pair of silver and brass dueling pistols.

When he had loaded one gun, he locked the box away again, then put the pistol down on the carpet, and lay beside it. He tried to pray, but he was empty. All his prayers had been spent in futility during the past few months, and now there was nothing to say. Groping for the pistol, he checked with unsteady fingers that it was cocked. He pushed it up until the muzzle grated against the dry roof of his mouth. Taking a deep breath, he pulled the trigger.

Bess Myers was the only person in the house who heard the shot. She had been awakened by a bad cramp in the calf of her right leg and was tenderly massaging the affected muscles when the crack came. For a moment she sat still, listening. Then she poked her husband's shoulder with her thumb. "Myers, wake up. There's somebody downstairs. You had better check."

His hand groped drowsily to her body. "There's nobody there."

"Oh, do be sensible," she said irritably. "I mean it. I think there's somebody down there. I just heard the strangest noise. Nothing like I've ever heard before in this house."

"What did it sound like?" Myers was not interested in being pushed from a warm bed he occupied for too short a time tonight.

"A loud popping noise. It only went the once."

He sighed and rubbed his chin on the turned-over sheet. "It was probably one of your infernal cats after the food scraps."

"It can't be," she said, ruminatively scratching between her breasts. "All of the cats were shut in the stable yesterday and they've not been let out yet."

He squinted at the little candle flame on the nightstand. "Perhaps somebody found one of the fireworks left over from the display. One of those crackers."

It was a feeble offering and he knew it. "At this hour?" she asked.

"All right, all right. I can see I'm not going to get any sleep until I go." He sat up resignedly and shoved his feet around, groping for his slippers.

He set off in his long gray nightshirt. In a short while he was back, scrambling in beside her.

"I couldn't find anything, lass. I checked the front door and the back, and the conservatory and the tradesmen's door. God in heaven, but there's a mess down there. I don't look forward to starting on that. We have a big day's work in front of us."

She snuggled up to him. Friendly now that her cramp had eased, she felt soft and smelled of warm sleep. "Mmmmmm," she said in his ear.

"That tickles, lass."

"What about that? Does that tickle too?"

"Do that again and I'll not be liable for my actions," he warned her sternly.

Suddenly he sat up. "The study!" he said. "When I was in the conservatory, I noticed a faint light in the study. I went to the front door and then I forgot to check where the light was coming from."

"Put your greatcoat on!" she ordered from the bed.

This time he complied.

Ten

When Millie came in at nine next morning with a tray of tea, toast, and crab-apple jelly, Victoria was asleep. As Millie set the tray down, the noise woke Victoria and she jerked bolt upright. Millie drew the curtains back and opened the windows.

"No wonder this room smells musty," she remarked cheerfully. "Not a breath of air gettin' in."

"Millie, we shall be going home today," Victoria announced.

"Yes, miss?" Millie poured milk and held a perforated china spoon in the flow of tea to catch the leaves.

The hours of darkness when Victoria crouched against the headboard, fearfully awaiting his return, had given her ample time to think things through. There was no explanation possible except drunken insanity. She had done nothing to warrant such cruel, perverse punishment and could not understand the way he savored doing those dreadful things to her. Though the prospect of re-living the night filled her with loathing, she knew that she would have to tell her parents all that had taken place. She must make her parents see that she could not be allowed to remain married to such a vile, twisted man.

Without comment Millie handed her mistress the cup of tea and held the sugar bowl ready. The spoon clattered about in the saucer as if it had a life of its own. Millie wondered how much sleep her mistress had had.

"I cannot stay here," Victoria explained earnestly. "I shall send you to fetch Mother and Father, yes, as soon as I am dressed. However, I shall remain here in my room until they come for me. I do not wish to see or speak to Lord Benchley again."

"Did 'e really give you such a bad time, then?" Heedless of all Miss Beatrice's careful instructions about what topics of conversation could be mentioned and what must never, never be discussed, Millie had crossed the line between servant and friend without pausing.

Victoria nodded, flushing to think that her screams had penetrated the house as far as the servants' quarters. "I don't wish to discuss it," she said.

"Of course you don't, miss," soothed Millie. Her face was earnest. "But you don't want to fret too much. It's always bad the first time. So I've 'eard, of course," she added hastily.

"Millie, I don't think you understand at all," frowned Victoria. "Of course I don't mind being away from home as much as all that. No, it's Lord Benchley. He had far too much to drink last night but that cannot explain his horrible behavior..."

"I know exactly what you mean, miss," said Millie calmly. "I know all about men an' what they like to do. Beasts, all o' 'em are at 'eart."

Could Millie possibly know what had happened? "Tell me exactly what you mean, please, Millie."

Millie was happy to oblige. "It's what they all do to their wives, of course. They do summat down there," and she pointed vaguely to the area covered by her apron.

Victoria could hardly believe it. "Is that normal?"

"They all do that," Millie assured her cheerfully, pouring another cup of tea, for the first had been gulped in two desperate swallows. "It's summat in their nature makes 'em act that way. That's what they gets married for. Didn't you know that, miss? Didn't nobody tell yer?"

Feeling like the victim of a monstrous practical joke, Victoria shook her head. "Nobody told me anything. If they had, I would never have agreed to get married. Never. I wouldn't have done it no matter what it meant to my family."

What strange people these rich folks are, thought Millie. It was incredible that a young woman could be led right up to her own wedding night without one word to cushion her.

"Drink your tea, miss," she said, settling herself uninvited on the edge of the bed. "Oooh, miss, but I do feel sorry for you, not knowin' what you were in for. Beggin' your pardon for askin', miss, but did 'e hit you with 'is fists at all? Did 'e beat you?"

Victoria shook her head. Being beaten was preferable to what had happened.

Millie spoke kindly. "That can't be 'elped, miss. It's bound to 'urt the first time. Next time it won't be so bad an' then, after that, you get used to it. Some women even get to like it."

Millie must be mistaken. Of course she was talking about common men, men of her own class, when she said that "all men" were like that. A true gentleman would never inflict such an ordeal on his *wife*!

"I don't believe you," Victoria said flatly.

Millie set the cup and saucer aside, saying patiently, "It's expected of us women, miss. We 'ave to put up with it. All married women do. Their 'usbands expect it. What other way can you get babies? You want a baby, don't you, miss? There ain't no other way to get one."

This was too much. Now Millie had the impudence to imply that her own mother, Aunt Penelope, Charlotte, all of them, went through that same revolting business. "Don't lie to me," she said angrily.

Millie's eyes were full of sympathy and inescapable truth. "I ain't lied to you, miss. I am tellin' you the truth. All men 'ave that in their natures so we can get babies."

Suddenly Victoria remembered her mother's faint, veiled warning about not liking but having to endure. Then she realized that it *was* the truth. Heartsick and nauseated, she fell back against the pillows. Her parents had conspired against her. She had agreed to the marriage because it would help them, and they had pushed her into it, knowing full well what would happen to her. How could they have done such a monstrous thing when for all her life she had been dutiful and obedient and loved them with all her affection? They had dressed her in a beautiful white dress, taken her to a beautiful church, thrown a lavish party to celebrate, and all the while a filthy painful obscenity lurked at the bottom of everything.

Millie tried to soften the facts. "If you love a man, it's different then. You want to please 'im, an' 'e tries to make it easy on you, so it don't 'urt. Or so I've 'eard, of course."

Victoria thought about Charles. If such a thing had happened between them, it would have been quite different.

Drowsily she said, "Please close the curtains, Millie, and see that I'm not disturbed."

"That's the spirit, miss," said Millie approvingly. "Once you've 'ad a good, long rest, you'll feel different. Wait an' see."

I doubt that, thought Victoria wearily. I shan't feel one speck differently. One thing was settled though. She could not go to her parents for help, not when they had conspired in this dirty assault on her person. She closed her eyes, clinging to a small grain of comfort—she was the mistress of her own house now. If she wanted to stay in bed all day, she could. There would be no Nana rushing in to bully her out of bed.

Millie returned to the room in the early afternoon. "I'm sorry to 'ave to wake you, miss, but Lord Benchley wants you to go downstairs to talk with 'im."

Victoria's voice was chilly. "Go and tell him that I shall not be down at all today."

Millie stayed where she was, uncertainly.

Victoria frowned. "Did you not hear me, Millie? I am *not* going down. Tell Lord Benchley that I gave you strict instructions not to be disturbed. And you might tell Mrs. Foster that I would like my dinner on a tray this evening, please. Tell her I'm unduly fatigued from the wedding."

Millie bobbed respectfully. "Very well, miss."

But Millie was back within a few minutes, visibly agitated. "I'm real sorry, miss, but you 'ave to go on down. 'E says 'e 'as to talk to you. I think you better go."

Victoria's anger flared. Not content with physical abuse, he was ordering her about. Well, she had no intention of taking any notice of him.

Millie said unhappily, "Miss, it ain't for me to tell you this, but . . ."

"Then refrain from doing so, please," Victoria said coolly. "You and I will get on much better if you do not succumb to the temptation of telling me what I should and should not do. I am still undecided about whether I shall stay here at all."

Tears were flowing down Millie's thin cheeks. "Miss, I *'ave* to tell you. Summat terrible 'as 'appened at your 'ouse, an' that's what 'e wants you for . . ."

Victoria snapped upright. "What is it?"

"I can't tell you, miss. I ain't exactly sure."

Rushing into the dressing room and trailing the maid behind her, Victoria grabbed a dress from an open trunk and pulled it on over her nightdress. "Here, do me up. Hurry, Millie. See if you can find a hairnet. A thick one; there's not the time to fix my hair. It will have to be covered up. No, not there, in the little red case. Good. Now splash some water into the bowl while I find my shoes."

She fidgeted impatiently while Millie smoothed her hair into a black lace net, then jumped up and hurried downstairs.

Lord Benchley and Mrs. Foster were sitting in the musty-smelling parlor.

He was holding a glass of brown liquid in each hand. Though he glanced at her when she entered, he did not stand. Instead he held out one of the glasses. "This is for you. Drink it quickly."

She kept her distance, standing behind one of the sofas and facing but not looking at him. "Tell me what has happened. Is it Father?"

He didn't answer her question right away. Turning to Millie, hovering at the door, he barked, "Go away." To Victoria he said, "Sit down and drink this."

Anger flashed through her, blocking her fear. There had been little difference in his tone when speaking either to her or Millie. As coldly and as haughtily as she could, she said, "You wished to speak to me. Then speak, please."

He was indifferent to her hatred. "I strongly advise you to do two things. One is to sit down, the other is to drink this brandy."

She obliged, but only because her attention had fastened on a letter, lying open on a table at her husband's elbow. She recognized her father's extravagant penmanship. "When did that come?"

"An hour ago."

"Did the police arrest Father?"

"No."

She sat down, suddenly giddy. She'd been so sure it was the police, when Millie mentioned trouble at the house. Mrs. Foster leaned over, pushing the glass rudely at her lips, and Victoria shoved her away impatiently.

"You must drink it," she said sternly.

"I don't want it." As she spoke, the rim of the glass clacked against her teeth. She rightened her lips and pinched her nostrils against the fumes, pushing the glass aside firmly.

The housekeeper looked at Lord Benchley and shrugged.

"There has been an accident at your house," he said.

"To whom?"

"Your father."

None of this was making any sense. The brandy, the mystery, the letter. Why would Father write a letter if he were involved in an accident?

Mrs. Foster offered the brandy again, but Victoria swatted her hand away.

"Your father was shot. He is dead."

"Oh."

"It happened early this morning."

"Oh."

"He took his own life."

"Oh." She stood up, swayed, and began to scream. "I want to go home," she cried. "I want to go home!"

Part Three

Autumn into Winter

One

Somewhere up there in the hazy blue-gray sky a lark was singing its delicate tremulous tune. Birdie stopped her swing to listen. As she squinted at the sky between the gaudy creeper that roofed the pergola, she listened. There it was again, trilling a lovely song to the lazy afternoon. Birdie wondered if Father could hear it too. He was somewhere up there, in heaven.

A push of her feet and the swing was in motion again. Tucking her feet up under her loosely bundled black skirts, she relaxed and closed her eyes, feeling the rush and pull of the air brush softly over her face and neck, back and forth, back and forth. When she let her head flop, her hair swung across her back like a flag; when she tilted forward, whispering auburn tendrils brushed against her face, tickling. She floated to and fro in airy suspension, humming an echo of the lark's song.

Birdie liked it here on Bolton Street. This house which Lord Benchley had lent them was certainly not grand, but Birdie was unimpressed by many things that seemed important to grown-ups. What did it matter if they no longer had a carriage and had to be driven to church with Aunt Brownie and Miss Manfred? That was more interesting anyway. She could sit by Miss Manfred and thrill to the way her booming voice soared over the choir's singing. And what did it matter if the house had only three bedrooms? It was fun sharing with Albertina and being able to play with all the porcelain toys and richly colored picture books which Albertina had jealously kept to herself when they lived on Clarence Street. It was even more fun to be able to play outside in this marvelous large garden. Who cared if Hyde Park was too far away to visit, when you had your very own fish pond with silver and gold carp longer than your forearm, rose gardens lush with pink and yellow blossoms, whose fragrance you could smell in every room of the house, and a row of fruit trees promising pears and peaches soon. It was the kind of garden made for children and nature lovers like Myers. He had already spaded and raked a black velvety plot for the winter cabbage, sprouts, and broccoli.

Birdie kicked harder, forcing the swing into longer arcs. This was much more fun than sitting in a dreary classroom studying. Since Father had died, there had been no lessons because Miss Boswell had to spend so much time looking after poor Mother. There had been a shelf full of books to be read, but reading was so enjoyable it could hardly count as lessons. Albertina didn't have to practice her piano even though they had been able to keep the old attic one. The noise of music distressed Mother. Any noise distressed her. It was just as well that they never had any visitors except Lady Longworth because Mother was so ill over Father that she couldn't be sociable. Secretly Birdie hoped that this would continue. Albertina griped because she missed sitting around like a lady and talking about gowns and gloves and hats, but Birdie hated afternoons "at home" because ladies often brought bratty little children along with them and *she* had to entertain them.

Everybody except Myers and Bess seemed so crabby these days. It had to do with grief. Birdie had grieved too. She missed Father and thought of him a lot, remembering how he had smiled at her and cuddled her. Now she had even forgotten what he looked like and wouldn't be able to find out until his picture was back in the parlor. Mother kept it in her room.

"I just can't remember what Father looked like," she had confided to Albertina one day. "Can you?"

163

Albertina had flounced out of her bed and marched to Birdie's, whereupon she had slapped her smartly across the cheek. "Don't you *ever* talk like that again," she had said. "Father is in heaven and his death is sacred. His memory is sacred too. Don't you *ever* talk about him again as though he was an ordinary person."

Birdie had been too bewildered to cry. Now, tired of swinging, she put down both feet to stop the rocking and fetched Clara from the seat where she had been lying. She was nursing Clara on her lap and tucking leaf stems up around the edge of her mobcap when the carriage rolled into the driveway. At first she didn't recognize the man who alighted and stood with pursed lips surveying the house and garden. It was not until he had been admitted to the house that she realized who he was.

"Uncle Wilton!" she whispered. "Uncle Wilton has come home at last!" Picking Clara up, Birdie skipped across the lawn and up the path to the house.

Miss Boswell was in the hall, taking a sheaf of towels from the linen press. It still seemed odd to see her doing maids' work, and Birdie smiled impishly at her. Nana surveyed the child in dismay.

"What in the world...?" she began crossly. Setting the towels on a hall chair, she seized Birdie by the shoulders and made her face the large oval mirror that was fixed to the wall. "Look at yourself!" she ordered.

Birdie regarded her reflection solemnly. The mirror was stained with age so that she had a brownish cast, and there was a faint wave in the glass. But despite the distortion she could see that her face was clean and her dress properly buttoned to the chin.

"What's the matter with me?" she said.

Miss Boswell burst into tears, her face wrinkling up in an ugly pucker. "Haven't you any respect for your Father or your poor Mother?" she cried angrily, spinning Birdie around and shaking her again. "You are in *mourning*! Don't you know what that means?"

Birdie nodded dumbly. Clara had fallen to the floor.

"Mourning means no vanity," instructed Nana coldly. "Mourning means soberness. Mourning means respect. Now fetch yourself upstairs and brush your hair one hundred times to clear out all the twigs and bugs and whatever else is in there.

Then stay in your room until you are called to say good afternoon to Lord Longworth. No," as Birdie stooped to retrieve Clara. "As a punishment your doll can stay in the cupboard for the rest of the day. You may have her in the morning. Now, up to your room this minute."

Stumbling and crying, Birdie fled to her room, tripping on the stairs and fumbling blindly with the door handle. In anguish she dropped facedown onto her bed and sobbed for poor Clara.

Albertina was reading in a chair by the window. She glanced at Birdie's quivering shoulders.

"Oh, do be quiet," she said, turning a page of the book. "It is *impossible* to concentrate with that wailing going on."

Two

Wilton, Lord Longworth looked out of place in the Fieldings' parlor, a mean, cramped room hastily furnished with the remnants of their once splendid household fittings. Only one of the four Brussels sofas had been smuggled out. Now it dominated the room, nudging a brace of velvet-covered wing chairs, neither of which matched the brown-toned Persian carpet which had been rescued from Birdie's room because the auditors would never have missed it from there. Contrasting with the meager furnishings, the walls were crammed with photographs, mirrors, and etchings, all of such sentimental value that Grace had refused to let any of them be sold.

Lord Longworth's face was in inscrutable repose as he noted all this. When he had finished, he nodded thoughtfully to himself, drew a string of Turkish ivory worry beads from his pocket, and counted them like a rosary as his gaze rested shrewdly on Andrew.

Andrew, who had shown him to the parlor, now regarded him with a succession of very mixed feelings. First he had been stunned. The last time he had seen Lord Longworth, he had been clad in a heavy gray coat and a striped muffler, such a familiar costume that he tended to think of him always as wearing those garments. Today he presented a different figure. He was costumed in an elegant dove-gray moleskin jacket cut in the French style, poppy-colored trousers with a fretting of silver embroidery up the outside legs, a black velvet waistcoat with silver buttons, and a poppy silk cravat stuck with a black-pearl pin the size of a grape, matching the black pearl rings he wore on the middle finger of each hand.

Lord Longworth, Andrew felt, had hardly come to pay his respects dressed like that. It was ill manners to flaunt worldliness in a house of grief, especially since Matthew had been one of his best friends.

They stood in silence for a few minutes, the older man leaning with the merest inclination of his body against the polished slate mantlepiece, the younger man a black silhouette framed in the crepe-draped window. Lord Longworth spoke first, observing idly in his flat, confident drawl, "I don't hold with this mourning business, and I don't think Matthew would have either. I saw young Beatrice out in the garden looking like a little black crow. Your father wouldn't have approved of that."

Andrew flushed, furious with himself for not speaking up immediately to tell this man that his attitude was impertinent and disrespectful, and above all because he had the prickling feeling that Lord Longworth was perfectly correct in his observations. "Mother wants it this way. She is desolate with loss."

"Good," Lord Longworth replied bluntly. As Andrew gasped, he explained, "The grief is coming out now, and that means that she will be recovered in a few weeks. It is when a widow appears serene at first that the pain and the shock are worse."

"Mother loved Father deeply," said Andrew. "She is taking his death very badly." The thought of Mother recovering seemed vaguely indecent.

"Of course. When I was with her just now, she was quite incoherent. She knew who I was and begged for my help but I was at a loss to understand her request. She insisted that someone had stolen the silver."

Andrew laughed to cover his embarrassment. So Mother was still having hysterics over that! "We had to sell the silverware. Teapots, coffeepots, warmers. They were valuable and there were debts to be met."

"Tell me the name of the firm which bought them and I shall purchase them for your mother as a gift."

Gripping the back of the wing chair behind which he stood as if for protection, Andrew said flatly, "I cannot allow you to do that."

"Nonsense. We are your oldest friends outside your families so nothing we do for you could possibly smack of charity or anything equally unsavory. You need us, my lad, like it or not. The scandal..." Lord Longworth let his voice drift off and then resumed on a stronger note but with an air of detatchment. "Alice has been glad to do all she could for Grace, coming to see her every day, helping to organize the household, finding employment for the extra servants..."

It irritated Andrew to be reminded of the debt he owed. Sharply he cut in. "We appreciate that." And on a softer note, "Your wife has been very kind to Mother. I don't know how she could have managed without Lady Longworth."

Silkily the lord said, "*Do* you appreciate everything?"

Andrew felt his shoulders tighten. "Indeed we do," he said.

A thin smile, and the eyes flashed at Andrew a second before returning to the black pearl. "Come now, son. There is no call to be so formal with me. You must be aware of what brings me here, apart from paying my respects to your very dear mother. I am disappointed in you. When I came here, I expected to have your assurances that you would not speak against me. I never suspected that I would have to be the one to broach the subject."

Andrew turned away and looked unseeingly out through the window.

"Lieutenant Fielding!"

The words and tone had the effect of a whip. Andrew snapped around and faced the older man, then paused while the courage rose in him to a sufficient level to force the words out. "I am deeply sorry, sir. I regret that I cannot discuss the matter you have come to see me about, and I apologize for the fact that your errand has been in vain."

"I demand that you do discuss it!" the nonchalant attitude was gone.

"This is my house, Lord Longworth, and while I am in it, you cannot order me about in that way."

Lord Longworth pursed his thin lips and sucked in a deep breath through his nostrils. When he spoke, his voice was as satiny as his cravat. "*Your* house, son? I had been given to understand that this was Lord Benchley's house."

In the uncomfortable silence Andrew stared at his knuckles knotted white on the moss-green velvet.

"Well?" inquired Lord Longworth. "That is the point, is it

not? This is Lord Benchley's house and that is the reason you are so ill at ease with me now. He might as well be here, in this room with us. That is the reason you will not freely give me the assurance of your allegiance. Oh, don't look so guilty, son. I know Lord Benchley well, and he is no friend of mine." He laughed softly. "I was drinking a goblet of claret when Alice told me about his marriage to Victoria. Literally, it was almost the death of me. I choked on the wine and had to be thumped most vigorously on the back. Fortunately Parkinson is a quick thinker." In a conciliatory tone and with a friendly smile he said, "Don't stand there looking hostile, son. You are inexperienced in the ways of the world. Come and sit down so that we can talk better." He seated himself in the gold velvet chair and put his hand out in a supplicating gesture. "You must not allow yourself to become so set in your opinions. There is a great deal about the world that you do not understand."

Father had said much the same thing when he had ordered him not to speak against Lord Longworth, Andrew recalled, but he had taken his position and must be unswerving in his maintenance of it. Ignoring the invitation to be seated, he said, "What I saw at Sebastopol. . . . I understood that well enough. I swear I feel ill just to remember it. It wakes me in the night. . . . There are many things I understand only too well."

Lord Longworth raised his eyebrows a fraction and said mildly, "So you have declared yourself now. Good. That gives us a start, a point at which to begin."

"There cannot be a start between us, nor a middle, only an end." In his own ears the words sounded impotent and hollow.

They must have appeared that way to Lord Longworth, too, for he leaned back on the dimpled velvet and regarded Andrew with tolerant amusement.

Andrew was beginning to despair. When he had practiced his "regret-I-cannot-discuss-the-matter" speech, he had foreseen that Lord Longworth would rage violently or appeal to his mercy and family duty. He had never envisaged that Lord Longworth would act as though Andrew was merely bargaining for position. His commanding officer was apparently not in the slightest afraid of him and yet *he*, Andrew, had the power to bring him into disgrace and dismissal from his prestigious rank! It was beyond understanding.

"Your family will have good cause to be grateful to you if you listen to your common sense instead of that bloated brother-in-law of yours," said Lord Longworth.

Andrew burst out angrily, "Grateful for whoring to you? I cannot do it! I will not!"

"Tell me, son," he said, blowing at the tip of his cigar. "Exactly what can you not do?"

He would have to say it to this man whom he remembered so well from countless outings with his father, the three of them at country race meetings, at club dinners, at cockfights, for they had treated him like a man and stood him handles of ale like theirs, drink for drink. A man he would have to be now.

"I cannot lie to the inquiry about you," Andrew said, almost shamefaced.

To his astonishment Lord Longworth tipped back his head and laughed. "Oh, sit down, son. Who is asking you to lie? *I* am not. Don't you think I understand and respect your integrity? Of course I do! What I am proposing is infinitely more ethical than it would be to *tell the truth for material gain.*"

Andrew could feel the heat in his cheeks and was aware of Lord Longworth's shrewd eyes on him. He struggled to keep his convictions steady.

Lord Longworth pressed home the advantage which Andrew's confusion had given him. "My proposal is simple. I think a good deal of you, as I have said. I feel deeply for the way your family has been left in such desperate circumstances, not only economically but socially as well. To plunge from such heights to such depths in only a few weeks must be an appalling shock for you all, and we wish to help you."

"Lord Benchley is helping us." If only he could speak out like a man! Why couldn't he state his case and bid Lord Longworth good day?

"If you cannot obey me as an officer under my command," Lord Longworth said good-naturedly, "please be at least a good host and listen to your guest until he has finished."

The rebuke was fair. As a host he was neglecting every duty. Andrew leaned forward and swung the little brass bell that hung in an arch of wood on the table between them. The door opened.

Lord Longworth did not see the servant enter and continued, "I propose that you marry Noelle as quickly as is decently possible. I am prepared to offer you one hundred thousand pounds as a dowry, plus an annual allowance, of course. Think

169

on that, son. One hundred thousand pounds is ten times what those army contracts are worth."

"They are worth fifteen thousand a year," Andrew corrected him.

Violet stepped forward from where she had been waiting for instruction near the door. "May I fetch thee tea or coffee, sir?" she asked.

"Coffee, please," Lord Longworth said and waited only for Violet to begin moving away before continuing. "You don't think Lord Benchley wouldn't ask for his share, do you? The man's a jackal where money is concerned—not that it does him any good for all the use he makes of it. But they say it's the richest ones who live the barest lives. No, son, you don't have an easy decision to make and I don't want your word on anything today. Lord Benchley won't take it kindly if you let him down, but you owe him nothing. He's done well from your father, damned well. He carved his slice of fat off every contract he drew up, and your sister took him a dowry besides . . . yes, she did. Every bit of cash and bond left in the house was padded into Lord Benchley's letter, and he received it the morning your father died. He was given it to help you— apparently Matthew was afraid the police would take it—but I doubt that you'll see much of it. *He's* called it a dowry."

"That's a lie," choked Andrew. "You're making it up."

Violet brought in the tray and served the coffee before silently withdrawing.

"How do you know all that?" Andrew demanded.

"My half-brother is his banker, and he doesn't know the connection." He stirred the coffee and laid the spoon daintily on the saucer. "*That* is a confidence, I stress, which you would pay dearly for breaking."

"I give you my word."

"Lord Benchley can help you, but I can help you more. As my son-in-law you would not be allowed to testify against me. There would be no deceit, no lies, no unpleasantness. Think it over. Noelle is a sweet girl, completely innocent of course. She'll cause you no trouble as a wife if you smile at her occasionally and pat her on the head. She's never had an evil thought or a temper tantrum in her life, and she adores you. Worships you. These bright young confections with exaggerated ideas of their own charms and their own worth . . . nothing but trouble. Nagging, unfaithful, shrewish, spendthrift . . ." He stood up. "Think it over, son, and listen to that common sense of yours. No, I'll see myself out. Tell your mother I shall call again on Friday."

Then he was gone, leaving Andrew staring morosely at the black-draped mantel and wondering what had gone wrong. He had made no concessions, yet the feeling of depression was stifling him.

It was the rightness of it all. Everything the man said made sense. Yet when he was with Lord Benchley, everything he said made sense too. Both men were offering him advantages, but both men, too, wanted something in return.

The coffeepot was cold. He swung the bell and paced up and down, thinking. Myers came in.

"Where is Violet?" Andrew asked, glancing at the butler in surprise. And then he thought. Of course, Violet! How could he have been so inconsiderate, so stupid?

"She seems to be nowhere about at the moment, sir."

"Please find her for me, would you, Myers? And ask Bess if she would mind brewing me a fresh pot of coffee."

"Very good, sir."

When Violet entered, it was obvious at once to Andrew that his fears were justified. She had been crying.

With brave dignity, and with hands clasped tightly at her waist, she said, "I'm sorry, sir, I did not hear thee ring."

His heart went out to her. He held out his arms. "I've neglected you shamefully," he said. "There have been so many worries . . ."

She was in his arms, her warm breath damp and sweet in the hollow above his black collar. "If only we could have been together sometimes, Andrew, I could have helped thee. My heart has ached to see thee so unhappy, so downcast."

And he had scarcely missed her. She had often crossed his mind, but very fleetingly and always nudged out by the weight of a more pressing worry. This house was not conducive to trysts or dalliance, so many people squashed into so few rooms, and Miss Boswell prowling the house in the moonlit hours when her rheumatism troubled her.

"I know," he said fervently against her hair, content for the moment to breathe in the clean honest smell of her soap. "I love you. I do really love you."

"I could have helped thee," she repeated the reproach gently.

"Why were you crying?"

She did not answer.

"Has something upset you?" He held her by the shoulders and pushed her away a few inches so that he could look at her face.

"You heard what Lord Longworth was saying, didn't you?" She nodded.

Folding her in his arms again, he said, "You must not let that worry you. Promise me you won't. I've told you what I want for us, and I'm going to keep to that plan."

"Thee must see that it is different now," she replied in a hopeless tone. "The family needs thee, Andrew. Thee cannot go and leave them now."

"Violet, Violet!" he said in alarm. "You mustn't sound so pessimistic. You *must* trust me. Everything will work out, you will see. It might take time, that is all." Swiftly he kissed her before she could say anything else to cast the day in even deeper gloom.

Late that night, when the house had fallen into silence, Andrew sat alone at the dining-room table. Three candles dribbled wax onto their bases. In their light Andrew pored over accounts, shuffling, sorting, adding figures and making notes in a ledger. So absorbed was he in the task that he jumped with fright when a hand was suddenly placed on his shoulder.

"Nana!" he said when he had recovered his composure. At any other time he might have smiled at the sight of her in her mouse-gray wrapper, warming her hands in a fur muff. But now he could not conceal his displeasure at being interrupted.

"May I have a word with you, Andrew?"

"What is it, Nana?" he said with forced patience.

"I offered my resignation to Mrs. Fielding this morning and she refused to take it."

Andrew slammed down the pen and rested his face in both hands. He felt like crying out in sheer weariness and frustration at this latest gesture of his mother's. Only a moment ago he had gazed disbelievingly at an accounting of ten pounds for engraved calling cards. He had only just stopped himself from observing cruelly that in as much as they were being shunned by all their past friends, they needed no calling cards at all. What capriciousness had made her order two thousand? Now here was Nana offering some real help, and Mother, blind in both eyes where money was concerned, refusing to take it.

"Do you think you could confide in me and tell me how

172

bad things are?" she was saying.

Andrew rubbed his eyes. "Nana, things couldn't be much worse. Brooke and his companions have taken the house at valuation."

"That seems fair," nodded Miss Boswell innocently.

"Fair! Valuation is two-thirds to three-quarters of what we might get if we were able to sell it, but unfortunately, the way things are, we have no option. No," he sighed. "Brooke is doing extremely well out of this unpleasantness. Not only does he get the house to do with as he likes, but the bailiffs have awarded him two thousand pounds more out of what the furniture fetches when it is auctioned. If we are very, very lucky, and if the sale goes well, we might recover two or perhaps three thousand after that."

"But that furniture costs a fortune! "Dear boy, I could weep. This is truly dreadful."

"I just don't see how we are going to manage unless Mother can be made to realize our situation. Do you know how much she spent last year? Over four thousand pounds! That doesn't allow for any of the household expenses, either. Mother cannot seem to understand that now she can spend nothing." He shook his head. "Four thousand pounds!" he repeated in awe.

"There were a lot of expenses this past year," Miss Boswell pointed out defensively. "Mrs. Fielding needed new carpet for the hall and reception rooms, that new carriage was expensive, and then there were all the costs of the wedding."

"I haven't even begun to worry about the wedding yet," said Andrew in quiet desperation. "*I* have to somehow find the money to pay for all of that. Look at these." He thumped a pile of papers with his fist. "These are overdue accountings for the wedding. Take a glance at these." He dealt the bills in front of her like cards, one at a time.

"There are over eight hundred pounds' worth there. Father calculated that we could live for a year on one thousand pounds. He must have been dreaming rosy dreams. He said in his letter that it would be necessary for us to exercise the strictest economy. Nana, how am I to make Mother see that? She hasn't taken that kind of exercise in years!"

"Not ever," remarked Miss Boswell dryly.

"I despair to think of what we can do. My army retaining pay at the moment is two thousand pounds a year, but *everything* has to come out of that. I do have expectations, but they could take a year to fulfill, and what do we do in the meantime? The tiniest unnecessary item will reduce the time our money will last, and after that who knows that will happen? I dread to think of it."

"This is going to be hard on Mrs. Fielding and the girls."

"It's hard on us all."

"Little luxuries mean so much to them, and when they come out of mourning in a few weeks, they will so much look forward to new dresses and pretty hats . . ."

Andrew's irritation mounted.

"The hell with fashions!" he shouted. Looking at her shocked face, he said, "I'm sorry, Nana. You came to me for help, and I've done nothing but unload my problems onto you. How can I help you?"

Giving her all his attention, he was astonished at what he saw. Nana blushed.

"I have received a proposal," she confessed shyly.

It couldn't be. . . . "Someone has offered you a job then?"

"No, a real proposal." He stared at her pink-quilted cheeks as she hurried on in embarrassment. "I thought it would be tactless of me to explain to your mother why I wish to go. This gentleman," and she blushed again "his name is Mr. Robert Hove. He is a businessman and quite well established."

"A gay old bachelor, then, hey? And where did you find him?"

"Oh, no!" she protested. "I have known Mr. Hove for thirty years at least. His wife died recently. She has been ill for a long time now, and needing lots of care. He found out where I was, and that I had never married . . ."

"So," wondered Andrew. "A romance from your youth."

"You could say that." She met his eyes with a touchingly shy defensiveness. "I'm not too old to marry, am I?"

"If he isn't too old, how could you be? I hope that you will be very happy."

"I haven't accepted him yet," she said, plucking at the corners of the bills with her gnarled fingers. "He does expect me to, though. He pointed out that I am not needed here any longer, now that Albertina has finished her education and Birdie can read well enough to continue hers with her mother's help. Birdie is such a bright little girl that it would not matter if she suspended her education completely. When the family's fortunes change, she could perhaps have special tutoring in languages or music, but for now Albertina could help her. If she were helping her sister, it would give her something useful to do to take her mind off moping. It's not natural for a girl her age to be in mourning and missing the season, Mr. Hove says. He thought it would be good for her to have an interest."

"Your Mr. Hove sounds like a very . . . forceful character."

"He is very determined," said Miss Boswell. "I gravely doubted the wisdom of his proposal at first, for we have both changed so much that I feared we may not suit each other."

"He proposed straight away, then?" inquired Andrew delicately.

"It is wrong of me to discuss it, but I feel so excited and thrilled that it is an emotional relief to be able to confide in someone," she said. "It was such a surprise. It *was* romantic! He wrote to me, then we met in the park two weeks ago, and he presented me with a beautiful bouquet of roses and carnations and said that he should have married me years ago because we have wasted all this time. Isn't it fortunate that it is not too late and that we can marry after all?"

Doubts began to whisper in Andrew's tired mind. "And have you seen Mr. Hove since?"

"Just the once. He was so impetuous! He is anxious to marry me, Andrew, and it is the strangest feeling! I have never thought of marriage before, but it seems that in only six weeks I will be a wife."

"That is very sudden, isn't it?"

"Mr. Hove is firm that it would be best to marry as soon as the family is out of mourning. He says that Mrs. Fielding will be strong enough to manage without me then."

"And has he a family of his own?"

"Oh, my, yes. I have not had the pleasure of meeting them yet, but Mr. Hove assures me that they are eager to see me. They miss their own mother dreadfully, poor things, but of course she was never a real mother to them, being bedridden for so long."

"How many are there?"

Her eyes slid away under his. "Ten. There were fourteen but two died and two of the older girls have recently married."

Pity welled up in him. He wanted to put his hand over hers, where it still restlessly plucked at the papers, and say, "You don't have to go." Instead he said brightly, "You will have plenty of love and interest to keep you happy."

She looked at him gratefully, and he could plainly see his doubts reflected in her eyes as she said, "I do hope that this is the right thing to do. But Robert is so tender and so attentive . . ." Her cheeks flushed pink again.

It was funny, thought Andrew when she had gone. Nana with a suitor after all this time. It should strike him as really amusing. Somehow, though, he could not even summon up much relief at the thought of being rid of the burden of her wages.

Three

Victoria stared at her husband across the breakfast table. All she could see of him were two sets of plump fingers with scrupulously clean nails. The fingers were holding the morning paper as they did every breakfast. If she did not find the courage to speak to him soon, he would fold his paper like an Arab packing his tent and go without a word to her, and yet another day would be lost. She wondered how to begin.

"Excuse me, sir," she ventured.

To her surprise the newspaper flapped shut. His round face regarded her uninterestedly, as if his brain were still digesting the news he had read.

"There is a letter for you." He took a large black-bordered envelope from the tablecloth beside him and handed it to her. She glanced at it briefly. The handwriting was unfamiliar to her—probably someone who had just heard about her father's death and didn't know about the scandal. It was sealed with black wax. "I expect you to put the letter on my study desk when you have read it."

This was unheard of. "But it is mine!"

"You will do as you are told," he said flatly.

This was no time to argue. "Yes, sir."

His thick lips pressed together approvingly.

"Sir, I beg a word with you," she said, anger giving her the impetus she needed.

He looked at her blankly.

"If I am your wife, as indeed I am, then this is my house, too, is it not?"

"Indeed it is, and I hope it pleases you," he said.

"Then might I be permitted to have some word in the running of it?"

"What on earth do you mean, child?"

"The parlor and this room are so dreary. . . . I was wondering if I might not redecorate?"

"We have no money to spare for such nonsense." He flapped the newspaper open again.

She leaned forward eagerly. "Please let me finish! When I was at Bolton Street, Myers told me that all the plants in our old conservatory are ailing for need of care, and nobody wants them. There are any number which would brighten up the house."

"Plants! What would you want with such nonsense? And who would look after them? Mrs. Foster has too much work to do as it is."

Not that she ever does any of it, thought Victoria. The house would be gritty underfoot and dust all around if it wasn't for Millie. "*I* will look after the plants," she said. "I used to take care of the conservatory at home, and I know those plants well. Please let me rescue them. They should thrive here, and cheer the house up wonderfully well. Plants are so fashionable nowadays."

"Very well, as long as you don't put any of the messy things in my study."

The newspaper billowed as he opened it to the middle page. "Please!"

He lowered it a trifle and looked at her over the top.

"May I please ask you about the food . . . about our meals?"

"What about them?"

"Could I please ask Mrs. Foster to serve a variety of food? I have been here two months now and every day for luncheon she has served me a piece of fish and a slice of fried potato. Every night at dinner we have had cabbage soup, stew, and bread pudding with plum jam. It is very tiresome."

"I hadn't noticed it being tiresome," he said coldly.

"But, you are never here for luncheon and are only here for dinner once or twice a week." She smiled to make a joke of it and said, "I suspect that Mrs. Foster makes one pot of soup, one of stew, and a huge dish of bread pudding every Monday and makes them do for the whole week!"

He gave her an odd look as he rang the bell. When Millie appeared, he asked her curtly for Mrs. Foster.

"Please," said Victoria, slightly alarmed, "I am not meaning to *complain*, exactly. I only wish to have your permission to speak with her. When I asked her for variety, she insisted that I discuss the matter with you."

He ignored her.

"Well, sir?" Beaming at him, Mrs. Foster jutted out her bosoms and folded her arms below them.

"Lady Benchley is not pleased with the standard of cuisine offered in this house," he told her with more than a hint of malice. "As you know, *she* comes from the house where Bess Myers does the cooking, and everybody has heard what a marvelous cook Bess Myers is."

Mrs. Foster lowered her curly braided head like a ram about to charge and said indignantly, "Oho! And all very well it is for her too! All Bess Myers has to do all day is cook! *She* doesn't have to do the marketing! *She* doesn't have to run the house! *She* doesn't have to clean and sweep and wash dishes! How dare anybody compare her lot with mine!"

Victoria could hardly let that pass unchallenged, and she was thoroughly sick of Mrs. Foster's slovenly, insolent manner. Clearly and precisely she said, "You will kindly retract every word you have just said. My mother now has only three servants. Bess, her husband Myers, and one maid. In other words her situation is the same as yours, except that Bess has *five* other people to cook for and most of the time you have only me."

Mrs. Foster gaped at her. Victoria stood up slowly. Her letter was crumpled tightly between her hands. She faced Mrs. Foster unblinkingly. "Do you retract those ill-considered remarks?" she demanded.

Mrs. Foster's jowls quivered. "Yes, ma'am."

"You will write out a menu card for luncheon and dinner for every day of the week and give it to me tomorrow. The card can do for every week as long as there are no repetitions at all on the card. Is that understood, Mrs. Foster?"

"Yes, ma'am!" The older woman stared at her in surprise.

Slowly and deliberately Victoria turned and walked out of the room, conscious of the housekeeper's eyes on her back as she crossed the hall and ascended the stairs. She was halfway up when the explosion came.

"The hussy! The cheeky, impudent young hussy!"

Lord Benchley's laughter echoed around the hall. "So she's

178

stood up to you, has she, Enid? You'd better start writing those menu cards."

Victoria scuttled along to her room and dived into it like a rabbit into its burrow. She leaned against the door, feeling ill.

Millie looked up from where she was smoothing the counterpane over the freshly made bed. "Ooooh, miss! What on earth's the matter? You look like you saw a ghost!"

"Nothing, Millie," she managed to say.

"Are you sure." Millie peered anxiously into her face. 'Ere, miss, you come an' sit by the window an' I'll go down an' fetch you a nice cup of tea." She picked up the black tin dustpan and red-handled brush and was gone.

There was no point in saying so, but the gloominess of this house depressed Victoria so unutterably at times that sometimes she lay on her bed heartsick and gave in to her misery. But that solved nothing. Her whole family was in a wretched state, and there was no longer any doubting Andrew's wisdom when he dissuaded her from eloping. Lord Benchley *was* being a friend to the family. He had made all the funeral arrangements. He had given the family a house, rent free, for as long as they needed it. He had seen to all the details of the estate, and most important of all he was arranging some kind of a business with Andrew that would mean financial security— modest, but far better than the poverty they were otherwise faced with. For herself he was no friend. Had her father not died, she would have left him as she had vowed on that first horrible morning of being a wife. Almost every night he brought his loathsome attentions for her to suffer. In the first few weeks she was numbed by such crushing unhappiness that when he came to her room, she stayed listlessly still, only turning her face away. More recently her hatred of him made her struggle, but instantly she sensed that he liked resistance. Somehow it made the unspeakable performance more fun for him, so with that realization came the end to her resistance. If she kept still, it didn't hurt much. But every time he violated her with his gross body, her hatred of him deepened still further.

Once she could look past the gloom and the presence of her husband, her life appeared brighter. She had a lot of things to be thankful for, the main one being that she saw him so seldom. They breakfasted together, but he never spoke, and then she would rarely see him again until dinner, and then only occasionally. Because of her mourning they did not entertain, so she was spared the humiliation of trying to act as hostess for a stranger. He did not go to church, a fact which she found strange at first. But now Aunt Brownie had developed the habit of calling for her, so Sunday became a happy day, one she could spend with her family, lunching on Bess's lovely cooking at Bolton Street after the service. Sipping at her tea, she gazed out into the street.

The scene outside was neither beautiful nor interesting. Opposite squatted a row of dull brown-terraced houses all so alike that only the puffing chimneys and neat front doors showed where one house ended and another began. The upstairs windows were all of a set, a neatly spaced row of dull glass oblongs uniformly screened from within by white lace curtains. Though she had sat at this window for hours, she knew no more of her neighbors than when she had first arrived.

She had asked Mrs. Foster about the people who shared their street, and as usual the housekeeper had been bluntly discouraging. "They keep to themselves, and that's the way it should be. Folks don't like other folks prying into their business," she said. Victoria dropped the subject. It was the only thing to do with any subject after discussing it with Mrs. Foster.

Today Victoria had a longer wait than usual before Mrs. Foster appeared below her, clad in her street-length gray coat and her gray felt bonnet over her head. On her arm she carried a deep round reed basket. This was the signal that she and Millie had the house to themselves.

Mrs. Foster had made clear her strict disapproval of servants fraternizing with their betters, and Victoria was powerless to brook her on this, for Millie was under her direct supervision and had to obey the housekeeper on pain of dismissal. So while Mrs. Foster prepared herself for marketing, Millie would brew a pot of china tea and butter a plateful of Mrs. Foster's crumbly cheese biscuits. The moment the housekeeper left, she would pop an extra cup and saucer on the tray and hurry up to Victoria's room with it. They could count on at least an hour to talk and laugh and enjoy each other's company before she returned. If they did not hear her coming until her boots beat up the stairs and along the corridor, when she came in Millie would be innocently dressing Victoria's hair while Victoria read to her from *Great Expectations*, a work which Mrs. Foster approved of for its uplifting qualities.

This morning as Millie set the tray down on the hall table, she noticed a pale, crumpled card on the floor beneath. When she retrieved it and smoothed it out, she could see that it was an envelope. Millie couldn't read, but she had seen the words "Lady Victoria Benchley" often enough to know that they referred to her mistress. Indignantly Millie opened the door and bore it in on the tray.

"Oooh, miss! Just look at what that old cow's done now! This 'ere's a letter an' it's meant for you an' she threw it down in the 'allway there!"

"Oh, dear . . . it's probably a condolence card."

"Well, she 'ad no call to mess with it!"

"It wasn't Mrs. Foster, Millie. I dropped it there this morning. I forgot it, and it must have slipped from my hand." She took it and picked at the wax with her fingernails.

Millie poured the tea and gazed reflectively out at the sky. "Looks like it might be nice enough this afternoon. If it is, I'll go for a stroll when it's me hour off. There's the prettiest tree you ever saw up the road aways. All bright red an' orange it is. Ever so gorgeous. Makes me feel grand just to look at it." She glanced at Victoria sharply. "What be the matter, miss?"

"It's from Charles," said Victoria in a colorless voice.

"Charles?" repeated Millie blankly, puckering her narrow brow. "Ooooh, miss! You don't mean Captain Lawrence!"

Victoria nodded, her head bent over the letter.

Millie sighed with rapture. "Oooh, miss, 'ow *romantic*!" She longed to discreetly inquire what the letter said, but even with the closeness they shared, she could not presume to do that. Instead she placed the teacups out, helped Victoria to a cheese biscuit, and wriggled in an agony of anticipation.

Victoria read slowly.

Princess, I am taking a fearful risk, I know, in writing to you like this, but having seen your new husband with my own eyes, I realize that your situation could not possibly be made worse than it already is. I am ashamed to confide my suspicions to you. When you would not meet me in the park, I decided that you must have fixed your heart on this lord as much for his person as for what he was offering, but when I saw him, I knew the truth, that you would never have sacrificed yourself willingly. If only you were mine! Oh, how happy ı would be, and how happy I would make you! I cannot forget you, for no matter how I try to put you out of my mind, somehow you seem to be there again within the minute.

Princess, it might be wrong of me to declare myself when you are so newly married, but one day I am determined that you will be mine and nothing will ever part us again. If you love me, as I dare to hope you do, please keep that vow in mind and look toward it. In the meantime, may I see you occasionally? My intentions are honorable, but I need to see you, to just be close to you and know that you care care for me too. If you have a servant you can trust, please send him with a letter to me at this address. As you can see, I have found lodgings only three streets away. I had to be close to you, my love.

Charles.

"He wants to see me," she whispered.

"'Ow romantic! 'E wants to be your lover!"

"Oh, Millie!" she protested chidingly. "Have you no sense of moral values?"

"What's moral values, miss?"

"Exactly," scolded Victoria more firmly. "Now fetch me my black-bordered writing paper and my plain paper. I have two letters to write and I had better be quick about it if you are to be out of the house before Mrs. Foster comes back!"

"Then you *will* see 'im, miss?" Her small round eyes glowed.

"I'm not at all certain about that, but he will be worried about whether I received the letter safely, and I want to reassure him." She pushed her half-finished tea away. "Put the black paper there, Millie. I have to write a letter to myself with that."

"To yourself?"

"Lord Benchley said that I was to put that letter on his study desk when I had read it, and tonight he is going to expect to see a letter there. So I must compose one, mustn't I?" Carefully unstoppering the glass bottle, she dipped her pen into the dark green ink and began her letter to Charles.

Four

"What's the big news to be then, Violet?"

Violet stirred her mug of tea with a knife handle as she glanced curiously around at Mrs. Foster's domain. She ignored Millie's question. "It's a fusty old hen that runs *this* place," she ventured. "Tell me, Millie. Why is it that this kitchen looks as though nobody ever cooks in it?"

"She's a right weird one," said Millie. "I been watchin' 'er real close an' I think there be summat wrong with 'er eyes. I mean she don't seem to see dirt an' dust even when it's lyin' thick right under 'er nose! An' she can't cook to save 'erself. *I* could do better than 'er, an' I ain't no cook m'self!"

"An' how is she with Miss Victoria?" Violet asked.

"She 'ates 'er," said Millie frankly. "She told 'er to keep out of the kitchen. Miss Victoria made 'er write out a menu so she could 'ave summat different for tea every day, an' the old biddy just says, 'I was unable to purchase the veal you requested, ma'am, so I *do* hope this beef stew will please you instead,' an' slaps down a plate o' stew she warmed up from yesterday! An' when Miss Victoria tries to say summat, she just cuts in an says, 'You can leave it to me, ma'am. I am perfectly capable of arranging it.'"

Violet laughed at the mimicry. "Thee sounds precious! Thee should practice and talk like that all the time!"

"Like *'er*?" snorted Millie. "Not flamin' likely! But I feel right sorry fer Miss Victoria at times. Married to a lump like that an' 'im not the least bit of company for 'er. It wouldn't be 'alf so bad if she was the mistress like, an' able to 'ave 'er say, but Mrs. Foster treats 'er like a kid. Oooh, but I feel sorry for 'er!"

"And thee told me before the wedding that thee was never going to feel sorry for her. Leaving that nice captain and marrying Lord Benchley for his money. Thee said she didn't deserve pity."

"No, Violet," insisted Millie. "She'd not 'ave done it if she knew what she were in for. Gave 'er ever such a shock, it did. She did *not* marry 'im for 'is money. When she came 'ere, she 'ad ten pounds in 'er purse. I been on messages buyin'

183

little things for 'er, an' now she 'as only seven pounds an' sixteen shillin's left. I know 'a 'cause I seen it, an' she said she don't know what she'll do when it's gone. 'E's given 'er nowt, Violet. Not one dress nor bonnet nor nothin'."

Violet sighed morosely.

"Now come on, Violet, an' tell me your news. You'd not 'ave asked when the old biddy 'ad a day off, then walked all this way over if it wasn't to tell me summat right important. I can see you're down about it, but you'll feel better once it's shared! Truly you will."

"Thee is right. Ted asked me to marry him, and I said that I would. I gave my notice in for next Saturday but one. That's when the wedding is to be, Millie. Can you come?"

"Try an' stop me." She took both of Violet's hands in hers and peered anxiously into her friend's face. "What did 'e say?"

She shook her head dumbly.

"You mean you ain't told 'im?"

"He thinks I'm going to help my mother in Chester. She's a widow, and Andrew knows all about her. I told Bess and Myers about the wedding. . . . They are the only friends I've got except thee. Bess is ever so thrilled. She's going to bake me some pies and they are both coming. They won't tell anyone in the family. I told them it would be cruel to say why I'm going when they are all in mourning, so Bess said she would box *my* ears for me if I let the real reason slip!" Violet's lips tightened in determination, but Millie could see frightening depths of unhappiness in her eyes.

"Why don't you at least tell 'im? I mean . . . 'e might 'ave plans of his own."

"Oh, Millie," and her voice trembled as she began to cry. "He says he has plans, but they will take months, perhaps more than a year, and I have to be wed or settled now! It's a *baby*, Millie! I can't make the baby wait. It will grow and come and nobody on this earth can change that. He can't help me, Millie."

"'E said that?"

"Of course not." Violet had to smile through the tears. "If it were thee, thee wouldn't be able to tell him either. Thee should see the worries he has! The whole family destitute and none of them facing up to it but him. They carp at him every day, asking to buy things. Albertina is the worst. She blames him for everything. Oh, but he has his troubles, Millie. All

184

the bills and no money to pay them."

Millie stared thoughtfully into her mug and remarked quietly, "It seems to me that you got worse troubles than any of 'is, Violet. An' it seems to me that 'e *ought* to know, since 'e made them for you."

"It's no use thee telling me what I should do and should not do," Violet said defiantly. "Andrew cannot leave his family to look after me. If I marry Ted, then he can marry a rich lady and help his family. I'm no use to him now! Surely thee can see that."

"Oh, Violet!" Millie said in anguish.

Sturdily ignoring her, Violet went on practically. "If I didn't do something for myself, I'd be taken to the workhouse the moment I couldn't hide it any longer. Thee cannot get out of that place, you know. Imagine how bad Andrew would feel if that happened to me!"

"It would serve him right," muttered Millie, already beginning to hate Master Andrew.

"I thought of getting rid of it."

"Oh, no, Violet. Never, never that!" She got up to refill the teapot from the hissing kettle. "Fancy another brew? All this talkin's makin' me mouth dry as a well on washday. Don't never think on gettin' rid of babies, Violet. Not now an' not ever." She gave the teapot an experimental splash and shoveled in another scoop of tea leaves. "Me auntie did that when me uncle was in prison, an' she 'ad this feller 'oo were kind to 'er like. Mind yer, she 'ad nine livin' already an' no way to keep their bellies full. Died summat terrible she did. Screamin!" She shuddered. "There was blood. . . . It was 'orrible! If I ever 'as to do for meself, I'd go for summat quick. Jump off the bridge. Don't never go to one of them old women. They can fix you, but they can kill you too."

Violet stirred her fresh mug of tea thoroughly. "I thought on it and thought on it, but in the end I couldn't do it. It would be killing a wee bit of him, wouldn't it? I'm hoping it will look just like him. I can watch it grow and love it, and for the rest of my life I can have Andrew's child with me."

"I feel so sad for you, Violet."

"Now don't thee start getting soft," warned Violet. "The more I think on this, the better I feel. I can't have Andrew now that he has to look after his family, but this way I can have a very good second best. This could be the biggest blessing of my life! Ted will be a good father, and I will be so sweet to Ted. . . . Millie, I know I'm doing bad by him, but I'll be so kind to him and his two poor motherless young ones that he'll never regret it . . ."

"I know you will," sympathized Millie. "But what if the baby *does* look like Master Andrew?"

"I hope it does!" said Violet stoutly. "Ted doesn't know about Andrew and once the baby is born, my servant days will be long behind us. I've thought it all out. Ted's young ones are a mixture, one fair and one dark, so unless this one has red hair like Birdie, it should be safe. Why should he suspect anything? The baby will be a bit early but babies often are! He'll be pleased with it. Besides, there's a nice twenty-pound dowry I've put by, saved from a bit each year since I started working. That will be a nice surprise to sweeten his wedding day."

"It will be a happy day for you both."

Violet stood up and lifted her gray bonnet from the peg next to the window. "Mind that thee praise my cooking after the wedding! I'm having roast beef and oysters, and Ted is buying a whole ham."

"Then I'll come for sure," laughed Millie, rising to see her to the door. "You got a real fine way with words, Violet."

"Is it my words or the ham that's bringing thee?" she asked archly.

"We don't get much 'am 'ere," Millie said.

Five

The afternoon air was balmy and soft on their faces as the carriage rolled along leisurely behind the smartly trotting chestnut horses, whose heads were high at the scents of home, hot oats, and rubdowns. Albertina listened to the slap and jangle of their harnesses behind her and sighed inwardly with irritation. The day had not gone at all as planned.

She was riding in a small landau with three other young ladies, so squashed in that their dresses were all crushed together like many colored blooms—the red-and-pink sprigged muslin of the girl beside her, the foamy sea-green poplin of the girl diagonally opposite, and facing her the lemon and spice muslin dress adorning the plainest and noisiest girl she had ever met, a young lady called Miss Enid Watkins.

They were moving between rows of oaks between which they could occasionally see the faint outline of Sedgewick Hall, far away across a glittering silver ribbon of water and a soft green spread of lawn. Miss Watkins was right; it was almost invisible. Only the basic rectangle and the taller tower at the front showed against the wave crest of cliffs a bare quarter of a mile beyond.

Albertina craned her neck. They were in the fourth and last carriage of the procession. Behind them rumbled the two carts bearing the picnic furniture and depleted hampers on which perched the half-dozen servants who had attended them. Judging by their laughter and high-pitched conversation, they had enjoyed themselves even more than the "gentry."

The front carriage was turning now to cross the bridge. In that carriage sat Elizabeth with her husband and three other gentlemen, Francis Blake, Viscount Marley, and Mr. Barnes's younger brother. Albertina sniffed sourly to herself. The pattern had been clearly established last evening, and it had been the same all day. Elizabeth collected all the presentable young men around herself and only occasionally, when the whim moved her, did she include another female in her enchanted circle of conversation. So far this weekend Albertina had found herself listening glumly to an unrelieved marathon of Miss Enid Watkins's gossip and an endless dissertation on guns by Mr. Francis Blake. The other two young ladies had sat stodgily together the whole time with nothing to say for themselves and no expression on their whey-colored faces. Albertina guessed that they were sisters but was not sufficiently interested to inquire. Miss Watkins was enough to cope with, for the present.

Now the carriage slowed down until the girls could hear the soft crunch of gravel under the wheels. The driver snapped the whip and shouted to clear a drift of bleating sheep from their path, then on they rolled again up the drive between the stands of enormous autumn-tarnished oaks until now, when she craned her neck, she could see the moss-stained gargoyles leaning hideously out from the roof line, their grotesquely yawning mouths open to spit the accumulation of rainwater from the guttering. Above the huge brass-nailed door the crest loomed, a creamier stone than the rest of the house, for it was kept scrubbed and free from mold. The carved lion and the deer, placidly standing side by side, regarded them as they alighted from the carriage and ascended the sandstone steps to where Elizabeth was beckoning to them.

"We have been here hours already!" she lied laughingly.

"*We* had to slow down for fear of running over the sheep," replied Miss Watkins.

Francis Blake came down the steps to meet them. His fawn breeches were grass-stained where he had been kneeling to aim at the target. Holding out a stiff elbow to Albertina, he smiled down at her, the whole side of his face falling into pleats where it met the scar. "You look tired," he said kindly.

This was too much! She had been neglected all day . . . a *servant* had to help her to tea at the picnic . . . and now this! To be told one looked tired was tantamount to being told one looked frightful! Instead of bursting into the scalding tears that lurked dangerously close, she said, "I do feel rather fatigued. It must be the air, I think."

"You *poor* thing!" cried Elizabeth in genuine concern. "Mabel can show you upstairs to your room and you can have a rest. We don't want to do without your company tonight, do we?"

"Of course not," said the men obediently.

Gilbert Belton was gazing at her with his usual detatched and rather superior expression. Albertina felt that his eyes missed nothing—neither the crumpled flounces of her dress, where she had been squashed with the others into a landau meant for two, nor the damp spot on the front of her skirt where Miss Watkins had joggled her elbow in excitement and spilled her tea.

Holding her chin high, Albertina said in a low voice, "Could I please have a private word with you, Elizabeth?"

The look of annoyance was fleeting, then Elizabeth beamed dazzlingly and said, "On you go, everybody, into the morning room! There's hot punch to refresh you after the drive! I shall be back with you in no time at all!"

She and Albertina lingered at the foot of the gently curving wine-dark stairway until the others had drifted in to the re-reshments.

"Elizabeth," said Albertina, "something quite unforeseen has happened! Violet did not pack my evening dress, and I have *nothing* to wear this evening! She is such a stupid, forgetful girl," she continued, hoping she sounded convincing.

"What can I do? I must stay in my room all evening, for I can hardly wear this. See how crumpled and stained it is!"

"You goose! Of course you won't miss this evening. There will be a special dinner, music and dancing. I wanted it especially to cheer you up. Mabel!" she called. "Do come here! Mabel will show you my wardrobe and you may choose anything you wish. Mabel knows what I am wearing tonight, so she won't let you choose that. You had better do it now so she will have time to run a tuck in the hem for you. Have a good sleep, now." With a rather patronizing pat on her cheek and a warm smile Elizabeth turned and hurried toward the morning room.

In the dressing room Mabel looked at her figure shrewdly. "We got all sizes here. Madam's weight goes up and down, but no matter whether she's been poorly or eating well, she's got something to fit her. There should be something for you." She took down a padded hanger from the rail and held up a fall of soft blue silk to Albertina. "Look in the mirror and see what you think."

Albertina winced at what she saw. She did indeed look tired, but more than that, her face was hollow-eyed and drawn in pain.

"Well, what do you think?" asked Mabel. "That's one of the prettiest madam has, and the color will suit you very well."

"It's lovely," said Albertina miserably.

"Hold it there, no, there. That's right. Now keep still a minute so I can see how much to shorten it by."

When she was finally able to creep into bed in her softly dimmed room, she felt better. Her eyes were soothed by moist drooping lids, and her skin had been pampered with a swirling massage of Rimmel Pearl Cream which made it feel more supple at once. As her spirits lifted, she slipped away into deep, velvet sleep.

Albertina awoke feeling marvelous and full of hope, eager for the evening to begin. The rest had refreshed and revitalized her. With one swooping tug she opened the curtains and looked at herself anxiously in the dresser glass. The late afternoon sunlight blushed her skin with a warm apricot tinge and her dark blue eyes sparkled back at her. She grinned at herself impishly.

Behind her, spread invitingly over the back of a chair, was the blue dress. This time when she held it up in front of her, she had no cause to wince at what she saw.

Only ten minutes after the musical cascade of chimes announced that it was time for before-dinner sherries and conversation in the parlor, Albertina approached the top of the stairs. She held a half-open silver-fretted fan in one hand and placed the other gracefully on the stair rail as she walked down slowly with her head high, confident that she looked her best. Mabel had cosseted and groomed her magnificently, had brushed her hair and styled it into a frankly darling arrangement of ringlets with a bunch of shining golden curls hanging above each ear like catkins. The dress fitted perfectly and needed only the loosest of stays.

If any dress was designed to disguise plumpness, this one was undoubtedly it. Cut plungingly low to emphasize the bosom, it hugged the waist gently and then ballooned out suddenly under the high draping around the hips, falling gently to a wide, smooth hemline. The sleeves were high little puffs after the Russian manner. Below them her upper arms looked positively slender, she noted with satisfaction, though she colored to think of what her mother would say if she could see her exposing so much of her breasts.

But she did most definitely want to be noticed and to make the kind of impression on Viscount Marley that would stick in his mind. What she would do when she had loosened him from Elizabeth's side, she had no idea, but with all the confidence of a young lady who knows that she has never looked more beautiful, she descended the stairs to begin her performance.

Just as she stepped onto the polished floor of the hallway, a door opened opposite and Gilbert Belton came out of the room she knew to be the library. He stopped with a smile of delighted surprise. Barely able to conceal her triumph, she nodded to him politely, ringlets bouncing at her ears and silver earbobs brushing her cheeks, before drifting past close enough for him to notice the lavender water with which she had generously splashed her throat and arms. Pausing only a moment at the parlor door, she fastened her gaze on Elizabeth and moved toward her determinedly, smile fixed, expression pert, brave as a crusader setting out to conquer the world.

When Gilbert joined them a few moments later, she did not deign to notice his approach and chose that exact moment to see Miss Watkins sitting alone in a corner, whereupon she rushed to her in a swirl of blue silk as if there were nothing she wanted more in the world than to see her. Only when she was settled and already feeling the twinges of boredom, her jaws aching from the effort of stifling a yawn, did she allow herself the distraction of peeking to see if her maneuver had been effective. No, he was chatting earnestly to Elizabeth as always, and Mr. Barnes was nowhere in sight. You would think that one husband would be enough for her, thought Albertina cattily. Anybody would think they were lovers! As she watched, Elizabeth smiled up at Gilbert and plucked at his floppy, white silk bow tie with her long, aristocratic fingers, then placed her hand on his wrist and began the procession in to dinner. In helpless frustration she saw a beaming Francis Blake walking toward her, proffering both elbows.

"It seems that I have the pleasure of escorting both you beautiful young ladies in to dine," he said gallantly. And, to make matters even worse, she found herself stuck at the bottom of the long table, isolated with Francis in a sea of Mr. Barnes's teen-age children.

"I asked to be seated with you," he confided with a grin.

Smiling back at him, she amused herself with the idea of leaning over, lifting the revolver from its holster, aiming it at his chest, and pulling the trigger. His confidence explained a lot of things. Of course Gilbert Belton would not be so grossly ill-mannered as to flirt with a young lady already tacitly claimed by his best friend!

The meal did little to add to her pleasure and made her realize how well they ate at home. She was astounded to hear the comments of delight from the children around her that greeted the procession of courses, comments that revealed this was festival fare for them. The soup was thin and poorly flavored, the fish overcooked, with a sauce in which floated rubbery lumps of cheese, the entrée of partridge was tender enough, but the wine-and-butter sauce was burnt and bitter tasting, and the main course was a culinary disaster. Somehow the cook had contrived to overcook the carrots and peas until they had turned into coagulating pastel mushes, yet the roast pork and baked vegetables were not "done" at all. After chewing for several minutes on a sliver of pork, Albertina swallowed it whole and daintily placed her knife and fork at the side of her plate.

"Saving some room for dessert?" asked Francis, who had

munched his way purposefully through all the courses.

Albertina smiled at him without replying. Idly she glanced around at the other guests, most of whom were silently chewing to the accompanying click of silver on eggshell Wedgewood porcelain. At the far end of the table Gilbert Belton lounged back negligently, picking at his teeth with a gold-handled tooth probe. He was staring at her; his lean, olive-skinned face was frankly admiring. He lowered the tooth probe and ran his tongue around his lips, still fixing her with his hard, wood-brown eyes. Then, abruptly, he smiled right at her.

Albertina flushed, angry with herself for looking at him so long when she had only intended to take a quick peek. She tossed her ringlets and turned to Francis, but beyond him she could still plainly see Gilbert in the corner of her eye. He appeared to be laughing. She didn't look at him again for the remainder of the meal, nor did she glance at him when the gentlemen rejoined the ladies in the drawing room after dinner.

It must have been midnight when Gilbert at last decided to acknowledge her presence. He cut in on Francis. Even if this was not the heart-stopping moment she had hoped for, she would have been grateful to be spared the arguments for and against the new Winchester repeating rifle. Sweeping and guiding and propeling her around the polished square of dance floor, Gilbert held her so perilously close that every breath she drew brought the tangy scent of his hair pomade.

She placed one trembling hand on his shoulder and glanced quickly about the room, hoping to see what Elizabeth's reaction to this desertion might be. But there was no sign of Elizabeth, only Mr. Barnes, standing by the shiny aspidistra, who smiled at her as they whirled past. I should think of something clever to say, she told herself. He will think me fearfully dull if I don't. Smiling and arching her neck she racked her mind and came up with nothing at all.

It was Gilbert who spoke, and when he did, his words were even more astounding than the decisive way he had whisked her from Francis. Murmuring into her ringlets, he said in a low voice, "I am enchanted with you, utterly enchanted."

"Thank you," she said in surprise and immediately cursed herself. What had happened to her wit?

But perhaps she had no cause to worry. Gilbert smiled and squeezed her waist very slightly, with just enough pressure to compliment and not enough to offend. "I have been gazing enraptured at you all day, and I think that—well, can you guess what I think?"

She shook her head. "What do you think?"

"I have never seen anyone quite as beautiful as you are. It frightens me."

"Why should it do that?" She glanced innocently into his face and thrilled at the earnest expression she saw there.

"I'm afraid that I might be falling in love with you."

Albertina was swept by such a strong feeling of mingled happiness and triumph that she felt quite dizzy. This was the moment she had dreamed of, where someone rich, handsome, and gallant declared his love to her. Oh, wouldn't Mother be pleased!

"I beg your pardon?" she asked his questioning face, so close to hers.

"Dare I hope?"

"Of course, of course," she babbled. "Oh, please could we sit down for a moment? I feel rather faint."

"We can do better than that." Swinging away from her as they reached the edge of the carpet, but still holding her hand, he guided her boldly through the open doors and into the dark conservatory. There was no time to protest that she did not mean *this* before he moved in front of her, put both arms savagely around her in a gesture that was far more constraint than embrace, and kissed her passionately full on the mouth.

Her first reaction was shock. Mother would never let her go away alone again if she could see this! But her next reaction was pure pleasure. This man who was making such ardent love to her was the Viscount Marley! The kiss was wonderful. She had never felt so completely powerless and she enjoyed the sensation. He tasted like all the manly smells she loved, tobacco and port, pomade and warmth.

"I love you. I know it now," he whispered at the corner of her mouth.

She heard herself say, "I love you too. I've thought about you so much..."

"May I see you later?" He pulled his head away from hers so that he could study her reaction. His eyes gleamed liquid in the darkness.

"Of course you may," she said, surprised at the question.

"Then let us be getting back before we are missed," he said and gave her another swift kiss on the mouth.

As he walked just ahead of her, nobody seemed to take any notice of them, and once they were on the floor, she took his arm for the short walk over to where Francis was still talking about Winchester repeating rifles.

Gilbert bowed formally. "Thank you for the pleasure of your company, Miss Fielding." The look of mischief in his eyes was a pact between them.

Francis glanced at her. "Are you enjoying yourself?"

"Oh, yes, Mr. Blake!" she said. She seemed as fresh and glowing as a just-opened rose. He wondered whether he was merely strongly attracted to her or whether he was actually beginning to care for her.

Clinging to his arm breathlessly, she said, "I do declare that I feel quite exhausted after that last dance, Mr. Blake. Do you know where Elizabeth is? I should like to thank her for the dinner and the delightful evening before I retire."

"She went to bed earlier with a severe headache," Francis told her. "It has been developing all day, brought on by the sun no doubt."

"I shall say good night then," she said, curtsying to them each in turn, drawing only the sketchiest of veils over her impatience to get away. She had been with Gilbert such a short time, but in that time her whole life had changed course.

She remembered to lock the door to her room, thinking as she slid the brass bolt that she would be able to report fulfilling *that* part of her orders. What a catch she had made! Hastily she told herself that his wealth meant nothing to her; she loved him for his handsome leanness and his romantic spirit alone. All through the night she alternated patches of light sleep with long, achingly beautiful interludes when she lay awake thinking of him. Several times she was shaken from her shallow sleep by the sound of her door handle turning, and she smiled at the fancy that it might be Gilbert come to give her another of those tender, thrilling kisses. If only it were! She wondered if he, too, was lying awake, his mind stirring with thoughts of her. Toward morning she slept more soundly.

The next day brought bitter disappointment. There was no sign of Gilbert at breakfast, and of course she could not be so forward as to ask Francis where he was. Then at services in the tiny paneled chapel, there were only a few of the older men present. Later Elizabeth was heard to complain that one of the village tenants had come to report fox trouble so the men had taken the hounds and gone off to help. Albertina hoped that Aunt Brownie's carriage would be late in coming to collect her, so she might have the opportunity to see him before she left, but when the familiar carriage with Garth on the box waited at the steps, as she said her farewells to Elizabeth, the men were still out after the fox.

She was still able to hug herself happily as she gazed back at Sedgewick Hall, watching it blend gradually into the cliffs beyond, watching the autumn oaks fade as the road turned and they left the river behind them.

Two or three miles up the road was an inn, an old white-washed inn built in Tudor times, with sagging black timbers, crazily sloping roofs, and hanging eaves. A chipped picture of a highwayman swung above the door. Albertina sat up and moved to the other side of the carriage in order to get a better view as they clattered past.

She saw men on horseback shouting to each other as their horses moved edgily back and forth amid packs of brown-and-white splotched hounds gamboling around their hoofs. A coarse-featured girl in a rumpled apron was carrying a tray on which rested tankards frothing over with ale. As she passed amongst the horses, the riders leaned down and helped themselves.

Albertina cried out in joy as the carriage slowed to avoid a tumbling rush of dogs. These were the gentlemen from the Hall! And there, close by, were Francis Blake and Gilbert Belton, facing her as they sat side by side in their saddles, talking earnestly. She waved and Francis saw her and waved back, a grin splitting his good-humored face. Gilbert glanced up too, then deliberately turned his head to continue talking. As the carriage moved away, she took with her a picture of him sitting there, bare-headed, his hair shining and sun warmed, his tall boots gleaming brown, his jacket and trousers an immaculate creamy chocolate color, and his tanned profile turned cooly away from her. As she subsided, frowning, into the buttoned leather seat, a small, cold kernel of doubt sprouted inside her mind. He *had* seen her; he could not possibly have mistaken her for someone else. She didn't understand his hauteur, but one thing seemed certain. She had no news that she could properly tell her mother.

Six

"Do you like it here, lass?" asked Myers.

They were alone in the pale, scrubbed-wood kitchen at that mellow time of the day when the dinner things have been tidied away and there is still enough of the evening left to enjoy.

Bess pulled out a chair. It scraped on the cold tiles. She settled herself down, wriggling her haunches to and fro until she felt completely comfortable. "I like it here well enough, now I'm getting used to it. Reminds me of the old days, it does. When we were wed. Do you remember?"

"Aye, their house were a lot like this one, and I spent more time in these clothes than in a butler's jacket and gloves. You may not think it, but I've missed having a proper garden these past years. Chasing after the maids, always checking on their work, it gets a man down."

"I thought you enjoyed chasing after the maids," said Bess slyly.

Myers didn't answer. Many quarrels had been avoided because he simply decided not to hear her innuendos. Rising slowly, he went to the cupboard where the brandy bottle was kept. "I miss the master, though," he confessed wistfully as he poured.

"I know, love. We all do, don't we?"

"He must have been driven by the devil himself. He'd not have done it otherwise."

Bess took the thick tumbler he offered and set it down on the bleached table top. "Do you remember how it was with just you and me and Bessie, and not even Miss Boswell to look down her nose at me?"

"And that funny old tart with whiskers who used to come in and wash?"

"Belle. I haven't spared her a thought in years. She's probably dead by now." She sighed and tilted the glass toward her lips.

"Do you miss the dinner parties . . . all the fancy cooking?"

"Ah, that's good! I do, love. More than I miss the house, the two Wills, and even the master. It's odd having to worry about every tuppence, but it's good practice for later when we're on our own."

"You do right well, lass. Real well. You can make a piece of stewed meat taste every bit as good as the best roast."

"Not quite."

"Better." He smiled at her affectionately.

Reaching over with both hands, she carefully removed his glasses and pushed her face forward to kiss him. Her breasts bumped against her glass.

"You're in a right good mood."

"Every time I think of Miss Boswell going, I'm in the best mood I've ever known. I laugh to think of it. How is she going to take to being married when she's too high and mighty to touch the chamber pot when she uses it? She'll die of the vapors on her wedding night!" Bess leaned both elbows on the table and roared. "She told me... she told me that the main reason she's accepted is that the Fieldings are so poor that they will be better off without her wages to pay. 'Salary,' she called it. For a moment I thought she was talking about *celery*! She said that if she wasn't going to be married to Mr. Stove..."

"*Hove*," said Myers. "Mr. Hove."

"Then she would have offered to work for half her *celery*! I told her that she couldn't do half as much work for that since she does none worth speaking of now!"

Tugging at his black side-whiskers, Myers said seriously, "You realize that the Fieldings might get to the stage where they can't afford to pay us? We get good wages, lass. Twenty pounds apiece more than the Emery family pay their cook and butler."

"How long before we can emigrate and start up our own eating place?"

"Two years. Less, if we throw away the bottle."

She stroked his face with a rough, dry hand. "We can't do that. Brandy keeps my wheels running."

"How would you feel about going to work for someone else, then? We keep getting offers, and the money is good."

"Myers! You don't mean that! This is our family. How would we know what we were getting into? Another master and mistress might have all sorts of silly rules for their servants. No, Myers, we stay here, then off we go on our adventure."

"Aye, our adventure." He uncorked the dark bottle and refilled the glasses.

"Oh, Myers, it's been all these years in the dreaming, and now its getting closer I'm starting to get churned up about it.

A little eating house of our own! Plain dishes for plain folks, but cooked so special with those extra touches, and served pretty as a princess, so those who eat in our place will be impatient to be hungry again so they can come right back for another meal."

"And a garden," drawled Myers. "A garden to catch the sun with a wall to keep the wind out, where I can grow you asparagus and broccoli . . ."

"And cabbage and carrots," continued Bess with a smile. "We'll be serving plain folks, remember?"

"Overlooking the sea, with a little curl of sandy beach and rocks to fish off."

"And the salt smell in the wind."

"And I'll have a strawberry patch! We have to have a strawberry patch! Folks like strawberries and cream."

"Where will it be? The Canadian territories? Capetown? New Zealand? Australia?"

"I rather fancy Australia."

"With the convicts?" They had traced the path of this conversation many times before, mellow-voiced with brandy, warm and inconclusive.

"There will be many freed by now and anxious to start good lives. We'll not be troubled."

"True, love, true. Oh, Myers, I hope that nothing goes wrong to spoil it all."

"Hey, lass, don't dwell on the might-be. Let life take you by the hand and lead you along."

Bess grinned as she said, "Bats might fly in the dark, but I like to see where I'm going."

Seven

The publicity accorded the opening of preliminary hearings in the inquiry into the behavior of officers at the Crimea was more intense than any fanfare ever played to greet the queen's newest baby. Newspaper printed thick black headlines above stories that hinted of startling revelations to come. In no time the sparks and flickers of public interest had been fanned into a roaring blaze which the press eagerly fed, blew on and prodded, then warmed its hands at the flames.

Not a single family in London had escaped suffering, either

directly or through close friends, neighbors, or relatives. Nobody was unaffected by the reports of the wanton waste and negligence of the war. Months ago, as the trickle of home-coming soldiers had swollen to a ragged tide of misery, and the soldiers told their families what and how they had suffered, the low buzz of indignation had begun. At every hearth in the city one could hear the sentiments: "It's a disgrace, the way our loyal men have been treated." Or "Something must be done; somebody must pay."

The noise of protest grew louder as groups got together. Ghastly reminiscences were exchanged, each tale of horror capping the one before, until the suffering reached gothic proportions. It grew louder still as bitterly disillusioned men, seeking jobs in vain, began to feel the bite of injustice and watch their families go hungry with the prospect of a bleak, starving winter ahead. Something had to be done. Somebody had to pay.

At the height of the anger, at that flashpoint when the heat was at its fiercest, the inquiry began.

On the first morning only a huddle of poor people filled the front benches in the public gallery, but by the third morning there was a queue over a mile long waiting in the hopes of securing a place on the benches. There were mothers who had lost sons, widows with young children, grandmothers, and bereft sweethearts, all silently standing in line, their breath softly pluming on the crisp morning air. There were war veterans anxious to see that justice was done and eager to entertain the others there with their own magnified stories of the fighting. With them they carried hunks of bread wrapped in grimy cloth, tea in small earthenware crocks that snuggled under the top layers of clothing and warmed the chest, and sly bottles of stuff much stronger than tea that could warm best of all.

The high double doors opened at ten. By a quarter past ten the benches were all full and more than half of those who stood in line were turned away, disappointed.

Andrew Fielding was called to the stand late in the afternoon of the third day. There was time enough only for him to be sworn in and questioned about his particular position on Lord Longworth's staff. A murmur of interest rippled along the row of judges as it was revealed that Andrew Fielding was in such a sensitive position that he would probably be the key witness to the whole inquiry. He was bold and direct as he answered the questions, and nodded solemnly when the judges, members of Parliament for the most part, warned Andrew and the other witnesses that, though they might not be called for days or weeks, they were still under a sworn oath and owed all their loyalties to the court. All other allegiances were ordered suspended until the inquiry was completed.

Directly the hearing was over for the day, Andrew drove to Lord Benchley's house. They had met for prolonged discussions each afternoon for the past few weeks. This afternoon he was not yet home, and Victoria received him in the morning room, a room now warm with the sweet autumn smell of earth and leaves, and green with the lace of potted plants.

"It seems odd seeing them here," he said. "They seem to be doing well, though."

"They brighten the room marvelously well," said his sister with a smile as she gazed affectionately at the rows of plants on the mantel.

"Hm," said Andrew. Lord Benchley would be pleased with his report of the afternoon.

Victoria left her color-splashed tapestry resting in her gray silk lap and stared at him seriously. "Please sit down and let me ask you something."

"What is it, little sister?" He smiled at how grave she looked her eyes rounded and her mouth set in a straight little line that she could not quite hold still, for her lips trembled nervously. Reaching over, he tucked a stray wisp of hair into the netted bundle at the back of her neck. The warm gesture gave her confidence.

"Mother is very unhappy," she began.

Instantly he was on guard, and she cursed her clumsy approach.

He stood up before speaking. "If you want me to stop giving evidence, I'm sorry, but it can't be done."

"I understand that you have strong principles and that you feel deeply about this, but surely you could back down for Mother's sake?"

"It cannot be done," he said, walking away from her to the window.

"Why not?" she begged. "Surely it is no more than you asked me to do."

He looked defensive when he turned to face her, for he felt a lingering guilt over what she had sacrificed. "That was quite different. In the long run, your marriage to Lord Benchley will help us all."

"But do you need to do *this*? Lady Longworth is Mother's only friend apart from Aunt Brownie, and she can't be good friends with Aunt Brownie the way she used to because she dislikes Miss Manfred so much. Mother needs Lady Longworth, and you know that she will lose her if this continues."

She already has, thought Andrew, but there was no need to tell Victoria that. Mother would tell her soon enough about the cold letter cutting off their friendship.

"I have to think of our futures," he said. "Lord Benchley is helping me, and my evidence is essential to that. Now leave it be, please, Victoria. Let me assure you that it isn't pleasant having Mother weeping and nagging at me every day. I do know what I'm doing. My way is best for us all."

"How can it be when you will alienate so many people?"

"Leave it be, Victoria. Lord Longworth does not deserve your consideration."

"How can you say that? How would you feel if he had done something like this to Father? You are behaving no better than those businessmen who hounded Father to death and then forced all our family onto the charity Lord Benchley gives us! It's all the same thing."

His face went white. For a long time he said nothing, and when he spoke, his voice was dull and level; she knew that he was extremely angry. "You and Mother have an odd picture of Lord Longworth," he said with deceptive mildness. "You seem to think that he is Saint Wilton, guardian of the poor, or something equally ridiculous. I tell you, Victoria, that man is a murderer. He does not deserve one scrap of your compassion."

"I cannot believe that. If he did wrong, then it must have been because the strain of the fighting distorted his judgment."

"Strain of fighting! Ha!" When he threw back his head to laugh bitterly she could see that he had lost most of his back teeth. The sight jolted her. "He saw less fighting than Mrs. Duberley. Let me tell you something about your precious Lord Longworth! We were at Varna, awaiting instructions from England before proceeding. Some of the lads became ill with fevers, vomiting, stomach cramps. They had cholera, though by the time it was properly diagnosed, it had spread like a fire and nothing could be done to check it. Lord Longworth knew the men were ill, and he could see it was serious, but he told me that it would delay our departure if he worried about having medical treatment made available. When the orders came to sail for Sebastopol, he was in such a hurry that he insisted all men transfer to the ships which had been waiting for three weeks at anchor. We were packed in so tightly that there was scarcely air to breathe and we had to take turns at lying down. I shall not describe the conditions of our quarters, with sick men helpless to look after themselves properly. But it was a miracle so many of us reached our destination alive. All the medical supplies and other goods were left behind because the transport carts were full of Lord Longworth's furniture and wines and there was no room for them. When we arrived, Lord Longworth decided that there was nothing wrong with the men, though by this time more than half were ill. We arrived in the middle of the night, and orders were given to disembark straight away. Heaven alone knows why. At the time I thought Lord Longworth was commendably eager for battle, though later observations proved this wildly wrong. Anyway, there we were in the dark on a rough sea, freezing cold. One longboat tipped over and the men were too weak and ill to save themselves."

"They all drowned?"

Andrew nodded. "Next morning, after a night spent in the open, the beach was littered with dead and dying. The rest of us were weak from the journey and much in need of rest and hot food, but that madman gave the orders to begin marching to the battle site, across the River Alma. There were no animals to carry what few supplies we had, and most of the men could carry little besides themselves, but we managed as best we could. Any army who wanted to follow us could have done so easily by tracing the line of men who fell, too enfeebled to go any further."

"He left them to die? With nobody to care for them?"

He nodded.

"But they had food and water, of course?"

"Gracious, no!" snorted Andrew. "What little there was of that—and there was precious little—was needed for the strong ones, the well ones, the ones who were going to give battle for the glory of England and Lord Wilton Longworth."

"Why was he so unfeeling? Do you think he might have been suffering from cholera, too?"

"He was in perfect health, more's the pity. I argued with

him several times, requesting that we pitch camp for a few days to allow the men to recover to full strength. If we had done that, a lot of lives would have been saved. It was the pace he set that killed those men."

"What did he say when you asked for a rest?" asked Victoria, struggling to reconcile her very different ideas of Lord Longworth. She was incredulous, yet knew Andrew was not lying.

"He told me we were not there for fun and games. This was war! In all fairness to *him* he *was* getting orders from home, but instead of using a bit of common sense and his own judgment he was carrying the orders out to the last letter. The men at headquarters here did not know of the conditions we were under when they framed the orders. They didn't know of the senseless waste of good life, or of the cholera that was thinning the men down like saplings in a gale. And as for Lord Longworth, he was there for the glory. He's a murderer, Victoria! Don't waste compassion on him. He will lose prestige, and he will lose those contracts he's grown fat on all these years, but neither is punishment enough. Turn your back on him, Victoria, and encourage Mother to do the same. We need the contracts more than we need them as friends!"

"You *are* getting the contracts? Those army-supply ones?"

He nodded. "Lord Benchley and I will. They will give us a good income. Mother will have a higher standard of living, and as for me . . ." He sat close beside her and held her hands. His eyes, all anger burnt out, were moist and warm. "I'm going to get married! I've made up my mind to it."

"Andrew!" This was a subject much more exciting, and she was relieved to drop the other business with the thought that it was no concern of hers. "Who is it to be? Have you told Mother?"

"Not yet, and neither must you. It all depends on the outcome of the hearings, but I want you to know that this is one of the main reasons I am doing it. She has no money and so I *must* have an income!"

"Oh, Andrew! I never suspected. How long have you known her? Do I know her?"

He kissed her forehead. "No guessing games. I shall tell you soon enough. But wish me happiness."

"Of course I do. Mother will be disappointed that she has no money, but *I* think it's splendid!"

Tapping rather brusquely at the door, Millie came in a pace and stood staring at them both.

"Excuse me, miss, but Lord Benchley is 'ome an' in 'is study."

"Thank you, Millie. We didn't hear him, we were so busy talking."

Andrew stood to leave, but Millie doggedly blocked his way and said, around him, to Victoria. "Might I please still be 'avin' tomorrow off to go to the wedding?"

"Of course," said Victoria, puzzled by the hostility in her tone. Perhaps Mrs. Foster was being tyrannical again.

"Not your wedding, is it?" began Andrew, but with a glare she cut him off in mid-sentence by shutting the door almost in his face.

"How odd of her," said Victoria. She was going to make some light remark about Violet's wedding, but Millie's behavior perturbed her. Absently she accepted Andrew's kiss of farewell, frowning as he left the room.

Eight

Violet's wedding cake was exquisite. Bess couldn't make it in the traditional shape for fear someone might ask questions if they saw her icing a three-tiered white and silver confection, so she chose a shape which could be passed off as a birthday cake she was icing for a friend who cooked at a neighboring house. Bess often did such favors in return for bottles of her favorite tipple. This cake was in the shape of a cottage, a whitewashed cottage with a swooping thatched roof and an arch of red roses above the doorway. She had tinted the icing golden to make the straw and mixed a bright blue for the shutters and the front door.

Bess and Myers had managed with considerable intrigue to keep the cake secret even from Violet. They waited until the last minute before leaving for the little church, and when they got there, the service was already under way. Millie, standing beside the bride in her best brown dress prettied up with red ribbons Victoria had lent for the occasion, had turned slightly as they came in, wondering why they were so late. It was not until the procession of laughing well-wishers had trailed from the church and around the corner into Ted's narrow street that she realized why. The white sheet, spread over the table to protect the dishes from the flies was lifted. There among the pink sliced ham and succulent roast beef, the deep tureens of stewed peaches and the pickle saucers, there amongst that royal bounty stood Bess's glistening cake, like a queen among her subjects.

Violet gasped in wonder that so much time had been spent on *her*. "Bess, this must have taken thee days to make," said Violet, overcome.

"I have plenty of time these days," Bess said blandly.

"I can't thank thee for it. It's too grand for thanking," said Violet impulsively and stood up high to plant a kiss on Bess's downy cheek.

"You'd better give me a kiss too, for I helped stir the batter," decided Myers. Swinging her into his arms, he dealt her a thumping kiss.

"Come, everybody, sit thee down!" cried Violet when she recovered her balance.

They needed no further invitation, and soon everybody was jostling elbow to elbow, chattering and eating and laughing and joking and drinking, while Edward Baker, father of the groom, and his tow-haired, blotchy-faced, unmarried son Joe carried jugs of ale to fill the glasses.

Millie had little appetite, for her attention was so fastened on the groom that she had no thought for food. Ted was overweight, narrow-eyed, and slack-jowled, with a complexion almost as florid as his brother's. Shaking her head, Millie wondered how Violet could have turned her back on Master Andrew and married this man, no matter how kind and good he was reputed to be. Master Andrew loved her. She had seen it herself the day he returned from the war. How could he be so blind? Surely he must have guessed that Violet was expecting a baby even if he didn't know about the wedding. Even Millie could see the signs of pregnancy thickening under the pink silk waist.

Violet and her Ted sat at the head of the table with Ted's children, Daisy and the four-year-old, serious-faced Patrick. Violet ate busily and helped the others to more of everything. Mr. Baker kept himself busy dredging up scraps of vulgar advice which he gave Ted in a loud voice so that everybody could benefit from his years of accumulated wisdom in matters of the bedroom. Ted grinned at each new gem, while Violet blushed and looked down at her plate. Millie wondered if poor, deaf Mrs. Baker had any idea of what was being said about her.

Everybody helped to clear away. The dishes were stacked in a tub in the yard and two of the neighbor's big girls were given tuppence each to wash them. All the food was collected and packed into covered dishes and pots to be brought out again as the party wound on into the evening. By now it was midafternoon. The men scraped the chairs back for dancing, and Mr. Baker warmed up his concertina with a lively jig tune. More ale foamed into glasses, more people arrived, and with them the unwashed street children who bunched in the doorway and at the windows, craning for a glimpse of Violet in her pink wedding dress. Soon the cramped little room was packed inside and out. Ted and Violet led the dancing while Joe, heavy with drink set out to ask Millie to partner him but was intercepted by a hand on his arm as his sister claimed him instead.

Daisy tucked a hand in Millie's.

"What do you think of your new mam, then?" asked Millie.

"She's pretty," smiled the big-toothed, skinny and freckled Daisy. Millie hugged her wishing that she could steal her and take her home. A house needed children, and this one could be guaranteed to dispel gloom.

It was hot in the cramped room, and presently the party grew quiet. Someone put the children down for a nap. Someone else fitted a spigot to a new keg of ale. The sun went down and the lamps were lit. Everyone felt tired, damp and sticky. Mr. Baker, Ted, and Joe stood on a bench and sang a song from *The Beggar's Opera*:

> Pretty Polly, say,
> When I was away
> Did your fancy never stray
> To some newer lover?

Millie was sitting opposite Violet, watching her. The room smelled of ale and pipe smoke. Violet gazed steadily at the scuffed, dusty floor. A tear was rolling halfway down her cheek. She dashed her hand absently across her face to wipe the tear away. Then, suddenly, Millie saw her whole face and bearing change. Daisy tugged at her pink silk sash.

"Look, Violet! There's a gentleman!"

The song faded. The whispers hushed.

Andrew was standing in the doorway. Though everybody gaped at him, Andrew saw only one person in that cramped and stuffy room.

"Why didn't you tell me?" he said.

Violet said nothing. Her fingers rubbed convulsively over each other. Nobody but Andrew looked at her. All eyes were on him.

Millie longed to haul him away. Couldn't he see what damage he'd do if Ted and his family suspected the truth? She was relieved to see that they were staring at Andrew with genuine bewilderment plain on their simple faces.

"Why didn't you tell me? Why should I have to hear it from Birdie of all people? She heard Bess and Myers talking in the garden, and she told me not an hour ago. Why did you do it, Violet? Why, after all I promised you?"

"Please, it's too late," cried Millie, jumping to her feet, desperate to stop him before he said more. Violet was doing nothing to help matters herself, merely gazing at him with a sick, helpless look on her face.

Finally, understanding dawned on Ted. He seized Violet's arm and dragged her to her feet. "What's this, then?" he asked in a coarse voice. "What's this toff to you?"

"Violet didn't give proper notice!" invented Millie loudly. "This is the master, and he's angry because she's gone and left them without any help!"

It did no good, for Andrew seemed suicidally bent on getting answers to questions it was fatal to ask. He brushed Ted aside as if he were a beggar and directed himself to Violet. "Why, Violet?" he demanded quietly. "Why go and marry someone else when we mean so much to each other? I've planned everything, everything . . . all because of you."

The baffled pain in his voice enraged Ted, who already felt like a cuckold. On his wedding day! In front of all these witnesses! People would never let him forget it. He placed a fist on Andrew's shoulder.

"Let's be gettin' you out of here," he said.

Then Andrew made a fatal mistake. Shrugging Ted off, he grabbed Violet's shoulders and shook her gently in despair. She looked at him helplessly, her eyes enormous with tears, her mouth trembling.

"Why, Violet?"

Ted clawed at Andrew with a hand on each wrist, pulling him away from Violet. As he tottered backward, momentarily losing his balance, Ted punched him with a crunching thud on the side of the face, flinging him backward on to the floor. The women squealed in horrified delight and picked up their skirts, retreating to the corners of the room like so many mice. All except Millie. She tried to stop Ted, tried to drag his fists away, tried to reason with his deaf determination.

It was Joe who restrained her in the end, to prevent her from being hurt too. But later, when Andrew had been flung like a sack of rubbish into the black alley, nobody stopped Millie from going to help him. Satisfaction had been extracted, and nobody was interested in Andrew's fate.

Millie bathed the blood away from his eyes and nose with a rag which she kept wringing out in warm salt water. Andrew groaned and tried to roll away from her ministrations.

"Leave me be," he said.

"I damned well should!" scolded Millie. "I don't know why I'm 'elpin' you after what you done! Put 'er in a real mess, you 'ave."

"Why did she do it?" Weakly he tried to sit up on the cobblestones. "Why did she run away like that?"

"Because she's 'avin' a baby, that's why! *Your* baby, sir!"

"I don't believe you. She would have told me."

"But she didn't, did she?" said Millie coldly.

Wearily Andrew realized why and came closer to self-hatred than he had ever come before. With a moan he rolled away from Millie and retched his heart out, convulsing in misery.

Her anger turning slowly to pity. Millie waited for him to finish vomiting, wringing the cloth out. Then she pulled Andrew's head into her lap, sponged his mouth and chin again, and said, "Come, Master Andrew. I'll see that you get 'ome safe."

Lord Longworth was waiting in the parlor of the Bolton Street house. Right up to the time when Andrew was sworn in at the inquiry, he had not really believed that the boy would act in such an ungrateful and disloyal manner. Now he cursed himself for not trying harder. He had handled the lad too delicately, had not been forceful enough.

With a much higher price and a freshly marshaled set of arguments, he heard the front door click sharply and waited confidently to begin his last assault on Andrew's will. Scrambling to his feet in mingled horror and dismay, he regarded the dirt-smeared figure that swayed in the doorway. Andrew's face was only just recognizable; at first Lord Longworth had believed him to be some wretch who had burst in off the street.

"My boy! What has happened?"

"I was set upon," said Andrew through split, swelling lips. He flung himself into the moss-velvet chair. "Pour me a whiskey," he muttered.

"I want to assure you that I had no part in this," said Lord Longworth, handing him the glass.

Andrew snorted. "You'd dearly like to have watched it happen, however. Don't deny it."

"I didn't pay to have you beaten," said Lord Longworth, ignoring the truth of Andrew's remarks. "On the contrary. I have come to offer you a two-hundred-and-fifty-thousand-pound dowry for Noelle. I realize now that my first offer was ill-advised and ungenerous."

"That's a lot of money for you to give away," Andrew observed sarcastically.

"On one condition. You marry Noelle before the week is out. I want you to be honeymooning in Florence when the hearing calls you again."

Casually he said, "I prefer Paris, actually."

For a moment Lord Longworth almost lost his cool demeanor, the second time in a matter of minutes. "Then you accept?"

"I may as well," said Andrew bleakly. "There is no reason not to accept you now." For a long time he sat silent, staring into the fire, the glass cradled in both dirty hands against his torn coat. Suddenly he stood and smashed the glass into the fireplace, scattering sparks and coals all over the carpet.

As he left, Lord Longworth could see that Andrew was crying.

Nine

Victoria went alone to Andrew's wedding. As if she were preparing for church, she dressed in her black mourning taffeta with the rows of mother-of-pearl buttons at wrists and neck. She had Millie dress her hair smoothly to go under her stiff black bonnet with the mother-of-pearl buckles at the side to anchor the black satin chin ribbons.

"It's funny, miss," said Millie, her head held to one side. You look better in black than in your pretty dresses. It brings out the color of your skin an' your eyes."

Mrs. Foster did not agree. "What's this, then?" she asked rudely. "It's not Sunday. There's no call for you to go getting up like a witch on a Thursday."

"I'm going to a special church service," said Victoria calmly, pulling on her glossy black gloves and checking her reflection in the mirror near the door. Through the open fanlight came the sound of a carriage rumbling to a stop. That would be Aunt Brownie, punctual as ever. Aware of Mrs. Foster's curiosity, Victoria opened the door and stepped outside. She hurried down the steps and across the pavement. Garth pulled the step down for her.

Miss Manfred and Aunt Brownie sat opposite her, side by side. They too wore black: Miss Manfred in a severely tailored suit with a full, piped skirt and a double-breasted piped jacket; Aunt Brownie in a ruffled, pearl-pinned confection of frothy black lace.

"What did he say?" said Aunt Brownie, leaning forward anxiously. "Was he fearfully cross?"

"I haven't told him," said Victoria. "I didn't have the courage. This morning I was all prepared, but he hurried through his breakfast and left so quickly I didn't have the opportunity."

"He'll find out soon enough," smiled Miss Manfred. "With luck the news will give him apoplexy!"

"Eunice! We're on our way to church!"

"That doesn't stop me from thinking the truth," Miss Manfred said comfortably with a grin at Victoria.

Aunt Brownie broke in. "Your mother is delighted about this wedding," she told Victoria. "It has come like the answer to a prayer. Did you know that Lady Longworth had cut her friendship? Yes, she had, and of course this has mended everything. Lady Longworth came around when she heard the news and the two ladies fell on each other's necks. It was so touching."

They were early at the church. The two older women went on in, but Victoria elected to walk awhile in the grounds. She loved this plain old church. It had weathered humbly and settled its cracked, humped stone floors right into the ground it stood on, looking up toward heaven through thickly leaded stained-glass windows which still glowed richly as faith. The grounds were simply laid out and surrounded by a squat gray stone wall, partly smothered with a creeper which flamed bright red and orange.

Victoria walked slowly amongst the graves and the trees, which dropped brown leaves crisp as bank notes that crunched under her buttoned boots. The air was cold and sharp on her cheeks. Leisurely she walked to the end of the path where the old lych-gate stood among tall fronds of blond autumn grasses. Nobody came this way any more. This roofed gate, which long ago was used to shelter coffins until the vicar came to officiate at the burial, was never needed now that funerals were held in church. Some of the tiles had fallen off and straw poked out, showing where birds had been nesting in the early summer. The little cross on the top of the roof had been broken. Shivering, Victoria turned to go back.

Facing her, Charles Lawrence stood in the middle of the path!

"Hello, princess," he said. "I got your note."

"Did you come to the wedding?"

He shook his head, smiling at her. She was much smaller than he remembered, and even more beautiful, her eyes modestly downcast. "Andrew invited quite a few of us, but I came only to see you. I thought that if I didn't manage a chance to talk to you before the service, the opportunity would come later."

It took an effort at will to raise her eyes to meet his. He was exactly as she remembered him—the merry eyes, the drooping sandy moustache, and the rumpled curls of straw-colored hair. "I was so grateful for your letter," she told him. "I never meant to hurt you, but I had to go ahead with the marriage. I'm glad that you understood why."

"Your family *is* in rather serious straits," he said. "I gather that Andrew is sacrificing himself too. There are all kinds of odd rumors about his bride."

"Noelle will always be a child," Victoria said gently. "She seems to worship Andrew, but I know he doesn't love her. Charles, I don't have the slightest idea what is going on. Only last week Andrew told me that he must oppose Lord Longworth, and he hinted very strongly that it had to do with his being married soon. I *know* he didn't mean Noelle. He had such passionate ideals, such a crusading zest for this inquiry.

And now he's giving it up. I've not seen him since he changed his mind, but I heard that he's been in some sort of a scrap and his face is bruised and beaten. Aunt Brownie told me he looked frightful. You know Lord Longworth, don't you? Do you think he might have set someone onto Andrew? Has he threatened him, do you think? I know such things happen."

Charles took her gloved hands and held them against his jacket front. The trees above them shuddered in the wind, and whirling dry leaves flew in circles.

"Put such thoughts out of your mind," said Charles. "He would never do that. What happened to Andrew was a mischance, that's all. As for the other business, I think that your brother has seen reason."

Frowning at him earnestly, she protested, "But he was so desperate to incriminate Lord Longworth. He hated him for the way he acted in the war."

Sandwiching her hands between his large brown ones, he squeezed them gently, saying, "Andrew *is* doing the right thing. He is only a lieutenant and has a very small voice. He can't change things. This way, staying in the army with Lord Longworth as his patron, he could rise far up in the system. Then, when fighting comes again, he will be in a really strong position to do some good. The things he was railing about will happen again unless there are passionately right-thinking men like Andrew to prevent them. No, princess. Your brother *is* doing the right thing."

She searched his eyes, longing to be convinced but still unable to reconcile Andrew's words of last week with his actions of today. Finally she sighed. The answer would come in time. "Thank you for explaining it to me." She smiled warmly at him, marveling at the way she felt so *right* with him.

"What are you thinking, princess?"

"I'm thinking that I could tell you anything at all, and you would understand. You are the only person I know with whom I feel completely safe. With everybody else I always feel the need to keep something back, hide something of my thoughts. But not with you." The wedding party would have arrived by now. She should be ashamed not to mind that she was going to have to sneak in at the back like a fugitive.

Charles still held her hands, but it was obvious that he wasn't going to kiss her. He could have done so without anybody seeing them, for the trees grew close together here and a rise topped with a cluster of mossy tombstones hid the church door from view. What a hussy I am! she thought, astonished at the intensity of her disappointment. Why else would she keep thinking of that morning inside the park gates if she didn't want him to kiss her again? Hoping that her thoughts didn't show on her face, she glanced quickly away, her cheeks hot.

He was saying, "I want you to tell me honestly, princess. Are you happy being Lady Benchley? Is your life pleasant?"

"I am utterly miserable. More than that, I'm afraid. Lord Benchley doesn't yet know that Andrew has deserted him. They had some scheme to get Lord Longworth's contracts for themselves. Now, with this happening, I fear Lord Benchley will be angry and take the blame out on me."

"You are right to be afraid." He led her to where the trees thinned toward a gray-painted bench. "Now, princess. Do you remember how I once said that if you were married already, I would be plotting to steal you from your husband?"

"And I was shocked."

"Would you be shocked if I told you that I am doing exactly that? Plotting to steal you away?"

She felt suddenly dizzy. He put out an arm to support her. Searching her face, he said, "Are you all right, my dear? Are you quite well?"

"I haven't slept since I heard about Andrew," she confessed, pressing the scented handkerchief to her nostrils and breathing deeply. "And I've been thinking too about you. Since I received your letter, I've been quite agitated, Charles. I don't know whether I'm shocked or not. I love you very much. I should be aghast at telling you that, but I'm not. I was brought up to be a lady, Charles. Do you think me brazen?"

His laughter seemed out of place in the misty surroundings. "Of course you're not brazen. Lovers have a license to act differently, for different standards apply. I'd best let you go now, but first there is something very important I must do."

"Yes, Charles." She hoped it would be a kiss.

"You are to be clear in your mind that this misery of your marriage cannot last much longer. Soon I am going to take you away. I cannot do it yet, because you'd be found and brought back home, but it will be soon. If he is unpleasant to you, keep that in mind. If he hits you, go to your aunt or your mother. I can fetch you from there when the time comes."

"Charles, I don't know *what* to say."

"Don't say anything, then," he said, helping her up. "I love you and I cannot live without you. What you must do now is come to my rooms. I shall expect you at ten thirty on Wednesday. Would that suit you?"

Her eyes snapped wide open as she turned to him in surprise. In her feminine dreaming she had imagined that he might beg her to come and visit him, or might ask politely if she would consider bestowing on him the honor of her company, but never had she pictured so bold and abrupt a summons as this.

"Bring your maid," he said urgently. "She knows where to come, and there is a garden outside where she can sit and keep watch." He tipped her chin up and grinned at her. "I do believe that I *have* shocked you now!" he laughed. "Don't worry, princess. I shall not compromise you." He embraced her lightly and laid his warm cheek against her cool forehead. "I love you," he whispered.

"I love you, too," she said, keeping very still and listening for his heartbeat.

"Until Wednesday then."

A small figure in black, she turned at the top of the rise and looked back. Her face was white in the mist. She looked lovely, vulnerable and lovely. He did not wave or smile, but he remained there on the bench for a long time after she had gone.

There was no reception after the service, but the guests were invited to the Longworths' home to take tea and sandwiches, sherry, cold roast meats and cakes. Victoria rode in the same carriage, crowded now with Albertina and Birdie, both hooped, ruffled, and bursting with things to say. Albertina was almost weeping with indignant rage.

"Mother says that we have to *entertain* Noelle and treat her like a *sister*! I couldn't bear to have a sister like her! She never has anything to say for herself, and she stuffs herself with cakes, leaving none for anybody else! Have you noticed how fat she is?"

"Why should that worry you?" asked Victoria, amused by the strength of the outburst and by the description of mere chubbiness as "fat." From long experience she guessed that something else, something quite different, was bothering her sister.

"When I get married," said Albertina loftily, "I shall have to impress people. And Noelle will ruin things for me, absolutely *ruin*..."

Albertina broke off, staring, as Victoria tipped up her face and broke into merry laughter. The others laughed too.

"I don't see anything to laugh at," grumped Albertina.

"We are laughing at you, dear," said Aunt Brownie quickly, for fear one of her sisters would put it less kindly. "You should be the happiest person in this carriage today. You are young, healthy, beautiful, and quite free, and as if that were not enough, you have another wonderful holiday at Sedgewick Hall to look forward to! Or perhaps that is the problem? Perhaps you feel you must go and yet do not want to? I can help you to decline the invitation if you wish."

"What do you mean, another holiday at Sedgewick Hall?"

"Grace is so absent-minded," soothed Aunt Brownie. "But she has had a lot to worry about lately. Don't tell me she's forgotten to tell you. It's losing Miss Boswell, I fear. Still Andrew will be able to afford to hire a gracious and genteel companion for your mother now. I expect she will be full of her old spirits very soon, don't you think so, Eunice?"

"Oh, definitely," said Miss Manfred.

Victoria was watching Albertina's face with interest. It had transformed completely, softened with the faraway look in her eyes. "I see that there is someone special there," she whispered to her sister.

Albertina started guiltily. "Oh, I hope so," she replied passionately. "Oh, I do hope so!"

"Well, so do I," said Victoria firmly. "We have all been far too unhappy lately. It is time for a change for us all."

"Happiness is vitally important to the human condition," droned Miss Manfred. "Gracious, Beatrice! You really must have a word with Garth. I declare he almost tipped us over at that corner."

The carriage had reached the Longworths'.

Aunt Brownie laid a warning hand on Albertina's wrist. "You will be kind to Noelle, won't you, dear?"

Albertina seemed to have forgotten her outburst. "Of course I will," she said with some surprise.

That afternoon Lord and Lady Longworth left for a weekend at Maidstone, abandoning the house to Andrew and Noelle. After a lengthy dinner the servants withdrew discreetly, as the young couple settled on the high-backed sofa in front of the fire. The evening yawned ahead of them. Andrew tried not to realize that this was the first evening of the rest of his life, and that all of those evenings now belonged to the young lady beside him. Noelle seemed quite at ease, but then this particular evening was probably little different to her than the many others she had spent on this very sofa, the only difference being that Andrew was here now instead of her parents. At the generous curve of her elbow rested a large blue box with a design of pressed wild flowers on the discarded lid. Inside had been packed row upon row of fat white-sugared almonds, but the rows were unraveling as Noelle plucked out the almonds one at a time and crunched them noisily. The sound grated on Andrew's nerves so much that he shuddered. When she offered him one, he rejected it violently.

Andrew had still not recovered from his beating of five days before. To make him presentable for the wedding, Lady Longworth's maid had rubbed his face with grease and dusted it with rice powder, but now the purplish bruises were showing plainly through the eroding mask. The general opinion was that he was fortunate not to have had his noise broken or to have lost his front teeth. All had sympathized with his physical injuries, quite unaware that Andrew barely felt the effects of them now. Even the cracked rib only gave him a twinge now and then, when he moved suddenly and it caught him unawares. But the other hurt was monstrous. Although Andrew nursed a large brandy which Parkinson had set out for him, and although his head was swimming from the wine he had quaffed at dinner, that other pain was as fierce as ever.

What kept the pain at full strength was the fact that he correctly blamed himself for it. Violet had honestly believed that he had lost interest in her; this was the reason she'd been forced to make her decision. She was wrong, of course, but by the time he found out, it was too late. He had married Noelle in a state of wounded shock; now all he could do was hope that he hadn't hurt Violet with his clumsy interference. Only one thought comforted him. Millie had assured him that she'd tell whatever lies she could to save Violet's fate and Ted's face, and that if Violet was in any physical danger, she would come straight to Andrew for help. He reflected bitterly as he stared into the fire that he could now give Violet anything money could buy—now that he was no longer free to love her and she no longer free to accept anything from him. Perhaps he could help her through Millie. She had promised to keep him in touch with what was happening and to give Violet messages from him.

"Would you like an almond, Master Andrew?" asked Noelle again, pressing one damply into his hand.

"No, thank you."

She peered owlishly at his bruised face. "Oh, *poor* Master Andrew!" she exclaimed.

That grated even worse. Every time she had looked at him today (including twice during the service), she had cried out, "Oh, *poor* Master Andrew!"

"I'll cheer you up!" she cried and leaped out of her seat. For a ridiculous moment he thought she was going to sing or dance, the way Birdie did to entertain captive guests, but she fled up the staircase. He heard her satin slippers beating on the floor above before she dashed back down, panting, and thrust a china doll into his arms, bumping his glass and spilling his drink over his moleskin suit.

"This is my best friend!" she cried. "Her name is Ethel. Do you like her?"

Andrew barely glanced at the doll's painted porcelain face. Shoving the thing back into Noelle's lap, he said grudgingly, "I suppose so."

"You don't really like her, do you?" said Noelle.

Andrew was at the dresser by now, replenishing his brandy glass. Noelle twisted around on the sofa, watching him, a hurt expression on her face.

"I don't think you really like Ethel at all, do you?" she called plaintively. When he returned with his drink, she held Ethel out toward him. "Give her a kiss to show her that you like her!"

Andrew, his nerves already frayed, exploded: "Of course I don't like dolls!" he shouted, dashing poor Ethel to the hearth. "I don't like dolls, and I don't like sugared almonds, and most of all I don't like being pestered when I want to be alone!"

But Noelle hardly heard him. At the sound of the ominous crunch she flew to Ethel and picked her up, cradling her like a baby. Her face crumpled, her mouth opened and her eyes screwed up, tears dropping from the corners.

"Oh, my God," he said disgustedly, realizing what he had done. He stood up and put an arm awkwardly about his wife's shoulders. She shrank from his touch, clutching the doll protectively. Ethel's face had cracked and there was a gaping, triangular hole where one eye had been. "We can have her mended," he said.

"She's dead," sobbed Noelle. "Mama told me I must be careful of Ethel because if she broke, she would die, and now you've killed her."

"I'll buy you another." He pulled her unresisting head against his chest. "I shall buy you another doll with prettier eyes and prettier hair, and a much, much prettier smile."

"Will you really? Do you promise?"

"Of course I promise." He took the doll from her grasp and put her high on the top shelf of the mantel, out of sight. "I shall take you out tomorrow and buy you the most beautiful doll to be had anywhere. What do you say to that?"

"Master Andrew," she said shyly, hanging her head. "Can I have a real one? A real, real, doll?"

"What do you mean, a real one?" he asked rather uncomfortably, suspecting what was coming.

Her cheeks shone wet with tears as she smiled eagerly up at him. "You know, Master Andrew! A *real* doll that cries, and moves, and drinks, and makes funny little noises! I saw one once when Aunty Miriam came to visit. She had a real, proper little doll but Mama wouldn't let me touch it. Aunty Miriam said that one day when I grew up properly, I might have one of my own. Can I have a real doll, please? I'll be so careful not to drop it."

He pulled her against him, knowing that she couldn't. He would never be able to touch her in that way. It would be as grotesque as molesting Birdie. Very tenderly he said, "We shall look at all the dolls in all the shops, and then you shall choose. Will that please you?"

She sighed and tucked both arms about his waist. "Oh, Master Andrew, I do love you."

For the first time in five days he smiled.

Ten

Outside Charles Lawrence's apartment was a row of trees, huge trees with full-spreading branches that blocked every window of his rooms. Being late deciduous, the trees were now laden with translucent leaves, pure gold in color. The apartment had south-facing windows, and every scrap of light that reached the windows was first sieved through this delicate gold filter. Inside, the atmosphere was clear amber liquid and now, in the afternoon, every object that met the light was instantly gilded to the tone of rich copper.

Victoria lay in bed and stared up languidly at the slow-moving patterns on the ceiling.

Charles moved drowsily beside her. His hand caressed her hip. The sheets were pulled up to their necks, and underneath their bodies touched smoothly.

"Are you happy, princess?"

She smiled sleepily at him, nuzzling her tumbled glossy hair in the curve of his shoulder. "I don't want to go home," she confessed.

"Soon, princess," he promised. "Soon you won't have to."

"Won't you change your mind and tell me? Where are we going, and when?"

"Let it be a surprise," he said, kissing her forehead.

"I can't help being impatient to know," she sighed. "Oh, I am glad I came. I want to remember every moment of it until I see you again. This has been the most wonderful day since . . . since forever."

"There will be better ones than this. Much better. When we are used to each other and can go about together, and when people call you Mrs. Lawrence . . ."

"Charles! How will you manage that?"

He laughed at himself for letting slip so much of the surprise. "I am being posted abroad soon. And, my princess, I have stated in the applications that I am married, so all preparations for the journey are being made for a married couple."

"But don't they know these things at the army?"

"Why should they? It is nothing to them. As far as all the world knows, once I collect you from that man, you will be my wife. But, princess, will *you* mind the deception?"

"Not really and truly being your wife? No, Charles. After this afternoon I realize a very important thing." She smiled softly at his face, bent close over hers, and with a fingertip traced the fan of crease lines beside his eyes. "I realize that I've been your wife all along. In my soul and my heart I've always belonged to you. I had the misfortune to be made to stand beside the wrong man in church, but that changed nothing. I love you and I am most definitely your wife."

Wordlessly he folded his arms about her and kissed her. As she sank and floated in happiness, she wished that the afternoon would never end.

The day had not started promisingly. Not until yesterday had Lord Benchley found out about Andrew's defection, and then he was made aware of it only through a chance remark. He had come home doubly enraged, not only at Andrew's treacherous behavior, but also because he realized at once that his so-called friends had spent the best part of a week laughing at his expense. After raging at Victoria, to whom the flood of abuse was almost a welcome relief when it finally came, he ordered her to her room and informed her that he did not wish to set eyes on her again until further notice. Mrs. Foster had served her dinner on a tray—a small slice of dry bread, an underdone pork chop, and a glass of milk. All night she worried that Millie was to be kept from her, but it was Millie who brought up the breakfast tray of tea and dry toast.

"Miss, we 'ave to think of some way to get rid of that old cow. Now that 'is lordship is mad, she's runnin' wild. Says it's 'er 'ouse again now, an' about time too. This mornin' when I came out to set up the dinin' room for 'is breakfast, she was in there, pourin' boilin' 'ot water into them pot plants!"

"Oh, no!"

"I'm real sorry, miss, but there was nothin' I could do. When I asked what she thought she was doin', she looked at me with them sour baggy eyes an' said she was givin' them a nice 'ot drink since it were such a perky mornin'. You lost 'em all, miss. These in 'ere are all you 'ave left."

"I could cry. . . . I really could cry! They were doing so well."

"I just 'ope things don't get no worse," said Millie.

"If they do, we shall try not to be discouraged," said Victoria. This seemed an excellent time to firmly remind herself of her considerable blessings. She still had Millie. The five biggest and most feathery pot plants graced her room, safe. Lord Benchley had not beaten her in anger as she had feared he might. And best of all, she had something special to look forward to. At ten thirty this morning Charles would be waiting for her. How could she be unhappy?

They left the very minute Mrs. Foster stepped out for her marketing. Victoria wore her black taffeta, partly because it suited her so well and partly because nobody would give her a second glance in passing. The anonymity of black calmed her mind a little. Before they left the house, they did one last thing to ease their minds. The five pot plants were locked into the dressing room, then the bedroom was also locked. Mrs. Foster wasn't likely to come snooping, but if she had any ideas of that kind, Victoria aimed to block them straight away.

They were quite a few minutes early but Charles was ready and very pleased to see them. "You have spared me two wrinkles and a dozen gray hairs," he joked to Millie, giving her a veal pie and a jug of cider as he showed her the sunny nook in the yard where she could wait in comfort.

"I'm glad you thought of her," said Victoria, impressed. "You have her to thank for my being here. I so doubted the wisdom of coming to see you. She persuaded me in the end."

"She is quite a character," laughed Charles. "Most of the maids I've met are either self-effacing and meek, or standoffish and cold. She's cheeky as a monkey and bright as a bird."

"I'm glad you like her," said Victoria. "You will take her too, won't you?" Hastily, for she could see instantly that he had planned no such thing, she went on, "I just couldn't leave her to Mrs. Foster's tender mercies. She will have to come with us, Charles."

"Of course," and he pulled out a chair at the table for her. "You'll need a companion, and she will do splendidly. I hadn't yet considered the matter, that's all. Now, princess, there are no servants here. You and I are quite alone, but I have luncheon for you. No, I didn't cook it. A fat old dear with chins like dumplings came in and prepared everything. All I have to do is pour water onto tea leaves!"

While he set out the morning tea things, she wandered about his living room, feeling strangely out of place. She examined his pictures (stags in Scotland), his books (Thackeray and Dickens), and his photographs. There were two in frames. One she guessed to be his parents, he with a moustache and muttonchop whiskers, she with an enormous dark hat shading her features. The other photograph was of a full-bearded young man who was so like Charles that she asked him if it was himself, newly returned from the war.

"No," he said, carrying in the teapot and hot-water jug. "That is Derwood."

She set the picture down amongst the books. "Your older brother?"

"Yes. He's the one with the good sense to be born first. Everything will belong to him. I shouldn't mind, but I do mind, dreadfully."

"Why? Because he has more money than you? Surely that doesn't matter?"

"In a way it doesn't. I've learned to appreciate other things, but my life will always be hard because I'm a second son, whereas his, because he's the elder, is going to be always easy. Oh, Derwood is indolent, and cynical, so I shouldn't envy him, but I doubt that I'll ever forgive him for being first."

"He can't help it," she said practically as she poured the tea. "I cannot for the life of me see that it matters."

"You *are* an innocent, aren't you, princess?" he teased. "If I were Derwood, you and I would be married by now. The one reason your father treated me so harshly when I appealed to him was money. Horrid, isn't it? However, it is true."

"Perhaps a law should be passed to declare that wealthy parents can have only one son," she said slyly.

"Perhaps. Oh, you minx! If it is in your mind that you would prefer Derwood to me then I must disappoint you. He is married to a lady who cannot string two consecutive words together without giggling in between them, and they have four bonny boys."

"Alas!" she cried mockingly. "I fear I am too late!"

"Drink your tea," he said sternly.

Their lovemaking happened naturally. They lunched quietly and rather messily on cracked lobster, a deliberate choice of Charles's, as it was impossible to eat cracked lobster and stay formal. With it they drank iced Graves, but only a little. Then they sat together on the tapestry sofa in the golden light and looked at his album of photographs, his family, his nephews, his regiment. Andrew was in some of them. She was able to discuss his souveniers intelligently too, for Andrew had brought back knickknacks from Italy and the Balkans. And then, when they were both feeling warm and pleasantly full, and gorgeously at peace with themselves and each other, Charles took her in his arms.

He treated her with leisurely gentleness, waiting and lulling her when her tense muscles and rigid back betrayed her terror, her memory of what was to come. They didn't speak, as though fearful that with words the spell would break. For him it was an exquisite pleasure he never could have imagined; for her it was wonderful. She marveled that an act which had so revolted her with her husband, could be so beautiful with Charles.

"What is the matter?" he asked from his pillow.

She began to say, "I'm crying because I feel so foolishly happy," but the other words came unbidden: "You've compromised me!"

That made him roar with laughter, which even Millie probably heard from her nook in the garden. Victoria laughed too; it was infectious.

He kissed the tip of her nose. "I shall compromise you again in a minute," he promised.

Eleven

Because her mother and brother were so preoccupied with their own worries, it was to Aunt Brownie and Miss Manfred that Victoria turned in the turbulent days following the news of Andrew's marriage when the house was permeated by Lord Benchley's rage. Her mysterious day out, reported with undisguised glee by Mrs. Foster, had been the spark that set off the explosion of violence. He stormed into her room, dashed all the delicate porcelain ornaments from her dresser, pitched her carefully guarded ferns out of the window and into the street below, and snatched up a pretty afternoon dress from where it lay on a chair, ripping the bodice completely away from the skirt. Victoria cowered on the far side of the bed against the wall, white-faced but determined to be brave, while Millie listened helplessly from downstairs to the crashes and shouts of anger. When it was all over, he forbade her to leave her room.

Millie found her kneeling on the floor, weeping and rocking back and forth over the broken porcelain figures.

"I loved them," she said. "Each one of them meant something to me. Oh, Millie, what shall I do?"

Victoria was not being rhetorical. She had learned very quickly that the best person from whom to seek advice was Millie. Her mind could calculate rapidly, sum up the problem, and invariably propose simple, if unconventional, solutions to

223

most difficulties. This time her answer was based on common sense.

"Write to your auntie, miss, an' I'll take it round sharpish. 'E'll never suspect that you'll do anythin' tonight. I'll be back quick as a wink. It ain't far."

And so it happened that a few days after this, following daily visits to Victoria in her room, Miss Manfred and Aunt Brownie announced openly to Mrs. Foster that they were taking Victoria out with them for the day.

"Lord Benchley won't like it," huffed the housekeeper, drawing herself up like a snake about to strike.

But Miss Manfred could swell to even more imposing proportions. "Lord Benchley is not invited," she snapped, deliberately misunderstanding.

"Lady Benchley is not permitted to leave her room," Mrs. Foster icily informed Aunt Brownie.

Adjusting the buttons on her gloves, Aunt Brownie said sweetly, "Lord Benchley has made a mistake, I fear. He took my niece as a wife, not a prisoner." She smiled at the older woman with all the Christian spirit she could muster and cooed, "Now if you will kindly excuse us, we shall see if Victoria and Millie are ready."

"You're not taking that scamp anywhere!" shouted Mrs. Foster. "There's work to be done here, and that cheeky scamp does little enough as it is. No, she's not going anywhere!"

Aunt Brownie's voice was like honey, and Miss Manfred was grinning broadly, aware that her friend was enjoying this in a most un-Christian way. "There *you* have made a mistake, my dear Mrs. Foster. Millie is Lady Benchley's maid, given to her as a wedding gift by her dear husband. I very much regret that for today you will have to manage as you did before Lord Benchley married!"

Leaving her gaping, the two ladies proceeded up the stairs. Millie met them at the top, scarlet-faced, her apron corners stuffed into her mouth, her eyes bulging with repressed laughter, for she had heard every word.

A few minutes later they were settled in the carriage, churning with excitement, as high-spirited as children on a picnic. Millie smoothed her gray cotton skirts down and jingled the calico bag which held her accumulated wages.

"Me Mam's goin' to be right surprised to see me an' you ladies an' all. An' this money'll please 'er no end! I'm thinkin' she ain't ever seen so much money as this in one 'eap before! But most o' all she'll be perked to see you, miss. I told 'er so much about you, an' she always asks 'ow you are. Now she can see for 'erself."

The carriage jolted into fashionable Regent Street, and Miss Manfred rapped the top of her ebony walking stick on the carriage roof to order Garth to drive carefully. Shoppers thronged the sidewalks. Victoria didn't know which to gasp admiringly over first, the stylish ladies or the shops themselves with their beautiful stone carvings and lacy iron balconies which bracketed and fringed the upstairs windows.

Soon they moved out of the fashionable West End and quite abruptly found themselves in a different part of town. At one point in the road Garth had to rein the horses up sharply to avoid running down a rabbit seller, rocking the ladies violently in their seats and prompting a "Really, Garth" from Aunt Brownie and another rapped message from Miss Manfred. They all heard Garth's mouthful of abuse, but the rabbit seller was quite unperturbed. He grinned and gave a jiggle to the bar on which his rabbits hung by their back feet, making them dance.

Suddenly Victoria felt almost carefree, and her heart gave a queer little skip of excitement. Because she now knew that she could go to her aunt if things were bad, and because there was now a short time limit on her marriage, she realized that she was no longer afraid of Lord Benchley. His rages now seemed like the outbursts of a child, aimless and impotent, for she had the promise of revenge. She was leaving and he suspected nothing. Like all ridiculous figures he loathed being laughed at, and Victoria got grim satisfaction from imagining the roars of laughter he would have to face at the news that his wife had run away. He wouldn't be able to show himself outside the house while the merriment rocked London. And she would be with Charles, away, far away, somewhere safe where Lord Benchley couldn't find her.

Then Millie was pinching her arm and crying triumphantly, "There you are, miss!" She pointed out a young woman with a tray slung from her shoulders by a dark-colored strap. "That be a cress seller, miss! There's 'ow I used to be. I 'ad a 'at just like the one she's got. It's a dandy, ain't it?" And she proudly admired the flat red hat with the stained white ribbons drooping from either side of the sagging brim.

The streets seemed to become dirtier and untidier as they

moved along. There were more street traders now, people selling all manner of wares from ice cream to bootlaces. The streets chimed with their calls, advertising their goods and shouting their prices. People wandered about, making little distinction between footpath and road, for there were fewer horse-drawn vehicles now and more leisurely barrows. Garth was forced, reluctantly, to slow his pace, and Victoria had more opportunity to observe. There was so much to see! In crumbling doorways crouched drab young women with babies and weather-wrinkled old grannies. There seemed to be many more men than women. Dressed in baggy dark trousers and wide belted overshirts, they sat hunched on the curbing stones or lounged against the shopwindow ledges, caps pulled low over their eyes. When Victoria asked why there were so many men, Miss Manfred explained that there were not enough jobs for soldiers returned from the war, and these men had to wait until times improved.

"But what will they do in the meantime?" wondered Victoria.

Aunt Brownie said, "It worries us all. There are soup kitchens in most of these streets where they can get one meal a day. We can keep them from starving, but unfortunately we cannot give them hope."

Miss Manfred smiled indulgently at the look on Victoria's face. "My dear, you must not worry about it. You look exactly as I felt when I first saw conditions like these, but it is no use fretting. What can be done to help is being done, and times will improve."

Aunt Brownie patted Victoria's arm. "Miss Manfred and I hope that you might be interested in helping us with our charity work, dear. I can see that you have sympathy in your heart, and your life at home seems so drab. Good Christian work might give it some purpose and joy."

"It would indeed, Aunt, and I would like that very much," said Victoria with enthusiasm before remembering that she would be of no charitable use while hidden away with Charles in some military outpost, but with the guilty thought came the comforting knowledge that these two dear ladies would never condemn her.

Rubbish carpeted the streets and choked the gutters, but nobody seemed to mind. In fact she saw many people idly poking about in the rubbish as if looking for things worth picking up. Victoria restrained herself from asking what until she saw a gang of youths with rusty tins scraping up what were unmistakably dog droppings.

"That's pure, miss," said Millie obligingly. "They use it to cure leather. Good bit o' money in pure, miss, an' my brothers did right well with it before they got reg'lar work." Millie wrinkled her nose in disgust. "Can you smell the river, miss?"

"Is that what it is?" Victoria had supposed that the combination of rubbish decay was making the smell which dug sourly into her chest. The others were pulling out handkerchiefs so she did the same.

Beatrice offered a bottle of cologne which they sprinkled on folded handkerchiefs to breathe through. The relief was instant and pleasant.

"Funny 'ow when I lived 'ere, I never noticed this smell," remarked Millie. "The river is right over there, see, by the dock gates. That's where me Da works." She pointed to where men swarmed around tall iron railings. "Them's extras, miss. Me Da used to be one of them. The docks take on reg'lar workers an' then if anythin' else wants doin', they 'ire the extra men to do it." She squealed, pointing out Victoria's side now. "Look, miss! There's the bath 'ouse!"

"What might that be?" inquired Victoria.

"The likes of us 'oo live 'ereabouts don't 'ave baths an' such. We goes there to clean up proper. I been there three times, once when me Uncle Jack got married, once when I slipped off the jetty—fishin' we was, an' I went right under water—an' once when I got ready to go with Miss Beatrice. This is me 'ome, round 'ere."

Beatrice and Miss Manfred were obviously well known here. There were hails and cries of "'Ello there, Miss Beatrice! Good day, Miss Eunice!" and several people kept pace with the carriage, talking and laughing, showing broken, decayed teeth. Vendors cheekily urged them to buy new mackerel, cough drops in twists of old newspaper, bunches of turnips, eels cut into chunks with bloody backbones showing at each end, coarsely chopped tobacco, chewing stuff, and elderberry wine to be drunk on the spot from a dirty glass provided for the purpose. Millie seemed to know them all, and she laughingly rejected their wares and called out saucily in return, tossing her plain gray bonnet and screwing up her nose in an impudent reply when they shouted that she was too grand a lady to trade with them now.

Suddenly, above the clatter and the din, came a shout and a cry, followed by a sharply piercing whistle.

"Over 'ere, our Millie! Over 'ere!"

"Oooh, it's Jack an' Sam!" Millie cried in delight. "You'll see 'em in a second, miss!"

Millie's two brothers stood on a flat-topped cart which was heaped with a steep-sided cone of rubbish. The driver, a tall man dressed in a frock coat and top hat, both soiled and shapeless, stood on the seat, jiggling the reins. The boys shouted to him and leaped off the dust cart, racing each other to the carriage, their faces splitting into grins. Victoria knew that the boys were either side of Albertina in age but they seemed smaller even than Birdie. They wore ragged calf-length trousers and women's boots with the toes cut out. Their too large coats seemed familiar, very familiar, and she frowned until she recognized them. Of course! They were Andrew's old hunting-style jackets, discarded years ago, long before he went away to war. The boys stood panting under the carriage window.

"'Ello, Millie. Good mornin', Miss Beatrice, Miss Eunice, . . . ma'am," the last uncertainly, for Victoria's was a new face. "'Ave you come to see our Mam, then? She'll be right pleased to see you. She's been poorly for a week now. Da said if she got any worse, we 'ad to come an' fetch you 'ome."

"Is she real bad then, Sam?"

"Nah," said Jack, stuffing his cap into his torn pocket. "She been worse by far. Yer gettin' to be a fine lady, Sis, ain't she, Sam?"

"Get away," said Millie, pleased, but her voice was sharp with the edge of anxiety. "What's up with our Mam, then?"

"Jes' 'er chest," said Jack. "Jes' poorly. 'Ad us scrubbin' an' cleanin' yesterday."

"Wouldn't 'arm you to scrub yourselfs neither," observed Millie tartly, ashamed that Victoria should see them looking like this instead of handsome and washed, dressed in their Sunday-service best.

When the cart owner called them back, they grinned at their sister. Jack said, "It's off to the dust yard we are now. Anythin' you fancy?"

Millie joined in the spirit of their childhood game. "Bring me back a gold necklace, an' earrings to match!"

"If we cain't find gold, will silver do instead?"

"No, gold or nowt!" she yelled after them. "I'm a grand lady now, remember?"

Almost immediately Garth swung the carriage into a narrow alley, scattering children from their play and sulky dogs from their resting places on the sun-warmed stone. Washing lines heavy with sheets and towels sagged above them as they drove in the shade of the double row of buildings.

"Mary 'Erbet is still keepin' busy," commented Millie.

They stopped in a large courtyard, walled all around by tall buildings so that sunlight fell only on a quarter of it. A group of men played a card game on the ground, marking the score on the wall beside them. Chickens strutted about. The air was thick with the stench of urine and rotting rubbish.

"Mind 'ow you walk," said Garth.

Victoria saw a little boy, squatting earnestly over an open drain. Millie laughed at her horrified face.

"That ain't nowt, miss! Look up there, at that window with the blue curtain. We live up there."

The ladies alighted and followed Millie and her calico bag. Brushing past a cluster of big-eyed children, they entered an open doorway. The passageway was dark, and their feet sounded hollow on the bare floor. They climbed a narrow stairway past two tiny landings and on up to a third. There Millie stopped, pushed open a door, and suddenly they were crowded into the Hamwiths' one-room home.

The cleanliness of the room came as an immediate and refreshing shock. The walls were bare but whitewashed clean, and the skirting boards were pasted over with bits of newspaper. Millie had already told Victoria about this when describing her home. The newspaper was liberally dosed with chemicals to discourage rats from chewing it. Because they took this trouble, their home was rat free, not like others around them. The room boasted one window. Victoria recognized the blue curtain as the skirt of one of her mother's old dresses. Some of the ribboned bodice trimming had been used to make the tiebacks, and more of the same skirt had been used to screen a set of wide shelves below the window.

There were only three items of furniture in this large, white room: an old wooden table of no particular color stood squatly in the center of the bare scrubbed floor, a chair stood near the hearth, and over by the far wall stood an enormous bed, the biggest bed Victoria had ever seen, so big that she guessed correctly that it had been made on the spot. Opposite the window was a fireplace, its embers cold under a black kettle. More shelves, holding household items and jars of foodstuffs, were beside the stove, above a cut-off barrel which had been made into a crude bucket, and which was half-full of water from the pump in the yard. And in the bed, her thin, wasted body barely raising a bump under the brown blankets, was Millie's mother.

Millie leaned over the bed and embraced her mother while Beatrice fussed with the basket, taking things out and putting them on the shelves.

Presently Mrs. Hamwith held white arms out to beckon the others closer, and Millie pulled out little donkey stools from under the bed for them to sit on.

"'Ow kind of you to call," she said in a voice as harsh as her daughter's but much quieter. She looked like Millie too, thought Victoria, bending over the bed to greet her.

"You must be Lady Benchley." The old woman smiled. Like Millie, her teeth were her best feature, strong, white, and even. "You been so kind to Millie, I 'ardly know 'ow to thank you," she said.

"I don't know what I would have done without her," Victoria said frankly. "She always seems to know what to do and her ideas are so sensible that I've come to rely on her judgment."

"Always was a busybody, our Millie," whispered Mrs. Hamwith proudly. "I'm 'appy she puts it to good use."

Then Aunt Brownie took over the conversation. Victoria glanced around the room, trying to fit all the stories, all the anecdotes Millie had recounted into the background. How had they managed in just one room? Where did the boys sleep? Where did Millie sleep when she was home? Surely they didn't all sleep together in one bed? Perhaps there were more beds underneath.

Her thoughts must have been plain on her face, for Mrs. Hamwith suddenly laughed.

"You never been in a place like this afore, 'ave you, dear?" said Mrs. Hamwith kindly.

"No," said Victoria. "You've made it very nice and cozy. How many children have you, Mrs. Hamwith; how many of you live here?"

"Ain't Millie told you? I 'ad thirteen children, I 'ad, but

only two boys an' Millie livin! The rest all died one way an' another. The Lord God is kind to take 'em so young. 'Ard enough tryin' to make do an' feed what's left."

Millie poured tea and added some of Aunt Brownie's sugar and milk to the handleless cups.

Mrs. Hamwith twisted her head to see Beatrice more easily. Beside her near the pillow was a shallow basket overflowing with creamy silk glove segments, backs, palms, gussets, thumb pieces, all waiting to be sewn together.

"It's said that they're goin' to pull this 'ole place down soon. There'll be thousands o' us 'omeless, they say."

"Who said that?" asked Miss Manfred, easing her tightly knotted cravat a trifle.

"Down at the corner, they said it. It's for the railways, they said. Won't be wantin' much more rent, goin' to let us stay free after six months, but what 'appens then? Got to live somewheres."

"Perhaps the railway authorities will find new homes?"

Another laugh, and the wrinkles on her old neck quivered as though they, too, were amused. "Not a likely thing, Miss Eunice."

"Perhaps it won't happen," soothed Beatrice. "It might be only a rumor. You know how these tales spread."

"True ma'am," chirped Millie. "No sense in borrowin' trouble. 'Ere. Sit up an' drink your brew."

Mrs. Hamwith gazed thoughtfully into her cup. "It 'ud be nice to do what them Wilks down the 'all are doin'. Off to New Zealand, they are. Paid the fare, steerage on the *Kitty 'Awk'*, an' off they go in two weeks. Oh, they're too good for owt now, an' all talk 'ereabouts is of nowt else. Jack an' Sam are all for goin', but at twenty pounds the fare, 'oo can scrape it up?"

"It's Tom at the ale 'ouse gets most of the spare from round 'ere," said Millie contemptuously.

"Not from your Da. Not from 'im, 'e don't. 'Ave ter watch Jack an' Sam, though, with one leadin' the other off the path. What do yer know on this 'ere New Zealand, Miss Beatrice?"

"I hear that the land is good, and the air is clean, and that the countryside is rich and beautiful."

"There are chances there for all to do well," said Miss Manfred. "We have speakers at church who have been there and return to tell us about missionary work with the natives."

"My cousin and her husband went there to go farming," said Victoria. "They went because there were no opportunities here to buy a farm of their own."

A pale light shone behind Mrs. Hamwith's eyes, and again Victoria could see how like Millie she was. "What a dream that 'ud be. Trees an' grass an' clean air all round. Still, we've only thirty-five pounds put by an' a long way to go 'afore I can be dreamin' on that."

"Well, mam," said Millie with deceptive casualness. "'Ere's summat to add to it. It's five pounds an' four shillin's—all I got except what I give Miss Beatrice back to pay for me uniform dress an' the other thin's she bought me to start with."

"Oh, Millie love . . ."

The others left, then, for it seemed the only thing to do.

"She seems so ill," remarked Victoria on the stairs.

"She may well die," said Miss Manfred behind her in a voice that sounded like the pronouncement of doom.

Aunt Brownie shushed them both. "Voices carry here, and you may be sure people will be listening to everything we say." But once out in the open again, she said somberly, "Mrs. Hamwith certainly does look worse than I've ever seen her. She shouldn't be left untended from morning til night. I'm glad that Millie will be staying with her." She should be left alone so long."

They waited in the carriage for Millie. This courtyard was where she had played as a child. A young girl in a red skirt was feeding pigeons in a wire cage. She had a cob of maize and was snapping the kernels off, one at a time.

Millie was red-eyed when she returned to say good-bye. Victoria climbed out of the carriage to meet her. Then she climbed back in, alone.

Garth whipped up the horses, and Millie watched them rumble out of the courtyard. Victoria waved, and she waved back. Aunt Brownie took out her cologne bottle.

When they were almost home, Victoria began to realize what she had done.

"He's going to be so *angry!*" she said. "Millie does most of the work around the house. She presses all Lord Benchley's shirts—he used to have to pay a washerwoman before—and she keeps his study tidy. I promised Millie that her wages would be paid just as if she were here! He will never agree to that! Oh, I wish Millie was here to tell me what to do!"

"You are not to worry," said her aunt. "Surely you don't think Eunice and I would drive off and leave you alone, not after virtually kidnapping you this morning?"

"Thank you," breathed Victoria, but though she smiled bravely, both of the ladies sitting opposite noticed her chalk-white face.

Their timing was perfect. As Garth was helping them down from the carriage, Tom Booth turned the landau into the street and Lord Benchley's rounded shoulders and top-hatted head swung into view. The three ladies waited on the footpath to greet him. His eyes narrowed when he saw Victoria, out of her room, blatantly disobeying his orders.

He would deal with her later and show her how angry he could be. For the present he masked his feelings with a polite, if insincere, smile. These two zealous ladies always made him feel uneasy. He had heard the whispers about them, of course, but quite frankly he couldn't bring himself to associate such salaciousness with these two. Being a nonbeliever, and never having committed a completely unselfish act in his life, he couldn't help being awed by women who lived for church and charity.

"Good evening, Lord Benchley," smiled Aunt Beatrice as polite as if he were an out-of-work mill hand. "We wish a word with you."

"Certainly, certainly," he said graciously, ushering them into the parlor and ringing the bell for tea. "Send Millie in with tea for us all, would you please, Mrs. Foster?" he said when the housekeeper appeared.

"The little tramp hasn't bothered coming round to the kitchen, yet!" declared Mrs. Foster angrily, and to Beatrice she said, "I sometimes wonder where you found that little wretch."

Cooly Beatrice replied, "Millie is only sixteen, and I should think that running a house single-handed would be too much for her, capable though she is." To Lord Benchley, who was seated with a whiskey glass, she said, "I'm afraid that Mrs. Foster will have to do without Millie for a week or two, perhaps even longer. We went to see her mother today, and"—she winced as the door slammed indignantly behind the house-keeper—"Mrs. Hamwith is very ill. Eunice and I will go again in a fortnight, and if she's no better, we'll arrange to have her cared for in a little hospital we are running experimentally.

Otherwise, perhaps Millie can stay there until she is properly better? Oh, good!"—for Lord Benchley was gaping wordlessly—"I *knew* that you wouldn't mind, just as I know that you wouldn't mind our taking Victoria with us! She looks so pale and listless we thought a drive might do her good, didn't we, Eunice?"

Victoria did indeed look pale and listless, and she suddenly felt as though she was literally wilting, with all the blood and thoughts and feeling draining from her head and down through her weightless body. Without a sound her eyes closed and she slumped across Miss Manfred's lap.

She awoke to find the room crowded, expanding, contracting, the faces around her looming huge and pale and then shrinking away small and white. Time passed. . . . Nobody was looking at her, they were staring at each other. Their angry words pounded at her ears.

"You've exposed her to some disease, some horrible infection," Lord Benchley was saying.

Aunt Brownie snapped back angrily at him, "I must have heard you say that twenty times in the past half hour, and I am heartily sick of it! The trouble *you* have caused is fathomless! Poor Matthew would never have landed in such a financial mess if you hadn't led him there. Oh, yes, you did, and don't deny it! But you managed to step out of the muck yourself, didn't you? Then you married this poor child, and she has not been at all happy since, so it's plain that you've done nothing to please her or make her life more comfortable."

"It's up to her to make herself comfortable," blustered Lord Benchley.

Victoria closed her eyes, hearing her aunt say, "Yes, with that dragon of a housekeeper circumventing all her orders, treating her with rudeness, killing her pot plants! No, she's not been telling me tales. I can see that they're dead, and they'd not die on their own or from want of care with Victoria looking after them! And look at her family now, out of one house and into another again. No time to settle anywhere!"

"I didn't evict them," he said sulkily. "They deserved to be tossed out, but I didn't do it. They left of their own free will."

"No?" spat Miss Manfred, unaware that Victoria could now hear what was being said. "I suppose it wasn't you who had

234

the water cut off and all the front windows smashed with broken bricks?"

Victoria opened her eyes in horror. Nobody had told her about that. All she knew was that her mother had moved to a lovely little cottage near the large home where Andrew and Noelle would live when they returned from their honeymoon.

Aunt Brownie was saying, "And now you accuse us of making Victoria ill! Really, Lord Benchley, the only infectious disease she has been near is yourself."

"You had better explain that before I have you thrown out," he said halfheartedly, for they knew it was a toothless threat just as he did.

"I mean, sir, that when Dr. Fry arrives, he will confirm what I have suspected all day. Victoria is going to have a baby. I am convinced of it. If she is, then Miss Manfred and myself will move in until you hire another maid and a part-time nurse to look after her! I mean it, sir! I mean it with utter sincerity."

"I believe you," he replied gloomily.

"Oh, look! She is waking up at last," said Aunt Brownie. "Victoria, dear child, the doctor is coming to see you."

Miss Manfred wrote something down on a card from her purse. Handing it to Lord Benchley as if he were a servant, she said, "Send your man to this address, and ask him to bring back these two young ladies. One is a maid, the other will nurse this poor child until she recovers. Both will inform us if you so much as raise your voice to her."

Grumbling, Lord Benchley went to do as he was bidden.

Twelve

Most of the golden leaves had fallen now; the branches were skeletal, the last of the leaves impaled among the twigs like scraps of rag.

Victoria hurried up the steps to Charles's door. He was not expecting her and answered the door himself, dressed in his shirt-sleeves, his hair rumpled, and a bluish tinge on his chin. It did not matter. The look on his face told her he was overwhelmed to see her. He pulled her into the living room which was in careless disorder. Obviously she had interrupted his work, for paper was scattered over the table and the ink bottle stood open on a stand with the wet-nibbed pen beside it. The room smelled of pipe smoke.

She sat on the red tapestry sofa; he knelt at her feet and looked into her face.

"I've been frantic with worry, princess. Four weeks and no word. Have you been ill?"

"In a way, yes." She tried not to smile.

"Are you better now?"

"In a way, yes." Would he guess? She was longing to tell him the secret and see the incredulous joy on his face. Not only was he going to get a wife, but a family was well! She could hardly wait to tell him, but perversely she wanted him to guess that she had marvelous news and coax it out of her. How she would tantalize him, tease him, until he finally managed to wriggle the secret out.

But he didn't notice her ebullient mood, though he was staring at her as if evaluating her condition. "Are you well enough to travel, princess?"

"Oh, Charles, how splendid! Are we going soon?" She clapped her brown-gloved hands together.

"In less than three weeks we will be on our way to India. Captain and Mrs. Lawrence until we reach the ship, and then, my dearest princess, it will be *Major* and Mrs. Lawrence." His eyes sparkled at her. "What do you think of that? I'm not supposed to know, but somebody tipped me off to the news."

"Charles, that's wonderful! You are way above Andrew now! He is still a lieutenant!"

"Not for long," said Charles wryly. "Not with all that money behind him."

"I suppose you are going to tell me that Derwood managed to make the steps to major in half the time you did?"

"He did indeed. So you, princess, must fuss over me and congratulate me twice over, for the news will not rouse much of a cheer at home. My father will say in his gruff voice, 'What took you so long?' and my mother will say, 'How very nice, dear. And what do you think of my new afternoon gown?'" He laughed, and she laughed too, then they kissed and whispered to each other before Victoria pulled away and sat up primly on the sofa with a determined look on her face.

"I have some wonderful news too."

"Oh? And what might that be?"

Her eyes widened and grew large with sparkling excitement.

"Charles, it's marvelous! It's so splendid I can hardly wait for it to happen! Charles, we are going to have a baby! Isn't that wonderful!"

She waited breathlessly for him to shout with joy, to cheer or to laugh, but he did not. His eyes slid from her expectant face to her waistline.

"We can't be," he said. "It's not possible."

She could hardly believe her ears. This was ridiculous! Men were supposed to know everything, and Charles was more ignorant than she! "Of *course* we can have a baby, and we are, Charles, we are! Dr. Fry told me so himself! It's true, I tell you, true! Oh, Charles, isn't it wonderful? I still feel excited and I've known for over three weeks! I've been longing to see you to tell you. Millie is with her sick mother, so I haven't been able to send you a message, so don't be cross with me for not telling you sooner! Oh, Charles, I could die with happiness! There's nothing I want more than to have your baby, and for it to happen right away like that, why, it's a miracle!...Charles, whatever is the matter with you? Please, dearest, don't confess that you loathe children!"

"What exactly did Dr. Fry say?" he asked in a strange, quiet voice.

"He asked me a lot of questions..." She colored, remembering the details. "Then he said that I was going to be a mother, and that it would be in early spring. February, he said. Why, Charles? That won't affect our traveling plans, will it?"

"Don't worry, princess," and he patted her hands. Her face was beginning to acquire a pinched, frightened look. She knew that something serious was the matter.

The pinched look intensified when he handed her a small glass and said, "Drink this. It's brandy. Drink it quickly." As if to set an example, he downed his own with a toss of his head.

Ugly echoes whirled in her mind as she stared suspiciously into the glass. Brandy meant bad news, ghastly news: "Your father had an accident. Your father is dead, dead, dead, dead..."

Charles was urging her very gently, "Drink it, princess."

"You drink it," she handed it back to him. "It seems to me that you have something unpleasant to tell me, and that you're reluctant to do so. Please, you drink it. I won't need it. I *want* to hear what you have to say."

"Very well." He sipped at the glass and set it down on a side table. "You and I, we are not having a baby together. It is you and Lord Benchley who are having the child, Victoria. He is the father, not I."

"Oh, no," and she laughed to show that she knew he was only teasing her with another of his silly jokes. He did not smile in reply, and there was no hint of mischief in his eyes. "It can't be true. It must be your baby. It *has* to be. I hate him, and I love you. Don't you see, Charles?" She shook his hands in a panic, her nails denting the skin on his knuckles. "You *must* see that it is yours, Charles. It *has* to be yours!"

"Princess, feelings have nothing to do with a thing like this."

Helpless tears blinded her. "I refuse to believe it. You just don't want it to be yours, do you?"

"Now stop that," he said angrily, and she did, looking dumbly at him. "We have to face this honestly. It looks as though nobody told you much about babies, but they take nine months from when they first happen until they are ready to be born."

It took her a few minutes to digest that news, then she said hopefully, "But does it really matter, Charles?"

"Not to me," said Charles. "If you already had six children, I would gladly look after them, but it matters to the child if he is a boy. No, let me finish. If this baby is a boy, he will be the heir to the duke of Lanark, isn't that correct? That *is* so, isn't it?"

"Yes, but what difference . . .?"

"A big difference. Do you know what the duke of Lanark will leave him? Enormous estates, a country house that is the envy of all of England, town houses in every town you would want to visit, places in France and Italy, and that is merely all I know about. There is probably much more."

"There is much more." Mother had bored her endlessly with the details in the weeks before the wedding; she felt she could itemize every possession of the duke's worth naming.

"Do you know what your son will inherit if you come with me now? Nothing, Victoria. Absolutely nothing."

"Oh."

"Look, this might not be as bad as it seems. You sit there and I will make us a cup of tea while we think it over."

"Yes, Charles."

When he came back, she was crying. "I don't want the money and the estates, and the town houses," she sobbed as he tried to comfort her. "I just want you, and to be with you. This baby means that you won't take me with you, doesn't it?"

"Now, now, princess..."

"You won't say so outright, but that's what it really means, doesn't it?"

"Young lady, you are going to listen to me, and listen well. Do you understand?"

She nodded, accepting a cup of tea and letting him spoon in the sugar and stir it for her.

"You are going to trust me, and above all be sure in your mind that I love you and intend to have you. No more hysterics and crying. It unsettles me to see you cry, and it won't help the situation."

"Yes, Charles." The hot tea soothed her and she lapped it in quick little gulps.

"You say you don't want the estates and the money, and I believe you, but what about the child? He will be Lord Benchley's son, like it or not, and if you try to cut him out of his due, that is like stealing from him without his consent. He might have a different idea about money. Believe me, princess. You *cannot* do this to your son."

"That means I can't come with you," she said flatly.

"It is quite out of the question." He put his arms around her and crushed her against his chest so that she couldn't see his face. "Once the baby is born, *then* you may come. If it's a girl, you may bring her with you. A girl won't stand to inherit anything, and in that case all the estates go to Lord Benchley's cousin."

"You seem to know a lot about it."

"I found out because I was afraid this would happen before I could get you away."

"You were well prepared."

"Not well prepared enough." There were only a few more months to wait and in his mind he knew that the time would pass swiftly, but he was ill prepared for the disappointment that was seeping through his whole body. "It won't be long, princess, truly it won't."

"I wish I hadn't found out about the baby until we were safely on the ship and out on the ocean!" she exclaimed miserably. "You'd not have been able to send me back then."

"Be thankful you did find out," he said unexpectedly. "A baby grows into a child, then into a man, and that man would have found out the truth and hated and resented us both for all his life."

"Charles," and her fingers toyed with the edges of his silk cravat, "I've just had a horrid thought. If my baby is a boy, won't I be able to bring him with me? You said I could if it's a girl . . ."

"Princess, I'm afraid that if it's a boy, you will have to leave him with Lord Benchley. It's only fair. He will be able to hire a nurse and a governess to look after him. The boy will have the best of care."

"I suppose you're right, but . . ."

"We will have lots of other children, God willing."

"It seems so heartless! I want to keep the baby! How could I be so heartless as to abandon a child like that?"

"Not nearly so heartless as robbing him of his inheritance, I assure you! Look, princess. Most babies in his position have nurses and governesses anyway. My mother certainly didn't bring me up. I hardly knew who she was for the first ten years of my life! . . . You still have doubts, don't you?"

She nodded. "I was so happy when I came here this morning, and now everything seems so dismal."

He sighed and straightened her bonnet for her. "You will have plenty of time to think about it before the baby comes. I shall have to trust you to do what you think is best. Princess, I don't want to persuade you against your will. I'll give you a card with a name and address on it. Keep it safe, and after the baby is born, all you need to do is get in touch with him and he will take care of all the arrangements for you, even send a carriage to collect you when the time comes for the ship to sail. You will come, won't you, even if it is a boy?"

His face, his voice, the whole room seemed to be swimming in a dull sorrow. She burst into tears and flung herself into his arms. They closed like a welcoming harbor around her.

Thirteen

Flurries of snow brushed against the windows and Victoria could see that it was dark outside already, though the afternoon tea things had only just been cleared away. A good log fire leaped cheerfully in the grate and the room glowed soft yellow from the light of four wall lamps, lit an hour before and turned down, to be adjusted as the room darkened. Moving slowly and awkwardly, for she was now heavily pregnant, her figure thick under her fur-trimmed emerald wool robe, Victoria got up from the table where she was busy with the Christmas decorations and moved over to close the curtains.

"Don't do that," said Andrew from behind her. "The carol singers will be along soon. Parsons heard about them from the butler next door, and Noelle is so excited. She doesn't want to miss them, do you, Noelle?"

Noelle looked up from her hassock beside the fire and smiled obediently, though she did not look in the least excited. Victoria had never seen any expression on Noelle's face except utter blankness or a babyish smile, though Andrew said that she did get happy and sad at times.

Faint lights glowed from the other houses in the street and carriage bells jingled as they passed. What a night to be out! Victoria smiled to think of how she'd be sleeping here in Andrew's house in a warm, fire-lit room instead of huddling damply in her own cold bedchamber.

Ever since the doctor confirmed her pregnancy, Lord Benchley had been marvelous to her. He had supplied the maid and nurse Aunt Brownie had demanded, and even kept the maid on after Millie returned from her now recovered mother. This had put Mrs. Foster in a better humor, and though she had still not spoken one pleasant word to Victoria, she was more careful to be respectful, and had finally obeyed her in the matter of the menus. However, her cooking was still atrocious, and Victoria's mouth watered in anticipation of tomorrow's Christmas dinner which Bess was coming over to cook, allowing Andrew's cook, Mrs. Whyte, the day off to spend with her family. Victoria sighed happily. She had so much to look forward to, so much to be thankful for.

Because Lord Benchley didn't celebrate Christmas Day, he had allowed her to come here and spend it with all the people she loved most in the world, except for Charles. Her husband now indulged her in every way he could. This beautiful robe was just one of the "waiting" dresses he had ordered for her, and her dressing room overflowed with the butterfly-bright gowns she'd be able to wear later. And best of all, because he was so concerned for her health, he never came to her room at night. Victoria remembered how, as in a nightmare, she used to lie awake waiting for the thump of his study door and the creaking of the stairs. She would pray desperately that once he was in his room, his door would not open again, lying stiff with terror until the tight, sharp groan of his bedsprings told her that it was safe to go to sleep. Miss Manfred had also said, to jolly her up, that she was safe from "the brute" for a long time after the baby came, news that heightened her spirits even more. She could confidently suppose that she had suffered Lord Benchley for the last time. As soon as the baby was born, she and Millie would be on their way to India—and very probably the baby too.

This was the first problem Millie had been set to unravel on her return, and it was a knotty one even for her, but she had come up with a really clever solution this time. Why not, she suggested, take the boy to the duke of Lanark and tell him the truth? Not the whole truth of course, but enough to impress on him that Lord Benchley was intolerable as a husband and that she could not stay with him. Then she could give the old duke the option of taking the child to rear himself. Millie was sure that the duke would agree to let her keep him, and Victoria felt so optimistic that she ceased praying that the child would be a girl and was content merely to be happy. She smiled at the silently falling snow, thinking that in less than four months she would be with Charles. In four months her life would begin all over again.

Andrew turned to her. "I'm so glad you could come today," he said."

"I wouldn't miss dressing the tree for the world," she replied with a lump in her throat, for Andrew had not been able to hide his unhappiness from her. Andrew was so kind to Noelle; he treated her with unfailing tenderness and courtesy, yet she knew he was suffering torments. Why, she wondered? What had happened to the mysterious marriage plans he had hinted at so joyfully? Since he had already rebuffed her delicate questioning and gentle offer of comfort, she could only give him silent sympathy and hope that soon he would feel better.

"No pain lasts forever," she had said soothingly.

"It does when it's of your own making," he had told her, and she was powerless to answer that.

Absently she saw him turn as the door opened and heard him speak to the butler. The next moment Millie dashed in, snow dripping from her bonnet and dark brown cloak onto the floral carpet. She was gasping and wild-eyed, not at all like Millie.

Victoria started toward her, frowning. "Is Violet all right? Does she need a doctor?"

To her astonishment Millie turned to address an equally astonished Andrew. "She needs 'elp bad, sir. You said to come if she were in trouble, an' this is terrible, Master Andrew. She's callin' for you, an' you must come!"

"Has she had her baby?" urged Victoria.

"Twins, miss. Dear little twin boys they are, an' ever so . . ." She crumpled up and began to sob. "Oh, please, sir, come right quick. She's dyin', Master Andrew. She's dyin' an' 'e won't do nowt to 'elp. Oh, do come on, sir!" She seized his arm. "It ain't far but we 'ave to 'urry!"

Victoria followed them into the front hall. Noelle, lamblike, tagged behind. "Could I send for Dr. Fry? Would that help?"

Millie was helping Andrew with his coat. "I doubt if he'd come out in this weather," he said. "Not to where we're going."

"It's too late fer the doctor, miss. I seen a 'undred babies born an' this one is far too late. Oh, poor Violet! 'Er of all people, an' she never 'armed nobody. It ain't fair for 'er to end up like this!"

Andrew kept his composure with the greatest difficulty. He hadn't expected this for another month, and knowing very little of babies and birthing he didn't know whether or not Millie's alarm was justified. Violet *couldn't* die. If she did, then her sacrifice of their future had all been for nothing. She must not die!

"Send for the doctor, Victoria," he said. "Millie, go with her and tell Parsons what the address is. He knows the district and he can go and give Dr. Fry proper instructions. Go, go . . . do as you're bidden!"

"But we ain't got much time!" argued Millie. "She's dyin', I tell you!"

"Say that once more and I'll slap you scarlet," said Andrew quietly. "Now, go along! I'll wait for you."

Noelle and he were left alone in the hall. She raised her pale green eyes and smiled at him. "A baby! A real baby doll! Oh, she is so lucky!"

"And you are lucky too," Andrew said with a shaking voice, relieved that she had understood only what interested her. "You have as many dolls as you could possibly want." Millie hurried back, and together she and Andrew hastened out into the winter evening.

A cab waited at the curb. Millie had ordered it to wait for her. On the way to Violet's house Millie recounted what had happened.

She had been sent for by Ted's sister, a kind woman who had been forced to interfere constantly in the marriage, for Ted had grown possessive and so suspicious that Violet was virtually kept a prisoner and never allowed anywhere alone. When the pains began the evening before, Violet had tried to hide them from her husband. She had been hoping against hope that the baby would be born at least two or three weeks late so she could pass it off as premature, but instead it was several weeks early. She had been married to Ted barely five months. Toward morning she had been unable to contain her cries, and Ted had guessed the truth at once. He was no fool, and had seen his first wife through two pregnancies. His anger had apparently been dreadful. Arming himself with two sharpened knives and a flintlock pistol, he barricaded the door and refused to let Violet out or anybody in to help her. "Let the bitch die," he had said to all who implored him to be merciful. "Let the bitch die and the cuckoo she's brought with her. I'll not have my house shamed." Millie did not repeat these and other unprintable things to Andrew, but merely told him that Ted had sat listening to her screams and been as deaf to them as to the pleadings of family and neighbors, all of whom liked Violet and admired the way she had so lovingly mothered Ted's two children.

"She was a saint," sobbed Millie. "I loved 'er with all me 'eart. She was so sweet an' kind an' good. She never 'ad a bad thing to say about nobody. Oh, Master Andrew, life ain't fair at all an' God ain't fair if 'E lets 'er die."

"Stop it, for God's sake," said Andrew, aghast at the way Millie spoke of Violet in the past tense. "Tell me, how did you get in?"

"Joe thought to get Ted drunk, an' then get 'im out of the way, but 'is Da said no acause Ted can get real nasty when 'e's 'ad a few."

"I know," said Andrew flatly.

"A'course you do! So that idea was no good. In the end some o' the men thereabouts tied three ladders together an' I climbed up that. So did Meg Tarrant—she's a midwife. Well, Master Andrew, you ain't never seen so much blood. Poor Violet 'ad birthed the babes all by 'erself an' 'er life were just bleedin' away out o' 'er body. It's too late. Even a doctor couldn't 'ave saved 'er. She was such a little thing. One babe would 'ave been too much, but avin' the two . . ."

"She won't die," said Andrew savagely.

Millie opened her mouth to contradict him, but she could see how anguished his face was. Dutifully she said, "I 'ope you're right, sir."

Andrew paid the driver and asked him to wait half an hour, and to direct the doctor in when he arrived. Spurning Millie's urgings that they go around to the alley and up the ladders, Andrew strode inside and up the stairs, pushing through a crowd of silent neighbors. One sought to restrain him. "He's in an ugly mood, sir!"

"So am I!" Andrew shook off the hand without glancing back.

He caught Ted by surprise. Lolling against the upturned table which he had propped against the door to effectively block it, Ted was idly playing with the pistol, pointing it at the wall and sighting his eye along the top ridge. The hair on the back of Andrew's neck bristled and he paused, soft on his feet, waiting his moment. Ted was whistling to himself in the way that some people do when they are artificially manufacturing cheer. Andrew stood back in the shadows and waited. The moment came when Ted turned away slightly to set his sights on something further down the dingy corridor. With a leap and a kick that crunched Ted's hand against the table leg, Andrew sent the gun flying. Then, before Ted could react to the attack, Andrew punched him full in the face.

He had done little more than disarm and stun Ted, for he was soon on his feet snarling oaths, but what he did was enough. At the first sound of battle the narrow passageway filled with men and Ted was overpowered before he had time to recognize the man who had defeated him.

"You cuckolding bastard," he spat.

"And you, sir, may yet be a murderer," said Andrew in disgust. "Lock him up, somebody, will you.—until we are finished here."

He was glad that Millie had prepared him. If she hadn't, he might have wept. Andrew had seen nasty sights in battle,

245

so the warm, bloody stench of that tiny room did not affect his senses. Violet had been cleaned up by Mrs. Tarrant and lay on a high pillow with clean blankets over her. What he saw and understood was terrible. She lay peacefully on the snowy pillowcase, her hair combed, her face sponged, her dark blue eyes turned toward the door and the ruckus behind it. She looked ethereally, unutterably lovely, but her face was thin and pale. She was obviously dying. Had she been in a torment of pain, her face contorted and racked, he would have been able to smother his distress in the covering activity of comforting her, but she looked so beautiful, so tranquil. Andrew knew enough of death to see, even as he paused on the treshold, that a hundred doctors could not save her now.

She smiled at him with the faintest movement of her lips. He knelt beside her and she whispered, "I'm so glad thee came. I knew thee would. I loved thee, Master Andrew. My life was happy because of thee. Will thee promise to think of me sometimes?"

He pressed her pale, lifeless hand to his mouth. "I think of you always. I've never loved any woman but you."

"Don't thee cry. I'm not sad to die. Truly, Andrew, truly! Has thee seen the babies? Ted would have hated them, and been cruel to them. Aye, it's harsh to say so, but it's the truth. Will thee please look after them and love the poor, motherless creatures?"

"They'll have more love than anybody could want."

She smiled, an echo of an old, tender joke between them. "Don't thee spoil them, mind."

The words hit him like a blow. Instantly he was back in his old room and she was with him on the bed, laughing up into his face and chiding him, "Don't thee spoil me, mind!"

"Oh, dear God!" he cried. "Don't go, Violet! Please don't leave me!"

"Thee must be happy," she sighed gently, "for I will be . . ."

She was interrupted by Millie and Mrs. Tarrant, who placed a bundle each into Andrew's arms, so that he had one red face in the crook of each elbow.

Violet smiled at the sight of him gazing bewildered at first one, then the other. Both tiny faces seemed to be regarding him as seriously as he gazed at them. Feelings of love and fear and awe struggled inside him until pride triumphed, and he realized in a wave of exhilaration what it was to be a father.

He glanced up at Violet to tell her, but her eyes were closed. She had gone.

The doctor still had not come. Parsons waited in the carriage outside with the message that Dr. Fry was ill with a serious cold. Someone inside the house had told him he was too late anyway, so he paid the hansom cabdriver and waited for his master. The babies caused him some surprise, and he suggested that Mr. Fielding would be needing a wet nurse, would he not?

"Millie is bringing one to the house within the hour," Andrew said wearily. "Not a word to anyone, Parsons."

"No, sir," said Parsons, with only the slightest rise of his eyebrows. He pulled his hat down over his eyes and dusted the snow off the driver's seat.

At the house Victoria was looking out for him, and she flew to the door anxiously. As he entered with the gray-wrapped infants, Victoria stepped back a pace. Had the world gone mad?

"What are you doing with the babies, Andrew? It's wrong to take babies from their parents! You must return them at once!"

"Violet died," he said calmly. His face was cold and numb.

She backed away further as he made to hand her the babies. "Andrew, you cannot! It is terrible that Violet has died, and all of us will be sorry this thing has happened to her, but what about her husband? Andrew, you are kind, and good, and very protective, but you don't think before you do things! Father used to accuse you of that and it is so true now! You *can't* bring them here! We can't look after them! They will starve! What will their father say? He will come looking for them . . ."

Noelle came through the doorway and stood between Victoria and her brother. Tentatively she put out a trembling hand and touched a red, velvety cheek.

In a voice filled with wonder Noelle said, "Are they both for me?"

"Yes," said Andrew softly. "Will you promise to be very careful with them?"

"Oh, yes!" she breathed. "Real dolls! Two real dolls!"

Andrew explained, "We shall have to hire a nurse to look after them, but you will be able to sit on the sofa and hold them every day when the nurse says you may. Would you like that?"

"Oh, yes!"

Victoria was horrified. She stepped forward to put a stop to this insanity, but something stopped her. Andrew was looking down at the babies with such pride and awe in his face, with such overwhelming love, that it shook the jumble in her mind into a readable pattern.

"They are *yours*, aren't they?" she whispered.

He looked deep into her eyes, paused for a moment holding her gaze, calculating whether or not he could trust her, and said, "Yes, they are mine. I'm all they've got now."

Dumbly she followed her brother into the warm, gaily decorated room and stood near the Christmas tree. Tomorrow afternoon the family would be here to exchange gifts. Already some were stacked up: Aunt Brownie's plainly tied blue-wrapped parcels, and Aunt Penelope's artistically decorated with homemade pictures of angels. What on earth was Andrew going to tell everyone about the babies? Mother would collapse on the spot at the scent of yet another scandal. How was Andrew going to explain this?

He seated Noelle on the sofa, placing one of the tiny babies in her arms. Victoria's heart ached as she watched him, and mingled admiration and pity welled up in her heart. He must have loved Violet very much if she was the mysterious woman he had wanted to marry. And Violet must have loved him equally if she ran off with another man to save Andrew from ruining his life over her. She recalled distinctly how Andrew had come and almost shaken her in his impatience to find out where Millie had gone, where Violet's wedding was to be held. It was the day he had been set upon and beaten, and only then had he agreed to marry Noelle. Poor Andrew! He must have tried to take Violet away and been thrashed by her husband. Well, he was doing right in taking the babies. He could hardly have left them in the care of ruffians.

Noelle looked up at Victoria. For the first time Victoria saw genuine expression in those strangely pale green eyes.

"Isn't young Master Andrew kind to me?" Noelle said joyfully. "I asked him for a real doll and now he's given me one!"

"Two," Andrew corrected her. "It's your birthday tomorrow, remember? Your birthday is always on Christmas day."

"Is it?"

"Yes, it is. So one of these babies is for your birthday, and one is for Christmas."

"That's wonderful," said Victoria. Foolish tears fell down her cheeks.

Noelle sat very still, gazing at the tiny sleeping face. "She's lovely," she crooned.

"*He*," said Andrew gently. He leaned over and kissed his wife very softly on the forehead. "Merry Christmas and happy birthday," he said.

Fourteen

Victoria was up and dressed before anybody else next morning. Carrying her boots, she tiptoed along the corridor and down the stairs.

Millie was prodding the fire when she reached the kitchen.

"Merry Christmas, Millie," she said.

"Oooh, miss, you gave me ever such a start!" cried Millie, turning abruptly with the poker still in her hand. "I was miles away!"

"It's the first Christmas you've spent away from home, isn't it?"

"Yes, miss." After a dismal moment of reflection she brightened up and said, "I'm real glad I'm 'ere, though. I'd not 'ave missed them babies for the world. An' it's fun bein' 'ere, just us in this 'uge big 'ouse."

"Bess and Myers will be here soon, with Mary and Eliza, the new maids. I hope you don't mind Bess being here?" she added slyly.

"Oooh, no, miss! This may be me first Christmas away from 'ome, but it will sure an' certain be the best one! I cain't wait to see what she gives us to eat!"

"I thought you didn't like Bess," said Victoria innocently. "You once called her a cow."

"I wasn't talkin' about 'er cookin'," said Millie stoutly. "If I call Mrs. Foster a cow, I mean *everythin'!* Well, breakfast won't be up to much. I 'ope everybody likes boiled eggs, miss, acause that's all I can do proper. There's chicken, too, for the wet nurse."

"Boiled eggs will be fine, thank you, Millie," said Andrew behind them. He gave Victoria a kiss and said, "You look pretty this morning."

"It's this dress. Albertina gets disgusted with me because I wear this one all the time when I have others to choose from, but I like this one, so why not wear it? Did you sleep well?"

"The boys woke me once, and I went in to check on Hetty. She was awake and feeding them. They look healthy and strong, but I'll have Dr. Fry look them over as soon as his cold is better. He's no gossip, and he *is* the best doctor in London."

"That's true."

Millie set the pot of water to boil and turned to where they sat at the kitchen table. She was frowning. "We'll 'ave to talk about summat, Master Andrew, an' it's best to get it over with."

"Violet's funeral? We'll go, of course," said Victoria.

"Beggin' your pardon, miss, but I think it's best you don't."

"But she was with us for eight years..."

"Ten," said Andrew.

"It wouldn't look right if we stayed away."

"Beggin' your pardon, miss, but it wouldn't look right if you went. Violet wanted the babies looked after, but other than that she didn't want no trouble. Violet's got lots of friends to bury 'er proper, an' I'll go of course, but that Ted.... 'E'll be there, miss, an' e'll be nasty. 'Is Da said for me to ask you all very nicely to keep away. 'E said takin' the babes to bring up, that's the main thing, an' Violet would want it this way."

"I should be there," said Andrew.

"No," said Victoria. "Millie is right. You have the boys to think of now."

"An' a good thing too. Do you know what 'e was going' to do? 'E said 'e'd dash their brains out if 'e got 'is 'ands on them. No, Master Andrew. Violet died 'appy acause of you bein' there, an' them boys will 'elp you no end. I ain't never seen a widower mope if 'e 'ad a son to look to, an' you got two."

The pot began to bubble. Wisps of steam filled the space above the stove. Millie ladled boiling water into a china teapot and then placed a wire basket of eggs into the pot. She sliced bread and laid the slabs on a wire grille to be slipped into a slot above the coals. While they were browning, she set out cups and saucers.

"I'll take some up to Noelle," offered Victoria.

"No," said Andrew. "I'll go and fetch her down. We have to explain everything to her and it might take some time. Last night she was too excited to see reason."

For it had to be a secret today, of course. There was no hope of keeping them hidden for long, but if Andrew broke the news to his relatives individually when he sensed that they were in a receptive mood, the opposition would be overcome gradually. To tell them all today would be a disaster.

Millie listened for his footsteps before saying, "You know, miss, Master Andrew is real kind to Miss Noelle, ain't 'e? I seen the way 'er Ma an' Da treats 'er. They talk like she was a dog or a cat, but Master Andrew, 'e treats 'er like a real person."

"That's right," said Victoria, thinking that if Lady Longworth had not been so ashamed of Noelle and kept her shut away all her life, then the girl might have grown up to be quite different.

"Acourse she's got summat the matter with 'er," said Millie, turning the toast slices. "Anybody can see that in a minute. She ain't right. But there ain't nobody perfect, an' plenty o' people got worse things the matter in their natures."

"I wish Albertina would see it that way," sighed Victoria. "She is so sensitive about her own feelings and so careless of everybody else's. I worry over her at times." She laughed. "I wonder what *she* will say when she finds out about the babies?"

Noelle pouted stubbornly when Andrew and Victoria explained that she must not say anything about the babies.

"Real dolls are special," said Victoria. "We have to wait until they grow bigger before we show them to anybody."

"Can't I just whisper?"

Andrew snorted in exasperation. "No! You must not tell anybody at all about them. Not *anybody*, do you hear me?"

"I want to tell Mummy and Daddy," she said, smiling. "Mummy said I couldn't have a real doll but you gave me one." She frowned, thinking. "Two!" she remembered.

Andrew gave up being kind. "Noelle, if you tell anybody at all about them, I shall take them away and give them back to the shop. No, I won't get you any more, either. Now will you promise to be good?"

She nodded sulkily, reluctantly. It was so mean that she was forbidden to tell anybody, when she was so terribly proud of them!

"If you tell anybody, the dolls will be taken away," said

Victoria. "You *must* be quiet about them."

Noelle began to weep. "I don't know how to *not* tell. I don't know how! I just say things. I don't know how to be quiet!"

"Then I will help you. Andrew and I will stay with you all the time, and if you start to say anything, I will pull your sleeve like this."

Noelle stared at her sleeve uncomprehendingly.

"Let's practice," sighed Victoria. "The others will be here soon."

"Oooooh!" squealed Millie. "I'd better look sharpish an' get this room clear. Bess won't 'alf be cross if she comes an' finds the breakfast things all in a clutter."

Andrew had already lit the fires, a skill he had learned in the war and which he proudly demonstrated now. Fires now blazed in the morning room, parlor, dining room, and in the upstairs bedroom where the babies were being fed by the wet nurse. As Millie carried a tray of food up to her, she heard Andrew welcoming the family at the front door.

"Don't forget," Millie told the wet nurse, "keep that door locked. There's a right imp of a lass comin' today an' we don't want 'er bustin' in! An' keep the babies quiet if you can."

"I never nursed a noisy babe yet," said Hetty with pride as she seized a chicken leg from the tray. "Good, rich milk I got, an' plenty of it."

"I ain't surprised," said Millie dryly, noting the relish with which she ate the food.

The table had been prepared the day before and laid with festive napkins, nuts, sweets, and bonbons. Bess surveyed it critically and had to admit that Mrs. Whyte did have a way with artistic table decorations, there was no denying that. Though Bess grudged giving credit to others, she privately admired the diminutive, feathery Christmas trees which sat in front of each setting, holding the place cards. Mrs. Whyte had fashioned them exquisitely from fir twigs and decorated them with dainty strings of red and yellow glass beads and starry glass flowers.

Before dinner, as everybody sat in the parlor in a state of pleasantly hungry anticipation, Aunt Penelope read from Charlotte's letters. The story of their New Zealand venture ran through them like an unbroken thread.

"Isn't that exciting?" said Victoria when she had finished. "Charlotte is so clever! I never imagined that she would have the talent to bake a dozen loaves of bread at a time, or wash clothes in a kettle over an open fire. What a fine, healthy life she must be leading!"

"It sounds horrible," declared Albertina ungraciously. "*All* of it sounds horrible. An uncomfortable, endless journey and primitive conditions."

"We had much worse conditions in the war," Andrew said. "No, Albertina, you are too pampered to understand what life is all about. When you have a husband and family of your own, you will appreciate challenges, satisfactions and all the better qualities of life."

"Well spoken," applauded John Fielding.

"Nothing that I ever say is right!" Albertina flung at them. "Nobody cares what I think!"

"Of course we do," said Victoria.

"It's all very fine for you, *Lady* Benchley," she said bitterly. "You've got everything you want."

"I don't understand her," said Grace helplessly as the door banged shut behind her prettiest daughter. "Yesterday she received a beautiful pendant necklace from that wealthy young American she met at Victoria's wedding. Oh, I do know it is not proper for her to accept such a thing usually.... It was frightfully expensive, an enormous sapphire! But with the necklace came the most beautiful card, with a charming note proposing marriage!"

"Oh, my dear, how splendid!" cried Alice Longworth.

"I think so too," said Grace. "But the child is behaving so oddly about the whole thing."

"Shut her in her room," said Alice positively, nodding at Grace. "Shut her up until she sees reason."

Penelope looked shocked, and Miss Manfred said, "What a lot of *fuss* about nothing. If the child doesn't want to marry this gentleman, leave her be. Far too much unhappiness is caused by forced marriages."

Hear, hear! cheered Victoria silently.

Grace glared at Miss Manfred, who returned the look with a jolly smile.

"If he is so rich, she should be persuaded..." said Alice. "Wilton, won't you help? Poor Grace has no man to call on for advice."

"She has me," said Andrew quietly.

Lord Longworth's aristocratic lip curled expressively. He

would never forgive Andrew for his day in court. Although nothing damning was said, the clear intent was there. Lord Longworth would never forget that Andrew had defected for one reason only, money. Someone who could be bought could not be trusted. The two were incompatible.

"She should marry in wealth and repent in luxury," he drawled.

Then Myers swung open the double doors and announced that luncheon was served.

Bess had surpassed even the delicacies she had prepared for the wedding breakfast. Ecstatic over the challenge of an unlimited budget, she had spent weeks planning for this meal, then tasted and seasoned until she could rest, satisfied that she had created a masterpiece.

Throughout the leisurely meal and the crossfire of conversation that went on all the way through each course, Noelle was a constant source of unease to Andrew and Victoria, sitting on either side of her, they had to be on guard every time she began to speak. But all went smoothly, to their vast relief.

When everybody had gone home laden with gifts and good cheer, Victoria and Andrew sat on either side of the fire surrounded by the cheerful debris of the afternoon. The babies had been looked at, and Noelle, sighing with contentment, had been put to bed too. Brother and sister were alone in the silent room sipping strong coffee from the black winter pot which sat near the grate to keep hot. Victoria's baby kicked under her ribs. She smoothed her emerald dress and remarked, "I'm looking forward to being a mother myself now. Your two have inspired me. They are lovely babies, Andrew."

"Which do you want, a boy or a girl?"

She considered. "A girl. Less complications."

"Someone once said wisely that it was always best to want a girl, for if it turned out to be a boy, there was never any disappointment."

"What a *masculine* thing to say!"

Andrew laughed. "Wasn't Flounce funny with the snowballs?"

"He's like that everytime it snows. What about the way he howled when Noelle wound up her music box! She thought it was so funny she kept doing it to tease him and make him howl louder."

"I wasn't so amused. Flounce's howl reminded me too much of the timber wolves we used to hear way back in the mountains. I rather think that Noelle's pretty music box might be mysteriously lost whenever Flounce is here with young Birdie."

"I was worried that the babies might start screaming."

"They have been marvelously good, haven't they?"

"You sound like the stereotype of a proud father. No, seriously, I agree with you. And Millie said they were quite exceptionally good babies. I'm so happy to be able to be here with you for a whole week and help you get settled with them. Isn't Lord Benchley thoughtful to go off and let me stay here until New Years? And won't Millie's family be surprised to see her? You know, I thought it was kind of Bess to make up that hamper for her to take. She never liked Millie, not from the first. Even now she doesn't, which makes her gesture doubly generous."

"Generous, nothing!" snorted Andrew, filling her cup again. "Bess and Myers both were so overwhelmed to receive that case of brandy instead of the bottle each they've had other years, they'd have given Millie almost anything she asked for. She knew it and that's why she asked."

"A whole case of brandy was a lot, Andrew. I saw Mother's eyebrows go up, and Aunt Penelope looked shocked too."

"They deserve it. Bess and Myers stood by us when I know for a fact that they were getting offers almost every day for better wages elsewhere.

If I had brains like Bess and Myers, and organizing ability, I'd be in business for myself and a millionaire in no time." He sighed. "As it is, I'm afraid I have no great potential in any direction. Still a lieutenant, and not a shining one at that."

"Father used to say you had the heart and the right ideas but you never seemed quite able to marshal your energies in the most efficient way."

"That's putting it politely! I'm a bungler, Victoria."

"Oh, surely not!"

"I am. Not in big things but in lots of little ways. Quite enough to give my superiors an impression of hopeless ineptitude! But I care about my men, my fellows, and I chafe to improve things."

"You should use all the influence you can to get on, up above the petty level, so then you can help to improve all the conditions that have made you feel so bitter! As a lieutenant you have a small voice, but as you go up the ranks, your voice will carry more power."

"Exactly!" He stared at her curiously. "I thought you knew nothing about the army and cared even less?"

"That must be Albertina." She smiled at him wickedly. "One hears things here and there."

"Obviously!"

"So you're remaining in the army?"

He nodded. "We could be posted abroad soon."

"*No*! I hope not."

"It's only one of those vague, fluffy rumors that take months to verify."

"I want you to be here when you become an uncle. It's the least you could do since I've so obligingly become an auntie twice for you!"

"You've been marvelous."

"I approve, you know. All the way along. Everything you've done. Everything."

"After what's happened to you, that means more than I can tell you. But, oh—I shall regret Violet for the rest of my life. There's nobody to blame but me. That's what makes it all so hideous. I won't ever forget her."

"She wouldn't want you to," said Victoria gently, standing behind his chair with her hands on his shoulders. "She'd want you to remember her, but not in any guilty way. You have to stop blaming yourself. Millie said that Violet would have died anyway, doctor or no doctor. That would still have happened even if you'd been married to her. This way she felt that she did something to help you. The other way, if she'd let you take her away, she'd have died believing that she had turned you from the family right when they needed you most. If you had married Violet, she would be just as gone now, but what sort of life would the boys have had? Look what you can do for them now! And for Noelle! Andrew, you have altered her whole life. Noelle has already changed so much since you married her."

"I've impressed on her that there are certain things we don't say and do in public, and she's learning," he said dryly, toying with his coffee spoon.

Victoria sat down again, facing him earnestly. "They kept

her shut away all this time, and all she needed was to be a wife."

"She's not a wife," said Andrew slowly. "Not in the real sense. I couldn't do that to her."

Victoria stared at the graying coals, knowing there was no need to voice further approval.

"She needs protecting, and I like that. One of the things I liked most about Violet was her vulnerability. I always sought to protect her. When I was away, I never even wrote to her for fear the letter would find its way into Bess's pocket. She would have had Violet dismissed, and I wasn't willing to risk it. I'd have done anything to look after her, and I suppose that's why it's so difficult remembering."

"You made it all better in the end."

"She smiled when she saw me holding the boys. That's what I was doing when she died. It was the last thing she saw." He looked at his sister in quiet amazement. "I can talk about her already and not break down."

"It's those boys, you know. Now you have *three* people to protect." She glanced up quizzically. "I was idly gazing around the table today wondering what the different ones will say when they find out."

"I'm glad you know already. You will be the one I feared most."

"Why?"

"After my speech about duty to you. There wasn't any other way for our family, but I felt so wretched later, especially as all along I was indulging my own happiness. I could imagine what you would think of me when all this came to light."

"Oh, *Andrew!* You spend far too much time feeling guilty about things you can't change. It is so needless! Millie has been giving me instruction in this very thing. She says to think very carefully first, then do what is best *for you* and not worry any more. *All* the thinking must come first."

"I shall have to have some long talks with that philosophical young monkey. At least she approves of the babies."

"So will Aunt Brownie and Miss Manfred, though Miss Manfred is a wee bit well . . . snobbish about servants. She likes them in their place. In fact, I don't think you should tell anybody the truth. Aunt Penelope will love the babies, and when you tell Uncle John that you adopted them because you can't have your own, he will support you too."

"Mother had better not object! I'm keeping her in very splendid style. And even if nobody will call on her, she's having a most delightful time with dressmakers and milliners."

"What about the girls?" asked Victoria.

Andrew laughed. "They can worry about that, for I'll be damned before I shall. It's Lord Longworth who worries me. You've seen him make cruel fun of Noelle, criticizing her, ignoring her when she's trying to tell him things . . . For all that, he likes to pretend she's normal. I was with him one evening recently at the club when someone made a slighting remark about Noelle. Lord Longworth nearly had a seizure and we were asked to leave by one of the waiters. It was embarrassing, but it told me a lot about our elegant Wilton. *He* will be extremely sensitive about the babies."

"Surely Noelle's feelings will count for something?"

"He doesn't even *like* her. I rather think that he was more pleased to be rid of her than he was to remove the danger of my testimony. *Both* of us were a source of potential embarrassment to him. Our elegant Wilton does not like to be embarrassed."

"Then let him worry about it," said Victoria. "You shouldn't. Noelle certainly won't and I shan't. *I* intend to be as happy as I can."

"What a good idea," said Andrew. "Is it another of Millie's?"

"I do have some ideas of my own," said Victoria, pretending to be offended. "It's late. Will you light my way up the stairs please, dear brother? Now I have the truly delicious problem of how to spend your Christmas gift."

"It was nothing."

"Two hundred and fifty pounds and you say it was nothing! Andrew, it was manna from heaven!"

"I was going to buy you something, but then it occurred to me that Lord Benchley probably doesn't give you much of a cash allowance."

Later, before she went to sleep, Victoria decided that it was probably the best Christmas ever. Her heart was full at the prospect of a brave new year.

Part Four

Spring Again

One

Tom Booth sat up on the hard leather carriage seat with his toes scrunched into knots in his boots and his fists plunged deep into his pockets. With all his might he wished it didn't take women so long to have babies. If it were not for Lady Benchley's condition, he would be at home now relaxing near the kitchen stove with his pipe lit, a mug of hot cocoa warming his hands, and a plate of cheese biscuits ready to eat. He was hungry now, and thirsty, and cold. How long was the master going to be?

Lord Benchley was inside some grubby whore's room doing what a man must do. When the master was wed, it was an enormous relief for Tom to be able to stop these degrading missions, but he had been pleased too soon. Since Lady Benchley had taken to her room, the master had reverted to his bachelor habits, and twice a week Tom had to drive him to the seedier streets off the West End, find someone no older than thirteen who would suit, bring her to the carriage to be inspected, and then wait an interminable time for his master's return.

Tom bunched his damp collar higher around his neck. With irritated boredom, he watched the traffic pass, carriages moving slowly with lanterns swinging from the harnesses, an occasional horseback rider holding a lamp on high as he ambled along, and a few pedestrians with their firebrands. How much longer was Lord Benchley going to be?

He had decided that something must be wrong when two faces swam up out of the haze and a scrap of card was thrust into his hand. "Do this 'ere belong to your master?" said a man, his dark face urgent.

Tom held the card near the bracketed carriage lamp. It was one of Lord Benchley's calling cards. "What 'as happened to 'im?" he asked.

Looking closer, he saw the girl he had found earlier. Eleven or so she was, just the kind the master liked best with a pale face and dark hair. She was clinging to the man's arm, crying with low, long moans as she cringed half behind him.

"You'd best come wi' me," said the man. "Your master be ill. Summat weird, real weird."

Tom trusted nobody east of Regent Street. He gave the man the lamp to carry in order to free his hand to bring the iron pipe as he followed a safe pace and a half behind. The girl moaned like a ghost trying to haunt him. Tom hated them both.

Later, when Mrs. Foster questioned him about the room, Tom was sorry that he had not noticed much in the way of detail. It stank unpleasantly of sour ale and mildew. The walls were coated with peeling, brown newspaper, and old sacks hung at the window. Tom had noticed these things as he cautiously entered the room, but what he mainly saw was the enormous body which lay like a beached whale on the sagging iron bed. He had never seen his master with less than his underclothing on before, and Tom was fascinated with a sort of crawling revulsion. The whole of the body was covered with a thick dusting of short black hairs.

The girl began to scream. "'E were all right," she said. "'E were all right, an' then 'e just went all over queer. It was nothing I done."

Tom turned back to the bed. His master lay on his stomach

with one hand flung over the edge of the filthy mattress as though reaching for something on the floor. The skin on his body was paper-white, but his face was distinctly blue. Grasping the shoulder nearest him, Tom tried to roll Lord Benchley over onto his back, but only succeeded in raising him a few inches before he fell back down again. The outflung hand knocked against Tom's shins.

Looking in helpless disgust, Tom thought how pathetically sordid the whole thing was. How could Lord Benchley bring himself to even walk into a room like this, he who was so fastidiously clean in his own person? The girl clung crying to the man. . . . Her brother? Her father? Tom felt ill.

"You will 'ave to 'elp me dress 'im and take 'im to the carriage," he said resignedly. "I need to get 'im to 'is doctor quickly."

"But 'e's dead, aint 'e?" said the pimp. "We thought . . ."

"'E's not dead," said Tom, for a split moment wishing that he was. "Stupid bloody fool that 'e is. 'E's 'ad a seizure, that's all, more's the pity."

Two

The Fieldings' position in society had always been tenuous at best. In the Clarence Street days it had promised to firm and develop into something solid, thanks largely to the patronage of the Longworths. Too, Matthew Fielding was fast earning himself a reputation as a shrewd and flamboyant businessman. Besides, they were a likable couple, eager to please and genuinely friendly. They also set what was undoubtedly the best table in the whole of London. Their star was rising in the society firmament.

But Matthew's death changed the whole picture. The cause of his death was unpardonable. Adultery was winked at, desertion was a source of merriment, murder was discreetly ignored (if the murderer could get away with it), stealing (from those less fortunate) was tolerated, and gambling, whoring, and cockfighting were tacitly encouraged. But apart from insulting Her Majesty, there was only one real crime, and that was to lose one's money.

Though Lady Longworth loyally tried to smooth their path

once the mourning period was over, it was no use. Grace and her family had become a rather pathetic embarrassment. Nobody called and nobody sent cards. Victoria was unable to help. It had been expected that she would lead a glittering social life accompanying Lord Benchley to the royal galas, the important balls, and the dinners to which he was always invited, in his capacity as heir to the duke of Lanark, but none of this eventuated. It was not Lord Benchley's fault. Just before the three-month mourning period ended, Victoria found that she was pregnant, and of course no pregnant lady danced at the balls or twirled a parasol at garden parties. As time went by, Grace began to accept that her dreams had died and the people she had once called friends would never be friends again.

Grace didn't know it but she was spared a great deal of nastiness. Because she never heard the accusations that were whispered all over town, they couldn't hurt her. Rumors abounded: Matthew had sold Victoria to Lord Benchley. He had been keeping a mistress in a town house near the Mall, and the extravagance of this young lady was what had bankrupted him. He had not committed suicide at all but had been killed by a jealous husband who had discovered evidence of an affair. There was no way these vicious lies could have reached Grace because the only person who could have told her was Lady Longworth. But Lady Longworth, while she loved gossip and was malicious to the point of bitchiness, would never tell friends unpleasant things about themselves. Grace also held to that precept. When Albertina returned from Sedgewick Hall in tears over unkind things which had been said about Noelle, Grace kept silent.

This mutual respect only stretched far enough to cover immediate family, however, and it was with gleeful undertones that Lady Longworth told Grace all about the scandal and disgrace which had come about because Lord Benchley had the stupidity to suffer a heart attack while lying stark naked in the arms of a child prostitute.

"Everybody is so consumed with sympathy for Victoria," she assured Grace. "It reflects no ill on her, of course. On the contrary, the general feeling is that a man with such coarse appetites would have been better to die while he was about it and make the poor girl a widow! They say that the duke of Lanark is disgusted, especially when Victoria is so close to her time. The shock could have harmed her irreparably. The old duke has sent an extremely stern letter of reprimand to Lord Benchley, I believe."

If so, Lord Benchley was unable to read it. The heart attack had been so serious that Dr. Fry, sent for by Victoria when she was not satisfied with her husband's doctor's bumbling indecision, ordered that Lord Benchley have complete bed rest, no access to business papers or letters of any kind, and be kept in semidarkness. Mrs. Foster nursed him constantly, and another cook was hired to run the house. Victoria felt sorry for him; not knowing what had really happened, she believed him to have had an accident while out on business, but she kept out of his way, for her time was close.

Less than a fortnight after Lord Benchley's mishap, and in the very early hours of the morning, Victoria's son was born. The labor was brief and merciful. When it was over and the child had been washed and dressed in a soft flannel gown, Victoria was well enough to sit propped up with a tumbled heap of pillows and nurse him. As she cuddled him against her breast, she knew that, no matter what had happened to her during the past months, this moment made all of the pain and unhappiness shrink away to nothing. He was perfect. She marveled over the delicate translucence of his nails and the wonder in his slate-gray eyes that went in and out of focus. The helpless grasping movements of his hands fascinated her, and the endearingly odd shapes he made with his mouth. Too excited to sleep, she played with him, supporting him on a pillow so her arm wouldn't go numb. She blew at his wispy blond hair and held a finger in the palm of his hand until his fingers closed around it in a surprisingly firm grip for someone only a few hours old. But as soon as the tiny face bunched into a scowl, she held him against her shoulder, gently rubbing his back the way Millie showed her.

Millie was as peacock proud as if the baby had been hers. From the moment Victoria rang for her when the pains started, she had not left her side except to send Tom Booth scurrying for Dr. Fry. The doctor had ministered to Victoria with a capable but most unwelcome female assistant, for he liked to make his own decisions and Millie tactlessly and cheerfully told him that there would be no complications, that the baby would be born within the half hour, and that all the stages of birthing were proceeding in the correct order. She was right. When she had tidied up and taken the soiled linen to be burned, she sat on a chair beside the bed holding a fresh cup of tea for Victoria and offering welcome advice on the feeding.

She was every bit as hurt and disappointed as Victoria when Grace and Lady Longworth called late that afternoon to see the baby and barely looked at him. After a few conventional remarks and speculations on whether he looked like his mother, they settled down to the real reason for the visit.

"We don't know what to do," flapped Grace, looking distressed.

Alice Longworth's purple bonnet quivered in righteous indignation as she struggled to compose herself. "Your brother has completely taken leave of his senses," she said.

Somewhat annoyed at their perfunctory attentions to her baby, Victoria said cooly, "Are you referring to the adoption?"

Lady Longworth flared. "So you know about it?"

"How did *you* discover it?" smiled Victoria. She rarely said anything which caused such a start of astonishment, and she found the feeling agreeable.

"We simply don't know what to do," cried Grace, "This morning when we called to tell Andrew about your baby, Noelle was at home alone, and..."

"And she showed you the babies."

"Noelle told us that Andrew gave them to her for Christmas! What an utterly preposterous notion!"

"Only one was for Christmas, Lady Longworth. The other was for her brithday."

"But it is scandalous!" flustered Grace. "Poor Noelle didn't know where they had come from, but Alice and I could tell by one glance at that revolting wet nurse! They are slum children, aren't they? Oh, imagine, slum children being brought up as Fieldings!"

Even if she had been free to tell these two anxious mothers the truth, Victoria would not have done so. It was too amusing to see their panic and horror over something which mattered not at all. The real issue seemed to have been so completely overlooked that it might as well not have existed.

"But Noelle wanted a baby so much," said Victoria. "You must have been aware of that. She was always asking Andrew to give her one."

Grace gasped and Lady Longworth crimsoned. She almost choked as she said, "Then he should have given her one of her own. There is no physical reason why she cannot have children.

265

Andrew is being quite outrageous taking babies in off the street, when those same children will inherit from us! How dare he do that without our consent!"

Victoria could see that there was little she could do to improve this woman's outlook, but she said gently, "If you say anything to Andrew, Lady Longworth, please consider your daughter. She loves those babies and it would break her heart to lose them." Then, because it was teetering on her tongue to tell this woman a few home truths about Noelle, she turned to her mother, changing the subject with determination. "How is Albertina? Has she made a decision yet about the proposal?"

Grace sighed and looked even more worried. She pulled at a loose thread in Victoria's cream lace bedcover and then brushed the thread off her pale blue gloves, the same shade as her new woolen gown. "I wonder if she would listen to you, Victoria? She has always envied your life as a married lady and said how she longed to be married too. This young man of hers is quite captivating, wouldn't you say so, Alice?"

"Once the initial impression of his ill looks is overcome," agreed Lady Longworth in vinegary tones. "Of course he does have that certain crassness which unfortunately plagues all Americans, but he is undoubtedly very rich, and that should count for everything."

Victoria smiled, saying, "I shall talk to her."

Albertina came to visit a week later, reluctantly, as if she knew what was planned and suspected that her sister was going to deliver a lecture. Victoria covered her shoulder with a fine white shawl to hide little Mattie while he fed, for he was pulling at her nipple with a suddenly firm and hungry mouth. Always he dragged at her until he was full, then the tugs became weaker and further apart until they stopped altogether and he fell asleep with the nipple in his mouth.

Albertina held him while Victoria buttoned her pink silk nightdress up to the lacy collar. Staring down at the tightly wrapped bundle, she observed, "He's got a much redder face than the other two babies."

"They are almost eight weeks older," Victoria said. "And what do *you* think of them?"

Albertina shrugged. "I don't care what Andrew does, now that he's married to that creature. Do you know what she's calling them? Andrew let her decide!"

"I don't know what she's calling them. I've not seen him

for some time... Please Albertina, do ask him to call. It's quite all right if he does. Lord Benchley is still so ill that he sleeps most of the time. He doesn't even know about Mattie yet."

Albertina sighed with annoyance. "Nobody ever lets me finish anything I want to say."

"Sorry! Have the babies been named, then?"

"I started to tell you! She has called them Abraham and Isaac, of all things! Isn't that dreadful? If Andrew was stupid enough to bring brats in from the slums, he should at least have given them sensible names like you did. It's lovely that you're naming him after Father. Noelle isn't capable of naming a puppy!"

"At least they are not family names. If she'd called them Andrew and Wilton, Lord Longworth would have had apoplexy!"

"He had it anyway," said Albertina. "Mother says that in all the years she has known him, she's never seen him so angry as when he found out."

"Poor Andrew."

"It's his own fault," pouted her sister. "What a stupid thing to do."

Victoria sighed. She might as well talk to any of them in Chinese as try to offer sane comments on the situation. They were all determined that Andrew had done something dreadful. What if they knew the truth!

"And what about you?" Victoria asked. "Are you going to marry this wealthy American?"

Albertina's pretty mouth went sharply down at the corners and she said plaintively, "I sometimes think I just may do that, just so Mother will cease badgering me about it!"

"What is the problem?"

"There isn't one. I just don't want to marry him. Oh, I suppose I like him well enough, even if he is ugly and rather boring at times. You would like him too, I think. He's very kind, but I don't want to *marry* him!"

"Then don't."

"If only it were so simple! I'd like to marry someone dashing and romantic, someone like Captain Lawrence! He would have been splendid, but I suppose the scandal chased him away, too."

"Have there been others?"

But Albertina only shrugged. The shame of that evening was fading, and she had no interest in refreshing it by confiding the details. "I shall have to make up my mind soon, I suppose. It is awful being dependent on Andrew and Noelle, for Mother makes us go and visit them twice a week!"

"Is that really so bad? Noelle has changed. Those babies will do her good."

"I suppose she is improving but Andrew is so *soppy* over her that it makes me sick to watch him."

Albertina would never change, thought Victoria. When she was a little girl, she couldn't bear to see anybody else getting love or attention, and when she became an old woman, no doubt she would be the same. "Please don't begrudge her Andrew's attention," she said gently. "He is only being kind to her."

"I don't begrudge her anything," protested Albertina indignantly. "I just don't like Noelle, and I hate having to see her all the time. Now that there's all this row about the babies, it is simply intolerable. It makes me think I might marry Francis and go to New York. He said that Mother and Birdie could come too, and they like that idea. Mother will never be accepted again here, you know. She could have a fresh start over there."

"Albertina, I must warn you," said Victoria slowly. "Don't marry this man unless you really care for him. If you think he is ugly and boring now, then you will find his company much worse when you are married to him, for you will have to endure..." Despite her brave ambitions to tell Albertina the mysterious facts about marriage, she was unable to finish. Instead she said, "You would do better to endure Noelle twice a week rather than marry someone who irritated you all the time."

"I suppose you're right," said Albertina, frowning. "Oh, I do wish somebody interesting would come along. I wonder what happened to Captain Lawrence."

Andrew could have answered that question more accurately than Victoria, but Albertina never thought of asking him, for every time she saw her brother, Noelle was also there, and whenever she was in Noelle's presence, all she could think of was how much she disliked her. How, she often wondered, out of all the girls in London, could Andrew have brought himself to choose *her*! But the next time she saw Andrew, she passed on Victoria's message.

"I was coming to see you anyway," Andrew told Victoria as he bent to kiss her soon afterward. She was up now and dressed in a loose yellow robe with long, flowing sleeves trimmed with black braid. He sat on the sofa opposite while she rang the bell twice.

"So that Millie will know it's for her," she said in reply to his quizzical glance. "What brings you, then, if it isn't my request to see you?"

Millie entered and was dispatched to fetch the baby. "I must warn you that *lots* of compliments are in order," she said, satisfied to leave her first question unanswered for the moment. "Mother and Lady Longworth barely looked at him, they were so aghast about yours. They've made up for it since, of course, and are most attentive. Lady Longworth gave him a silver rattle and Mother brings baby clothes and toys every time she comes! As for Birdie . . . If I don't take care, young Mattie will be the most spoiled child in London!"

"While mine are ignored," said Andrew, adding quickly, "That is not bitterness. It might be different if they knew the babies were mine. Mother would be different anyway, but I'm not going to tell her. It's not worth the risk."

"I agree!"

"Acceptance may take some time, but soon it will matter very little that Lord Longworth is making life intolerable for me."

"Is he?"

"Most certainly. He wants me to give the babies away now, before their existence becomes common knowledge. He's even found a shopkeeper in Yarmouth who is willing to adopt them and give them a good life, so I won't have to suffer any conscience pangs about 'throwing them back into the gutter,' as he puts it. As I found with Lord Benchley, once a man has given you money, he thinks he has put a bridle on you."

"He won't give up easily either."

"Oh, no, not our elegant Wilton. He is at our house every day telling Noelle that she *must* give them up. Now, when she sees him enter the room, she begins to cry and runs upstairs to shut herself in the nursery. I can't even begin to tell you how difficult this is. I can't even have him thrown out because it *is* his house!"

"You were right about him having no concern for Noelle, then. That poor child! How insecure she must be feeling, fear-ing that her father is going to take the babies away."

"She has nightmares every night. I have to go to her at least twice, trying to calm her. I've tried appealing to him, but all he will say is that when I give in, he will stop his persuasion. Do you remember the rumor that my regiment is being posted abroad?"

"Yes, I do."

"Well, it's not, but I have arranged a transfer and with it will be becoming a captain!"

"How wonderful!"

"Not when you hear the rest. I'm off to New Zealand to join the Sixty-sixth there."

"New Zealand! Oh, Andrew!"

"Don't look so stricken. It won't be forever, and it really is the only thing for me to do. The boys will get a good start in life without any taint of unsavory gossip . . . And we *do* have family there in Charlotte and Martin. I've examined some maps and they don't look like being too far away from Auckland. I imagine they trade there for the things they need."

"What does Lord Longworth think?"

"He doesn't know, and he'll be furious, of course, but when he really thinks about it, he is certain to change heart. This way he'll be completely rid of Noelle, and people do forget, you know. Besides, he has worries of his own. He is on full suspension until the inquiry is over, which means he can't do a thing officially to stop us from going. And Noelle's dowry is safe. He can't take any of it back."

"New Zealand," said Victoria, smiling at him. "Just think of it! Pour me a sherry, will you, dear? This needs a toast." She glanced toward the door. "Ah, here he is!" For Millie had entered with Mattie. "What do you think, Millie? Andrew is going to New Zealand!"

"It's a secret," said Andrew, alarmed.

"Don't worry," soothed Victoria.

Millie's thin face brightened. "Me Mam an' Da say there ain't no place they'd like better to go than New Zealand. Me Mam's been savin' since I don't know when for 'em all to go."

"Is that right?" said Andrew politely.

"Come on, Uncle!" coaxed Victoria. "It is time for you to excel yourself with flowery compliments. Your nephew is waiting to be praised."

"With pleasure," said Andrew, setting the sherry glasses

down beside her. "What a bonny fellow young Mattie is. He'll probably be a fine big lad when I next see him."

"Why? You're not going so soon, surely?"

"I was speaking figuratively. We shall be leaving in four weeks and two days on the *Princess Mary*. A comfortable ship, I believe—and fervently hope!" He laughed. "I detest sailing and am a poor sailor, I'm afraid. It is to be hoped that Noelle fares better, for someone must look after the babies. There is plenty of room left on board, which surprised me. Apparently it was block-booked for a party from Yorkshire and many of them were stricken with that dreadful yellow fever. I'm rather hoping Mother and the girls will agree to come, too."

"What a splendid idea!"

He joggled Mattie on his knee, laughingly ignoring Victoria's protests that he was too young for rough horseplay. "Never too young for that, are we, lad?"

"Do you think Mother and the girls will go with you?"

He grinned wickedly. "Albertina will leap at it when I tell her what I discovered this morning! The Sixty-sixth is on transfer from India and you'll never guess who is with them!"

Victoria could, but she silently sipped her drink and tried to appear inscrutable.

"Major Charles Lawrence!"

"What a coincidence!"

"He will be surprised to see me."

"Indeed!"

"So, I think I shall use him for bait to encourage our recalcitrant sister. She needs the change of scene just as Mother does, and I'm of the firm opinion that after a long sea voyage, when she is forced into Noelle's company a lot, she will change that poor opinion of her."

"She is certain to . . . But Andrew, it might be rather cruel to use Captain Lawrence for a lure. He could be married by now."

"*Major* Lawrence, please! And *Captain* Fielding too!"

"Very well *Captain* Fielding! . . . Andrew, would you please do me a favor, apart from being kind to Albertina, of course? Nana came to see me yesterday, and she looks so old and ill that you would barely recognize her. If I give you her address, will you please get in touch with her and offer to take her with you? That man she married only courted her because he wanted a free governess for his children. Oh, she didn't complain to me, you know Nana wouldn't do that, but I could see how unhappy she is. She loves babies, and you need a governess, and I think she would welcome a chance to escape...She doesn't owe him anything....Do you know she had over three hundred pounds saved and he took it all? She was saying that she would love a holiday but had no money...Oh, please..."

"Enough, enough!" he cried in mock alarm. "Of course I'll rescue the old dragon. I might even tell her our secret. Nana keeps better secrets than anybody I've ever met, and if there is spice, danger, and intrigue, she's sure to agree to come!"

"And *don't* tease her by telling her what Charlotte said in her latest letter, about the dozens of gentlemen who wait for the ships to come in, hoping to find a wife. She will have rather a sour view of marriage now."

"That's hardly surprising," said Andrew. "I had a feeling about that marriage, and if I'd tried, I could have stopped her. But I didn't try because we needed the saving of her wages."

Victoria held out her arms for the baby, who had gone to sleep in Andrew's arms. "Remember what I told you about self-reproach?" she whispered. "It's pointless! Besides, you have the chance to make it up to Nana." With one gentle fingertip she brushed the velvety cream cheek. "I wonder what name he will be christened with?"

"I thought it was to be Matthew?"

"No, that's only what *I* shall call him. Didn't Mother tell you? Millie and I are off to Lanarkshire on Friday. He will be christened there..."

Three

The duke of Lanark had been flattered and pleased that Victoria was bringing the child to him to be christened and sent a comfortable brougham and two footmen to escort her. The journey to Lanarkshire was a tedious day's traveling, but with considerations for the baby it was divided into three brief stages with overnight rests at respectable country inns in between.

Spring was gentle on the land. Daffodils were scattered in thick swatches like carelessly flung gold coins, bluebells raged rampant in the woods, looking like fallen scraps of summer sky, and deep pink creepers blushed at them from hedgerows as they passed by along the rain-damped cobbled roads. Victoria leaned from the carriage windows to gaze at the flower-starred apple and peach trees, bridal and glistening pink and white in the early sun. Her heart ached. Never before had she considered her feelings for England. It was a place she had never really expected to leave, but now the prospect of going away for an interminable time loomed close. Looked at from this proximity, it seemed more of a threat than an adventure. From Charlotte's descriptions she knew that New Zealand had an untamed nature, where wild, dark trees clambered down steep slopes right to the water's edge, a place all evergreen so that the seasons had no touch upon the land. Flowers were scarce and then only white. Her cousin had written home begging for daffodil bulbs, for seeds of pansy, stock, wallflower, peony, petunia and "any kind of wildflower" that could be gathered for seeding. For the moment all the plus considerations fled Victoria's mind, and she bleakly considered the cheerless prospects of living in a flowerless land. Already she anticipated the lonely pangs of homesickness.

As they bumped and jolted along, her hand frequently stole into the cradle. Her fingers would touch the soft cheek, or follow the curl of a downy gold lock of hair, or fasten gently around an already chubby wrist. What if she had to give him up? On this point Victoria had been optimistic since Millie first proposed that they go to the duke; she had not seriously considered the possibility of refusal until she was confiding her plans to Aunt Brownie. Both she and Miss Manfred agreed emphatically that Victoria must offer the child to the duke, but neither seemed confident that he would let her keep Mattie. They pointed out that if she became a widow, she could remarry. "You will have other children, dear" was the refrain they repeated, until it seemed like the chorus of a well-known song, and utterly comfortless. She had not told Millie this, but if it meant giving up the baby, she might well change her mind and remain in London. Charles did not need her so intensely as the child; he was grown up, far away, and would find someone else to marry (though the thought made her feel ill). Mattie was a helpless baby who needed his mother. With all the protectiveness in her generous soul she understood Andrew and what motivated him. Before, she had considered his actions to be a vague tangle of impulsive ideas. Now she could see that the same thread of caring traced through everything he did . . . his concern for his fellow soldiers, his longing to make a home for Violet, his deep tenderness toward the babies, and his protective attitude toward Noelle. If he were in her place, would he be able to go away and leave Mattie? Life in London would be drab, but there would be a few compensations. Lord Benchley would never be able to visit her in her bedroom again. Miss Manfred had assured her of that with a coarse laugh and the comment that "his capering days are over, thank the Lord," saying that one child was enough for anybody to cope with.

Millie, sitting jauntily erect opposite her mistress, could see that she was depressed and tried to cheer her up.

Millie twisted one of her green sash ribbons between long, bony hands, looping it and smoothing it in her flouncy-muslin green and lemon lap, and tried to think of something else to say. Despite the sunshine and the green shawl about her shoulders, she was shivering, for this afternoon they would be meeting the duke. Millie had resolved that for such an important occasion nothing would do but her beautiful new Christmas dress. Victoria had tried to dissuade her by pointing out that it had been meant as a morning room dress, or for summery afternoons, and today they would be exposed to chilling Lanarkshire winds and the icy breath of early evening frost. But Millie couldn't wait to wear it. She had tried the dress on a dozen times and had visited it on the peg behind her door on a hundred other wistful occasions as if marveling that it had been actually made for her. It was an extravagance on Victoria's part, for when she bought the fabric and had it made, it cost almost every shilling of the four pounds still remaining in her purse. But it was a purchase she had enjoyed making, if only for the creative satisfaction in choosing a material in a color to suit Millie's features, and a style to minimize and soften her angular figure. It had a ruffled bodice, a gracefully swathed skirt, and puffed sleeves to hide the scrawny arms. Millie still had the look of a wading bird about her; no dress could disguise the beaky face and roundly staring eyes. But she now had an air of feminine prettiness and a glowing pride in herself, which showed in the way she pertly peered out at the world from under the brim of her new green bonnet.

"Two an' a 'alf days travelin', an' to think I used to fancy it a long journey from me 'ome to Clarence Street! I really am gettin' a good look at the world!"

Victoria nodded tiredly and closed her eyes.

"'An' just fancy us goin' all the way to New Zealand an' takin' five months to do it! You know, miss, I cain't even start to think of what it'll be like! I wonder if Miss Beatrice 'as been to see me folks yet an' told 'em they're comin' on the *Princess Mary* with us? Oh, miss, I don't know 'ow to thank you for what you've done. Miss Beatrice told me that you saved me Mam's life, acause she'd not live out another winter stayin' 'ere. I wish I could 'a been there to see 'er face. It's goin' to make it 'appier for me to 'ave them there."

Victoria smiled. "Please, Millie, let me rest for a while. If you see any more hayricks or ploughs or scythes, or anything else that interests you, remember where they are and ask me about them on the way home. I'm sure Aunt Brownie has been to see your parents. She was as excited about the idea as we are."

For Nana was not the only person who enjoyed intrigues. Aunt Brownie and Miss Manfred snatched up Victoria's plans and from then on they were no longer hers. This was a welcome relief to her, for she was exhausted with postnatal weariness, and Millie was of no assistance with the practical details of their escape, for she knew nothing of shipping offices, tickets, or luggage. At first Aunt Brownie had been somewhat doubtful of the scheme, but Miss Manfred was for it at once.

"You are magnificent!" she had roared, heedless of the laughtears that dribbled over her pitted cheeks. "To think that all these years I've thought of you as a meek, quiet little thing, and here you cooked up this marvelous idea all on your own!"

"Not quite on my own...", said Victoria hesitantly. She had resolved that nobody but Millie must even suspect Charles's influence behind this. To be fleeing from an unhappy marriage was one thing and acceptable, but to be rushing to the arms of a lover was quite another—and decidedly *un*acceptable.

Her guilt about unwittingly using these two kind ladies intensified when Aunt Brownie said with sweet approval, "How very thoughtful it is of you to go on the same ship as Andrew! Noelle truly loves you and will be much happier when she knows that you are going too."

"Please don't tell anybody," begged Victoria in alarm. "I

shall tell Nana, to help persuade her to go as the twins' governess, but nobody else, not Andrew or Noelle—not even Mother."

"Why not, dear? Grace and the girls are shilly-shallying back and forth. Even though Andrew has reserved cabins for them, I doubt if they will decide firmly until the last minute. Bess and Myers are surprisingly keen to go, but the others change their minds from hour to hour. If you confided your plans, it would settle the matter for them."

"I *couldn't* tell Mother!" protested Victoria. "You both know what she is like. Secrets seem to burn her tongue and she *has* to spit them out. If we told her, then it would be only a few days before Mrs. Foster or Tom Booth heard of it, and though Lord Benchley is ill, he is quite capable of confining me to my room and hiring men to stand guard outside the door. I would love it if Mother and the girls came too, but you must see that I cannot be the one to persuade them. Now, you are to swear that you won't even hint to them about this!"

"You are quite right," sighed Aunt Brownie. "We shall try to tactfully help make up their minds for them, and not a word about you will enter into the persuasions. Grace would like to go to New York, but Albertina is set against marrying this Mr. Blake, and the harder Grace tries to sway her, the more obstinately she refuses. I rather think they *will* be on the *Princess Mary* when it sails."

"And won't they be surprised!" boomed Miss Manfred, her jolly face shining with enjoyment at the prospect. "They will think that you are there to say good-bye, and when the ship pulls out into the river behind the tug, there you will be, standing at the rail beside them!"

Miss Manfred reveled in the details of the plot. She dragged Aunt Brownie to the shipping office and reserved steerage space for the Hamwiths and a first-class cabin for Mrs. Forsyth, widow, and her companion Miss Peale, gleefully noting over the clerk's shoulder that the cabin was next to a double, connecting cabin for Mr. and Mrs. Andrew Fielding and governess. All the tickets were paid for with Victoria's Christmas present from Andrew. Miss Manfred solved the luggage problem too. For this journey to Lanarkshire Victoria and Millie packed all their belongings, half of which were stowed in trunks furtively smuggled to them by Miss Manfred. These were dropped off at the beginning of this journey, to be labeled

"Mrs. Forsyth" and "Miss Peale" and delivered to the ship.

The actual escape promised to be fun for it involved sneaking out right under Mrs. Foster's nose, a prospect which gave Victoria as much satisfaction as firing the bullying woman. Millie was sure it would be easy. Mrs. Foster was so devotedly nursing Lord Benchley that Millie declared they could have cleared the whole house of furniture without her noticing anything amiss.

"You know, miss," Millie had reflected, "I don't think they'll even miss *us* when we've gone. All them two really need is each other. 'E don't need no wife an' she don't want owt else to do but fuss over 'im. 'Ave you noticed 'ow she whispers to 'im for hours at a time in there? An' 'e don't care owt for the babe neither, so you don't need to fret on takin' 'im from 'is father, that's for sure!"

But all of that rested with the duke.

Millie saw the castle first. It was in the late afternoon when the setting sun slanted in across Victoria's black lap making the taffeta shine like coal. Millie had quietly lowered the carriage blind to shade her face while she slept, nodding in the slow rocking of the carriage. It was impossible for Millie to sleep. She had no secret worries to tire her, and more than a thousand wonderful things to see. But of everything she had exclaimed over during the last three days, Lanark Castle was the most exciting by far. The sight of it caught her with a shaft of delight.

"Oooh, miss, I'm sorry to wake you," she said ruefully as Victoria jerked awake, her eyes opening in fright.

"What on earth is the matter, Millie?"

"It's the castle, miss. Look!"

They were cresting a hill and descending a long pale ribbon of road cut out of the grassy, rock-patched hillside leading to a wide, shadowed valley. Across from them was another long rib of hills, lit gold and standing cleanly against the sky. And there, directly opposite, sitting astride the hill like a crown, was a fairy-tale castle with turrets, high crenellated walls, cone-peaked towers, tall slits of windows clear and black, and a huge, arched gateway that seemed to reach halfway up the sloping walls.

"Oh, Millie!" Instinctively she reached for her baby, staring at him in disbelief. Suddenly the phrase "heir to the duke of

Lanark" took on a real and awesome meaning.

There was nothing in the least awesome about the duke, however. He hustled out to meet them when the carriage clattered into the yard. his square, rimless glasses magnifying the pleasure in his eyes. A smile was wrapped from one side of his fluffy-whiskered face to the other. Victoria remembered him only vaguely from the wedding, but enough to know from his dome-shaped head and gingery fringe of hair that this was the duke himself and not a butler. He helped them down, elbowing the footmen aside, and insisted on carrying the cradle up the steep stone steps on his own.

He was the soul of kindness, insisting that they wash and sleep before dinner, leaving Mattie in the care of a maid so that they could rest fully. But Victoria's heart sank as he showed them to the stairs with the words. "I have been in this world for long enough to guess that there is another reason you are here besides the obvious one. I would like to know it this evening, please."

Aunt Brownie was right, she thought, as she trudged miserably up the endless mahogany staircase. The duke will never agree. Nor, despite his friendly kindness, will he even be able to sympathize with me.

Millie was saying, as she shut the door behind them in the cavernous room they had been given, "Ain't this the strangest place, miss! All these rooms an' only 'im to use them! Did you notice all the furniture with them covers over them? An' the dust an' cobwebs everywhere?"

"Loosen my stays, please, Millie," Victoria said dejectedly. "I must sleep so that I can think clearly."

An hour later she awoke refreshed but with a tightness in her breasts that warned her Mattie would be feeling hungry. Leaving Millie dozing on the other enormous four-poster bed, she buttoned her dress over the loosely tied corset, smoothed her hair, and repinned her hairnet, splashed some icy water over her face, and crept downstairs. On the way she noticed what Millie had mentioned earlier and she had been too depressed to notice. She passed room after room filled with shrouded, dusty furniture. Every room seemed like the one they had been given, vast, richly carpeted, with ornate plaster ceiling decorations and heavy chandeliers, beautiful but unused and therefore useless. Downstairs it was the same—even to the odd detail of the doors being left open so that each ghostly room could be seen clearly. It was indeed a strange place. Perhaps, filled with people and servants, with dogs underfoot and children romping in the hallways, with the curtains flung wide to let in the sunshine, and the chime of harpsichord music floating high above talk and laughter, perhaps then it would be a magnificent house. But with only one man living here and the rooms all hushed, it seemed sad, like an elaborate mausoleum waiting for the one coffin to rest in it.

Mattie was being hugged by the little maidservant. She gave Victoria a friendly grin and said that she had just dried the baby and dressed him in clean clothes from the supply in the basket.

"'E's real 'ungry, me lady," she said. "'E were tryin' to suck me front. I 'ope you don't mind but I dipped me finger in 'oney an' give 'im that to quiet 'im down."

"That's very kind of you," said Victoria, and she settled by the fire to feed him while the maidservant bowed out, drawing the doors closed behind her. When Mattie was content again, she wrapped him in a white shawl and checked her appearance carefully in the mirror above the mantel.

She found the duke in the library across the hall. He was seated at a broad leather-topped desk with a spread of clutter around him, but when he saw her hesitating at the open doorway, he rose from his chair and beckoned her in.

A brace of wing chairs stood at either side of the fire and he waved her into one, taking the other himself and putting Mattie on his knee. The baby waved his arms, clenching and unclenching his fists. The duke smiled at him.

"This is an odd moment for me."

There was a long silence. Victoria was not at all sure what he meant by that remark, so to make a conversational path to what they must discuss, she said, "What work are you engaged in here, my lord?"

"Ah!" he said. "Ah! You might well ask!" There was another silence before he continued, "I, my dear, am engaged in translation. When I was a young man, I was fervently religious. Fervently! I made pilgrimages to the Holy Land. I have stood on the site of the stable and on the hill of Golgotha!"

"Why, that is most impressive," said Victoria.

The pale eyes gleamed behind his square glasses. "I learned Hebrew . . . studied it for years, then studied it in ancient and ever more ancient forms."

"I had heard you were a respected scholar," said Victoria politely after another long silence when she thought that some comment might be expected from her.

"All these books are in Hebrew. All!"

She could hardly believe that, for as her eyes roamed the room, hundreds upon hundreds of book spines met her gaze. Then she saw that he was pointing to a glass cupboard beside the fire which held perhaps two hundred volumes.

"Are they really?"

"I, my dear, since you were so kind as to ask, am engaged on my life's work, a work which has turned me from a fervent religious devotee to a skeptical unbeliever."

"Oh, my lord, what do you mean?" for she began to wonder in a tiny corner of her mind if the duke of Lanark was perhaps weak in his mind. He couldn't be senile, for he seemed younger and sprightlier by far than her husband, despite the few years' edge he had on him.

"I'm serious, my dear," he said, joggling Mattie gently on his knee. "My life's work is to translate early editions of the Scriptures. Now, you would consider that to be an ideal occupation for a religious gentleman such as myself, would you not? Of course! But ah, you might well be wrong! The more I read, and the longer I work at it, the more visible is the mind of man behind these words of God. As is the hand of man who wrote them down."

"If you have come to such an opinion, why do you not cease work on the translation? Surely it is harmful to become cynical?"

"Not *cynical*, my dear. Merely skeptical, and to be skeptical is to be healthy in mind. I would not have it otherwise. Take youself, my dear. If I were merely a foolish old man, I would think, 'How very pleasant! This young lady is honoring me with a visit!' But because I am a *skeptical* old man, I think, 'How very pleasant! This young woman is honoring me with a visit *for a purpose*!' Do you see the difference?"

"I do, and of course you are correct, my lord." There seemed little point in delaying things. He was looking at her kindly, his domed head gleaming like a polished apple and the gingery hair glinting in the firelight. Taking a deep breath and looking bravely at him, she said, "I came hoping to take leave of you, my lord. I am bitterly unhappy with your nephew. It is no fault of his, but we are so unalike in age and nature that I am desperately lonely in his house. Now my family is all emigrating to New Zealand, and I wish to go with them. If it were not for the boy, I would go without your leave, but if he is to be your heir, then you must take the responsibility of deciding what I must do. I was going to offer to give him to you to bring up as your son, but I cannot do that. I love him too much to be parted from him. I want desperately to go with my family, but if you feel it would be wrong of me to leave my husband, then I will respect your wishes."

"My dear!" he cried in agitation. "You cannot give me a decision like this to make! I am a scholar, not a Solomon! How would I know what is the right thing for the boy?"

"Sir, I cannot take him away if it would jeopardize his chances of being your heir . . . Not for myself, for please understand I want nothing at all from you, but Mattie has a breathtaking future as your heir and I cannot steal that from him! You can see how wrong that would be. My Lord, if you agree to let me take him away, I shall undertake to send you frequent reports of his progress. I shall have photographs of him taken every few months so that you can see how he is growing up, and I shall bring him back to England when he is twelve so that he may be educated under your direction and influence."

The duke chuckled. "You have plans for my longevity, then?"

She blushed. "I think you will live many years longer than Lord Benchley, for all that he is receiving the best of care."

"That housekeeper of his, hey? Always doted on him, she has. I'll wager that she didn't take kindly to you coming into the household."

There was a long silence. Victoria waited in an agony for his decision, but instead the duke said, "We shall christen the boy tomorrow, I think. The bishop of Sandbarnes is coming in the morning to perform the service. What names have you chosen?"

"Lord Benchley has chosen none, so I thought to ask you to decide, if that will please you. Only, would you mind if I call him 'Mattie' for his everyday name, regardless of what names you give him?"

"Matthew was your father, was he not? Ah, yes! A nasty business altogether. Not the first client of Henry's this kind of unfortunate . . . Ah, well! Perhaps it is all for the best . . . Emigration can soothe many ills, I've been told. Society is cruel, very cruel. Worse than children, the way they peck and peck at a weakness. And to lose one's money!" With a sigh he handed Mattie back to Victoria and then, as if forgetting that she was in the room, he returned to his seat and bent over the papers again.

"My lord!" she begged from across the breadth of his cluttered desk. "Can you tell me of your decision?"

He glanced up in surprise. "Do you like the names Mark or Edward? They are mine. Would they do, my dear?"

"Splendidly . . . But as to the other matter? May I have leave of you, sir?"

When he frowned, only the lowest fraction of his forehead creased. "Henry is my nephew," he said at length. "I am not qualified to help you."

"But, sir," she pleaded. "Unless I have your blessing, I cannot go with my family. Please tell me what you *think*, at least. It would help to guide me."

"I'm truly sorry, my dear. Ah, well." He bent his head again, and she stared at the top of it for several seconds before quietly leaving him there, surrounded by his towers of books, his face worried as he pretended to concentrate on the page before him.

The chapel had been scrubbed out for the christening service, the first service to be held there since the funeral of one of the gardeners eight years before. The altar cloths had been aired in the spring sunshine, all the pews had been polished with beeswax and rubbed until they gleamed with the red and blue from the stained-glass windows. Spring daisies had been crammed into silver vases, and the font was scoured out and ready to hold the bottle of holy water the bishop was bringing with him.

Millie stood beside Victoria, shivering in her best dress, bonnet, and shawl again today. But despite the cold, which made her grit her jolting teeth together, she was too worried about Victoria to give herself a thought. There was definitely something ailing her mistress, something which frightened Millie, for it reminded her uncannily of those first days of her marriage when the shock of her father's death had caused her to drift specterlike about the room, blank-eyed and inhumanly passive. This morning, when Millie had taken her first shocked look at Victoria's haunted face, she tried to talk to her about it, but instead of Victoria's usual warm courtesy, there was a snappish retort that Millie should learn to hold her tongue and mind only what concerned her. If Victoria's happiness didn't concern her, Millie wondered, what then did?

Miserably she stood there, ready to hold Mattie if Victoria's arms tired, so worried that she hardly heard a word of the bishop's opening remarks, even though she was staring unseeingly at him from across the font. She jumped when Victoria moved, but relaxed when she realized that it was that part in the service where the baby is handed to the clergyman to be named. Millie shivered and hunched her shoulders under the thin shawl.

The bishop and the duke whispered together, then the bishop dipped his fingers into the water and solemnly made the sign of the cross on Mattie's forehead. The water must have been very cold, cold enough to startle him, for he began to shriek. Millie giggled in embarrassment. She didn't hear the bishop's words, but Victoria did, despite the screaming.

"I name thee Matthew Edward Mark Benchley, in the name of the Father and of the Son and of the Holy Ghost, Amen."

"Thank you, sir," whispered Victoria through the sudden constriction in her throat. Mattie was still wailing, and she thought that the old duke hadn't heard her, but he found her gloved hand, squeezed and patted it, and only relinquished it when the bishop bundled the red-faced baby back into his arms.

Shushing him with an odd, old-maidish tenderness, he joggled Mattie until the crying stopped and then rocked him, crooning aloud through the bishop's final brief prayer. He was still holding the baby later, on the sunlit gray steps outside, when the bishop shook hands with Victoria and wished her well, chucked the baby under the chin with false heartiness, and bade the duke good day with even falser bonhomie. The little encounter was not lost on Victoria, who deduced from the duke's previous comments that he and the bishop had engaged in many bitter theological arguments over the years. Yet the bishop was dependent to a large degree on the duke's largesse for the wealth of his diocese. An intriguing situation, that, and the duke's unexpected generosity in naming her child helped to lighten Victoria's mind. But she was still feeling drawn and weary from the long journey, and utterly miserable at the prospect of a life with Lord Benchley and Mrs. Foster— a prospect she had resignedly faced as inevitable after yesterday's chat with the duke. All that remained was to break the dismal news to Millie, and while the two elderly gentlemen talked briskly behind her, she turned to where Millie stood in the sheltered vestibule nook, rubbing her arms, her face pinched and bluish.

Victoria smiled wanly at the sight. "Vanity ill becomes you, Millie. Don't you think gray wool would have been a wiser choice?"

"Not when it's 'is christenin', miss. Not an' 'im goin' to be a duke 'imself one day. Look at 'im there, so peaceful in that dear old man's arms! 'E's a fine feller, ain't 'e?"

"The duke? Yes, Millie, he is. You wouldn't guess that he was somebody so important if you met him, would you? He has this awesome responsibility of property, and people who have to depend on him, yet he hasn't let any of it affect his life. He enjoys himself doing the things he wants to do."

"Not like Lord Benchley, you mean, miss, always workin' an' never seemin' to really enjoy 'imself?"

Victoria nodded. "In there I prayed as hard as I could that Mattie will grow up to be more like his uncle than his father. A life driven by greed is a wasted life. I do pray that Mattie's will be to some purpose, some meaningful purpose that satisfies him."

The duke stood beside them, pointing across the valley. "All this will be his . . . as far as those hills and out to the sea."

"It frightens me, sir. It terrifies me."

"It holds no fear for me!" The duke retorted with a dry chuckle. "Ah, well! As long as the tenants are well cared for, I take no interest. It is done for me, and it will be the same for Matthew when his time comes. You have done well to produce such a fine heir for me, my dear," he said, carefully placing the sleeping boy into her arms. "Before your week is over and your visit comes to an end, you and I must draw up some kind of a fund for him . . . something to last until he is twelve."

"I do not understand, my lord," she said politely. A combination of bright sunshine and exhaustion was making her feel faint and depressed. She could barely concentrate.

"When he is twelve, you must bring him back to England, my dear," he explained, and when she stared at him uncomprehendingly, he sighed and said, "Ah, well! You *will* look after him for me in New Zealand, won't you?"

All the remaining color drained from the squarish little face, the pointed chin quivered, and Millie hastily rescued Mattie as the tears spilled out in a scalding torrent. The baby wailed in sympathy and the duke fussed about in alarm, proffering more handkerchiefs and apologies than she could cope with.

"My dear! Don't cry! I was going to wait and tell you later, but, ah well! You looked so distressed I couldn't bear it. I'm a poor old man who has never developed any kind of immunity to feminine unhappiness."

"I'm profoundly grateful for that," sobbed Victoria.

With a tweedy arm about her he led her to a low stone wall where they sat. He hugged her shoulders gently as he talked. "I have to have an heir, and I'm pleased to have been able to avoid Henry. He has no feeling for people. None at all, and feeling for people is the only important requisite for the job of duke of Lanarkshire." He chuckled self-effacingly. "Frankly, my dear, I'm shocked but not surprised at your wanting to escape my nephew, and I'm skeptical enough to hope that divorce isn't part of your plans. But I'm glad the wee fellow will be brought up away from Henry's influence. Ah well! I have known Henry a long time and rather fancy that I have a good idea of what kind of a husband he is . . . Things do reach my ears, not that I enjoy listening. But you, my dear. You must have any number of grievances you could relate to me . . . Ah, yes! I do hear more than I care to know. Those plants of yours, for instance . . . Tom Booth used to work for my brother, you know. Henry's father. My dear, you have said not one word against your husband, and to me, a man inured to complaints of every kind, to me that is impressive. I admire your charity and your dignity and above all the fact that you put your love for the child first. I shall be deeply sorry to put so much time and distance between us, but go with my blessing. Keep your promises and return with the boy when he is older. Perhaps in twelve years I will have finished these accursed translations and will be able to turn all my attention to young Matthew."

"I shall bring him back to you, sir."

The eyes behind the glass squares were shrewd and wise but they looked at her with pure affection. "And as for you, my dear, I hope you will be happy. That is all! Ah, well! One can only hope. Happiness is the most difficult thing to attain in this world, and impossible to snare for too long, but from

285

what I have come to know of you so far, I see that you have the gift of recognizing happiness. Many people cannot even do that! Henry would not know a happy thought if one occurred to him, he is too busy looking for the next acquisition. When he married you, I hoped he might change, but it was too late for him, of course. I hope young Matthew learns your qualities."

Her eyes filled with tears again, but she looked at the duke's kind face and said steadily, "And I pray most fervently that he will grow to be like you."

"Thank you, my dear," he said, emotion thick in his voice. He rubbed her shoulder gently with his thin scholar's hand as together they sat there gazing out over Matthew's vast inheritance. The accord between them was so perfect that there was no longer any need for either of them to speak. Victoria knew with a sense of relief that she did not have to confess about Charles. Tacitly the duke had consented when he told her to be happy, and tacitly he had warned her when he said he preferred not to listen to gossip. Her responsibility was to be light. Though he warmly liked and admired her, it was Matthew he was interested in. All Victoria had to do was to be a fine, loving mother. For the rest, the duke had set her free to fulfill her destiny.

She smiled to think of what it would be like when the *Princess Mary* docked in Auckland. Charles would certainly be there, waiting for a letter from her. But Andrew had put it succinctly when he said:

"Won't Major Lawrence be surprised?"

He would indeed.